AT THE END OF THE EARTH

When he'd first come to Aotearoa the old Maoris had told many stories of the birds their ancestors had hunted. None of the settlers had believed them, until they found the bones. Elephant birds, the Europeans called them.

He rose warily, backing away from the broken egg. Then the bush itself seemed to rise on two immense splayed feet. From the top of the bush a neck extended that ended in an absurdly tiny skull. It towered over him, twice his height.

The elephant bird blinked at the ruined egg. Then its tiny hot eyes returned to the man standing close by. It let out a screech and trundled towards him, its weight shaking the ground, each clawed foot capable of crushing a man to death.

Coffin turned to run . . .

MAORI

ALAN DEAN FOSTER

ACE BOOKS, NEW YORK

This book is an Ace
original edition, and has never been
previously published.

MAORI

An Ace Book/published by arrangement with
the author

PRINTING HISTORY
Ace edition/February 1988

ISBN: 0-441-51925-3

Ace Books are published by The Berkley Publishing Group,
200 Madison Avenue, New York, New York 10016.
The name "Ace" and the "A" logo are trademarks
belonging to Charter Communications, Inc.

PRINTED IN THE UNITED STATES OF AMERICA

10 9 8 7 6 5 4 3 2 1

Te Atua. . . .
This being, as the Maoris say,
The Spirit of the rest of the Book

BOOK ONE

1839

1

"Why the divvul would anyone want to live at the end of the Earth, sor?"

Robert Coffin was standing by the bowsprit of the schooner *Resolute* when the question was asked. North Island lay north by northwest, South Island somewhere astern. "Aotearoa" the Maoris called this place in their melodious language; the Land of the Long White Cloud.

"I might ask you the same, Mr. Markham."

The powerful, battered face of his First Mate convulsed into a half-smile. Out in the vastness of the South Pacific it was considered impolite, not to mention potentially fatal, to inquire too closely into a man's background. Yet Markham didn't hesitate. There was very little he'd hesitate to do for Captain Robert Coffin. It was one of Coffin's great talents, a rare one among men, that others of his kind were eager to do things for him.

"Well sor, it were encumbent on me to leave the Blessed Climes of home in somewhat of a hurry. There were a bit of a problem with some cards."

"What sort of problem, Mr. Markham?"

The First Mate's contorted grin widened. "Too many of 'em, sor."

Coffin nodded. Lit by the flickering glow of the whale-oil lamp hung from the rigging, the First Mate's face bore more than passing resemblance to the impenetrable topography of South Island. Then he turned to stare out at the tar-black sea.

"I chose to live here, Mr. Markham, because I had nowhere else to go."

"Ah now, sor, be you meaning to say you wouldn't go back to Blessed England to live were the circumstances appropriate?"

"Mr. Markham, insofar as I am concerned, Blessed England

can sink to her gunwales and I'd shed not a tear for the scuppering."

The First Mate had seen a great deal in his lifetime. There was little that could shock him. But he was shocked now. He nodded somberly, turned as if to depart, and then recalled why he'd sought out his Captain. Finding him had not been difficult. Coffin slept less than any man he'd ever met. When not taking charge of his vessel you were apt to find him here, staring over the bow, as though searching for something only he knew was out there, somewhere ahead in the salty darkness.

Though he didn't turn he knew the Mate was still there. Coffin had the gift of the third eye, he did, and his men knew it and whispered. But not in front of their Captain.

"Something else, Mr. Markham?"

"Sor, Mr. Harley and the helmsman both wish to know if you intend to try a landing tonight or if they should search out a place to drop anchor."

"Forgive my absentmindedness, Mr. Markham. It's fore-thought that weighs heavily on me, not indifference to my duties."

Again the Mate grinned, a different sort of smile this time. Coffin could be ruthless, as was proper for a Captain, but he could also confess to his humanity. It was another reason others were willing to die for him.

"I know that, sor. 'Tis been a long night."

"Intended to bring us home in good weather. I would not be caught out even in these familiar waters in the storm which may be brewing."

Markham nodded approvingly. Coffin was twenty-six and the First Mate twenty years older, but each knew who the superior seaman was. Other Captains studied charts. Coffin memorized them, to the neverending awe and respect of his crew. The young Captain had a real brain.

If only he wasn't quite so driven.

He was pointing toward the shore where the first glimmering lights were coming into view. "I've not pushed the night watch since moonrise to stop half a league from home. We'll berth the *Resolute* in her own dock tonight. The men may berth where they will."

Markham chuckled. Tired as they were, once they made landfall only those few men with wives would repair to the comforting arms of Morpheus. The rest would awaken anew to drink and debauchery.

More of the harbor was coming into view. Markham squinted to port. "It won't be any easy thing to manage in the darkness, sor. I estimate there be near a hundred vessels at anchor tonight."

Coffin considered the same darkling panorama. Always ready with a joke, our Captain, thought Markham, but not what you'd call a jolly chap.

"Inform Mr. Harley and Mr. Appleton of the situation ahead. If there are a thousand ships we're still going in. Mind Mr. Appleton doesn't go ramming any clippers in the dark or I'll patch any hole in the hull with his buttocks."

"Aye, sor." As often happened, the First Mate was unable to tell if his Captain was being sarcastic or dead serious. Therefore he treated every ambiguity as gospel, preferring to be thought of as dour rather than stupid.

Turning, he unhooked the lamp and swung it from side to side as he yelled sternward. "Reef all tops'ls! Make for landing!"

The cry was taken up by the other mates, relayed sternward where it eventually reached the ears of the helmsman. Hands leaned on the great wooden wheel.

Coffin stood steady as a figurehead, gazing out over the bow. "Two degrees to port, Mr. Markham," he said calmly.

"Aye, sor." Once again the First Mate shouted orders. He joined his Captain in studying the crowded harbor. Running the gauntlet of anchored ships that lay in front of them would be no easy task, especially at night, not if Neptune himself were giving directions. The *Resolute* was in the hands not of a King but a Coffin. A bad name, he mused, for a good master.

It was a measure of the confidence they had in Coffin that not a man among his crew questioned his decision to try and dock in the darkness. There were only a couple of hours left until morning. It would have been simpler and safer to drop anchor outside the harbor and wait for daylight, but Coffin was not a man to tempt a calm sea. In this isolated part of the world, storms and typhoons could appear with astonishing speed.

Overhead the Southern Cross gleamed, a road sign fashioned of diamonds. The quarter-moon turned the shallower water the color of deep green glass. Luminescence boiled in the schooner's wake, caressing her bow as she disturbed billions of tiny creatures with her passing.

The very water seemed on fire as they entered the harbor.

Flames towered a hundred feet high, throwing the skeletal
spars of dozens of vessels into sharp relief. In addition to the
apocalyptic sight it presented, the air of Kororareka Harbor
was dominated by a terrifying, pungent smell. For while many
men spent the night ashore wallowing in the drunkenness and
debauchery of the part of town known as The Beach, others
toiled through the darkness on their ships, intent on the final
and most noisome stage of that business which brought so
many vessels from so many lands to this godforsaken corner of
the globe.

Of the hundred or so craft which bobbed at anchor in the
harbor, most were whalers. They roamed the vast empty spaces
of the Pacific seeking the great whales whose rendered corpses
would provide light for the lamps of Europe and America. At
Kororareka they came together to boil out blubber and flesh, to
restock stores and supplies, and to leave behind their gold.

The hellfire that flared across the waters came from gigantic
iron cauldrons on the whalers' decks. Fired by wood and
charcoal bought from New Zealand's fledgling merchants,
these seething black pits reduced tons of animal to gallons of
oil. It was said among the sailors that when God looked down
on Kororareka he had to hold his nose, for the stench from the
vats was strong enough to assail the nostrils of the Lord
Himself.

When the boiling and rending was done, the oil would be
dipped out with long-handled iron scoops. The reservoirs of
the whaling ships would be topped out with liquid gold enough
to build grand palaces in Newcastle and Nantucket, Salem and
London, Boston and Liverpool and Marseilles. The awful
business was better done in a calm harbor, away from the grip
of a raucous sea that could easily spill the precious bounty with
a single unexpected wave.

For more than a league in any direction from Kororareka,
North Island stank of cremated leviathans.

The natives were a fastidious bunch of savages. They kept
their villages and settlements well away from the rancid
vicinity of the town. They called themselves maori, which
meant normal. This in contrast to the *pakehas* whose odiferous
business clearly marked them as anything but normal. Those
Maori women who had joined their imported white sisters in
the business of attending to the needs of wild sailors breathed
as little as possible when they went into the town. Their habits

and barely veiled contempt for the seamen did not endear them to their customers. However, this did not interrupt the ancient commerce between the sailors and ladies-of-the-evening. The Maori women were comely, the Pacific was vast, and the polyglot crews that called at Kororareka were not interested in the social opinions of the women they solicited.

Fortunately there was little need for the two cultures to mix when not in bed. The permanent settlers served as go-betweens for ship's pursers and Maori suppliers. It was this business which had drawn respectable citizens to the hell that was Kororareka.

Coffin's opinion of the Maori was considerably higher than that of most of his colleagues. He was familiar with the savages of other lands: the aborigine of neighboring Australia, the blacks of South Africa and the Redmen of North America. From what he'd heard and experienced, the New Zealand natives were special, differing even from their cousins in the Tahitis and Samoas.

For savages they were good people. He enjoyed their company and had gone so far as to learn much of their language. This shrewd move gave him a decided advantage come trading time. Few of his countrymen had any interest in learning the speech of savages, preferring to rely on interpreters who often as not were in the business of taking kickbacks from the very Maori traders their European employers assiduously worked to cheat. Among the European settlers only the missionaries strove to acquire a working knowledge of the native language.

Coffin had first traveled to Australia as a common seaman. There he'd learned of the promise of still another new land lying farther to the east. And there was fortune to be gained in this New Zeeland, as its audacious Dutch discoverer had named it. Not in the form of gold to be scooped off the ground or spices to be plucked from trees, but from hard work and sharp dealing.

So he'd shipped to lawless, open Kororareka in the *Resolute*. Five years later found him her owner and master, as well as the founder of Coffin House, prime supplier and victualer to the insatiable whalers who crowded the harbor ahead.

In England a man couldn't rise far above his station unless he had friends at Court or in Parliament. The poverty-stricken

Coffins had none. At the ends of the Earth no such restraints were placed on a man's ambition at birth.

He was taller than most men, smooth of face but certainly not soft. Broad of shoulder and hip without being bulky, he was stronger than friends or enemies surmised. From a small, almost delicate mouth issued a voice of striking depth and power. The kind of voice, he'd been told on occasion, that belonged not in a mercantile establishment but in the House of Commons debating great issues. Coffin had no regrets that this was not to be. The life he'd chosen suited him well.

The wind shifted slightly, scuttling down out of the dark hills that ringed the harbor. The horrible miasma rising from the rendering kettles was momentarily diverted. The breeze blew Coffin's hair into his eyes and he brushed at it absently. Along with his booming voice, the young Captain's most striking feature was his silvery hair. It gave him the look of a man twenty years older. As it did not seem to put off the ladies, it never troubled Coffin. The first Maoris he'd met had promptly dubbed him "Makawe Rino." Iron Hair.

His attention shifted from the hellish harbor to the town beyond. There waited not just Coffin House but Mary Kinnegad. Irish Mary, the sailors called her.

She'd migrated to New Zealand several years earlier, leaving behind in Australia a convict past of unknown origin. It mattered not a whit to the men who frequented The Beach, where any member of the opposite sex more comely than a beluga was welcome with no questions asked. Set down among shop-worn painted doxies and dark Maori girls like a diamond among zircons, Mary Kinnegad found herself treated like a queen.

Then Coffin had found her and she found him, and the finding changed both their lives permanently.

She'd unburdened her history to him, confessing to the killing of another woman in England. She refused to say what had sparked the fight save that it was not over a man. There wasn't a man alive Mary Kinnegad thought worth fighting over. Coffin was doing his best to change that opinion.

Two fine, healthy children she'd borne him already: little Flynn, and Sally whose hair was as red as her mother's. A family as admirable as his business, he knew. Not a bad life for the sole son of a coal miner dead of the black lung these ten years past. His father would have been proud. Aye, there was a good life to be wrested from this far land, and he gave thanks to God that the Dutch who'd found it had decided they wanted no part of it.

He turned to gaze at the deck, stacked high with its heavy load of Kauri pine. The Kauri grew on North Island as well as on South, but with increasing demand came also increasing prices from those "ignorant" Maoris—who knew business as well as any of their European counterparts. Hence Coffin's risky voyages to South Island in search of high-grade trees and low-grade Maori traders. With a *pakeha* vessel still something of a novelty there, he'd managed to find both.

God seemed to have designed the Kauri pine specifically to serve the needs of sailing men. The tree soared straight and true to extraordinary heights before sending out its first branches. Coffin knew of emergencies where an untrimmed Kauri had been stepped into service as a mast without having been touched by the axe of a ship's carpenter. The saplings made excellent, perfectly straight spars.

Of the hundred-odd vessels that rocked at anchor in the Bay of Islands fronting Kororareka, many had been dismasted and many more limped in with broken spars. The Pacific seemed to strive to belie her name, and good quality Kauri was in short supply in the harbor now. Captains paced their quarterdecks and fumed at the delays; Coffin could expect a warm welcome for his cargo. Pine for masts, flax for sturdy rope, and the provisions for starving sailors—

The cauldrons of Hades receded as the *Resolute* moved on one sail toward the makeshift wharf. Not a pretty landing, not like Liverpool or Southhampton, but it was his. No one else in Kororareka could claim that. As an anchorage Kororareka left much to be desired. The wharf was the best he could do.

As the schooner bumped up against the pier the mates had to raise their voices in order to make themselves understood above the screams and shouts that rose from The Beach. Soon the sun would be up, but there would be no slowing of frantic activity. The taverns and grog shops and brothels never closed. Bartenders and whores and gamblers worked the whalers in round-the-clock shifts.

Lines were tightened around cleats and made fast to pilings. A ramp was extended over the side. Somewhere a musket went off and louder screams were heard.

Coffin had come home.

2

He approached the ramp. Markham was waiting for him.

"Orders, Cap'n?"

"We've been a month away from port, Mr. Markham. Once the cargo's been seen to, give everyone leave to visit their wives or sweethearts or both. Mount the usual guard. We want no sneak thieves making off with our profit."

"Aye, sor. I'm anxious to be off meself. South Island be a cold place, and not meaning only the weather, sor."

Coffin's gaze went to the head of the pier. Already seamen not utterly besotted with drink could be seen stopping to gape at the masts and spars-to-be that were piled high on the *Resolute's* deck. They would carry word back to their ships that the badly needed supplies had finally arrived.

"The market will come to us, Mr. Markham. Inform any who inquire that there'll be no sale of our Kauri until Mr. Goldman has had time to grade and price the wood. I'll not lose all our hard work to a panic selling."

"No sor," agreed Markham.

"Good. Arrange for your own relief when you're done. As for myself, I have business of my own to attend to ashore."

The Mate winked. "Don't we all, sor."

Coffin started toward the ramp, only for Markham to delay him. "One other thing, Cap'n." The Mate nodded across the deck. "What are we to do with *him*?"

Coffin's gaze followed Markham's through the waning darkness. He could just make out the spectral silhouette that was leaning against the far railing. The old Maori stood six foot six in his sandaled feet and was thin as a clipper's mizzenstay. He wore a dun-colored flaxen cloak and four feathers in his hair: three plucked from the rare kea and one from a bird Coffin didn't know, though it was easily the largest feather he'd ever set eyes upon.

The Maori had been taken aboard at South Island. From what they'd observed, the natives there were glad to be rid of him. His name was Tuhoto and he was a *tohunga*. It was not quite the same thing as a priest; more in the line of a spiritual adviser and wizard all rolled into one. If nothing else, he was a curiosity. In return for his passage he'd promised to cast a *karakia*, a spell for good weather. This primitive nonsense he'd backed with practical knowledge of wind and waves.

The crew didn't like him and made no effort to hide their feelings. "No place on a clean ship for a filthy savage" was how one sailor had put it. In conversation the native was dry and concise.

Despite this he was cordial to Coffin. For what it was worth, everyone admitted that they had enjoyed unusually calm weather during the homeward leg of the journey, though not a man-jack among the crew would dare give the heathen's incantations any credit for their good fortune.

One sailor who'd stood night watch claimed to have seen the old Maori conversing with dolphins. The mocking laughter of his comrades soon silenced him. It was amusing thereafter to observe this otherwise tough seaman going out of his way to avoid the *tohunga* whenever their paths threatened to cross on deck.

"I'll take care of him, Mr. Markham."

"Thank you, sor." The gratitude was plain in the First Mate's reply.

They're all afraid of him, Coffin thought as he walked across the deck. Maoris and sailors both. His crew barely acknowledged their Captain's presence as they scrambled for the ramp. By the time Coffin reached the port side of his ship, the schooner was quieter than it had been in weeks.

"*Tena koe,* Tuhoto."

The old wizard spoke without smiling. Coffin had yet to see him smile. "Hello to you, Captain Robert Coffin."

As before, Coffin was impressed by the old man's fluency. The Maoris learned English readily enough, but Tuhoto hardly seemed the type to have attended missionary school.

"What are you doing?"

Tuhoto pointed toward the harbor with his staff, a beautiful piece of hardwood covered with intricately carved whorls and scrolls. They matched the tattoos that covered his face.

"Those men on all the ships. They burn the flesh of the great fish, but not for food. For what, then?"

Coffin indicated one of the lamps which illuminated the deck. "They suck oil from its flesh, to put in containers like that one to give light."

"The *pakehas* value such lights highly?"

"Highly indeed." Coffin was a pakeha himself, of course, but he did not feel insulted.

"Then it seems to me you must fear the darkness very much."

"Some do. Is it not true of the Maori?"

"No, it is not, Captain Coffin."

"I think I know why this may be so. In the land where I came from there were and still are dangerous wild animals who hunt by night. Your islands seem never to have been inhabited by wolves and bears and such. You have no reason to fear the night because it has never threatened you."

Tuhoto mulled this over before replying. "That is a good thought, though I think there may be more to it. There is something in the pakeha that fears even the deserted darkness. I think many pakehas fear themselves." He gazed down at the young Captain. "I think your thoughts have teeth."

He turned to stare back out across the waters recently crossed. Coffin remained until the lamps were no longer necessary, giving the elder his due.

"You have been a good friend to me," Tuhoto said finally. "Moreso than any pakeha I have ever met. I sense something in you that is not in the other pakehas."

Coffin shrugged. "We are all special to ourselves, Tuhoto. I might say that *you* are unlike any other Maori I've ever met."

The old man did not laugh, but he smiled for the very first time. The smile was another curve in his face, a sweep matched by his intricate tattoos. They covered not just his face but his entire body, the most extensive Maori tattooing Coffin or any of his companions had ever seen. Upon being questioned, Tuhoto explained they represented the entire history of the Maori people. More nonsense, Coffin knew, but colorful nonsense it was.

"I wish you much luck, Captain Coffin. I think you like my country. I think it may like you."

"I'm very happy here, Tuhoto. Best have a care when you debark." He nodded shoreward. "Kororareka's become the wildest and most lawless pakeha community in this part of the world. A lot of badness all in one place. It's full of pakehas who don't like Maoris even when they're sober."

"I have tasted of the pakeha rum. I like the way it heats my belly, but not my head. I know what you warn against. Small men I do not fear. I have six gods. I will not be harmed."

"Maybe you could loan me a couple. I could use help these days." Coffin intended it as a jest, but the old man's reply was dead solemn.

"I wish I could do that for you, Captain Coffin, but it is beyond even my abilities. Besides, have you not your own god, your Christ?"

"I think he avoids Kororareka. Many of your people have already converted to Christianity, Tuhoto. Will you not do the same?"

"I already have six gods," the old man replied firmly. "It is too late for me to change."

"Couldn't you add another? I know some of your people do that."

"I think not. It would make the other six jealous."

Coffin looked toward the deck so Tuhoto would not see his smile. "Yes, I can understand that." He forced himself to adopt a serious mien. "If you should ever need to return to the south, seek me out and I will help if I can."

"Thank you, Captain Coffin, but I do not think I will be returning there soon. I have much to do here. *Haere ra*—good-bye."

Coffin followed the tall old man's progress as he strolled gracefully across the deck to vanish down the disembarking ramp. He immediately put the *tohunga* and his wild tales out of his mind. An entertaining diversion. Now it was over and there was plenty to do before the sun was well up. Notations to make, shares in cargo to be apportioned—and Mary Kinnegad. He was not long in following in Tuhoto's wake.

He paused halfway down the pier, frowned at the wooden planking. Footprints seemed to lead to the edge of the pier. Below, dark water swirled oddly. He shrugged and continued on toward town.

As he entered the ramshackle collection of small warehouses and storage sheds which lined the waterfront he could feel the first kiss of the sun on the back of his neck. By rights he should head straight home, but Goldman would be opening the store soon. It was vital that they get the Kauri graded, priced and sold as soon as possible, before some desperate Captain thought to send armed men to try to steal it. Even if law did come to Kororareka, His Majesty's troops would have an impossible time trying to track down criminals whose business took them clear around the globe.

Kororareka's streets were paved with the usual combination of mud and drunken sailors. It was quiet, but only by comparison with the debauched nights. The revelry, if so polite a term could be applied to it, never ceased. Whalers were often away from home three or four years at a stretch. When such men finally made port-o-call their pent-up desires manifested themselves in a paroxysm of pleasuring.

To the sometimes puritanical shipmasters Kororareka was truly a bit of hell on Earth. They forced themselves to turn a blind eye and deaf ear to the depravity of their crews, though the sight of nubile Maori maidens prancing about clad only in flaxen skirts was enough to tempt the thoughts of the most dedicated Quaker.

So they said nothing while good men sinned a little among the heathens. It kept the mutinous in check and the Captains knew that God would punish such men in His own good time. A Captain's task was to bring his ship home safely, its tanks brimming with precious spermaceti. To do that one needed the backs of strong men, not angels.

A few of the grog shops and stores now boasted wooden walkways which rose above the mud, while the less prosperous were as filthy inside as the streets they bordered. Coffin navigated around those bodies which did not stir, paused to permit lurching men to pass.

3

The proprietors of the shops that lined the town's "respectable" streets rose with the sun. On the fringe of The Beach, back behind the grog shops and gambling dens and the pens, were stores that sold tinned foods to homesick sailors, geegaws and gimcracks, ship's supplies and fresh victuals. The latter was purchased entire from the Maoris. Why farm for a living when one could buy from the natives? This was fine with the Maoris, who realized substantial profits from their virtual agricultural monopoly.

A few of the shops even specialized in primitive, heathen arts and crafts of the sort calculated to raise eyebrows and promote nervous giggles among the womenfolk at social gatherings back home in New Bedford or Southhampton. The Maori were deft craftsfolk, fashioning hooks and needles of bone, skirts of the everpresent flax, attractive baskets and heavy war clubs. The latter were made of intricately carved hardwood or a variety of South Island jade. The Maori called it greenstone and went to great lengths to obtain it. Sharpened and polished, a greenstone war club was a fearsome traditional weapon, though Coffin had noticed that any Maori warrior would gladly trade war club, wife and child for a modern musket and powder.

There were even more notorious souvenirs to be had.

The boy stepped out of a narrow alley between two stores. He couldn't have been more than fifteen: a cabin boy or sailmaker's apprentice, most likely.

"Your pardon, sir." He had a canvas bag slung over his right shoulder. "You look the sort of gentleman who might be interested in the unusual." There wasn't a suggestion of shyness or hesitation in his manner.

Coffin eyed the lumpy sack, had a fair idea of its contents.

15

He tried to go around the youngster, who moved quick as a crab to block his path.

"You haven't even seen my wares, sir. At least allow me that courtesy."

"I know what you're selling, boy. I've nothing to do with that filthy trade."

For a moment the boy looked hurt. Then his flinty stare returned. "It's not filth, sir, but a question of anthro—arthro—anthropology." He smiled, having pronounced the difficult word correctly. "It's science, sir."

"It's unwholesome, and though I am not a religious man I am dead against it."

"Perhaps you've not actually had the opportunity to consider it in person, sir." The boy hurriedly lowered the sack, reached inside, and extracted part of the contents. Coffin's suspicions were confirmed. He eyed the object with distaste.

It was a Maori head: smoked, embalmed, and exceedingly well preserved. A man of less refined temperment might have called it fresh. Teeth grimaced at Coffin. The eyes were shut tight.

"Half a quid, sir. That's a fair price. You won't find a better head for twice that anywhere on The Beach. I'll suffer a hiding if you can prove otherwise."

"I don't want to beat you, boy, though God knows you need it. Do you not know where these heads come from, nor why?"

"Of course I do, sir." The boy was trying to sound knowledgeable as well as important. "The Maoris themselves do them up, even to tying the knots in the hair." A youthful finger traced dry, dead flesh without hesitation. "Notice the tattoos here, sir. Are they not exceptional?"

Coffin leaned close and examined the gruesome object with clinical detachment. Sometimes you could tell if the tattooing had been added subsequent to decapitation. In this instance the tattoos appeared to be original with the deceased. The knotted hair was not the fashion among the Maori, but had been so secured the better to display the forehead tattooing.

"I am told, sir," the boy went on, "that the natives do up the heads of their own relatives this way, and keep them on display for visitors much as I keep a picture of my sister in the locket which hangs 'round my neck. It's their custom and habit. If they have a few heads to spare and if some jolly-boy wants to take one back home, why should I leave all the profit to the heathen who don't appreciate real money anyways?"

Coffin did his best to keep his voice even. "If you think the Maori've no sense of profit, boy, you're wrong there. They are as sophisticated and avaricious as any white man, much to the distress of the good fathers who proselytize among them. I fear that is reflected in this dreadful head business.

"I asked if you knew how you might've come by your stock. It's true they've had this habit for as far back as any care to confess to it, but what many fail to realize, or choose to ignore, is that being the natural merchants they are, since the arrival of the European they have expanded their interests to accommodate an increased demand for goods.

"I personally know of traders who've traveled to villages to bargain with the head chiefs, the *arikis*. The trader will set a price. Then the chief will line up some poor souls, usually prisoners of war, and let the trader walk down the line picking out the heads he likes. Come his next visit his merchandise will be waiting for him, like the contents of your duffle.

"A man can make a cannibal of himself with his eyes and purse as easily as with teeth and gut. The Maoris have no corner on degradation. If the pakehas exhibited less interest in such souvenirs there'd be a few more natives walking the island this day."

After digesting this information silently the boy responded with an indifferent shrug. "Of what concern is that to me, sir? If their own chiefs have no more concern for their own people than that, why should I worry myself about it?"

"Because you are not a damned naked savage, boy!" Coffin was unable to restrain his anger any longer. At his tone the boy took a wary step back. "You're an Englishman. A Christian youth of good stock who has no business mucking about with such filth."

"My age be none of your business, sir. If my wares put you off so, why then I won't try further to soil your fine hands with them. I'll take my trade elsewhere."

"Why you impudent little bastard!" Coffin made a grab for the boy, but his feet were as nimble as his tongue. He scampered out of reach and vanished back down the alley from whence he'd come. Coffin gave a brief thought to pursuing, then turned away. By his willingness to overlook the questionable activities of others he'd profited well. He was no reformer.

It was the youth of the offender that had moved him to anger. Kororareka was no place to raise children. Its air was full of poison, the missionaries' strenuous efforts notwithstanding.

Some day, he told himself. Some day something would have to be done.

High on the hillside above the clamor and gunshots and debauchery of The Beach stood a cluster of small wooden buildings. They were grander than the huts that sprang out of the sand below, but not by much. Coffin House was the largest of the lot. It boasted a rock foundation and a fireplace, the latter an unnecessary afterthought since it rarely grew cold in the Bay of Islands. Captain and sailor alike founded many a jest on the establishment's unintentionally morbid name. They appreciated the rough humor of it.

It did not hamper business. Coffin had built a reputation among the sea captains by giving quality for money received. He never tried to cheat a ship new to the port, and he dealt only in the freshest victuals and best quality stores the Maoris made available. In addition to Kauri pine and treated hemp rope, a ship's officer could find tea from India, coffee from Egypt and Turkey, tobacco from the Virginias and Carolinas, metalware from the mills of Birmingham and woolen goods from Edinburgh.

Word of mouth was the best advertising, and satisfied Captains gratefully passed the name of Coffin House from ship to ship. "Put in to Kororareka and seek out Robert Coffin!" it was shouted across gunwales slick with blubber and whale blood, "He'll not steal from you and his prices are fair."

It was comforting to set eyes on the familiar storefront, its sign hanging limp in the still morning air above the front door. Something else made him quicken his stride, however, and he soon broke into a run.

Fighting was as natural to Kororareka as whoring and drinking, but it belonged down on The Beach, not up here among the community's reputable businesses. Open brandishing of guns and knives was off-putting to customers.

The sight made his blood rise for another reason. Three against one are not fair odds in any fight, for all that the lone Maori appeared to be holding his own. Like many of his people he looked too fat to run, but Coffin was not deceived. He'd learned while participating in friendly wrestling contests at trading meets that the brown bulges which so often surged over skirt-tops were usually rock hard.

The native moved lithely, keeping his back to the building. He hefted a hardwood war club inlaid with sparkling *paua* shell. Both edges were lined with the inset teeth of some deep-sea monster. Using both hands, he swung the club in wide arcs sufficient to keep his three assailants at bay. They kept feinting, trying to draw his attention so one of them could slip behind those potentially disemboweling blows to cut the native's throat.

The shattered cutlass lying on the ground was testament to the force with which the Maori wielded his weapon. One sailor was bleeding steadily from a gash across his forehead while another's left arm lay loose and broken at his side. Blood flowed down the native's right arm where a knife had slashed home.

"HOLD!"

Coffin's voice could command attention from a topgallant lookout to the lowest bilge. It froze the three attackers. The Maori hesitated, then drew his club in close as he stared curiously at the new arrival. He was breathing hard, but so were his assailants.

One of them glared at Coffin. "This be none o' your business, sir." He turned back to the Maori. "We aim t'finish this cannibal for the insult he's done us."

Coffin lowered his voice as he advanced. "What insult might that be? As to this being my business or no, that is in truth my business you are fighting in front of."

The man with the broken arm spoke up. "Wouldn't get out of our way. Like to knock me over, he did. I take that from no savage. I've been all over the Pacific and Atlantic both, around the Mediterranean and three times 'round the Horn."

"Not in your present condition, I'll wager." Coffin eyed the other two. "You're all of you drunk. If anyone blocked anyone's path, I can guess who the trespassing party might be."

"Be you siding with the savage?" The tallest of the trio gazed at Coffin in disbelief.

"I side always with the right side. Deny to me that you're all drunk."

"So we've 'ad a spot o' rum or two," the first man growled. "What of it?" As he talked the fight was seeping out of him, just as Coffin intended. It's hard for a drunk to fight and think at the same time.

"If you're going to pick a fight in Kororareka, gentlemen, you'd best choose an opponent other than the Maori, much as they're delighted to oblige. That's my advice for this fine morning. My request is that you stop blocking the entrance to my shop. Go back down to The Beach if you desire to bloody yourselves, and leave this part of town in peace."

"What if we decide to include you in the party, good sir?" The speaker gave him a challenging stare.

Coffin's right hand drifted meaningfully toward the sword slung from his belt. "Why then," he replied slowly, "there'd be no containing the fury of your Captain, Kororareka being a difficult place in which to secure new seamen, and burials here being as expensive as they are time-consuming."

The man hesitated, glanced toward his companions. Neither showed an inclination to do battle with a gentleman swordsman. Furious, the leader of the trio glowered back at Coffin.

"What if we came back some night with friends, sir, and burnt your precious place to the ground?"

Coffin nodded toward the harbor. "Out there are a hundred Captains who regularly do business with me. They won't look kindly on the perpetrators of such an outrage. Given such a happenstance I wouldn't give you or any of your 'friends' the chance I'd give a Popester in Parliament." He waited quietly for the man to make his next move.

Instead it was the Maori who stepped into the breach, verbally and physically. He gestured with both big hands and smiled at the leader of his assailants.

"Come, come. Why you stop now? We fight some more!" He looked hopefully toward Coffin without bothering to ascertain whose side he might take. "You fight too?"

The tall drunk's expression twisted as he gaped at the native. "He's bloody mad, this one is. Come on, lads, let's shove out of here."

"Aye," said the man standing next to him. "What be the point o' fightin' with a crazy man? Nor have I a quarrel to pick with you, sir." He bowed slightly in Coffin's direction.

Bereft of his army, the leader of the trio turned and staggered toward The Beach, his comrades in tow.

The Maori let his shark-tooth-edged club fall to his side as he watched his assailants retreat.

"What for you interfere? It was good fight."

Coffin replied in fluent Maori. "Not a fair fight. Only three of them against you."

It took the native a moment to absorb this. Then he burst out in rich, appreciative laughter. His belly shook, but no more than the rest of him.

"Good man! You good pakeha fellow!" He gestured toward the building behind him. "I hear you say right you say this your store?"

Coffin nodded. "All men are welcome at Coffin House. If you ever have flax to trade or want to part with that oversized scalpel of yours, you'll find my people fair and honorable."

"Honorable pakeha? Interesting idea. I am no *rangatira*, not chief who does trading, but I will remember. *Haere ra.*"

"Good-bye."

Coffin watched as the Maori headed down toward The Beach. He'd heard seamen speak of savages who were ferocious fighters, and of aborigines who had no stomach for battle, but until he'd come to this New Zealand he'd never heard of a people who delighted in spilling blood for the sheer sport of it.

He stood and stared until the native had disappeared among the grog shops to make sure the three vindictive sailors hadn't set an ambush for him. Then he turned and mounted the wooden steps beneath the swaying sign.

4

The bell above the entrance jangled, prompting a reply from behind the main counter. The voice was reedy and heavily accented.

"Just a minute. It's early yet. We're not quite really open. Your business will have to wait."

Coffin strolled over to the counter and made his voice into a threatening roar. "A pox on your delay! Serve me now or I'll see you sold to the Kanakas!"

"What—ow!" The man bending over behind the counter straightened abruptly and smacked his head on the overhanging top. "Now you look here," he began, rubbing his balding pate, "whoever you are. . . ." His eyes widened behind thick glasses as he recognized the intruder. The anger melted instantly.

"Why Mr. Coffin, sir, you're back two days early! You gave me a start, sir."

"Fair weather and a favorable current, Elias. Sorry about the knock. I couldn't resist." The two young men, one thin and aging fast, the other powerful of frame but appearing older because of his gray hair, exchanged a firm handshake.

The young merchant had found Elias Goldman wandering dazed and drunk in a Beach alley two years ago this summer past. Goldman had shipped on a New Bedford whaler to see the world before settling down, and the world hadn't been kind to him. He'd gotten drunk, missed his ship, and quickly found himself relieved of what little money he had by the regular habitues of The Beach.

Coffin discovered that Goldman had a natural talent for figuring, if not for whaling. Coffin himself had little talent or liking for arithmetic. Quick to recognize ability in another, he soon had the grateful pilgrim installed as factotum of Coffin

22

House. During the past two years Goldman had never given him reason to regret his decision.

Adjusting his glasses, the clerk came out from behind the counter. "How did the voyage to South Island go, sir?" Without waiting for an answer he glanced over a shoulder and yelled, "Kamine!" A Maori girl emerged from the back room. "Mister Coffin has come back." He looked back to his boss. "What will you take, sir?"

"Some tea, Elias."

"You heard him," Goldman told the girl. "Don't dally." She nodded sharply, then vanished. Goldman found a high-backed wood chair while Coffin took a seat nearby.

"Now then, sir," Goldman asked eagerly, "tell me what you've brought back for us."

"Nothing much, I fear." Goldman's expression collapsed. Coffin didn't have the heart to tease his associate further. "A few logs."

"Kauri pine?" Coffin nodded. "How few?"

"I don't know. There are too many for me to count. You know how poor I am with figures." Goldman let out a delighted whoop and Coffin could no longer restrain his enthusiasm. "You should have been with us, Elias! It still grows on the South Island thick as the vines in south France. The best quality, and we had our pick as no vessel had called where we made landfall in many years. The locals had amassed a huge reservoir of logs, more than the *Resolute* could carry.

"Furthermore, as so few ships go there, the logs have been sitting out in the sun for months, curing fit to please the most demanding carpenter. There isn't a green one in the lot. Half a dozen men saw us tying up. By now the word must be all over the harbor."

"Wonderful, wonderful!" Goldman's eyes sparkled like those of a small boy at Christmas. "I'll get right down there and set to grading it. Do you wish it warehoused?"

Coffin shook his head. "There's no need, I think. You should be able to sell it right off the ship. Let someone else haul it for us. It's a fine profit we will have for a little difficult sailing. As soon as business here is finished and the ship made ready I'll be going back south for another load. Best to skim off the cream before our competitors think to try and retrace our course. I've sworn the crew to silence, but such a thing is scarce in Kororareka.

"Speaking of warehousing, how went business in my absence?"

"Most excellently. Every whaler in the Pacific knows our community for the friendly port that it is. There's no law here to irritate them as there is at Sydney, and not a tree in New South Wales to match the Kauri for quality. Nor do they have the Maori flax for making rigging repair. That's what we're really low on. We've had something of a run on rope while you were away. Every merchant in town is short stocked. Bidding will be spirited at the monthly sale several days hence. I'm glad you returned in time to attend. I can bargain with the natives, but not well in their own tongue. What besides Kauri? Gold?"

The eternal question. "Everyone knows there's no gold in New Zealand, Elias. We have a fair stock of foodstuffs. Kumara potatoes and some salt pork. Taro as well."

Goldman made a face. "Taro doesn't find much favor with a sailor's palate."

"True, but what I bought was cheap enough, and we can trade it to the Maori here. Taro for pork, say."

The clerk looked thoughtful. "I'll see to it."

"There's one other thing." Coffin dug into his coat pocket and extracted a small pouch. Rising, he had Goldman follow him back to the counter. Loosening the drawstring on the pouch, he dumped out a double handful of beautiful yellow-orange stones—except they weren't stones. They were soft and warm to the touch.

Goldman recognized them instantly. Picking up several of the largest specimens he held them up to the light. Bubbles and flecks of plant matter were silhouetted by the rising sun.

"Amber. Fine quality, too. Too fine for common sailors. They wouldn't know their value."

"No, but their Captains will. I've seen enough to know these are the equal of any to be gathered from the shores of the Baltic. If more was available we could make a good business of this, but supplies are scarce."

"A pity this is all this country has to offer in the way of gems."

"Who knows? The Maori have their paua shell and bone and greenstone. Perhaps someday the land will deliver to us some new surprise. There's much still to be explored. Ah, here's Kamine with our tea."

The girl's long black hair fell in lustrous waves from her shoulders as she bent to serve them. "It is good to see you home again, Mr. Coffin, sir." Her mission English, Coffin mused, was much improved.

"Thank you, Kamine. It's good to be back."

She'd been a prisoner of war. Her conquering chief, a *rangatira* named Waretotua, had not treated her well. The subchief was a drunkard and a frequent visitor to The Beach, where Goldman had seen him beating the girl unmercifully on more than one occasion.

With Coffin's permission, Goldman had bought her and sent her to the Anglican mission up the coast. Within a year she'd learned enough to begin helping out at the store. Now Goldman was teaching her figuring. She was valuable for more than tea-making and cleaning.

While they'd long since given her her freedom, she'd chosen to remain with Coffin House. She was a hard worker and invaluable to the busy Goldman, and she had a hunger for learning. Besides, Goldman's interest in the girl was beginning to be more than merely altruistic. As near as Coffin could tell, his feelings were reciprocated.

"What other news, Elias?" The tea was hot and sharp, though not sweet enough for his taste. Sugar was worth a King's ransom in Kororareka and the chance to buy it came infrequently. There was talk of settlers trying plantations in Australia's humid northlands. Coffin was intrigued. Sugar meant molasses, and molasses meant rum, and rum meant very happy whalers indeed.

Goldman didn't look up from his cup. "Nothing much, sir. Business is excellent. We did have a china clipper stop briefly. Caused a stir among the citizenry. Out of Boston bound for Canton. For tea, of course. Storms blew her south of her normal course and she made here for repairs. A beautiful vessel. Lost her top mizzen, among others. Sad to say we did not have the large log she required."

"A week too late." Coffin wasn't the kind to linger over missed opportunities.

"But," Goldman added brightly, "I did sell her a brace of topspars and plenty of rigging. Four barrels of pitch as well."

Coffin was nodding to himself, thoughtful. "Who had the pine big enough to replace the topped mast?"

This time Goldman looked away. "Tobias Hull."

"Damnation." Coffin's eyes narrowed. "Come, Elias, I know you too well. There's more. Bad news, I wager. The exchange rate in London?"

"No sir. Nothing of that nature."

"Then what? Don't try to hide it from me. You know I'll find out soon enough anyway."

"I can't actually say it's bad news, sir. It's simply—awkward."

"I'm not troubled by awkwardness. Enough fencing, man!"

"Sir, there were passengers on that clipper and they were not bound for Canton. She intended stopping here storm damage or not."

"Passengers for here?" Coffin looked pleased. "What's awkward about that? New settlers are always welcome."

Goldman took a deep breath and set his teacup aside. "Among them were your wife, sir, and your son."

Coffin looked like a man who'd just taken a musket ball through the brain. It was the first time Goldman had ever seen him so. "My wife?"

"I understand her name is Holly, sir. That's right, isn't it?"

"My wife." Coffin was staring blankly into the distance.

Goldman swallowed, continued. "The boy's name is Christopher. Fine looking young chap, sir. Has your eyes. Six, she said he was."

"Holly's here? Good God!" Coffin struggled out of his daze. "Where are they, where did you put them, where. . . ?"

"Rest easy, sir. You know I'd keep them off The Beach. Under the circumstances—your wife was most insistent—I thought it best as well as proper to install them in your house. I imagine they're there now."

"At the house? My house?"

"Sir, I didn't see that I had any other choice. I knew it could cause trouble, but the house was, uh, empty at the time and so far no one's come calling." Both men knew who might "come calling."

"If I've done wrong, sir, I apologize, but I. . . ."

"No, you did what you had to, Elias. As you always do. The problem is mine. Holly here, and Christopher too."

Three years since his last visit to England. His son would be walking now instead of tottering about on all fours like a bald dog. And what of his wife? What of dark-haired, delicate little Holly? Memories washed over him, all of them pleasant, all genteel. Memories too of the weeping and wailing that had accompanied his last departure. A long time ago, that. So long that he'd almost been able to forget.

Once a year he'd promised to visit home. For the first two years of their marriage he'd managed to keep the vow. But the endless ocean voyage took too much time away from business, time utilized by his competitors. He grew adept at devising new excuses for putting off the visits. During the last three years Kororareka had exploded commercially. Coffin House's growth had been proportional.

Unkept vows mattered not now. She was here, *here*, and the boy too. He could understand her longing and impatience, but to bring the child made no sense. Christopher had always been a frail lad. Hauling him halfway around the globe struck Coffin as dangerous to a fault.

Awkward, Goldman had said. Awkward was too pale a word.

"You might ought to go up and see her," Goldman prompted his employer.

"Yes. Yes, of course, Elias." Coffin's gaze remained distant as he stood. He glanced out a window, gazing down toward the raging depravity that was The Beach. "How much of the town did she see when you escorted her from the ship?"

"Enough, I should think, to make any respectable English-woman think twice about venturing there alone, sir."

"Good. Then at least she'll stay at home. Kororareka's no place for a woman of Holly's sensibilities, no place at all."

"I agree, sir, but it was not my place to tell her that. If I may say so, sir, she strikes me as a strong, independent person. Her stature is deceptive. The sights she witnessed didn't appear to faze her."

"Oh, she's strong, she is, Elias, and were she anything but independent she wouldn't be here now. She's always been like that. It was one of the things that first attracted me to her. I'll go up right now, of course. Bugger me if I'm not looking forward to it."

"That's good to hear, sir." Goldman had reason to fear his employer's reaction would have been otherwise. He was pleased it was not.

He rose and shook Coffin's hand a second time. "It's good to have you back again, sir. I trust this unexpected visit will only magnify your happiness."

"I imagine it will. It should be pleasant. What man wouldn't be thrilled to see his wife and son after three years?"

"Truly, sir. I envy you. Perhaps some day I will have the chance to experience such domestic bliss myself."

"I've no doubt you will, Elias." He turned sharply and headed for the door. "Mr. Markham will show you the cargo."

"I'll get right on that, sir. We should be ready for buyers by midday if not sooner. No dallying when there's money to be made, eh?"

"No indeed, Elias."

As soon as the Captain had departed, Goldman reclaimed his chair. Might as well finish his tea before fighting his way through town to the docks.

A soft voice materialized at his shoulder. "Mister Elias sir?"

"What is it, Kamine?" He saw she was eyeing the front door.

"Mister Coffin, sir, he doesn't seem much happy at the coming of his family."

"Oh, I think he is, Kamine. It's just that it won't be easy for him right now. The ways of the pakeha are not the same as those of the Maori."

"How is that?" she frowned. "Are not both women part of Mister Coffin sir's *whanau*?"

"Among the English there is no *whanau*, Kamine. No extended families as the Maori have. It's one man to one woman. I'd think they'd have told you about that at school."

"Mostly we talked about God, not men. So it is very different for the pakeha?"

"Very. As far as Mr. Coffin is concerned, this new lady and Kinnegad ma'm are truly part of his *whanau*, but it's kind of a secret *whanau*. You must help keep this secret from Mrs. Coffin ma'm as well," he told her sternly. "This is very important. As far as Mrs. Coffin ma'm is concerned, Kinnegad ma'm is *tapu*. Understand?"

"No, but I will do as you say, Mister Elias sir." She picked up the empty cups and the teapot and set them on an exquisite black lacquer tray which had been smuggled out of the Japans. She believed completely in the Christ God and was so grateful that Mister Coffin sir had paid for her to go to the mission school so she could learn the pakeha language.

Pakeha customs and ways, however, were another matter. She was afraid she'd never understand. What was the harm in one man loving two women, or three, or four, or in one woman sharing the same number of men? Truly the pakehas' ways were strange! It would be so much simpler if Mister Coffin sir were Maori. Normal. She hoped these peculiar customs would not make trouble for the plans she'd made for herself and Mr. Elias sir.

5

It wasn't far from the commercial part of town to the home
Coffin had built for himself. It crowned a slight rise overlooking the Bay of Islands and the forests of masts which filled it. It
was a simple, unornamented two-story structure of wood and
stone, its walls unpainted and unpapered, its furniture purely
functional. But it was a veritable mansion compared to most of
the local residences.

As he approached he found his pace slowing. Not ten
minutes ago his life had been ordered, settled, assured. He'd
known what the day would bring and had a pretty good idea
about tomorrow. Now all was in disarray.

The sale of the Kauri would bring a handsome profit. There
was flax and rope to purchase from the inland tribes, minor
accounts outstanding to be settled, and a few debts to be
collected before ships weighed anchor and slipped into the
untraceable reaches of the Pacific. All of which now must be
put aside while he coped with something of greater dimen-
sions: the arrival of his family. His real, his legitimate family.

Nearby was a rocky outcrop that formed a natural chair. He
sat down and stared out across the bay, brooding for the better
part of an hour. No nearer a solution to his problems when the
sun was well up, he rose and purposefully surmounted the rest
of the incline. Always the meticulous planner, he was at last
going to have to improvise.

The door was unlocked. Murder, rape, and barbarities
unnamed were common as fleas in Kororareka, but vile acts
were performed only within that clearly defined part of town
known as The Beach. Their perpetrators stayed clear of local
citizens. A merchant troubled could count on his colleagues to
boycott any ship whose crew caused him difficulty and no
Captain could tolerate that. Here at least Holly would be safe.

What do I say? he wondered worriedly. How should I act?
Most important of all, has Holly *heard* anything yet?

As he entered, sounds drifted from the rear of the house into
the front parlor. It would be like Holly to have already enlisted
the Maori cook and houseman, Samuel, in arranging things to
her liking. He took a step toward the kitchen—and halted.

Someone had emerged from a rear hallway to block his path.
The new arrival was small and lithe. It stared up at him out of
wide, solemn eyes, absently sucking on a finger.

"Hello, Christopher." It took Coffin a moment to identify
this child with the infant he'd last seen in London. At the
mention of his name the boy whirled wordlessly and vanished
back down the hall. Coffin heard another new voice querying
him.

"Christopher, what on Earth. . . ?"

A magical, soothing, miraculous voice. It wiped away all
the worries, all the fear which had nagged him during the endless climb from store to home. Long buried, half-remembered
emotions suddenly welled up inside him and took complete
possession.

Then she was in his arms, repeating his name endlessly. He
was holding her before he had a chance to really look at her. It
was some time before they separated long enough to inspect
one another.

"Holly," he murmured. "Holly."

"I finally missed you too much, Robert." She broke away
long enough to reach behind her and drag forward the reluctant
stripling Coffin had startled moments earlier. "This is your
father, Christopher."

Coffin leaned slightly forward. "Hello, boy."

The child looked wary, but allowed Coffin to place both
hands around his small waist. Suddenly he was high in the air
gazing down at a wide, illuminating grin, and everything was
all right. He giggled.

A peculiar sound, new to the recently erected home. Coffin
put the boy down gently. The lad promptly ran and hid behind
his mother's skirt.

"He looks well. Better than I remember him."

This time he thought her smile was slightly forced. No
matter. It didn't mar her delicate beauty any more than the full,
flowing dress could conceal her petite, perfect figure. She'd let
down her chestnut hair and bound it neatly behind her. He was

right: she'd already set to work making the house her own.
Holly Coffin had ever been as industrious as she was beautiful.
Only mention of her son's health seemed to sap some of that
beauty.

"Today he's doing well, but the voyage was hard on him."

Coffin shrugged it off. "The journey from London to here
would challenge the constitution of the healthiest man in
England."

That brought back the warm smile. "His attacks of the colic
are less frequent than when last you saw him, but his general
condition is not encouraging. The doctors fear his health will
always be at risk, but it is true he has made some gains. They
told me the climate here might be good for him."

"Certainly he'll be warmer than he would be in England, but
a visit won't have any lasting effects."

"Visit? We're not here for a visit, Robert."

He shook his head slightly. "I don't understand."

"Of course you do. We're here to stay, Robert."

"But you can't stay here!" He made helpless gestures with
his hands. His brain finally took control and directed them to a
window overlooking The Beach. "That's the worst hole in the
Pacific right there. Maybe the wildest place on the planet.
There are nights when it offers the Devil ten thousand souls to
choose from. Ten thousand wild, drunken, mindless men who
are not above committing any outrage that suits their rum-
sodden lusts. There have been times when permanent settlers
have been the object of their attentions. This is no place for a
respectable Englishwoman."

"Now Robert," she told him patiently when he'd finished,
"you know me better than that. I won't stand for any silliness.
I've made up my mind. If you'll recall I once told you that I'd
follow you to Hell itself. I don't make such promises lightly."
Her tone softened. Moving close again she put both arms
around his waist and leaned her head against his chest. She was
warm and smelled slightly of roses.

"Two and a half years, Robert. Nearly three counting the
voyage over. That's no life. It's certainly no marriage."

"I'm sorry." He resisted the urge to bury his face in her
hair. "I know I promised to come home once a year, but these
past three have been so full of new business, new enterprises. . . ."

She looked up and put a finger to his lips. "No matter.

Everything will be all right now. I understand. You were right to stay here and build our future, and you've done well. You can't be running back and forth to England just to sate domestic whims. Here, I have something to show you."

She slipped free of his grasp and disappeared into a back room, leaving Coffin and Christopher to gaze appraisingly at each other until she returned. She was wearing an elfin grin as she handed him the thin, wrinkled envelope.

"What's this?"

"Go on, open it." She looked like a little girl at Christmastime as she took a step back and gave him room.

He eyed her a moment longer, then slit the seal with a fingernail, slid the contents out and read. It took some time for the substance of it to register fully.

It was a bank draft, on the Bank of England, made out in the name of Robert Coffin, for the sum of two thousand six hundred pounds.

He looked up at her, whispered, "Where—*how* did you manage this?"

"I told you we've come to stay, Robert. To build a future here together. We'll have a real marriage again, and I will cope with the worst this bottom corner of the globe places in my path. So long as there is a church and one or two women of my own station to talk with I will be content. As to Christopher's schooling, I've no idea what facilities you have here but I can manage that myself if need be."

"You won't have to." Coffin was still in shock. The figures on the bank draft dominated all else. "There are several excellent mission schools. He can attend any of them provided you've no objection to him sitting next to a native."

"Anyone acceptable to the holy fathers is acceptable to Christopher. It will enhance his education."

He shook the bank draft at her. "You still haven't explained this." His mind was racing with previously unimagined possibilities. Twenty-six hundred pounds. In this part of the world that was a small fortune. Deposited safely in any sound financial institution, it would give him a line of credit usually available only to the wealthiest men in Australia. Never again need Coffin House worry about paying for goods in cash.

"I sold the house," she told him.

He blinked. "What?"

"The house; I sold it. It wasn't a home anymore, Robert. It

hasn't been a home for years. It was simply where we lived in your absence."

"But I thought that's what you always wanted. A fine city manse staffed with servants and. . . ."

For the second time she hushed him. "All of that I would like, Robert. I deny it not. But it's you I want most of all. The rest can come later."

"What, here? In Kororareka?" He burst out laughing. "Woman, there are no fine houses in Kororareka. This isn't Brighton." Turning a slow circle he indicated the absence of paint and paper, pointed to the cracks between the floorboards. "And this is the finest house in Kororareka."

"It could be made whole. Chink the cracks and put up some nice paper with flowers, a good painting here and there to break the monotony of the walls. Someday there will be craftsmen here along with the whalers."

"You are an incorrigible person, Holly Coffin."

She smiled. "I married an incorrigible man. It will work, Robert. You'll see. Leave the details to me. And now, if you can, tell me that our presence makes you truly unhappy."

He found himself unable to meet her gaze. "You shouldn't have come here. This isn't the place for you."

Her voice was soft, husky. "Tell me you're not pleased to see me."

"And there are the Maoris to consider," he rambled on. "They're not treacherous, but they are unpredictable. One will make himself your friend for life while his brother will cut off your head to sell on the open market when your back is turned."

She winced slightly at the image thus presented. "Say that you're not glad to see me."

Unable to look away any longer he turned back to her, and lost himself in those luminous dark eyes. "If I'd known. . . ."

Then he was stealing her breath again, locked in her arms, and he knew for a certainty he would never be able to reply to her question. The embrace was long, the kiss infinite.

"What about your parents?" he was finally able to say.

"As you might imagine, they objected to my decision far more strenuously than you ever could."

"How did you manage it? What did you tell them? I

would've thought your mother would have locked you up to prevent it.''

"It was simple. I told them they could have a daughter in New Zealand or no daughter at all.''

His wife's family was tight and close. It only made him admire all the more what she'd gone and done. "You didn't have to do that.''

"Of course I did. I had to do it for you, husband. For us. Is there any better reason for doing such a thing?''

For that he had no answer. "You shouldn't have burned your bridges this way.''

"It's done,'' she said with finality. "This is my home now, as it has been your home. You cannot be entirely displeased.'' She was teasing him now.

"I'd always thought to return to England after making our fortune.''

"You're not a man for theater and parties, Robert. I know you that well. Make a fortune if you must and we'll have a grand house here in this new land, but an English country gentleman you'll never be.'' She indicated the child hovering about her skirts. "And there's Christopher to think of. I would not see the boy grow up fatherless.''

"Why say such things? I've lived with the guilt of that for years.''

"I did not say it to make you feel guilty, husband. I said it because it needs be said. Do you find fault in it?''

"No, I can't. You've spoken nothing more than the truth.'' Something made him pause and look past her. "What's that?''

She followed his gaze. "What is what, husband?''

"That aroma.''

"Is there something wrong with it?''

"Wrong with it? It's wonderful! What is it?''

"Oh, I've already made myself known to your cook and houseman, Samuel. From what I saw of his kitchen I don't think I'd care for Maori cuisine.''

"He's a good man,'' Coffin protested.

"A mite old, I should think, for caring for this house as well as doing all the cooking.''

"There's little to care for and my wants are simple.''

"No longer. I will take charge of the kitchen.'' It was a statement of fact, not an issue open to debate.

"Samuel won't like that.''

"Samuel and I have already come to a meeting of the minds."

The warm smell drifting out of the kitchen was making him salivate. "What *is* that?"

"You will find out soon enough, husband. I promise that from this day forward you will dine properly and well, the efforts of your valiant but ill-educated Samuel notwithstanding. Why did you settle on so elderly a housekeeper?"

"The younger Maoris consider it degrading to work for hire. The attitude is changing slowly, but to take on work still requires the permission of one's chief and the chiefs are reluctant to grant such permission because they desire to keep all their young men available for fighting."

"Fighting? Fighting with us?"

He chuckled. "Generally no. God's blood but there never was a people who took such delight in slaughtering each other. They have not even the promise of a life after death, yet they take great pleasure in massacring their neighbors on the slightest pretext. It's all jolly good fun, you see." He waited with interest for her reaction.

"In that case they'll be too busy to bother the settlers, won't they? Poor things. Oh, and Robert, there's no reason to swear in front of the boy."

It required an effort to remember this was no insubordinate deckhand standing before him. Besides, she was right. She usually was. Holly Coffin's rightness was one of the things which caused him to visit England so infrequently. It was infuriating to be married to a woman so consistently correct, so regularly right in her opinions. Though it had to be admitted there were worse faults in a woman—though not many. The rich aroma coming from the kitchen mitigated any anger he felt.

"I made do," she told him apologetically, "with what I could scavenge from your larder. Tomorrow I will shop for proper foodstuffs. I will take Samuel with me. It will do him good to be of service. As there are other families in permanent residence here I presume there are reasonably safe places for an Englishwoman to do her provisioning?"

"There's one shop and one only that caters to the needs of the permanent inhabitants. Samuel can show you. I must insist you repress your natural curiosity, which I remember so well, and stay away from those businesses whose primary concern is the provisioning of ships. Any woman who strays into such places is regarded as fair game, and not even my name and reputation would be sufficient to protect you. Bear that in mind every time you set foot outside this house."

"They are Englishmen," she argued. "Surely Englishmen, however rough their company on board ship, would not presume to harm a lady."

"Madame, you presume too much. Englishmen there be in Kororareka, and Yankees, and Chinamen, Kanaks and Samoans and Fiji-men who still enjoy dining upon their fellows. All have their perception blinded by rum. Keep clear of them, woman. You're not setting up house in Queen's Court."

She put her hands on his arms. "I will take care, husband, though there's little after months at sea that I wouldn't risk for a basket of fresh vegetables. In any event I consider any risks I may take as less than yours. Now come." She drew him toward the couch, the single decorous piece of furniture in the entire room. "Sit down beside me like you used to. I have much to tell you of England and much to learn of this, my new home."

So Coffin sat, reluctantly at first, later with pleasure, and they talked of old friends and new. All this he did with half a mind. The other half was elsewhere, roaming the rooms of another house entirely, even as he wondered if a man could be condemned as guilty for being adulterous in his thoughts. Thoughts of the irrepressible, sensual woman of his recent life, of the woman who was not his wife.

6

"Well, husband?"

Coffin pushed back from the table. Everything edible had been swept from its surface as quickly as a puritan's vow on The Beach.

"As you promised true, that was the finest meal I've enjoyed since I was last in England."

She smiled contentedly. Christopher had long since finished his own dinner and was now exploring the land behind the house under Samuel's watchful eye. Master and Mistress had been left alone at their table.

"Especially the pudding." He still savored the flavor. He'd nearly forgotten what Yorkshire pudding tasted like.

"Thank you, Robert. I apologize for the setting."

"This is not a fancy house. I've no need to eat with silver. Simple plates are sufficient for me."

"I also, but someday it would be nice to have proper china."

"And so you shall one day. I promise you. Silver from Bond Street and the finest china Cathay can provide! Clippers sometimes put in at Kororareka on their return journeys as well as on their way out. I know a few Captains well. I could arrange for a pattern to be designed for you if you wish."

Her reply surprised him. "Not yet. House and furniture first," she said firmly. "China when we've a proper place to display it."

He stared at her admiringly. Can I truly be sitting here like this, he asked himself in disbelief? Sitting full-bellied and content like some pleasant Haymarket merchant across the dinner table from a lovely, demure wife, having just finished a meal fit for a lord? Or is it naught but a dream?

Distant echoes of musket fire breached the solitude of the dining room to assure him it was no dream. A party in progress

38

down on The Beach. Despite the sharp reminder, the debauchery of reveling whalers seemed miles away now.

A knock came from the door, a weak echo of the gunfire. He was puzzled. Visitors were not common here and those residents who sought him out were most likely to do so at the store. While Holly busied herself clearing the table he rose to see who had come calling.

She was handling it well, he had to admit. That could change in the days to come. She'd not been in Kororareka long enough yet to catch her breath.

A veritable army confronted him on the porch: men clad in work clothes, seamen's garb, and formal attire. His gaze flicked over them.

"Gentlemen, I hardly know how to greet you. To what do I owe the pleasure of this invasion?"

"We apologize, Coffin." The man who spoke tended to plumpness in his face and body. His muttonchops had turned white, bypassing the gray which so distinguished Coffin. He could not avoid sampling the air in the house. "I hope we're not interrupting your meal."

"We've only just concluded, William. Please come in." He stepped aside and let them pass. They filed into the parlor and settled themselves on the plain furniture.

"Well then, friends, what's this about?"

"It's about all of us, Robert," Jonathan Halworthy told him. Halworthy was tall, slim, and addicted to high collars. "This talk is long overdue." Murmurs of assent and nods came from his companions. "Together with you, the six of us represent the leading citizens of Kororareka and this isolated fragment of Australia colony."

"We're the ones with the most money, John, if that's what you mean."

A few of them laughed; not all did. They were a solemn bunch today, Coffin mused. He saw they were staring past him. He turned, spoke awkwardly.

"Your pardon, gentlemen. Allow me to introduce my wife, Holly Coffin, newly arrived from London via the Canton clipper. Holly, my colleagues, friends, and competitors." He identified each and they rose to bow in turn. "Titus Abelmarc, William Langston, John Halworthy, Marshall Groan, Safford Perkins. That fuzz-faced lad on the end is Angus McQuade."

"Gentlemen." She curtsied perfectly.

There were polite nods and a few awkward smiles which Holly did not penetrate. Most of the men in the room were at least marginally aware of Coffin's relationship with the fiery Mary Kinnegad. Each kept this knowledge to himself lest he provoke something stormier than a polite reaction from their host. Handshakes and welcomes were exchanged as she moved from visitor to visitor. That of Angus McQuade was especially warm. His young wife Charlene pined daily for one of her own age to gossip with. McQuade was the youngest of the group and acutely conscious of the fact. He was also, however, the second hardest-working man in Kororareka after Robert Coffin.

"You said the leading citizens of this fractious community were all here," Coffin declared after his wife had left them to their business. "I don't see Tobias Hull among you."

Uncomfortable glances were exchanged. "We've already discussed this matter with Tobias," Abelmare told him. "We supposed, rightly as it developed, that he would refuse to come into your house."

"Well, no matter." Coffin chose to spare them any additional embarrassment. "It's thought in some quarters that Tobias and I are not the best of friends." Only Angus McQuade had the indelicacy—or the boldness—to laugh at that sally. "It matters not. I confess I've no more desire to see him in my home than he has to visit it."

"Now, gentlemen, what brings you here at a time better spent on business? John, you said we had to talk. About what?"

"It's good that your wife is here now, Robert. Perhaps it will incline you more toward the opinion the rest of us have already reached. As you know, all of us are married, with the exception of friend Perkins." The saloon owner nodded. "Several of us have children, born here or brought with us from home. We believe we six here represent the feelings of the majority of the permanent settlers, regardless of their social standing in the community. We've talked, in groups and individually, with the tradespeople and craftsmen. Kororareka is for them as it is for us much more than a temporary stopping place. Some have dreams of making their fortune and then returning to England or Sydney, but most look upon this land as their final resting place. These are feelings of which you are doubtless already well aware."

"There's nothing new in what you say, John."

Titus Abelmare spoke next. He was senior among them and the weight he carried was not all in his belly. "Coffin, this is no place to raise a family. Despite all our precautions and safeguards children cannot help but be exposed to many, shall we say, degrading influences. To an impressionable youngster the lure of the sea as expounded by rootless, irresponsible, but voluble seamen is intoxicating. I myself have two grandsons verging on manhood. I see them look longingly at the ships anchored in the Bay and I know it for a fact they sneak away from their lessons to spend time listening to the stories spun in the taverns. Neither I nor their parents wish to see them swallowed by the Pacific."

"Whalers make good money," Coffin said with a shrug. "If it be the boys' destiny. . . ."

"That's no destiny!" Abelmare's whiskers quivered with the fury of his response. "Drunk and wild in places like Sydney and Macao, that's no life. Apprenticeship to a ship's officer I would consent to, but the other, never. I wouldn't think you want that for a family of your own, Coffin."

Marshall Groan spoke up, since Abelmare was turning red in the face and was compelled to resume his seat. "Only last week my wife Helen was accosted on the town's main street. Not The Beach, mind you, but our own section of the community. I was not able to learn the identities of these men so that I could deliver a protest to their Captain. Now Helen refuses to leave the house without an escort. That's no way to live, Robert."

"You've obviously all given the matter considerable thought," Coffin replied softly. "What do you suggest?"

Halworthy leaned over the back of the chair which held Abelmare. "I've nothing against The Beach itself, Robert. . . ."

"I wouldn't think so, since it provides most of your income." Of them all, only Perkins had more of an investment in grog shops and gambling dens.

"I do not mean to play the hypocrite. The Beach can stay as it is. We can't change that anyway. But Kororareka *is* The Beach, and as Titus says, it's not a fit place for women and children. We believe the time has come to find another townsite far from The Beach's influence, a place where honest folk can work in peace and safety, where God-fearing people can go to church on Sunday without worrying that their prayers will be interrupted by the shouts and gunfire of drunken, godless men and pagans.

"We must build a proper school for our children and be able to set out sheep and cattle on the land without fear they will be butchered at night for the larder of some ship whose luck has been too bad to permit them to pay for provisions."

"Are you worried they'll butcher your sheep, or your children?"

"It's no jesting matter, Robert, as well you know. I hardly need remind you of the fate of William's best mares this past month."

Truly that was no joke, Coffin admitted. There hadn't been much left of the horses. Heads, hooves, and skeletons showed signs of neat butchering and quartering. His own animals did their browsing under guard behind a high corral. Still, he found it hard to blame the unknown perpetrators of the deed. A hungry man seeks food wherever he can. But he could also sympathize with the unfortunate Langston.

"There's only one solution to our situation here, Coffin," Abelmare harrumphed. "We must find a new townsite away from these whalers and their ilk. Not in this area. Should we settle anew on this Bay we will quickly find ourselves inundated with the same riffraff all over again and our resettlement efforts would be for naught. Of course our new town must have a good harbor, but that need not mean disaster. With Kororareka already well established as a whaler's port I do not think they would be quick to switch anchorages."

Coffin didn't have to ponder long. "Gentlemen, I'm delighted to say I agree with you." A few tense expressions relaxed and smiles appeared among the visitors.

"Now that we have decided what needs to be done, how are we to go about it? Recognizing a problem is not the same as finding a solution. As we are all too well aware, the Maoris control all the land in this vicinity, land which they have refused to sell to us on more than one occasion."

"The savages are not entirely ignorant," Groan pointed out. "They realize if they were to sell us good planting land they might lose their monopoly on the supply of food and flax. We are dependent on them for our very lives."

"We must seek farther afield," declared Halworthy firmly, "so that we may establish ourselves in country beyond the reach of the locals who have grown sophisticated through their dealings with us."

Coffin had reason to believe the Maoris were sufficiently sophisticated in matters of commerce long before John Halworthy and his colleagues had set up shop in the Bay of Islands, but it would have been impolitic to say so.

"You've put your finger on it. But we cannot plant ourselves in the middle of North Island. As Titus says, it should also be an adequate port as well as having good land for farming."

"I still think such a move is liable to bring the whalers with it," said McQuade.

Coffin shook his head. "I think not, Angus. Nor does Titus, and with reason. If the grog shops and brothels stay here, so will the whalers. There is something else also, something which has long concerned me but which I have not had reason to voice before now. Surely it must have occurred to some of you as well. The Lord is bountiful, but I do not think he provided the oceans with an endless supply of whales to gratify the light-starved of London and Paris." There were a few protests, which Coffin proceeded to stifle.

"Nay, there are a hundred ships berthed here now, and this is but one such port among many. Already I hear Captains muttering of hunts taking years that once took only months, of having to wander into waters still more distant as familiar whaling grounds are hunted out. I believe, gentlemen, that ten years will find us witness to the beginning of the end of the whaling industry as we have come to know it."

Louder murmurs of disagreement, and a few of dismay, were articulated by Langston. "Then what should we do for business?"

"Not all the craft that ply the Pacific seek the great whale. These others will still need new masts and spars and stores and rigging. Such businesses may decline, but they will not disappear. Meanwhile we must develop other markets and industries. Our economic base balances on the thin fulcrum of whaling. We must strive to expand it." He focused his attention on Langston and Halworthy.

"You say we are dependent on the Maoris for our livelihoods. This is true. It must change. We must be able to raise our own food. The land here is fertile and rich and the Maoris leave vast fields fallow. Surely we could develop a market for whatever excess we might grow. New South Wales and the rest of mainland Australia is filling up much faster than we. All those new mouths will need to be fed."

Abelmare was uncertain. "You're talking about estates, Coffin, when we don't own enough land to run more than a few cows and horses."

"Look to your future, Titus. We'll get the land we need. We *must* get the land we need, or we may as well pack up and go back to England with our tails between our legs."

"We'll need more than just the land," Langston pointed out. "Land and crops are useless if they're going to be trampled every year by a people who've less love of peace than the headhunters of Cape Colony."

"Well said, William. Obviously we must have a treaty with the Maoris. Not just those we purchase our land from but as many tribes as we can bring into the bargain. We must move slowly in our dealings with them. As soon as they see our grain mills they'll want mills of their own. Build a dam and they'll duplicate it." He couldn't keep his voice from rising. "We must *never* underestimate the Maori! They're not like the blacks of Cape Colony or the Red Indians of the Americas.

"But we will have the land and the peace. Surely there is enough of both in this country for all."

"What of those who disagree and feel our future lies with the whalers? I, for one, am not ready to squat down in the mud and become a farmer."

"Nor am I, Safford," Coffin assured him. "My business now is as dependent on whaler trade as yours. But we may one day have no choice in what we do."

"I agree." Abelmare puffed out his stomach and regarded his companions sagely. "No need to rush into this. We're not about to abandon Kororareka in a day. We will maintain our businesses here while simultaneously establishing ourselves elsewhere."

That mollified the reluctant, suspicious Perkins, but it wasn't enough for Langston.

"There's something else to consider. I've heard talk that the French are thinking of setting a colony on South Island. Remember gentlemen, we are not a British colony but only a distant extension of New South Wales. If the French choose to raise their flag here as they have done elsewhere in the Pacific I am not so confident the Crown would risk a fight with them over so distant and underpopulated a territory. If we are to

secure Crown protection we must make this country into
something Parliament will want to retain. That means a real
settlement, not just a way station for drunken sailors."

"Aye—well spoken, William!—Let's get on with it. . . !"
declaimed several of the assembled men.

"How should we commence this enterprise?" McQuade
wondered aloud.

"It seems simple enough," said Groan. "We must get onto
FitzRoy to begin dealing with the local chiefs."

That suggestion brought forth a derisive laugh from Safford
Perkins. "FitzRoy? That pompous ass? He believes the Maoris
to be the same childlike, innocent heathen he's dealt with
elsewhere, and they in turn regard him as a weak fool. Deny it
not, gentlemen." Perkins's eyes flicked around the gathering.
"Understand that I am not attacking Mr. FitzRoy personally.
He is a good man, a decent man, if something of a prig. His
problem is that he seeks to do everyone well. Out of
compassion for the Maori's 'innocence' he'd let them steal the
legs off his trousers."

"We must decide how best to proceed." Coffin spoke
quickly, to forestall the brewing battle between FitzRoy's
defenders and detractors. "I'll set my own thoughts to the
project. I advise all of you to do the same. I thank you for
sharing this with me. It's reassuring to know that we're all
more or less of the same mind in this matter."

He turned toward the front door, a signal to his guests that
the conference had run its course. Hats were donned, jackets
straightened. As they departed, each man shook hands with his
host.

"We're agreed, then," said Langston.

"All?" Coffin smiled thinly at his friend. "What of the
absent Tobias Hull? What was his reaction?"

"The same. There'll be no conflict there."

"It's a rare day when Hull and I agree on anything." Seeing
that such talk made the rest of them uncomfortable, Coffin
dropped it. "It's also a rare occasion when all of us get
together," he said more cheerfully, trying to dispel the
momentary gloom his reference to his bitter rival had engen-
dered. He stepped in front of McQuade and shut the door on
him. "Take off your hats again, gentlemen, and stay a while
longer. Enough of business, and the future!" Striding over to a

rough-hewn cabinet he threw open the double doors to reveal the contents.

"A few poor excuses for cigars and a better class of brandy. We should celebrate our determination."

"Now that's more like it." Safford Perkins slipped out of his coat and immediately launched into an energetic discussion of fine brandy.

The leading citizens of Kororareka spent a leisurely afternoon in the house of Robert Coffin discussing the weather, the need to travel ever farther afield to locate sufficient stands of Kauri pine, gambling, horses, and the virtues of Maori women.

Coffin's gaze eventually drifted to the darkening sky outside. "Gentlemen, we've succeeded in wasting away the afternoon. I think we all have things best done before nightfall."

"Quite right, quite right, Coffin." Abelmare heaved himself out of his seat. His colleagues moved to follow him, making their farewells one by one, the brandy having put them all in a good humor.

As if on signal Holly Coffin materialized from the back of the house. She'd changed from the sturdy, multi-layered traveling dress into a thin skirt and blouse that enhanced her figure. She was slim but well-fashioned, like the *Resolute*.

"Did your discussion go well, husband?"

"Well indeed. There was much to talk about. The principal topic I think you'd find of particular interest."

"And what might that be?"

"No point in remarking on it until a final decision has been made." He was teasing her. She pouted, and he found to his considerable surprise that he was enjoying this little domestic tete-a-tete. He looked past her.

"If my nose tells me true, you've been working more magic in the kitchen."

"Samuel's a fast learner. I wouldn't have expected him to memorize my instructions so quickly."

He nodded toward the door. "I see that I'm going to have to remind you, as I do my friends, not to underestimate the intelligence of the Maori, whether it be in matters of war, business, or cooking."

She laughed easily. "I'll try to remember. But now while there is still light you must show me the rest of the house, and the grounds."

His laughter was sharper than her own. "The house you've seen. As for the 'grounds,' there are none."

She tried but failed to hide her disappointment. "You mean this single plot of land is all we own?"

"In Kororareka, aye. I've also purchased some land in the interior where some day I hope to run cattle, but it's too far from town for me to give any attention to it just now. Coffin House absorbs all my daylight hours and I'm not ready to give that up for the life of a shepherd, my dear."

"I could not envision you as such." She took his arm and led him toward the couch. "So be it, then. At least you can enlighten me as to the disposition of our immediate neighbors, and the location of the shops where I will have to go to supply the household."

It had been a long time since Coffin had spent an hour just conversing with a woman, a subtle pleasure he'd all but forgotten. In addition to her beauty his wife was industrious and intelligent. Her interests ranged beyond sewing and cooking and the arts of housewifery. Nor was she reluctant to dispute with him on matters she felt strongly about, arguing her points calmly yet forcefully. While they talked the boy was in and about underfoot, having already adapted to his new surroundings with the ease of the young.

Samuel was particularly taken with the child, though he agonized over Christopher's thinness. Maori children were much like their parents; healthy, large-boned, and tending to plumpness.

Supper was another minor miracle. The candles, which had come all the way from Boston, were used for the first time since Coffin had purchased them. Holly had somehow fashioned napkins out of rags, substituting imagination for linen. As he sat down to table Coffin was certain he must have stumbled by mistake into the house of a baronet.

"Holly, you are a veritable wizard."

"Thank you, husband." A violent boom from the vicinity of town made her to look up sharply. "What was that?"

Coffin reached for his wine glass. "Most likely someone being murdered."

"Please, Robert, not in front of the boy."

"Best he learn where he lives." Christopher was ignoring both of them, intent only on his food. "Better he learn of it here first than on the street."

"You did say that someday we might have a home away from this awful place."

"Did I say that?" He forked meat into his mouth, chewed hungrily. Had she been listening to the discussion earlier? No matter. "All things are possible, in the future. But I will not hide truths which the day will bring anyway. The boy must know."

"Very well." She conceded the point without further comment. "If that is how it has to be. As to this meal you find so extraordinary, it's only chicken."

Coffin gaped at her. "Chicken? I have chicken all the time. This is like none I've tasted before."

"You've forgotten, husband, what the hand of an experienced woman can accomplish." More gunfire from the vicinity of The Beach. This time she didn't look towards it.

"And now," she said, rising, "if you'll help me we'll see our son to bed." She picked up one of the candlesticks.

"There are other things that need my attention first. I have to check on the horses."

She accepted the rejection gracefully. "I realize we each have our duties, husband, but you must get to know your son. You're no more than a cipher to him."

"That time will come." He turned and headed for the door.

Have to see to a proper bed for the boy, he mused as he headed outside. In his mind he was already refashioning one of the empty upstairs rooms. Toys would be needed, too. Strange to think of a child running free through a house more accustomed to the shouts of drunken men and loose women.

The stable was peaceful, alive only with contented snuffling and the smell of new-mown hay. He returned to the house, his thoughts full of business more pressing than how to deal with an unexpectedly arrived wife and son.

It was a problem forgotten the instant he strode through the bedroom door. Holly stood waiting for him. Her hair cascaded across her shoulders and back, framing her upper body. The silk nightdress she wore clung to her like rain, while the candle on the dressing table threw delicate shadows into sharp relief.

He set his own candlestick aside, snuffing out the flame with damp fingers, wishing the other problem which tormented him could so easily be extinguished. No time to worry about that now. Time now for nothing save the heat of her in his arms as he lifted her and carried her toward the bed. She neither blinked nor looked away from his eyes.

Three years is a long time. Memories fade. More than food and politics and social life is forgotten. Holly brought the important things back to him in an overwhelming rush of passion. . . .

7

"Can you not stay a little longer, husband?"

She was lying on the bed, her head supported by one hand. Daylight outlined her body, giving her the look of fine sculpture. The silk nightdress was a small crumpled pile on the floor.

"Now Holly, we've had little enough rest this night and I've work that won't wait."

"Do you regret the loss of sleep?" she asked coquettishly.

He turned and walked back to the bed, bending to kiss her. He did it quickly, before she could wrap her arms around him. He'd forgotten how much strength that small body contained.

"Did I say that? But I can't linger. Already Captains and pursers will be fighting over the cargo I brought back from my last journey."

"What cargo is that?"

"Kauri pine, for replacing lost masts and broken spars. Much of my—of our business here is based on providing such supplies to the ships that call."

"This pine is good hardwood? Straight and true?"

"Yes, it. . . ," he broke off, smiling down at her. "Woman, I know that tone, and it has nothing to do with commerce. I heard it often enough this past night. It goes with a certain look."

"You saw that as well? In the dark?"

"Yes, in the dark. By the light that glowed from your face."

"If I glow, it's you who sets the wick afire."

"And I will do so again, but not this morning. There are nights to come."

"A lifetime's worth, Robert."

"But the day must be for work. You're a practical woman, Holly. You must understand."

"I understand, yes." She sat up in the middle of the rumpled

50

bed and stretched languorously. Watching her he nearly forgot
his resolve. "But I don't have to like it. Will you be able to
come home for lunch?"

"No. The morning is already lost. I'll be back for supper."

"For supper, and for dessert. Perhaps an English trifle?"

He all but fled from the bedroom, though it was a most
reluctant flight. Memories of the previous night flooded
through him. However, he'd spoken the truth. He was needed
down on the docks.

Those Captains most in need of wood for their ships were all
but attacking Elias Goldman by the time Coffin arrived. Rain
clouds mottled the sky above the Bay of Islands but the
occasional sprinkle did nothing to dampen the ardor of the
potential buyers. They pushed and shoved—decorously, as
befitted their status—for the best vantage point.

The Kauri had been removed from the schooner and stacked
neatly near the end of the pier. Ship's carpenters clambered
over it like termites, checking each log for grain, insects,
knots, wood rot and splits. Each log had already been graded
by Goldman, but each carpenter had to repeat the process to his
individual satisfaction.

The factotum's relief was palpable when he spotted Coffin
forcing his way through the jostling, arguing crowd. They'd
been told the sale would begin hours ago and they were
impatient to the point of violence. Goldman had already
sacrificed his hat to the mob. He was sweating profusely.

"Thank goodness you're here, sir." He ran a handkerchief
across his forehead. "I've had a time of it keeping them under
control." Coffin noted the presence of armed seamen from the
Resolute stationed around the logs and pitch barrels. He
clapped his assistant on the shoulder.

"I won't be late again, Elias. Come, let's make ourselves
rich."

A podium had been set up on the sloping land just beyond
the pier. Goldman stepped up behind it and rapped on the wood
with a hammer.

"Gentlemen, gentlemen! I apologize for the delay. The sale
will now commence."

"About bloody time, too!" yelled one of the Captains. A
roar of approval mixed with laughter seconded his opinion.

"I know you've all been waiting a long time." Obscenities

greeted this observation by Goldman. Without further ado he stepped aside. "I introduce to you the master of the schooner *Resolute* and her cargo, the honorable Mr. Robert Coffin."

A few cheers and not a few hoots greeted Coffin. Goldman picked up his heavy ledger and stood ready nearby as his boss surveyed the mob.

"Well gentlemen, I recognize some familiar faces among you, scattered in among the strangers. For benefit of the latter I'll explain the procedures of this sale. Each log will be sold individually, the smaller trimmed branches in bound lots. What is not sold will be available for later inspection in my warehouse, for those of you who might entertain second thoughts about putting to sea undersupplied." He gestured to his left.

"This is my assistant, Mr. Goldman. He will record the name of each buyer and vessel. Each log is marked clearly on both ends. Make certain of those you choose to bid upon, for once the sale is concluded there will be no exchanges, nor will I accept claims of mistaken identity. Those of you who wish to make your own arrangements for conveyance of your purchases back to your respective vessels can pay Mr. Goldman and remove your property thereafter. I can provide transportation for those of you without facilities. I realize some of you have been standing at anchor waiting for just such a sale as this, and I'll not delay a man among you any longer than is necessary to relieve you of your gold or sterling."

Good-natured laughter rippled through the crowd. One reason Coffin did as much business as he did with these men was that he was a seaman himself and understood their problems.

"I might also take this opportunity to remind you all that Coffin House stocks a large supply of ships' stores as well as such ephemera as brass spittoons and fine American and Turkish tobaccos. We'd be pleased to share a cup of tea with any of you, whether you make a purchase now or not.

"For those of you who've no inclination to depart these fair shores immediately I can provide storage at no charge for your purchases should an insufficient number of your crew be presently disposed to such labor." This was Coffin's polite way of saying he would hang onto any Captain's goods if his crew happened to be too drunk to walk.

"As you can all see, this pine is not your usual English or

American variety. More than that, this particular shipment has been dried and cured prior to delivery. You'll find no green wood here, gentlemen. Those of you who've used the Kauri before know that it grows straight, tall, and branchless to great heights. This is the seaman's tree, sirs." He leaned toward his assistant. "Announce the first number, Elias, and the minimum price."

A few outraged cries attended the figure Goldman cited, but these were soon overwhelmed in the excitement of the bidding. It took all the rest of the morning and into late afternoon before the sale was concluded. There was little left to be warehoused.

The total realized exceeded Coffin's wildest hopes. Now the services of the *Resolute*'s sailors were required not to watch the cargo but to guard the heavy iron and brass strongbox which held the day's receipts. In addition to the coin and paper there were a few signed IOU's. These last came from men short of ready cash but heavy-laden with whale oil. Coffin accepted the liquid readily. In Kororareka it was as valuable a medium of exchange as gold or silver.

Coupled with the unexpected windfall Holly had gifted him with, Coffin House would now be able to greatly expand its presence and inventory. There would be enough left over to begin buying property from the inland Maoris. The dream of a vast estate roamed by herds of sheep and cattle might at last become a reality.

Of course, as Abelmare and the rest had pointed out, such land was valueless without a comprehensive peace treaty that included all the relevant tribes. He mulled that problem over in his mind as he studied the small cluster of natives who had waited silently to one side of the pier. There were two low chiefs, no ranking arikis.

They'd been there for the duration of the sale, listening and watching, occasionally murmuring among themselves. Now that the sale was at an end they turned and marched away. Coffin knew what they'd been about. These "ignorant primitives," as Halworthy and others preferred to call them, had been noting the prices being paid for the Kauri with an eye toward raising the prices of their own supplies.

He wondered what they must be thinking of his journey to South Island. It showed they had no monopoly on the Kauri trade. Perhaps prices for local wood might even come down as a result. Keeping ahead of the Maori kept Coffin and his fellow merchants on their fiscal toes. No tougher financial wars were waged on distant Fleet Street.

The last bundle of spars was winched clear. Kauri-laden longboats scattered like waterbugs into the Bay. Coffin paused long enough to examine the contents of the strongbox a last time before securing the heavy padlock. For an exact total he relied, as always, on his factotum.

"How exactly did we do, Mr. Goldman?"

The other man's face was shining as he displayed a long sheet of paper covered with figures entered in his precise hand. The ledger book he clamped against his ribs with his other arm. He pointed to the last entry on the paper.

Coffin noted it, nodded appreciatively. "I'd thought as much. A memorable day's work, Elias."

"Memorable, Mr. Coffin."

"Take charge of this. For myself, I think I will pay a visit to Mr. Langston's shop and see to the arrangements for the enlargement of Coffin House." Langston's specialty was construction, though his people spent most of their time working on ships instead of in town. That was going to change, Coffin told himself.

"As you wish, sir." Goldman rolled the paper and slipped it under his arm atop the ledger. "Will I be seeing you later today?"

"I think not, Elias. You handle things."

"Very good, sir." He watched his employer turn and stride toward town.

Goldman knew it was premature to begin expanding their facilities despite the day's fine profit. He knew that just as he knew that Coffin had a destination in mind which did not include a meeting with William Langston. Goldman liked Coffin greatly, their business relationship aside. It pained him to see the torment that was raging inside his friend.

Suddenly he remembered to shout: "Mr. Coffin, Mr. Coffin, sir! This afternoon—remember the flax sale!" If Coffin was so inclined, they now had enough ready cash to purchase the entire Maori stock.

Coffin waved back without turning and Goldman was satisfied that his employer had heard. Thus assured, he turned to Markham and the sailors and led them back toward Coffin House.

It troubled Coffin deeply that he couldn't convince himself

everything was going to be all right. It seemed straightforward enough. He would break the news of his family's arrival to Mary Kinnegad, explain the new order of things, and life would continue as before, slightly altered in appearance but identical in substance. No different from changing parties in Parliament, really. It would be noisy.

However, what was so neat and clean in mind crumbled the moment he began mounting the steps leading to the front porch of the little house behind Kororareka's main commercial street. Nor did fate grant him additional time to marshal his thoughts. Before he could touch the handle the door flew open and his arms were full of Irish Mary.

"Robert! Ah, Robert, I'd wondered if you'd got back. Only this morning I heard that the *Resolute* had put in." Her legs went up over his hips and her arms around his neck so that he staggered and barely kept the both of them from tumbling backward.

"You're a damned rogue for not putting into port yourself last night," she chided him slyly. "Where the Devil were you?"

"It was an exhausting journey and we docked not an hour before sunrise." He hoped he didn't sound as awkward as he was feeling. "I didn't want to disturb you." That wasn't what he'd planned to say, but Mary's overpowering presence had already made a mockery of his careful mental preparations.

"Disturb me?" She laughed, throwing her head back, her red hair flying. "Damn me, Robert Coffin, but there are times when you puzzle me!"

Gently he set her on her feet. She was nearly as tall as he was. Her green eyes flashed and her smile was mirror-bright.

"There was cargo to unload and grade and only this morning a furious auction on the pier. My presence was necessary," he mumbled.

"I heard talk of such, though I wouldn't think a few logs would put such demands on your time. Did you well?"

"Well enough."

"That's not how I heard it. From what's being said about town you're now rich as Croesus himself. And here be I, a poor honest woman with nothing to tempt a businessman." She grabbed his wrist and pulled him through the open door, lifting her skirt with the other hand to keep it from dragging on the dusty, raw wood porch.

"What of the children?" He was unable to turn his eyes from her as she closed the door behind them.

"Ah, a restless pair, those two. Flynn's taken his little sister up into the hills to look for birds' eggs."

"You let them run off free like that?"

She eyed him uncertainly. "Now what strange weather did you run into on your voyage, Robert? Why should I worry about them? The Maoris don't steal pakeha children and the sailors have no interest in any girl under the age of twelve. They'll be safe enough, and more satisfied than their mother be at this moment."

The brass bed creaked as she pulled him down on top of her.

"Mary." He could feel the heat of her through her dress. "We have to talk."

"Sure and we do, luv." She put a finger to his lips. "Later. Later we'll talk all you wish. It's been more than a fortnight since last I carried you, Robert. A lonely time."

"What, with a thousand sailors roaming the streets?"

"As if a man among them could turn my head the way my Robert does. You know right well there's only one coffin I'm bound to lie with."

He tried to talk around her frantic kisses. "Someday you'll truly be the death of us. Then such humor will lie heavily."

"Lie heavily then, and I'll die happy." She was working the buttons on his shirt.

"I'm told," he said lamely, helpless against her intensity, "that we had better weather at South Island than you did here. Most unusual."

"So they say." She yanked his shirt apart as easily as she'd split a slice of bread. "Two nights of storm we had, a wet fury that tore in off the Bay and like to blew the whole town a mile inland. Even the Maoris ran and hid from it. I'm surprised it missed you." He smiled slightly and she grinned back. "Ah, now that's better."

"The weather," he murmured. "We had a wizard with us. Old character name of Tuhoto. I gave him free passage and he claimed to have smoothed the way for us."

"A real Maori wizard? Now that I would like to have seen."

"Not 'real,' Mary. A convincing old fakir he was, but nothing more." Though if that were so, he wondered, how had the *Resolute* avoided the storm which seemed to have smashed the rest of the islands?

It was difficult to think because of what she was doing with her hands, with those long, strong fingers, with her lips. Somewhere in the back of his mind another thought screamed a warning at him. It was obliterated by rising passion.

A devil, he thought wildly. The woman is a devil from her red hair to her painted toes. She has entrapped my soul.

He was unable to deny that he allowed himself to be trapped willingly.

8

Before the sun had fallen low enough in the western sky to suggest the onset of night, the first sounds of heightened revelry began to rise from the vicinity of The Beach. On the brass bed a naked Coffin lay on his back with Irish Mary Kinnegad slung sideways atop him. He'd been staring silently at the ceiling for some time before she sighed impatiently and turned to face him.

"You're silent as the sea, Robert. It's not like you. I want to hear all about South Island. They say there are mountains there high as the Alps, that fall straight down into the ocean. Some of the old Maoris who come into town claim monsters dwell in the mountain valleys, giant roosters big as giraffes."

"What?" The image she'd unwittingly conjured up gave him a start by causing him to remember the huge feather old Tuhoto had worn in his hair. "You mean moas. The Maoris exterminated them centuries ago. All that's left are bones." But Tuhoto's feather had looked fresh, he remembered. More nonsense.

"The Maoris are as adept at lying," he told her, "as they are at making war. You shouldn't be taken in by their tales."

"Oh, I don't really believe any of it. I just like a good story, that's all. Now tell me, Robert," she whispered as she snuggled closer, "all about South Island."

He pulled a pillow under his head. "Beautiful it is, and rugged and rough."

"Very different from North Island?"

"From the Bay Islands, anyway. The place is cold, Mary. Colder than you'd believe, colder even than Ireland. If you were to turn Britain on its head and put Scotland at the bottom I think it would be much like this New Zealand. South Island's damp as well as cold, with forests of ferns tall as trees, and mountains and gorges you can't imagine. Fine harbors, too, where a man can bring his vessel right in to shore with ice hanging over his head. Beautiful indeed, but no place to live. There's not enough flat land to grow a head of cabbage. Myself, I like to be warm now and then."

"As if you had to tell me." She snuggled close.

Enough! cried a resurgent voice inside his head. Tell her now, tell her quickly, before it's too late. Before she learns of it in some grog shop from one of Langston's garrulous employees or one of Perkins's serving wenches. Before she strides up to the house itself and knocks on the front door.

"Mary, I said before we have to talk. There's a—problem."

She eyed him innocently. "If it be Flynn's schooling that's troubling you again I promise I'll get him into the mission school and see to it the boy does his lessons."

Coffin shook his head slowly. "It's not Flynn's schooling. Not this time. It's something else." He didn't look away from her now. Desire had been replaced by determination and he plunged on. "Two days ago my wife and son arrived here from England."

He waited for a reaction but she just lay there next to him, silent and unmoving. Eventually she sat up, her smooth back resting against the brass headboard, and stared thoughtfully down at him. Just stared, as if waiting.

When it became clear she wasn't going to be the one to break the silence he went on. "I want you to know that I didn't send for them. You must understand that. They arrived here unexpectedly and without seeking my consent."

"Sure and that's fine, that is." No warmth in her voice now, only a crackling sharpness. "Since they've done this thing without your leave, you won't feel bad when you send them back again."

"I can't do that, Mary. They intend to stay. My wife wants to make a home here. The boy is sickly and there's hope the climate here might do him some good."

"Keep the boy, then, and be rid of the woman."

"She won't go and I can't force her. It wouldn't work in any event, since she's sold the family home in London."

"What care I for her damned problems!" Mary screamed it, unable any longer to control herself. "A pox on her and her life that's been and her life to come! As for the house sold, you can bloody well afford to buy her another!"

"It won't work, Mary. She's a strong-willed, stubborn

woman. She won't go back." He tried to calm her as best he could. "Don't be angry. There's no reason for us not to continue as we have, with me providing for you and Flynn and Sally. This isn't London, but a man may still maintain both wife and mistress. There's no sin in it."

"Don't speak to me of sin, Robert Coffin! You who go to church but rarely and then only when it suits your business."

"I believe in a God," he countered, hurt that she'd speak to him thus.

"And I believe in love," she shot back, "and it's you I love, Robert Coffin. I'll *not* share you with another. Unless," and the smile that spread over her face was positively feral, "yes, wife and mistress, so be it! Divorce the bitch and marry me and let her play the role of mistress!"

"Mary, the die was cast years ago. I was a child when I married her but what's done is done. I can't change the past. Would you have that destroy a happy future?"

"Happy? Happy for whom?" She slid off the bed and began pacing tautly back and forth, all the while gesturing with her hands, her hair flying, quite oblivious to her nakedness. At another time the sight would have aroused Coffin, but not now. Arousal was replaced with anxiety and a desire only to have peace between them. There was also a still slight but growing anger. He wasn't used to being on the receiving end of such a tirade.

"I've not given myself to you these past years, have not born you two fine children, to be suddenly put aside like old silver because some dried-up hag from England has decided it's time for her to act the wife!"

"She always thought it was time." He spoke softly. She didn't sense the change coming over him. "It was I who always refused her permission to come here. Finally she has decided to come without that permission. Nor is she a 'dried-up hag.'"

Kinnegad halted abruptly and turned to face him, hands on hips. It was a pose fit to defrock a priest. "Oh, so she's prettier than me, is it?"

"Not prettier, no," he conceded, "but equal in a different manner. There's some of you in her and some of her in you."

"I want none of her in me! But I see how your mind is working. You want both of us, is that not it? What a fine world you men make for yourselves, playing with women as if we were toys."

"I've never thought that of you, Mary. You know that I'll never foreswear my responsibility to you or the children."

"No, but you won't give us your name, either."

"That name's already been given. I cannot change that. But there is no reason why we cannot be happy together as well."

"We? Or you, Robert? What happiness would *we* have? Oh, sure and there's no doubt *you* would be happy. But what of me? How long do you think you could maintain such a duplicity, anyway?" She gestured toward the town outside. "In this whole country there are less than two thousand settlers. How long before your secret became common knowledge? No, Robert Coffin, I'll not be laughed at behind my back by every man and woman striding self-righteously down the streets!"

"Don't underestimate my resources, Mary. It could be managed. I could move you away from Kororareka, away from prying eyes. I have land in the interior and I'm planning to acquire more. I could set you and the children up in safety and quiet. A small farm, perhaps."

She could hardly contain her derision. "A farm! Me, on a farm?" In truth it was hard to envision Irish Mary Kinnegad, with her love of dancing and drinking and a good time, pining away her days caring for chickens and hogs. Coffin tried another tack.

"A boat, then, equipped with all the comforts of home, anchored safely by an island out in the Bay."

"Oh, you're a sweet talker you are, Robert. You'd have me well and truly marooned, would you?"

His voice rose impatiently. "I'm trying to find a solution to this, damn you!"

"I've already given you the solution. Send the witch back to England. Stay with me, Robert," Her tone softened slightly. "I won't insist that you marry me. But I'll not share you."

"I can't marry you. I've told you that before this."

"Aye, but I had hopes—perhaps someday. . . ."

"Such hopes were never encouraged by me. I've never concealed knowledge of this marriage from you, Mary, not from the first day we met. You've known about it all along. There were no attempts to deceive you. If there's been any deception in this it's you who've deceived yourself."

"Have I now?" she yelled. "Have I!" She searched for

something to throw at him. The pillow she heaved didn't make him flinch. "Lived my own deception, have I? False hopes—maybe you think my love's been a deception too? My love for you is real, Robert Coffin!"

"And mine for you, Mary. It can stay thus."

"The Hell it can! Not unless that woman goes back where she came from and leaves us be. Let her find another, Robert. She's not for the likes of you."

She wasn't pretty when she sneered, he thought.

"I can see her, here." She tapped the side of her head, by her flashing right eye. "Genteel she is, pouring her tea while her pinky flutters about like a little pink worm. Flying into a tizzy if the silver's not set all proper on the table. Sits with her back rigid as a foremast and wouldn't dare be caught dead naked before a man in the daylight."

"You wrong her," Coffin responded tightly. "Holly's a good person. Her patience these past years proves it. What little she's done the few days she's been here confirms it. I will no more abandon her than I would abandon you."

"Well now Mister high-and-mighty Captain Coffin, that's not your choice to make, is it? If there's any abandoning to be done here it's *I* who'll make the decisions. Go on, go back to her, get out of my house and my sight!" She turned and picked up a porcelain candlestick that had come all the way from Shanghai. Coffin had made a gift of it to her years ago.

"Get out, I say! Stay away from me and *my* children. We don't need your kind of help. I've never needed any man's help!"

The candlestick exploded on the wall behind his head as he ducked. He started climbing into his clothes, keeping his eyes on her as she searched for another missile.

"I know you're upset now, Mary, but think about what you're saying when you've had a chance to calm down. You know your temper."

"Aye, I know my temper, and my resolve as well, Robert Coffin. 'Think' about it? I think I can't stand the sight of you anymore. What do you think of that?" She threw a boot, but this time he was waiting for it and dodged easily as it bounced off the headboard. He edged toward the door.

"Come back to me when you've decided that I'm the woman for you," she growled. "I'll not have half a man. There isn't a one in Kororareka, nay, in all the Pacific who wouldn't sacrifice his life's blood for me if I but requested it of him. I won't take less from you, Robert Coffin!"

"Say what you will, I've an obligation to the children. No matter how you feel about me I'll continue to provide them with support."

"Hang your support! I don't want your filthy money. I never wanted your money. It's you I want, Robert Coffin, and by Heaven I'll have you! You'll see, you'll be back. I know what I have to offer and you can't resist that any more than any other man!"

She might have been right about that—at one time, he thought. She might have been right save for one thing: Robert Coffin was not "any man." What he was, was the type of man who reacts instinctively and strongly to anything resembling a threat.

"Think carefully on what you say here, Mary Kinnegad. I'm not a forgiving one. If you throw me out now, in this manner, I won't come back."

"Then don't come back, damn you!" This time it was a knife she threw. It imbedded itself in the wall not a foot from his face. He hadn't seen her pick it up. It was a kitchen knife, but she'd thrown it like a sailor.

He stared long at it as it hung there, quivering in the wood of the wall. Then his gaze returned slowly to its owner. She stared unrepentantly back at him. There was no doubt she'd intended to put the steel into his neck.

"Have it your way, then," he said quietly. "I've offered all I can offer. Spurn it at your own risk."

"Your offer's bilge, Robert Coffin! You know what it is I want."

"I know, and I can't give it to you. If we break like this now, remember always who fashioned the parting."

"To the Devil with you, then! I'll find me another man, and I won't wait six years for him to marry me. Some dark cold night when your very proper English wife is snoring away in her thick muslin gown on her side of the bed you'll remember me. Oh, how you'll remember me! And remember what you gave up."

"That may be." His tone was so cold that for a moment her fury was muted. He glanced casually at the knife imbedded in the wall. "I'll remember that as well, though it hasn't cut as deeply as your words. Have a care, Mary Kinnegad. I loved you and would love you still, but if that's not good enough for you. . . ."

"Not on your terms," she snapped.

"Then let there be an end to it." He pushed open the door. "Remember always this was not of my doing."

"Oh, you're so sure of yourself, you and your stinking righteousness!" She heaved a wash pan. It bounced off the door as he closed it gently behind him.

She was still screaming as he started up the street, not looking back. Her insults echoed in his ears as he strode purposefully away from the little house he'd had built for her and the children.

Her raving was soon lost amidst the rumble of The Beach. Coffin forced his mind away from the thoughts of the woman who'd been his close companion for half a dozen years. From this evening on, he vowed, he'd think of her no more. She'd made her choice. Let her live it.

The Crippled Raven was the nearest grog shop where a man could be sure of a tot of rum that wouldn't poison him. He angled toward it. In his mind there were no regrets. He intended it to remain thus. A few full mugs would help mightily.

"I tell you," he found himself muttering much later to the shop's manager, "there's nothing you can do with them. Nothing!" He stared gloomily at the floor as he cradled his tankard between his hands. "No matter how you strive to accommodate yourself to their wishes there's never an end to them."

"And who might 'they' be, sir?" inquired the barkeep politely.

"Women of course, you damn fool! Where are your ears?"

"Your pardon sir. I should have divined your intention."

Coffin guzzled from the tankard and wiped his lips with the back of a forearm. "She'll not get another shilling out of me. She does this by her own hand. I thought Kinnegad many things these past years but never a fool. Not this kind of fool, anyways."

"What's that?"

Coffin ignored the comment.

"I said, what's that?" The seaman now standing very close behind Coffin towered over everyone else in the shop. A small coterie of admirers bunched up behind him, nudging one another in the ribs and whispering like so many loquacious remoras hugging the belly of a shark in anticipation of its next kill.

"I've been listening to you, sir, for several minutes now. Do I understand that you be Robert Coffin, he of Coffin House?"

This time Coffin turned, curious. "I am that man."

"The one who's been squiring Irish Mary these past years?" Coffin nodded slowly. "And from your talk do I take it this is no longer the case?"

"You take it correctly, friend."

The man let out a rough guffaw. "This is a shining day, indeed! For two years now I've dreamed of little but lying in that Irish whore's bed. If you've no further claims on her, sir, then by God I intend to stake mine." This sally provoked laughter from the knot of hangers-on.

Coffin studied the man so solemnly that his attendants quieted rapidly. In the silence that ensued one of them muffled a nervous cough. Then Coffin turned to stare into his tankard.

"Do what you will with her, if she'll have you. I've done with her."

"So you say, so you say." The big seaman prodded Coffin with a knowing elbow. The barkeep discreetly edged away. "Bored with her, eh? I hope you ain't used her up, though from what I've seen of her on the streets there's still ample land left for plowin'."

Coffin slowly put his empty tankard aside and turned once more to study the man. Very big, with his hair cut short and his face scarred by some sharp instrument.

"Friend, Mary Kinnegad is no whore. If she were, that would make me a whorer, wouldn't it?"

The big man's eyebrows drew together. "I don't follow you, sir. You've just confessed to breaking with the wench."

"Her, yes. Her memory, no."

The sailor hesitated, then smiled and tried to recapture the jollility of a moment earlier. "It ain't her memory I aim to make use of."

"What might you be called, friend?"

"Shaun Connaught. Formerly of Liverpool, lately of New South Wales. I was told there were places down here where an Australian ex-convict could make a life for himself without police to harry him, so I've spent these past two years seeing to the cleaning of ship's bottoms, for I can hold my breath underwater longer than any man." He drew himself up, continued boastfully, "I'm always in demand, for 'tis a rare ship puts into Kororareka that doesn't have her bottom fouled."

"Yes, I can see that you're someone who's spent a lot of his time under water. The continual submersion has obviously softened your head. Otherwise you wouldn't be speaking of Irish Mary Kinnegad as you have."

Connaught's expression turned unpleasant. "Here now, Coffin, I don't care how much money you have or what your position in this port may be, but you can be certain there's nothing soft about me save my temper. Otherwise I'd have you by the shirt collar this instant and be shaking some manners into you."

"If it's manners you wish to discuss, friend Connaught, I'm willing to oblige you."

The man's companions retreated, murmuring excitedly. Connaught rolled up his sleeves and took a step back, curling his massive hands into fists.

"It seems I must teach you a lesson, sir, though it pains me to see a man take a beating for nothing. It's one thing to fight over a woman, but middlin' strange to do so for one you've confessed to giving up."

Coffin eased off his stool. "Let me be the judge of what I fight for."

"Hold!"

Both men turned toward the bar. John Fee stood next to his barkeep. The owner of the Crippled Raven faced the room holding a brace of naval pistols. He nodded behind him.

"Three times this year I've had to replace this mirror. Do ye know how difficult it be to find a mirror in this part of the world? I've no interest in your quarrel but much in its locale. Outside if you please, gentlemen." He gestured with the pistols.

Coffin swung a hand toward the door. "After you, Mr. Connaught."

"Nay, sir." The sailor managed a mocking bow. "Gentlemen first." Coffin nodded back and preceded his opponent to the exit.

A small crowd began to gather as the word spread. Not that fights were so rare as to draw attention in Kororareka, but there was plenty of novelty in the fact that this one involved a renowned bare-knuckler like Connaught and a reputable businessman like Coffin.

Connaught removed his shirt and handed it to one of his cronies. Betting had already begun. It favored the seaman two-to-one, for while Coffin was as tall he carried nowhere near as much weight as his challenger.

"A pound on Coffin!" shouted someone in the crowd.

"I'll take that!" came the instant reply. "You're a fool for betting on the squire. The sailor has a stone on him."

"I'll take it anyway." The wagering surged back and forth among the pushing, shoving onlookers as the combatants readied themselves.

A sailmaker Coffin knew took charge of his shirt and jacket. Both men faced each other and began circling the circumference of an imaginary ring while the crowd cheered them on.

"I'll try not to break anything vital, sir." Connaught was grinning widely.

"Have a care it isn't your hand," Coffin responded.

"Try to end it afore sundown!" yelled one of the watchers. "I've got to be back aboard me ship by dark."

By dark. Coffin hesitated as he glanced sideways toward the horizon. The sun was already low. How much time had he sipped away in the Crippled Raven?

"Bloody Hell," he muttered.

Connaught stopped circling. "Now what's this?"

"I can't fight you, son of Liverpool." Coffin's declaration provoked moans from the crowds. "I'm desperately late for a vital business gathering."

"Sir, I've no wish to harm your business, but I remind you we have important business of our own right here."

"Another time, Mr. Connaught. I promise you." Coffin was already redonning his shirt.

The sailor wasn't mollified. "I'm not one for appointments, sir."

"My apologies. Business first." Slipping into his jacket, Coffin prepared to leave.

Connaught reached out and grabbed him. "I'm not one for leaving a discussion half completed."

"Then we must make an end for it."

Coffin's fist moved so fast that several men in the crowd later swore they hadn't seen it rise. For an instant a couple thought

Connaught had been shot instead of struck. Indeed, the big sailor went down like a man who'd caught a bullet, a startled expression on his face. He hit the earth with a thud. Immediately his friends clustered above him.

One looked up. "He's out cold."

"Well struck!" shouted several members of the audience, while others yelled "Shame, shame!"

A well-respected merchant name of Briar stepped into the circle. "Nay. A bit of surprise there may have been, but the fellow was looking right at Mr. Coffin when he was hit. He had every chance to block the blow, dodge, or strike back. I declare Coffin a fair winner in the exchange."

Instantly half a dozen new fights erupted among the crowd as disgruntled bettors began trying to settle their own disagreements as to what had happened. No one paid any further attention to Robert Coffin as he hurried up a side alley. The black mare he borrowed kicked dirt as he swung himself into her saddle.

Then he was flying down the main street, scattering sailors and wide-eyed citizens with fine impartiality.

9

Two hours of daylight left. Coffin cursed himself for a forgetful
fool as he urged his mount onward. Goldman had reminded
him of the flax sale. Today the Maoris would offer three
months' accumulation of raw flax and rope for purchase by the
merchants of Kororareka. If he arrived too late, after everything had been sold, he'd have no rigging to proffer to ships'
pursers.

He forced himself to refrain from taking a whip to the mare.
She wasn't his and he didn't know her limits. If he ran her
down before reaching the trading site he'd be well and truly
stranded. So he let her set her own pace and tried to will the
setting sun to a halt. Once it fell below treetop level all trading
would cease.

The journey seemed as long as the cruise back from South
Island, but the sun still cast long shadows as he finally brought
the foaming, panting horse to a stop by the hitching rail.
Nearby, the ocean lapped at a rocky beach. Other horses stood
stolidly where they'd been secured. None glanced up as he
sprinted past them. There were a couple of imported buggies
and empty wagons awaiting their owners' purchases. Drovers
gathered in small groups paused in their chatter and gambling
to stare as he ran up the hill.

A few buyers turned to look at him when he arrived, out of
breath and concerned, but the attention of most was focused on
the center of the clearing where loud shouting was proof the
sale wasn't over.

Beneath the trees several crudely fashioned tables had been
hammered together. Each table displayed heavy bundles of
cleaned flax and raw rope. There was little remaining. Men
were already starting to carry paid-for loads back toward the
wagons below.

A few lean-tos stood off to one side of the clearing. They

shielded men in business suits from sun and rain. They were trading figures and gossip as the sale wound down. Coffin recognized most of them. Some were principals but most were Elias Goldman's counterparts, representatives of the leading merchants of Kororareka. Of the latter group only William Langston had elected to appear in person. Though Langston was a competitor, Coffin considered trying to buy some of his stock.

On the far side of the clearing stood a simple Maori meeting house. It was devoid of the elaborate woodwork for which the natives were justly famed. It was suitable as a temporary structure only, though it put the Europeans' lean-tos to shame.

Chiefs stood outside and conversed quietly. Their own finery was as elegant as anything one might encounter parading the Strand. One cloak in particular caught Coffin's attention; a full-length robe made entirely of rare kea feathers.

He started toward Langston. At the last instant he swerved instead toward someone clad differently from merchant and Maori, a man whose replies were less likely to be couched in commercial terms.

"Parson Methune?"

The man turned a sunburned face up to him. He was lean as a slab of salt pork and almost as young as Coffin. "Robert Coffin. I'm surprised to see you here so late. You've missed most of the business."

"I know that, Parson," he said impatiently. "What I need to know now is how that business proceeded, and who gained what?"

Methune smiled. "God deals equally with all men, Robert."

"All right, I know. A suitable contribution will find its way onto the collection plate. Now tell me: how went the bidding?"

"The heathen quickly disbursed nearly all their wares."

"Who did the buying?"

Methune didn't hesitate. "I think you know Tobias Hull."

Damnation! Hull wouldn't sell Robert Coffin enough rope to hang himself. He strained to search the crowd of buyers. Hull wasn't under the lean-tos. That was like him. He didn't fancy himself a gentleman like Ablemare or John Halworthy. Hull kept to himself except when business demanded otherwise. He was as ruthless as he was clever and he particularly disliked young Robert Coffin, who'd done so well in so short a time. This didn't disturb Coffin since the antipathy was mutual.

And because of his tardiness, Coffin berated himself, Hull had been able to purchase the bulk of the flax. What an idiot he'd been for neglecting business in favor of arguing uselessly with Irish Mary! Now it was going to cost him dear.

Well, he'd close down Coffin House before he'd beg an ounce of flax from Tobias Hull. Not that Hull would sell to him anyway.

The last of the trading tables were being cleared. No other Maoris stepped forward to submit rope or flax for sale. Despite his frantic ride it looked like he was still too late.

A hand clapped Coffin on the shoulder. As he turned, the hand dropped away and he found himself staring into the grinning face of Tobias Hull. How long his arch-rival had been standing close by Coffin had no way of knowing, but Hull looked quite pleased with himself.

He was older than Coffin by several years, of moderate height and already tending to fat. Hull could even envy the younger man his prematurely gray head of hair, for his own had already disappeared. His face, eyes, ears and nose were all quite round. A thick mustache shaded the thin slit that was his mouth.

"Well if it ain't my good friend, young Robert Coffin!" he intoned loudly and with false humor. "I don't recall seeing you earlier, Coffin. Can it be you've decided to forgo the business of supplying rigging to ships?"

"I was delayed." Coffin was cool but correct. "As you may have heard, I had to dispose of a rather large quantity of Kauri transported all the way up from South Island. Totaling the receipts and checking the disbursement is taking more time than I thought."

Hull's smirk vanished. Everyone knew of the bulging strongbox Coffin's men had hauled away from the Kauri auction.

"As I will be counting the profits from this day's transactions. Spars and masts are useless without rigging to run sails on them. Rigging which I will readily supply. Perhaps you'd like to buy some from me for your own establishment, lest you have nothing to show your regular customers."

"I think not. I have enough stock to carry Coffin House through to the next quarter's sale."

"Oh, to be sure." Hull smiled. "To be sure you do."

Conversation was interrupted by a small voice. "Daddy, daddy!"

Both men looked down at the little girl, a charming if solemn-eyed sprite of seven. She was tugging on one leg of Hull's pants.

"Can we go home now, Daddy? I'm hungry."

Hull kicked out his leg and sent her sprawling. Parson Methune's eyes closed and Coffin could see his lips moving in silent prayer, not for the girl but for the soul of Tobias Hull.

"Get away, brat," Hull growled. "We'll leave when I'm ready. Contain your appetite that long."

The girl rose slowly and wiped at her pants. She was dressed in boy's attire, rough and unfeminine. Nothing so frilly and cheerful as a skirt for her. She shed not a tear at her father's rough treatment as she slipped out of sight into the crowd.

Rose, her name was. Coffin had never seen her when her father wasn't berating her for some fault, real or imagined. It was widely known Hull blamed the girl for the death of his wife. Kororareka was not London and it was a long way from Queen's Hospital and decent medical care. There'd been only other women to try and help Flora Hull through the agony of a difficult birth. That good woman had lived barely long enough to name the infant before death had taken her like a thief in the night. From that day forward Tobias Hull had barely tolerated the unwanted girl-child.

Never known as a cheerful man, the death of his beloved Flora had ripped the last vestiges of decency from his soul. Now Hull barely tolerated the conventions of the law in his dealings with others. He was the most ruthless individual Coffin had ever encountered, and that ruthlessness extended to his treatment of his daughter. None dared interfere, however. Not even Methune. Whatever one might think, Hull was still the child's father.

Hull looked back at Coffin. "Then we might as well go our separate ways, eh? Say hello to your wife for me—and your mistress as well."

Snickering laughter could be heard from those merchants assembled nearby. This was silenced by a brief, cold glance from Coffin. The men turned away, as if aware they had trespassed on lethal ground.

Hull likewise realized he might have gone too far. Though he did not fear Coffin, neither did he press the matter.

Surprisingly, Coffin chose to elaborate. "As the Parson will tell you, Hull, my wife is a fine, God-fearing woman. As to the other lady in question I have broken with her utterly. It is hoped none would be so indiscreet as to mention the business to my wife. I'd take a dim view of that. Very dim."

"Have no fear on that score," Hull assured him. "I'm a businessman, not a scandal-monger. When I take the measure of an opponent it's in the books or on the boxing ground. I do not fight as some do with sly words or innuendo."

"I'm glad to hear that. I'd hate to think the latter true of anyone."

Hull ostentatiously extracted and studied the ornate gold pocket watch he carried with him wherever he went. He made a fetish of punctuality. "I must get back to town. It'll be dark soon, and as you can see I have a great deal of merchandise to move." He smiled curtly, nodded once, and turned to leave. Coffin looked after him. The little girl, Rose, was still keeping out of sight. Then Coffin turned and strolled back to Parson Methune.

"I can't believe I missed the entire sale. That I rode like the wind only to find everything gone."

"As I told you, my son, I have little interest in matters of commerce. However," he continued in a softer tone after first making certain Hull was well beyond earshot, "I have heard that one chief has been delayed in arriving. The Maori chatter incessantly about such things. For one such as myself, who has acquired some simple understanding of their language. . . ."

"Never mind that," an excited Coffin interrupted him. "What chief?" Maybe the day wasn't lost after all. His comment about having enough stock to carry him through to the next sale was nothing but bluff. He'd known it and so had Hull.

"His name is Te Ohine. An ariki."

"An important chief, yes. I know him well, Parson. I've supped with him." Coffin's eyes were already searching the path that disappeared into the trees, heading inland. "I believe I shall double my contribution this Sunday."

"I would rather see you in church than your money, Robert. Though the latter is, of course, not unwelcome. If you're to have reason to be grateful, why not come with your family and give thanks in person?"

"I'll consider it, Parson."

"God asks no more of you than that. May he be with you."

"And with you, Parson, as I've no doubt he usually is."

Methune smiled and wandered off into the thinning crowd in search of souls and contributions. The priest had more guts than most of those he ministered to. New Zealand weeded out weak ministers as quickly as it drove off the unfit sailor or tradesman.

10

He passed the time chatting with those merchants and drovers who still remained. As the sun continued to recede behind the mountains he worried that the Parson's well-intentioned rumor was no more than that. Only the continued presence of several Maori chiefs who'd already disposed of their goods convinced him to hang back. There was no reason for them to remain in the area, yet they continued to do so.

When at last it was certain the time for trading had passed and the only light came from torches and whale-oil lanterns, a line of heavily laden natives materialized from the trees. Slung between them were several huge baskets overflowing with finished rope. As Methune had indicated, the group was led by the massive figure of the redoubtable Te Ohine.

The few remaining merchants hurriedly gathered around the sorting tables as the rope was carefully laid out for inspection. The chief's representative gave the customary sales pitch, extolling the virtues of his tribe's product above that of all other tribes. No mention was made of their late arrival. It was not for a chief to offer excuses to common pakehas.

Then Coffin saw a familiar figure climbing hurriedly toward the clearing. He smiled to himself. While loading the last of his earlier purchases, Hull had heard about the unexpected late arrival. Now he was arguing vociferously with his assistants, who attempted to restrain him. Looking up the hill, he noticed Coffin watching and glared back wordlessly. Coffin nodded politely.

The remaining merchants bid enthusiastically as they inspected the fine quality rope. All were quickly eliminated save two: Coffin and Hull. Coffin didn't know if his arch-rival really wanted the rope or simply desired to keep it out of his competitor's hands. It didn't matter because Hull finally had to drop out of the bidding, having depleted his money with his earlier purchases. A delighted Coffin found himself sole owner of Te Ohine's produce, though he did not actually relax until the raging, cursing Hull had left.

His IOU was accepted, as he knew it would be. The chief consigned the paper to Rui, his beautiful fourth wife. She would see to it that the paper was exchanged for gold. That done, the chief concluded the bargain with a firm handshake.

"A good day's business, Te Ohine," Coffin told him.

"A good night's business, Makawe Rino. Come and smoke tobacco with me."

The chief wore an incongruous combination of sailor's dungarees and Maori feather robe. His great belly hung over the waistband of the pants. Tattooed whorls and spirals decorated his face from forehead to neck. Alien designs they were, though perhaps no more so than the bizarre inscriptions on the arms of seamen from Liverpool and New Bedford. "Is life good for you, Iron Hair?" the chief inquired pleasantly as he demonstrated his command of the pakeha language.

Coffin nodded. "Life is good. As is your English."

Te Ohine grunted appreciatively. He'd studied the pakeha language not out of any desire to please the traders but because it was good for business.

"I am much pleased to take your gold." An evening breeze ruffled the feather cape.

"I am much pleased to see you take it."

A woman produced pipes and tobacco. Fine American tobacco it was, too, Coffin noted. The Maoris knew how to enjoy life and did not hesitate to acquire pleasurable things from the pakehas.

"I am glad to see you here tonight, Makawe Rino. Business with you is always good."

"I enjoy our talking, Te Ohine, and your rope is always worth waiting for."

"I bring only the best quality. That is the best way to do business. Is it not so?"

"Very much so."

"I have heard you have just returned from Te Wai-pounamu."

That gave Coffin a start. "How could you know that? The *Resolute*'s only just docked."

"We hear much the pakeha thinks we do not." He smiled

again. "It is always a wise thing to know what visitors to one's land are doing."

"Very wise," Coffin agreed.

They settled down to enjoy the evening cool, puffing contentedly on their respective pipes. Only when it grew late did Coffin mention the matter most important to him and his friends.

"Yesterday I was visited by all the important pakehas of Kororareka. They came to my *whare* to talk. They are worried about many things. One thing they worry about is war."

"I could never participate in that."

"I know you would not, but there are other chiefs who would welcome the chance to fight. It is a big problem for us. Among other things, some of our own people cause us more grief than any Maori."

"That I can believe." Te Ohine nodded somberly through a veil of lantern-lit smoke. "The men who travel in the great boats and kill the big fish are falling-down drunk much of the time. The pakeha complain the Maori cannot hold his liquor, yet the pakeha sailors do no better."

"Not all of us are like the sailors. For many of us this has become our home. What we want are assurances from the Maori that we will be able to travel between our homes just as the Maori does."

"Do not talk in circles, Iron Hair. What is it you wish?"

"To be able to buy land elsewhere for such homes. For this we must have wide agreement with the ariki, as the Maori hold all land in common between the tribes."

"This is so."

"When we buy land from a tribe we must have assurances the business will be respected by all tribes, not just the one doing the selling. Te Ohine, we must make a treaty guaranteeing the peace between Maori and pakeha, so that we may live among you in peace and security."

"Iron Hair, you know that I have power only over my own people. No one chief can command more than that."

"I know. That is why the treaty we make must be comprehensive. It will do no good to sign separate treaties with one, two, or even a dozen chiefs if the thirteenth will someday decide to destroy us. We must have a meeting to discuss this important thing."

"Difficult to arrange." The chief scratched a cheek. "Very

difficult, my friend. Many of the chiefs who would willingly agree to peace with the pakeha will never do so with other chiefs. If they met in one place together they would spend all their time splitting heads instead of talking."

"I know of your feuds and rivalries. There's no reason why they can't be put aside for one afternoon. The peace could be assured by the pakeha representatives since they have no feud with any tribe."

"Still it will be hard, gathering so many ariki in one place at the same time. But I will talk to the *rangitira* and see if such a thing might be done."

"That's all I ask. I think such a treaty would be good for Maori and pakeha alike."

"I am a peace-loving man myself," Te Ohine declared. "I have killed in battle less than a dozen men with my own hand, and I have never begun a war."

No, but I bet you've finished plenty of them, you sneaky old devil, Coffin thought, though by Maori standards Te Ohine was a veritable pacifist.

"Tell me, friend Coffin; I have never been to Te Wai-pounamu, the place you call South Island. I am told it is different in many ways from our land. Speak to me of what you have seen."

Coffin found a place to sit. Then he regaled the chief with the details of the *Resolute*'s last voyage, omitting nothing he thought might interest the chief, even including the price the ship's cargo had fetched on the dockside market in the event Te Ohine hadn't already heard.

Eventually they parted. Working by lantern light the drovers Coffin had hired on the spot loaded his merchandise. He told them where to deliver the rope, then mounted his borrowed mare and galloped back toward town. In the light of the full moon the trail stood out like a silver thread dropped between the trees.

His mood sank as he neared home and the day's other business returned to haunt him. By the time he'd entered Kororareka's outskirts his thoughts were fouled with remorse and a personal fury that refused to subside. He stalked into the house wearing a storm on his face.

A voice came from the sitting room. It solidified rather than quelled the troubles which had stolen over his heretofore contented life.

"Robert? Is that you?"

She was sitting on the couch, sewing. How terribly domestic, he thought. Seeing the expression on his face she rose anxiously.

"I was worried, Robert. It's so late, and Samuel didn't know or wouldn't tell me where you'd got off to, and I. . . ."

"Upstairs," he mumbled.

Her own expression twisted. "Robert?"

"Get upstairs, I said."

She forced herself to smile. "Of course, Robert. If that's what you—oh!"

He'd walked over to her and lifted her like a chair. "Robert, you're hurting me!" Up the stairs he carried her, not even feeling her weight, his thoughts aboil.

The intensity of his passion frightened her, then consumed them both, until she fell into an exhausted sleep alongside him. This was just as well. The look he wore would not have reassured her. It was true his desire was sated, but something else was not. Something that stirred and roiled within him and would not let him be.

Guilt. Guilt because he'd made love to his wife, who loved him deeply enough to sacrifice comfort and friends to sail halfway around the world to begin anew with a husband she hadn't seen in three years. Guilt because in making love to her he'd really been making love to two women at once.

Adulterer! An inner voice screamed at him. Adulterer in mind if not in body.

Sweating, Coffin turned over and closed his eyes. It did no good.

That night the first of the dreams began. He was flying over an endless green landscape, omnipotent, all-powerful, lord of all he could see. Then the land exploded beneath him, turned to fire and brimstone, sucking him down and threatening to devour him. Two women stepped out of the fire: Mary and Holly. Each could save him. But Holly was an empty shell, a ghost, with no strength and no power. Mary Kinnegad just laughed at him, laughed and laughed until he struck at her. His fingers tangled in her red hair and he pulled her close, her mouth merging with his.

Then he saw that the fire was in her hair and the hell in her eyes, her hate as hot as burning pitch. With a cry he shoved her away, but her hair caught at him like the tentacles of a squid and clung tight. She pulled him close, with hands, with hair, with eyes, burning. He felt himself burning.

Off to one side stood a third figure. He recognized Tuhoto. The old wizard was staring at him, neither condemning nor approving. Just staring. Coffin tried to look away, but wherever he turned there were the old man's eyes. Just the eyes, detached from the body, hovering in emptiness. Accusing eyes.

When he awoke in the middle of the night he was inhaling so hard he thought his lungs would burst. He sat straight up in bed until his breathing eased, then looked down at Holly. She still slept, oblivious to his nightmare, the sheets rippling against her body. He stared a long time before lying down again. This time he slept.

11

Visitors to his home never mentioned Coffin's former mistress. His friends were too discreet and their own wives too far removed from the brutal gossip of The Beach to know of the life he'd abandoned the day of Holly Coffin's arrival. Those who might have been inclined to looseness of tongue had the vision of Coffin's sword to help them keep silent.

An innocence was preserved that allowed Holly and Christopher Coffin to settle into the routine of what passed for civilized life in Kororareka. For his part, Coffin ignored the occasional burning that dug at his innards and kept resolutely away from the little house down by the grog shops. He later learned that after throwing him out, Mary had taken up almost immediately with the sailor who'd challenged Coffin: Shaun Connaught.

It was just as well. Maybe Connaught could handle her. Perhaps she would see reason and at least seek some rapprochement with the man who'd shared so much of her life. But no letters arrived at Coffin House, no messengers brought requests for a quiet meeting.

Damn her, then. But he sorrowed for their children.

As days became weeks and then months Mary Kinnegad faded from his thoughts. Business and a new family occupied his time. Only at night, in the private, unsettled depths of his dreams did she return to plague him. Asleep, he was defenseless against her. He thanked God he was not one to cry out in his bed.

He was inspecting a newly arrived consignment of nails when the boy came into Coffin House. The youngster eyed him thoughtfully before venturing, "You are Robert Coffin, sir?"

"What is it, boy?" Coffin looked up from his work. From nearby, Elias Goldman turned away from the ledger he was setting in order.

"I've been sent by John Halworthy, sir." Inwardly Coffin felt conflicting emotions. No reconciliation with Irish Mary this, but no complications either. He wasn't sure whether he was more relieved or disappointed. "He says to tell you the great meeting is set. The Maori have agreed to discuss a treaty." For the first time Coffin noticed how tired the boy was and how hard he was breathing. He'd run a long way.

"That's what I was sent to tell you. That, and that your presence will be required."

"Wonderful news. Where is the meeting to take place, and when?"

"I don't know that, sir. Mr. Halworthy didn't say."

"Never mind. I'll find out. Where are we to gather first?"

"Tomorrow morning at the house of Titus Ablemare. I understand there's to be a formal parade to the treaty site. I was also told to tell you that Governor FitzRoy is already drawing up a treaty."

That didn't please Coffin. FitzRoy was well-intentioned, but pompous. Still, nothing mattered but the treaty's contents. If this was true, then a historic moment in the colony's history was approaching.

The boy goggled at the silver piece Coffin pressed in his palm, then whirled and bolted for the door before the merchant could change his mind. Coffin grinned after him before turning to the back room.

"Elias!"

"Yes sir, I heard. Great news."

"*If* it works out. You'll have to handle things while I'm away."

"Of course, sir. I wish I could go with you."

"You may be glad you didn't if the Maoris take a dislike to FitzRoy's wording." He didn't add the other reason. He didn't have to. Both men knew there were those among Halworthy's colleagues who would frown on Goldman's presence at such an important gathering, would feel it somehow demeaned them. They didn't speak about it.

Besides, someone *did* have to stay to attend to business.

"I've never seen you look so dashing, Robert. Not even when you were courting me in London."

Holly studied him thoughtfully as he struggled with the dress shirt. Still, he had no intention of being outshone at the signing—certainly not by Tobias Hull. The Maoris attached considerable importance to personal appearance.

Samuel had the buggy ready and waiting for him. Holly waved from the porch as he chucked the reins and headed out of town. As his horse trotted beneath the trees it occurred to Coffin that it might after all not be such a bad idea to have someone like FitzRoy preside over the signing. The Maori loved ceremony and FitzRoy could embroider language with the best.

By the time he drew near the chosen site he could see Maori chiefs and their entourages striding along parallel to the pakeha path, clad in flaxen skirts and elaborate feather capes and headdresses that shone in the sun.

The *pa*, or village, was not exactly Windsor Castle, but considering it as a military fortification entirely designed and constructed by savages it was quite impressive. A deep ditch encircled the whole community. This was backed by a high, stout stockade. Ports had been chopped in the palisade to allow the defenders within to make use of the firearms newly acquired from the pakeha. There was also internal scaffolding which permitted warriors to sling rocks and throw spears and clubs down on any assaulting enemy. As was typical, the *pa* had been built atop a steep hill. Coffin would not have enjoyed assaulting such a strong position, even one defended only by heathen.

Which was one reason why everyone had gathered here today, to sign the treaty that would ensure such conflicts never came to pass.

The village was crowded with spectators, both white and Maori. Ignoring the pomp and confusion surrounding them, the women of the village went about their daily tasks. Grain still had to be ground, garments had to be repaired, and children fed regardless of how momentous the occasion. One young woman sat beneath the arch of an elaborately decorated house reading a Bible.

The inhabitants wore an eclectic compendium of the traditional and the new. Christianized Maoris were as likely to stroll about nearly nude in their flax skirts as they were to don the trade clothing the missionaries favored, while their pagan cousins sported the latest in sailors' fashion.

The Maori adopted new ideas at their own pace. So far they seemed more taken with the pakeha religion than its culture.

Coffin jumped down from the buggy and tied the horse alongside a long line of similar vehicles. One thing he knew from his conversations with such men as Te Ohine: of all the pakeha gods, the gun was the only one all Maoris had immediately embraced. It answered the prayers of the Maori as quickly and efficiently as it did those of white men, while its doctrine was simple enough for anyone to understand.

A large table had been set up in the center of the village. Behind it stood Maori storage houses, intricately carved wooden sheds set high up on poles. Off to one side a cluster of children swung on vines that trailed from the top of a local version of the maypole.

Coffin was late. The ceremony was already underway. Chiefs marched up ceremoniously to the improvised stage to sign their names or make their marks on the paper while Kororareka's leading citizens beamed approvingly. As the signing continued FitzRoy rambled on in his impressive voice about what a great day this was for New Zealand, for Maori and European alike, and how this Treaty of Waitangi would go down in history as a model of its kind between settlers and native peoples. He conveniently neglected to point out that His Majesty's government had yet to approve so much as a word of it.

There was a tugging at Coffin's sleeve. He found himself looking down into the face of a wide-eyed Maori boy of twelve.

"You Coffin sir?"

"Me Coffin sir, yes."

The boy grinned. "You come." He turned and started away.

"Just a minute! Who wants me?"

"Priest-man." The boy struggled with the unfamiliar words.

Coffin hesitated, then followed the youngster. He was getting tired of listening to FitzRoy anyway. The boy led him to the large meeting house on the left side of the clearing. Removing his top hat, he bent to scramble through the low entrance. Unlike most Maori structures, this one proved spacious enough to allow him to stand up inside.

Carving decorated the walls and posts. That in itself was unusual since such decorations were normally restricted to the exterior of such a building. Glowering pagan faces glared back at him out of eyes of iridescent paua shell. The men seated inside studied him quietly. Among them was his friend Te Ohine.

"*Tena koe*," he said. "Hello, my friends."

"Tena koe, Makawe Rino." Te Ohine was not smiling. He gestured toward an unoccupied flax mat.

Coffin seated himself. "What troubles my old friend? Is there something wrong with the treaty?"

"Not with the treaty, no. But the treaty will not be complete if a certain chief does not sign it. His name is Wapatki."

"I thought everyone was agreed. Why is this one so important?"

"His tribe rules much of the land between your *pa* and the farms of the interior. If he does not sign then you will never be sure of safe passage from the sea to the land."

Coffin considered. The others watched him solemnly. "This Wapatki sounds like a stubborn man."

"He is." Coffin turned to see Parson Methune bending to enter. Evidently the boy had been sent to fetch him as well. He took the mat next to Coffin's.

"Why won't he sign, Parson?"

"He has been going on all day to whomever will listen to him among the Maori. He believes the pakeha are all drunkards at heart, that their leader, our estimable Mr. FitzRoy, is a coward, and that," he had to gather himself before he could exhume the last, "the God of the pakeha is an inebriate, a charlatan, and impotent to affect the lives of men."

"Then he is worse than a stubborn man," Coffin told the assembled chiefs. "He is also an ignorant one."

Despite his assurances Coffin could sense that this Wapatki had several sympathizers. If something wasn't done quickly the whole treaty signing might dissolve in a storm of Maori dissension.

One of the undecided chiefs didn't make things any easier. "If all Wapatki says is not so, let Iron Hair prove him wrong."

Coffin struggled to see which chief had spoken. Hunched over near the far end of the meeting house was a squat, unusually ugly Maori. He wore no decorated robe. His chest and belly were tattooed as elaborately as his face. There were two feathers in his hair. Other than the feathers and tattoos, the man was clad only in a simple skirt.

"I would gladly do so. How would the ariki Wapatki choose his proof?"

"From one among the pakeha who is not a drunkard, coward, or devoid of the assistance of his God. I am Wapatki, Iron Hair."

Am I never to be allowed peace, Coffin wondered? Must I always have to prove myself in this land with my fists instead of my brain? In truth, it was little different from the streets of London.

"Very well," he said with a sigh. "I will give chief Wapatki his proof."

The ariki's eyes glittered expectantly as he rose. Coffin began unbuttoning his shirt.

"It distresses me to see violence mar this historic occasion," Methune murmured.

"If I don't win this fight there may not be any historic occasion to worry about, Parson. Don't think of it as violence. This is just a friendly little Maori-type chat."

"One of you could be killed while 'chatting.'"

"Let's pray not, Parson."

One by one they exited the meeting house. Word of the fight drew curious Maori away from the signing ceremony. They were no different from the seamen who'd gathered outside the Crippled Raven, Coffin thought. He wondered if there was betting taking place and if so, what the line on him was.

Stripped to the waist, he turned to face his opponent. He was much taller than the Maori, though lighter. His greater reach did not make him overconfident. He'd seen "fat" Maori warriors move with incredible agility. He had no intention of underestimating this Wapatki.

"This is your fight. What will we argue with?"

"No guns." Wapatki sniffed derisively. He took a magnificently carved greenstone club from a waiting tribesman, shook it threateningly at Coffin and stuck out his tongue in typical Maori challenge.

Coffin surveyed the crowd that had surrounded them. "If someone would provide me with an equivalent?" It was Te Ohine who stepped forward to hand over his personal war club. It was made of wood instead of jade but that didn't trouble Coffin. The Maori's wooden clubs were solid as stone.

It began quietly, both men sucking in air and letting out little more than grunts, the crowd pressing close in silence. There was none of the boisterous shouting and shoving that such a battle would have generated in London.

Wapatki was as agile as Coffin suspected, but unlike most pakehas he was prepared for the chief's speed. Coffin had more trouble with the unfamiliar club. He gripped it with both hands while Wapatki switched his easily from one to the other. Coffin had to struggle to parry the steady succession of blows. If the jade club connected solidly it could shatter bone.

Once he stumbled and Wapatki rushed in to splatter his brains across the ground. Rolling just in time, Coffin heard the *boom* as the club bounced off the earth where his head had lain only seconds earlier. Each time he blocked one of the chief's blows a shiver ran up his arms. The Maori's strength was prodigious. Still he contented himself with parrying and defending, learning as he protected himself, content to let Wapatki do most of the work. His patience was beginning to pay off. The chief wasn't used to an opponent who dodged like a rooster. His face was now flushed and he was panting heavily, the sweat streaming off him.

Coffin managed a solid blow to his opponent's stomach, but the club simply bounced off, leaving behind a red mark but no visible damage.

Wapatki grinned tiredly. "You fight well—for a pakeha."

"Not all pakehas fight only with words, Wapatki." Coffin spoke without taking his eyes off the Maori's weaving club. "The men you see lying in the streets of Kororareka are not pakeha soldiers. They are a different breed of men than you have come to know."

"You must be such a soldier." He swung and Coffin jumped backward. The heavy greenstone cleft only air. The chief's wild swings were slowing.

"I'm not a soldier; only a merchant."

"Hard to believe, Iron Hair." Whereupon Wapatki charged with a speed and enthusiasm that belied his apparent exhaustion.

Coffin had anticipated the attempt to lull him. He ducked beneath Wapatki's swing and put his head into the Maori's solar plexus. At the same time he swung not up as his opponent expected but down with his own weapon. Wapatki let out a yelp of pain, crumpled, and lay on the ground clutching his right foot.

Gasping, Coffin stood over him. To his astonishment he saw that the chief was not moaning in pain but instead was laughing uncontrollably even though his foot had to be broken. The flow of amused Maori came too rapidly for him to follow. He turned to Methune as the chief's retainers rushed to assist him.

"What's he on about, Parson?"

"I believe he is decrying his own stupidity for permitting you to strike such a blow, my son." Methune listened intently to the tumbling vowels.

With the aid of his attendants Wapatki struggled to his feet. Using them for support he managed to hobble over to the sweaty, tired Coffin. The chief extended his right hand.

"I understand this how pakeha makes greeting." Coffin hesitated, then relaxed as the chief smiled. He took the proffered hand warily, still holding onto his club. A wounded Maori could be as treacherous as a wounded tiger.

But there was no deception in the handshake. "I was wrong, Iron Hair." Wapatki nodded toward Te Ohine. "He told me I was wrong. I did not believe him. Now I believe."

"Then you'll put your mark on the treaty?"

"Yes, I will sign. It is good that you struck my foot instead of my hand." This time Coffin found himself laughing with the chief. When the joke was translated the rest of the Maoris joined in, and Pastor Methune was hard pressed to maintain his priestly demeanor.

Wapatki became the thirty-fifth chief to set his name to the Treaty of Waitangi. When the last ariki had signed it was the turn of the pakehas. Led by FitzRoy they all proclaimed their devotion to the words they were committing to history. From this day forward Maori and pakeha would share the land and live together in peace and harmony for the sake of their children and their children's children, to the benefit of all.

When it came Coffin's turn to sign some mutters of disapproval could be heard from the more conservative citizens of Kororareka. Coffin looked down at his dirt-streaked self and smiled. Evidently they were unaware of his recent diplomatic exertions on their behalf. He signed boldly, as always.

At last it was done. The Maoris whooped and shouted and thrust their clubs and spears skyward while the pakehas cheered and let loose with musket and pistol. Coffin observed it all with a jaundiced eye as he wondered whether Maori or some member of the New Zealand Colonizing Company would be the first to test the paper words.

No matter for now. A temporary peace was better than none and who knew but that it might be the exception to the rule and last. He said as much to Te Ohine and his new friend Wapatki before climbing into his buggy for the long ride back home.

12

Holly was waiting for him with a kiss and warm embrace. "Everything went well, Robert? Are we to have peace?"

"For a while, it seems." He discarded the top hat as if it was a dead animal. "Some of the chiefs had their doubts, but in the end everyone signed." He was heading for the parlor as he shed his dress jacket.

"Robert, your face is cut!" Her hand gently touched his cheek, explored further. "And here's one running down your neck. You've been in another fight. What's this country done to you? In England you were no brawler."

"New surroundings dictate new approaches, my dear." He reassured her with another kiss before slumping into his chair. "It's nothing to fret about. I've suffered worse wounds from thorn bushes. Now, I'm hungry as a Welsh boar and if you don't watch out I'll have you for an appetizer!"

She giggled and scampered clear of his clutching fingers. Her laughter was music. "I think it's dessert you're referring to and we'll discuss that later. Oh, I nearly forgot." She looked embarrassed. "There's someone been waiting to speak with you and here I've gone and left him in the kitchen while we've been talking. I'll tell him you're back." She vanished through a rear door.

Coffin frowned. Who could be waiting on him? All the prominent citizens of Kororareka had been at the treaty signing.

Not quite all, it seemed. He'd forgotten Angus McQuade. He rose at the other man's entrance.

"Hello, Robert."

"Angus." They shook hands briefly. "You weren't at the signing?"

McQuade smiled. "It seems I'm considered a bit too young yet to be setting me hand to so glorious a document."

"The more fools they." McQuade was as sharp as Ablemare or any of them, he knew. "What will you take? Rum? Sherry?"

"A little time, if I may. I've something to show you, Robert."

"Then let me see it, man. I'm tired."

"It's not something that can be put in a saddlebag or box, mon. Kin you spare me a few days?"

"A few *days*?" Coffin eyed him in surprise. "I thought you meant an hour or so. I've business needs looking after, Angus, another trip to make to South Island, and a lot of drunken hands to seine from the depths of The Beach."

"Let Markham attend to your crew and that fine Mr. Goldman to the rest. This is more important. I must have your opinion on this, Robert. Without your support I cannot convince any of the others. They'll believe it if you're there to back me."

"Believe what?"

"What I've seen."

"And what might that be?"

McQuade's eyes glittered. "The future, Robert, the future."

"So it's time for highland riddles, is it?" But Coffin knew McQuade, a compulsive worker, wouldn't have taken the time away from his own growing business were it not a serious matter. He was intrigued.

"Samuel!" he yelled toward the kitchen. "Pack some dried beef and mutton. I'll be gone for a few days!"

That brought Holly out of the back of the house. She looked anxiously from her husband to their visitor. "Gone? But you've only just returned, Robert. Angus McQuade, what's this all about?"

McQuade looked apologetic. "I canna tell you now, Mrs. Coffin, but Robert himself will explain everything when we return."

Coffin tried not to grin. "You came here confident you could persuade me into joining this little expedition of yours, didn't you? This had best be a sight worth a King's time or you'll pay for it, Angus. Where are we going?"

"South and west."

His host nodded thoughtfully. "Yesterday I would not have attempted such a journey, but now the treaty gives us safe passage. It could still be dangerous. Almost as dangerous as

trying to leave Holly here again." He looked back at his wife.
There was a twinkle in his eye.

She tried to glare at him, failed and found herself smiling as
she shook her head despairingly. "I'll see to your horse,
Robert."

Trees full of yellow blossoms, brilliant flowers by the
wayside and strange creatures darting through the underbrush
held the attention of the two young men as they rode steadily
southwest. Never was there a country so devoid of dangerous
animals, Coffin mused. The countryside was as safe as
Regent's Park, if one discounted the occasional homicidal
Maori. Meanwhile the settlers of Sydney and Melbourne had to
deal with snakes so venomous their bite could kill a man in
minutes. Here there were no such serpents. Paradise before the
casting out, he thought. The Maoris thought so too.

Even with Goldman in charge he found himself worrying
about business. Time was precious and McQuade seemed
determined to guide them all the way to the tip of North Island.

Actually it was only a matter of days before they topped the
slight rise one morning and his guide was able to gesture at the
panorama spread out before them. It wasn't necessary for the
young merchant to speak. The view explained itself.

Below lay the future.

From the hilltop they could see the Pacific behind them and
the Tasman Sea in front. A town sited here could command a
harbor on both sides of the narrow isthmus.

McQuade was gesturing toward the western inlet as he
spoke. "I've done soundings there, Robert. Crude but ser-
viceable. This harbor puts the anchorage at Kororareka to
shame. See there, how the land bends to the south on the far
side of the harbor? A ship sheltering there could ride out the
worst of storms tied up close inshore."

"You were right Angus. It's a wonderful place. What about
the local Maoris?"

"None camped hereabouts. A deep-water harbor means
nothing to them. Manukau, they call the place. Several tribes
do have *pas* in the area, but their claims overlap. We should be
able to make a deal easily."

"The others must be shown this place." Coffin was still
entranced by the sight. "Ablemare, Halworthy, all of them.
How did you find it?"

McQuade shrugged. "A native friend told me of it one day. He has relatives here."

"And spotted potential profit in the revelation, hmm? I've seen enough, Angus. Here we'll build a town the whalers won't control." He started to wheel his horse around.

McQuade cut him off. "Nay, hold a moment, Robert. Why should we rush to inform competitors? Between the two of us could we not buy much of the best land here before extolling its virtues to the rest of the community?"

"You're losing sight of long-term goals in favor of short-term profits, Angus. Your instinct is correct but you've not thought it through. Were we to do as you suggest we'd have a much harder time convincing the rest to move their business all the way across the island. We cannot found a new town by ourselves. Rest easy. There'll be profit enough from this business for us both."

McQuade nodded somberly. "You're right, Robert. Still. . . ." He gazed longingly at the smooth, sweeping curve of the harbor. "It's hard to pass by so great an opportunity for gain."

"There's no gain without customers. We'll put together a consortium to purchase the land from the Maoris. Ablemare, Halworthy, Langston, Groan, Perkins and ourselves."

"What of Tobias Hull?"

That gave Coffin pause. It was with extreme reluctance he finally nodded and said, "Aye, Hull must be included as well. If he's left out he'll make trouble among the craftsmen and farmers. Much as it pains me to admit it we'll need his support. Perhaps we can arrange things so that his share consists mostly of marshland and rock."

Both men chucked the reins of their mounts and turned for home. Before evening McQuade finally had gathered sufficient courage to ask the question that had been troubling him ever since his arrival in the colony.

"How came this enmity between you and Tobias Hull?"

Coffin took no umbrage at the inquiry. It was a question others had asked. "Hull's a sour and soulless man by nature. At first I bore him no ill will, but he plays dirty and low and resents it when he's thwarted. Then too our businesses bring us head to head in a fashion you've not experienced. And it pains me to see how he treats that innocent child of his. The others say nothing about it but I make my opinion known. That infuriates Hull."

"I've heard about the girl," McQuade murmured. "It's said that after all these years Hull still pines for his dead wife."

"True enough. He blames the girl for the tragedy of his own life, though she bears no responsibility for it. I fear the girl's fate lies in the Lord's hands alone. I wouldn't bet a shilling Hull doesn't kill her some day in the course of one of his drunken rages."

"But that's monstrous! Can nothing be done?"

"She's his child. Legally he can't be touched. And Hull's capable of anything if he's enough rum in him." Coffin shifted in his saddle. "Enough of Tobias Hull. We've better things to talk of and much planning to do.

Holly stirred her tea, watching her husband closely. "What have you and young McQuade been up to, Robert? The town's abuzz with rumor."

He put his own cup aside. "Remember when you arrived here I told you how one day we might be able to live elsewhere, away from this noise and debauchery? I believe Angus has found such a place. A wonderful harbor nowhere near the Bay of Islands, on the western shore, yet not so far that business would suffer."

"Won't the whalers follow to the new port?"

"A few may, but such men are creatures of habit. If the grog shops and gambling dens stay here in Kororareka, so will those who frequent them. We'll be selective in the businesses we'll allow in the new community." He leaned forward over the table, his expression eager.

"Holly, the land through which Angus and I traveled is gentle and rolling, suitable not only for the raising of sheep and cattle but for crops. I believe, I've always believed, that the real future of this land lies not in serving as a waystop for nomadic sailors but in providing food for a hungry world. Well, for a hungry New South Wales, anyway. Being on the western shore the new town will reduce sailing time between here and Australia by several days at the least."

She reached out and took his hands in hers. "It sounds wonderful, Robert. Will we be able to buy land there?"

"Angus insists that we can. I'll build you a proper home, Holly. A real house, of dressed stone and milled lumber!" In

his mind's eye the grand structure stood finished and shining,
ready to greet them. "As fine as anything in England. You'll
have servants and live as a proper lady."

She rose from her chair, walked around the table and put her
arms around him. He leaned back against the softness of her.
"I knew I was doing the right thing, coming out from England
after you. I knew it."

"And I—I'm glad you came," he told her softly. He gently
disengaged himself, rising. "Now I must see to business. It's
time to broach the suggestion to the others. Not even gouty old
Abelmare will hesitate once he's set eyes on that harbor!
Someday it will be a fine city, Holly. Angus is going to propose
we call it Auckland."

"I've got to tell Christopher. He'll be pleased. He doesn't
like this place."

Nor do I, really, thought Coffin as he watched her depart.
Oh, Kororareka's been good to me. I've the beginnings of a
fine business here, something that would have been impossible
to accomplish in England.

He walked outside and leaned on the porch railing, gazing
down at the town. Sunset was near. There was a fire blazing
somewhere, he could see the smoke. Yells and screams filled
the air, floating up to him like the howls of the damned on the
day before entering Hades. Shots rang out fitfully, punctuating
the screams.

The Beach. Wildest street in the whole Pacific basin. Men
sinning on the carcassses of dead leviathans. Let it get wild
tonight. We have grander plans to implement.

Real money would be a problem at first, he knew. Credit
would be required for moving homes and businesses. The
Bank of England was far from convinced that the fledgling
colony at the end of the world with the notorious reputation had
a bankable future. He'd be better off than most, thanks to his
wife's foresight and courage. They'd be able to begin anew
without credit.

From then on success would be nothing more than a matter
of hard work. He was used to that.

He'd have to keep an eye on Tobias Hull. Despite the man's
crudity and coarseness he among all the other merchants
excepting Angus McQuade had an eye for the future. If given
half a chance he'd gladly swallow them all, most especially
Coffin House.

All this Robert Coffin could foresee and plan for. Only one matter was not so easily considered. He stood there listening to the shouts and laughter welling up out of The Beach, staring out across the sea of masts and the fiery cauldrons that turned the waters of the bay the color of blood. Only one thing he couldn't plan for.

Mary Kinnegad was still there, haunting his dreams when he let her into his sleep, disturbing his waking thoughts, unsettling his body. Damn the woman! He'd broken with her but still could not squeeze her out of his memory. She clung to his thoughts and dreams, holding his heart in a vise. He could sleep, but he could not keep himself from dreaming.

And why was Tuhoto there so often, expressionless, sorrowful, always staring at him reprovingly?

He rubbed tiredly at his forehead. An exhausting week it had been and he needed rest. Holly would help. She would understand and sympathize and help him to forget. He *had* to forget.

How the Devil could a man plan his future with ghosts clawing at his back?

BOOK TWO

1845

1

"Come on then, Christopher! Put some back into it. She's not that heavy."

The boy strained at the large packing crate, struggling to manhandle it up the boarding ramp. The past six years had seen him grow up but not out. A spindly toothpick of a lad, all gangly arms and legs, topped off by a knot of undisciplined blonde hair. He looked like an ambling cornstalk.

At his father's urging he continued the uneven battle until his breath began to come in long, ragged wheezes. Coffin could hear the rasp in the child's throat.

"All right, son, that's enough. You gave 'er your best."

Gratefully the boy let go of the crate, leaning on it for support. Coffin watched him closely until his breathing had stabilized. For an instant he worried he might have pushed too hard and he feared another of the boy's coughing spells.

At first they'd believed the spells were due to some persistent disease. Whooping cough, or endemic colic, or even worse. The doctors had assured them Christopher wasn't ill. Merely chronically feeble. They had no pills, no nostrums for that. It was not something they could cure, but there was the possibility the boy might outgrow it. That was why Coffin took every opportunity to expose Christopher to manual labor. He wouldn't grow stronger sitting home toying with the pianoforte Holly had bought for him.

As for Christopher himself, he didn't like heavy work, but then what child of twelve did? Coffin walked over to give the boy a hearty well-done clap on the back before lifting the packing crate easily in one hand and carrying it the rest of the way up the loading ramp.

"Mornin' to you, sor." Markham had left his duties to join them.

"Good to see you, Captain." Coffin's gaze swept approvingly across the deck. Everything in its place: loose ropes properly coiled, teak polished, brass fittings throwing back the sun. The *Holly* was a fine ship and Silas Markham handled her well.

She was larger and more modern than the sturdy old *Resolute*, which still plied its trade between North and South Island. The *Holly* was bound elsewhere. Not for her prosaic interisland shipments of pine and mutton. Already Coffin had sent her across the Tasman Sea to New South Wales. Next year, God willing, Markham would guide her to Shanghai for tea and porcelain. Aye, now that would be a cargo that'd raise some eyebrows along the Auckland quays!

One day he'd have a bigger ship still, one that would make the run all the way round the Cape of England, a vessel fast enough to compete with the clippers themselves. Markham would command her in turn. Already he'd done his former master proud, but that was no surprise. Coffin had always known that his old First Mate would make a fine Captain some day. Markham had repaid him for his confidence as such men always did, with loyalty and hard work.

He gestured with a nod of his head. "You know my son, Christopher?"

"That I do, sor." He extended a gnarled hand which Christopher Coffin shook as firmly as he could. The boy spent a great deal of time at the docks. He was fascinated by ships and the sea and enjoyed the company of sailors far more than that of boys his own age. The latter taunted and teased him, while the old seamen regaled him with tales of wondrous lands and exotic peoples.

Coffin was all for sending the boy to sea under Markham's supervision, but Holly wouldn't hear of it. Take him away from civilization? Away from his doctors? What if he has one of his spells out in the middle of the ocean? There'd be no one to treat him but clumsy sailors and the ship's carpenter, who doubled as barber and part-time surgeon.

You couldn't keep the boy in a cage and expect him to grow, Coffin had argued. Besides, he likes the sea. Yes, she replied, but would the sea like him?

Only one way to find out, he'd snapped back.

"No," she'd said with finality. "I will not hear of it, Robert. Maybe someday if we make that trip back to England you're always promising me he can go with us. We can bring along Dr. Flavia to watch over him."

"A nursemaid!"

"Well then, maybe when he's a little stronger."

"Stronger? Holly, the boy's eleven. When I was eleven I. . . ."

"I don't want to hear what you were doing when you were eleven, Robert. You're different. Christopher isn't well. Dr. Flavia says. . . ."

Coffin had turned away in disgust. "Flavia says, Flavia says! That quack!"

"He's the best physician in Auckland."

"I know, and that's not saying much." He'd turned back to plead with her. "Let the boy go, Holly. He'll manage. You'll see. He'll come back stronger and healthier than when he left. The sea does that to a man."

"Or he may not come back at all. I've seen the sea do that to men too. Besides which he's not a man. Not yet. He's still a boy, an unwell one, and it's too much of a chance." She'd smiled then and put her arms around his neck. "When he's older, then we'll talk of this again."

"Even Flavia says the sea air might do the boy some good."

"I know, but he's also said Christopher might not be able to stand the rigors of an ocean voyage. He wants to stay near the boy so he can be of assistance in any emergency."

"Aye, and so he can continue to dispense his pills and notions and bills. Christopher supports Flavia, not the other way 'round."

"Robert! How can you think of money where your only son is concerned?"

"I can always think of money," he'd replied, but it was a feeble riposte and he knew as much when he voiced it. Holly had retreated in a huff. Later on he'd managed an apology in his shambling, gruff way, but the matter was far from settled.

So every chance he had, which wasn't often given the press of business that seemed to fall heavier on him day by day, he took the boy down to the harbor. He let him roam the decks of whatever ship was at hand, watching with delight as Christopher studied the rigging and sails and asked question after question of the sailors as they worked. One of these days Holly would weaken and let him put the boy to sea, and when he finally went Christopher wouldn't be going blind. The child was bright and quick of mind. What he learned on these quayside expeditions would stay with him always.

Not only would the sea be good for him but he'd be good for the ship. No deadweight would Christopher Coffin be. He'd make a fine cabin boy. Markham would watch over him without coddling him. Exceedingly smart, his schoolmaster had called him. While Coffin wasn't much for books himself, he valued what they contained and respected those who could master their contents.

Take Elias Goldman, for example. Coffin House wouldn't have done near as well these past years without Goldman there to handle the ledgers, always peering over Coffin's shoulder, making quiet, unobtrusive suggestions about trades and sales, whispering whenever he thought something overpriced or undervalued. There were many times when it was Goldman who provided the edge over men like John Halworthy or Angus McQuade. Book learning was vital to any business's continued success.

He scanned the sky with a practiced eye. No rain today. His gaze roved over the busy waterfront. The *Holly* wasn't the only new ship tied up at the docks. Men were active everywhere: rolling kegs and vats on and off wagons, shuffling goods in and out of warehouses, checking lists and shouting orders and obscenities. Each week brought new immigrants to the growing city, a city that the old whaling town on the opposite coast could never have imagined. He and McQuade and the others had been right. Provide the proper environment and decent opportunity and people would settle this land in droves, even if it did lie at the end of the Earth.

It still amused him to watch the masters of Auckland's churches do battle for the right to save Maori souls. Theological argument had penetrated the mountains and countryside, converting the curious natives with ponderous regularity. Weslyan, Anglican and Catholic speakers were much in demand in the various fortified *pas*. His old debating colleague Father Methune presided over the second largest congregation in the city. Auckland's population could be counted in the thousands. Everything had happened as he and Angus had hoped.

He chatted awhile longer with Markham before letting the Captain leave to attend to his business. It was time to consider purchasing a third ship. By now shipwrights and carpenters aplenty called Auckland home, but there was nothing like a proper shipyard. He would have to buy in England. Markham couldn't go: he was too valuable on the Australia run to lose for a year or more. It would have to be someone else. Better all around if Coffin House had a full-time London agent to look after its business there. Some day soon he'd have to find someone to take up the English mantle.

A small voice at his sleeve, an anxious voice in his ear. "Father, Father! What ship is that?"

Coffin turned in the direction his son was pointing and promptly lost his smile. The three-masted square-rigger just coming into view was half again as large as the proud *Holly*. She was no transpacific clipper, but her mainmast towered above that of any vessel lying at anchor.

"The *Kensington*." He snapped it out, a dog bark.

"It's bigger than our ship." Christopher was leaning over the railing.

"Aye, but one day soon I'll have a bigger ship still, and don't forget that we own two."

"Yes, that's right, we do, don't we?" The boy dropped off the rail, his interest shifting as abruptly and unexpectedly as a compass north of the arctic circle. "Can I go now, Father? I'm tired and I still want to go to the warehouse." When he smiled he looked younger still, Coffin thought. "Mr. Goldman said he'd let me help him count today."

"You sure you're done with this, boy?"

Christopher nodded vigorously. "I've seen everything here, Father."

"All right then. Go ahead. Mind you stay out of Mr. Goldman's way if he tells you to."

"I will. Thanks, Father!"

The boy sped down the ramp, vanished into the quayside crowd. Maybe he couldn't pull his weight, Coffin mused, but he was fleet afoot. He could outrun anyone his own age and many of the older boys, but only over a short distance. Beyond a quarter-mile he broke down in coughing fits, like a fireplace whose flue had been abruptly slammed shut.

His son had been given the wrong set of lungs. Well, they'd damn well change that. Coffin would work it out of the boy no matter what Holly said. Hard work never hurt anyone, and Christopher was willing enough—when Coffin could slip him away from his mother. Bad enough she insisted on having him tutored privately. Public school would have been good for him.

Not for the first time Coffin realized how much he liked his son. If Coffin had insisted, the boy would have fought the packing crate until he'd collapsed. He would have to be brought along carefully, but bring him along Coffin would.

The *Kensington*'s crew was hastily reefing her sails as she steered for Hull's dock. Hull had bought her in Sydney, waving too much money beneath her master's nose for him to sail her all the way back to Portsmouth. She was bigger than necessary for the interisland trade, which indicated that Hull intended her to compete directly with the *Holly* on the Australia run. No matter. Now there was more than enough business to keep two such vessels gainfully occupied. And if there wasn't, the *Holly* would just have to sail faster and bring back better goods. He couldn't match the *Kensington*'s capacity but that didn't mean he couldn't undersell her, and in Markham he had the best Captain in the South Pacific.

None of which marred the tall ship's stature. She was impressive, and it galled Coffin that she belonged to Tobias Hull. Calm down, he ordered himself. Coffin House couldn't always be best, biggest, first. Not every time.

Besides, Hull couldn't seem to sever his emotional attachment to the sea. Inland he wasn't expanding nearly as fast as Coffin House. Too much of his business was concentrated in shipping.

Coffin immediately felt better. Let Hull boast of the biggest ship, then. There were sheep and cattle to be bred, corn to be raised, Maori trade to develop. Especially Maori trade, for despite strenuous efforts the growing colony was still dependent on the natives for the bulk of its food supplies. It was a tie that cut both ways, for the Maoris had come to look on the settlers as a source of manufactured goods they now regarded as staples instead of luxuries.

Six years of more or less continual peace had enabled that commerce to prosper. There was no reason why it shouldn't last for six decades. Of all the native peoples Coffin had heard or read about the Maori took the most readily to business. Rational people that they were, they saw that trade with the settlers was far more profitable in the long run than theft or war.

His relationship with the Maori, especially with the ariki Te Ohine, was his greatest advantage over Hull. Like so many in the European community his old enemy still tended to regard the natives as primitive and backward. Coffin knew better.

Te Ohine was much impressed with the white man's big pa and in particular with Coffin's new house. Occasionally he would pay a visit with Rui or one of his lesser wives to marvel at the china and silver, the big grandfather clock or the running water in the kitchen. Coffin's newly rich neighbors wouldn't think of having a native inside their homes. It pleased Coffin to ignore their muttered comments and whispers while escorting Te Ohine through the many rooms.

Holly's feelings wavered between those of her husband and those of her neighbors, but she tolerated her husband's guests, smiling at them while tagging behind like a nervous hen, chiding curious little girls like the frenetic Merita and mischievous Akini as they examined every drawer and utensil in her kitchen.

Coffin often reminded his friends that despite the fact that Auckland could now call itself a proper city, the colony still survived largely on the sufferance of the Maori. Whites were still seriously outnumbered. Parts of Auckland might now resemble those of an English town of similar size, but size alone did not ensure security. They still had no permanent armed garrison or standing armed force. If the Maoris ever chose to attack en masse there would be little the city's residents could do to stop them.

Unnecessary talk, Halworthy and the other merchants insisted. Why, the natives couldn't settle differences among themselves, therefore it was foolish to think they could ever pose a serious threat to the community. The Maoris who did not like the pakeha still preferred to fight each other. They held no ancient blood feuds with the settlers. All the New Zealanders had to do was stand aside, smile tolerantly at their bloodthirsty brown brothers, and look on as they methodically butchered themselves. Meanwhile the colony grew stronger with each passing day.

Maybe Halworthy and the rest were right. Everyone told him he worried too much. Holly was most concerned, convinced he would worry himself to death one day.

Something down on the docks caught his eye, breaking his reverie.

Christopher had not gone to the office. He still stood at quayside. Of all things, he seemed to be chatting with some filthy ragamuffin of a girl. She appeared to be about his age, a dark-eyed waif dressed in what once might have been a neat little pinafore. It was grimy and stained as a ship's bottom.

Coffin couldn't imagine what she might be doing here. This was no place for girls. They belonged at home with their mothers, tending to gardens or cooking or washing and cleaning, or if they came from a well-off family, promenading down the burgeoning shopping district. Not here alone among gruff and unpredictable men of a dozen races who hailed from every degenerate corner of the Pacific.

Yet as Coffin eyed her he saw she seemed quite sure of herself, not nervous at all. Her lustrous dark hair was cut unnaturally short. He wondered if she'd recently been in an accident. That's when he put everything together and recognition struck home. It all fit: the dirty dress, the confidence, the confidence at dockside, the severe, almost punishing haircut.

He shouted and saw Christopher turn to look at him.

"Boy, get your bum up here fast as she'll move!"

"But Father," the thin, piping voice protested distantly, "we were just. . . ."

"RIGHT NOW!"

Christopher turned to face the girl. He must have said something to her because Coffin could see her nodding her head. Then the boy turned to come running back toward the dock. As he did so the girl looked up and straight at Coffin. Noncommittal, her stare, but not vague either. As if moved by something unseen she suddenly turned and bolted up the road that lined the harborfront, a bit of leggy rag swept away by an unsensed wind.

Christopher slowed as he arrived at the top of the ramp, panting hard as always, eyes downcast. He was clearly puzzled, conscious of having done something to displease his father but utterly dumbfounded as to what it might be.

"Father, did I do something bad? We were just talking."

Kneeling, Coffin brought his face close to his son's. "Christopher, listen closely. I don't ever want you talking to that girl again."

"But Father." Christopher tried to make a joke of it. "What harm could it do? She's just a *girl*."

His father didn't smile. "My heart's in this, boy. Never again. You've plenty of playmates. If it's girls you want to start talking with, fine and well. But not that one."

Christopher didn't reply, turned instead to stare down into the crowded quayside. She was gone, that was sure. When his father roared like that it could frighten the paint off a man-o'-war.

"Where'd she go? Back to her mother, I guess."

"Her mother's dead. Been dead some time."

"Oh?" Odd how the boy could sound so grown-up all of a sudden, Coffin thought. "She didn't say anything about that."

"Wouldn't be likely to. Just stay clear of her, that's all."

"Her name's Rose." Christopher made it sound like a protest. "She knows who you are but she didn't know who I was. I don't understand, Father. It's not like she's dangerous or anything—is she?"

"No." Coffin rose and looked toward the city. "No, she isn't dangerous." He was aware that by making Christopher too curious he might end up achieving the opposite of his intentions. "I just don't want you associating with her. It's not her but her father who's the problem. Her father and I, we don't see eye to eye. Never have. I prefer it stays that way. Right through the entire family. Understand?"

"As you say, Father." Christopher was still enough of a child to shift emotions without warning. "I'm bored. Can we go home now?"

"I thought you wanted to help Mr. Goldman with his counting."

"Not anymore. I'm hungry."

That was an event in itself. It was a wonder the boy found the energy to arise in the morning, so little did he eat.

"All right. I'll take you home. But then you'll have to play by yourself. I've business to attend to."

"You're always doing business." Christopher started down the ramp. "I hardly ever see you. You don't get home till I'm asleep and you leave before I'm awake."

Coffin smiled and tousled the boy's hair as they stepped off the ramp together. "Someone has to pay for your toys and books and tutors. Hard work is what makes our fine house and the horses and ships like the *Holly* possible."

Christopher shrugged. "I guess so. Father, what do *you* do for fun?"

The question surprised Coffin. He smiled thoughtfully. "Your mother and I have our small pleasures, and I have toys you aren't old enough to understand. My work is part of my play."

Christopher mulled it over, discarded it. "Can we stop at Mr. Vanderlaan's for a sugar tart?"

"Of course! You can have anything you want, but you must promise to eat all of your lunch."

"I will, Father!" Christopher promised excitedly. His mother rarely took him with her to the city's best bakery.

They were nearly there when a Maori boy appeared on the street alongside them. He seemed to pop out of nowhere, though Coffin soon realized he'd emerged from the alley on their left.

He looked to be about fifteen. A battered cap rode his bushy hair like a skiff in a storm. His shorts and shirt had seen equally rough times. He was barefoot. Without preamble or introduction he stepped in their path and extended one hand.

"Sir, I was told give you this."

Coffin reflexively took the sheet of pounded flax and tossed the youth a coin. The boy turned to leave but Coffin held up a hand for him to stay as he unfolded the sheet. "Hold a moment, lad." The youngster paused.

The writing was crude but legible. The characters had been sketched in an odd sort of maroon ink, of a color and consistency one might obtain by mixing octopus ink with a bright red liquid. Paint, Coffin thought. Or blood. His brow furrowed as he read.

"'Robert Coffin. This city a good city for you. Make it your only city.'"

That was the entire message. There was no signature. He couldn't tell how fresh the letter was though it was fading already. He looked up sharply at the activity which filled the streets, found no gaze waiting to meet his own.

"Who gave this to you?"

"A normal person, sir. An old one."

"Tall?"

"Sir, he was the tallest person I have ever seen. I think maybe he was a tohunga."

Coffin's eyes snapped down to meet those of the youth. "What? What makes you think that? Did he tell you that?"

The native drew back from Coffin's sharpness. "No sir. Sometimes you can just feel it. The wise ones are different from the rest of us."

"Where did you see him? Where did he hand this to you to give to me?"

The youth turned to point. "Around there, sir, back in this alley."

Coffin started toward the narrow street. "Christopher, stay here."

"But Father, I want to come too!"

"Stay here!"

The alley running behind the row of shops and stores was deserted, the narrow accessway muddy and cut by wagon ruts. No sidewalk here to protect promenading citizens. He ran down the alley heedless of the mud and grime that splashed over his fine boots to darken the legs of his trousers. His eyes searched every recess and doorway. The road deadened in a brick wall fifteen feet high. He encountered no Maoris, tall or otherwise. A quick examination of the ground proved equally unenlightening, the slick surface a farrago of shoeprints, footprints, and the tracks of horses and mules.

It didn't matter. The youth's description was proof enough. Only one human being could have written Coffin the cryptic note. He was confused and puzzled as he slowly headed back towards the main street.

Of course the note had been penned by a tohunga. As it was necessary to read in order to study the Bible, many Maoris had learned to do so. But few could write. His eyes continued to flick over the recessed doorways and shadowed windows. He could still be here, hiding, watching. He raised his voice.

"Tuhoto!"

He called repeatedly, but there was no reply. Only the distant murmur of people out on the street mixed with the sloshing of horses treading the muddy road. Christopher was standing impatiently where he'd been left. Of the Maori messenger there was no sign, nor had Coffin expected him to linger.

"You didn't see him?"

"See who, Father?"

"A tall old Maori, like the native boy said. A very tall one."

"No, Father. I saw Mr. Voleinder. He waved to me, but I stayed here like you said to. I don't understand, Father. What's going on?"

"Nothing, son. Most likely just a joke." He put his hand on the boy's shoulder and turned him around. "Come on now. Let's get your sugar tart and hurry home. Your mother will be worried."

"Aw, Mother's always worried, isn't she? It's because of her I can't go to sea with Captain Markham, isn't it?"

Coffin hesitated, replied against his will. "No. Your mother and I make those kinds of decisions in concert. Perhaps next year you can go, when you're a little older and stronger."

Christopher looked away, his voice keen with disappointment. "That's what you told me last year."

The subject of going to sea was not mentioned again, for which Coffin was grateful. It made him uncomfortable to lie to the boy, but he had no intention of driving a wedge between himself and Holly in the child's mind, however wrong-headed was his mother's reasoning. Next year, he promised himself. Damn the bloody doctors! At least he could send the boy to Sydney, if not Canton or Shanghai.

He considered the strange message one last time before tossing it aside. Perhaps it hadn't originated with Tuhoto at all. It could be a veiled warning from any ariki with a grudge against Coffin. The warrior chiefs who lived near Auckland were not a happy lot, grumbling and complaining as the city expanded onto their lands. They got drunk and fought and argued among themselves. Any of them could have paid a wise one to write the note.

Coffin shook his head. If it was a warning it should have been made clear. They wouldn't frighten him with riddles.

2

The pa was full of dissension and bad feeling. There had already been two serious fights. That would solve nothing.

Now the chiefs sat in the meeting house and made faces at one another. They did not know what else to do and they were frustrated. Everyone calmed down only when Aruta spoke. As eldest present he commanded respect from all. As senior ariki he could remember the times before the pakeha had come to Aotearoa.

"It will only anger them," he finished.

"Then I say let it anger them!" This from Kaneho, one of the younger ariki.

"You would ruin our trade," said another of the chiefs.

Kaneho turned on him sharply. "In what? In kumara? In eggs? Is that how the Maori were meant to live, by growing food for the pakeha?"

"It is a good business," the chief who'd spoken reminded him.

"Pagh! We need nothing from the pakeha."

"No? Show me how to grow a rifle and I will think more seriously of what you say." There were murmurs of agreement from the assembly. The speaker rose, eyed his colleagues. "We need guns to fight our enemies in the south, the Opou and Arake. The only way to get guns and powder is to trade with the pakeha."

"The Maori do not need guns," shouted Kaneho. "We have defended ourselves before without guns." He held up his greenstone club. "This is all the Maori have ever needed. It will split the skull of a pakeha as easily as that of an Opou."

"But not from a distance," observed old Aruta sagely.

"We must do something." All eyes turned to the new speaker. Motawi had become an ariki through accomplishment and skill rather than heredity. He was proud but quiet, and men listened when he talked. Kaneho deferred to him immediately.

111

When he was sure he had their attention, the young chief continued. "We must show these pakeha they cannot treat us like chickens and kick us aside when it suits them. Te Rowaka is right: we must continue to trade with them, to get guns. We take from them what we need: their god, their weapons and their tools. But we must show them we can cast everything into the sea if it is our will to do so."

"Could we do that? They are many now," Aruta reminded him.

"Do not doubt it, wise one."

"I know what troubles Kaneho," said Te Rowaka suddenly. "He is not mad because we trade with the pakeha. He is mad because the tribes of the west now have most of such trade since the pakeha built their great new pa on the big harbor there."

"I have all the trade I want." Kaneho sneered at the older chief. "I don't need the pakeha."

"None of us *need* the pakeha," Te Rowaka replied patiently. "We deal with them not out of need but for profit. They sell us wonders we cannot make for ourselves for baskets of eggs and grain and piles of flax. We grow more than we ourselves can use. Why risk this trade over a war just to make a point?"

"Because they are growing strong," said Motawi. "We must show we are stronger while there is still time to do so."

"Must we be stronger?" Aruta sounded tired. He was old and wanted only to enjoy his grandchildren. "We are men, the pakeha are men. It is not necessary to fight to prove this thing."

Motawi shook his club, though not in the old chief's direction. That would have been unnecessarily disrespectful. "Many pakeha do not agree with you, wise one. They call us names and regard us as inferior to them. These new pakeha are different from those who first came to settle here. They have no *mana*. They care nothing for us or our ways. Many of us have learned the pakeha's words, but how many of them speak the tongue of the Maori?"

"We need to learn to live with them. They are here and we can learn from them even as we teach them our ways." Te Rowaka did not enjoy the position of adversary but he refused to let the young chiefs have their way. "They can be managed, as we manage our pigs. Take this business of their god, this

Christ, whom they insist is superior to all the old gods. We say
we accept him and this makes them happy. They need not know
we only put him in a place of honor alongside our own gods.

"This matter of writing, for example, is a good thing."

"We do not need it," Kaneho snapped. "It is not Maori. We
have always been able to keep our memories without it."

"Writing history is better than oral history." Te Rowaka was
not so easily put off. "Just as guns are better than spears. Now
that many tribes have begun to sell land to the pakeha we must
learn how the pakehas record these transactions." He shook his
head in wonderment. "They will not abide by word or promise
but must have record of it in this writing of theirs. We must
learn how they do this so we will not be cheated."

"You would have us become more like the pakeha each
day," said Kaneho.

"If there is good in it, then what is the harm?" Aruta
protested.

"The harm," Motawi put in quietly, "is that we will forget
that we are Maori and that this is *our* land. We will forget that
the pakeha are here only because we say it is all right for them
to be here." His gaze swept over the circle of chiefs. "Already
there are some among the pakeha who speak of taking all the
land for themselves."

That provoked some real indignation among the ariki, as
Motawi had known it would. Even Te Rowaka was stunned.

"Surely they cannot think such things! They must know we
would not permit it."

"I have heard such talk." Aruta made a dismissive wave of
his hand. "The pakeha are just like Maori. A few will say
anything when they have had too much beer." There was
laughter in the meeting house then.

When it died down Motawi continued. "I do not mind that
we trade with the pakeha. I do mind that they continue to buy
our land." He nodded deferentially to Te Rowaka. "You are
right when you say we should trade with them for guns and
powder to fight the southern tribes. But they must be reminded
who is master here and to whom they owe their continued
presence in this land."

Kaneho rose, too furious to sit still any longer. "What has
happened to the Maori, that they sit and debate this matter like
children?" He glared at Te Rowaka, impatient with Motawi's
conciliatory approach. "Does it not bother you that the pakeha

sailors take our young women? That they come back to us corrupted and despoiled?"

"Women will do what women will do," murmured one of the other chiefs. "You cannot keep them from the jewelry and money the sailors offer them. What is the harm in a little love between pakeha and Maori? Besides, many of those who go to the sailors have been corrupted before they lie with them."

More laughter in the meeting house. Frustrated and shame-faced, Kaneho sat back down, muttering to himself. "They must be *shown.*"

"I am not interested in showing them." Te Rowaka also sat down. "I am comfortable within my pa. I trade when I want to, not when they do. And if I tell them to go away," he made a broad, sweeping gesture with one arm, "they leave. They stay within their own pas. Those who buy our land are few while their animals are many. If we wish we could take the cattle and sheep at any time and blow these few pakeha away. There is no need to do this thing. Better to let the pakeha work hard. If we wish to taste of their animals it is an easy thing to borrow one or two."

By now the tide had turned in favor of Aruta and the traders. Kaneho was subdued and Motawi uncertain how to proceed. Therefore it came as a surprise when a new voice spoke up near the back of the meeting house.

"I agree with Kaneho amd Motawi."

Everyone turned to stare into the shadows as the speaker rose to address them. He was squat and powerful, clearly a warrior to be reckoned with. He did not look like an orator, but he spoke easily and fluently now.

"The pakeha grow too bold. Some take land without paying for it first. But trade is important too. What the pakeha need is a lesson, not a long war. I will not ask my brothers to join me in this thing, but will they stop me if I alone decide to show the pakeha who is master?"

Aruta was squinting, trying to see. "I know you. This is not a thing to do with reason. You fight for plunder and pleasure."

"I do it for both," the speaker admitted readily. "Is that not the Maori way? The pakeha can be useful if they learn their place."

Aruta sighed. "What is it you propose?"

"To show them what the Maori can do if they wish."

Kaneho's enthusiasm returned. "We will burn a farm and take all the animals."

The speaker eyed him contemptuously. "Any *tutua*, any commoners can burn a farm. We must make a lesson they will not soon forget. Only then will they treat us as equals in our own country. I, Hone Heke, would do this thing. I have a thousand warriors. Will any here join me?"

"I will," said Kaneho immediately.

"And I," Motawi added.

Hone Heke nodded. "Good. It will be enough." He gazed at his fellow ariki. "Will any here try to stop us?"

The chiefs looked at each other, finally back at old Aruta. The aged ariki considered carefully before commenting. "We will not aid you in this thing, but neither will we hinder you. The pakeha know how to fight. They will defend themselves."

Hone Heke spat on the floor. "Not these pakehas. They are drunk all the time. Though they have wondrous weapons they are not warriors. A *pu*, a gun, is only as good as the man holding it. The pakeha are soil-grubbers and fisherfolk, not fighters. You will see. I, Hone Heke, will show you!"

He turned and left the meeting house. Kaneho and Motawi went with him. The rest of the ariki began conversing excitedly among themselves. Te Rowaka had walked over to stand with Aruta. Together they stared at the door through which the young fighters had departed.

"This will be bad for trade," Te Rowaka said.

"Yes," said the old chief sadly. "And it will be worse if they win."

3

"Robert?"

At first he feared the onset of another of those unsettling dreams which had plagued him for years. Groggily he realized this was the waking world as he sorted out the sounds seeping into his brain.

Holly had rolled over and lay close to him, the soft folds of her sleeping gown pressing tight against his side. She was pushing against his shoulder as she whispered. "Robert, wake up."

He rolled over, still half asleep, confused. Slowly he opened his eyes, ready for the harsh burst of sunlight through the bedroom window. It didn't come. Slightly purpling sky was visible through the imported glass. He blinked.

"Woman, it's still night out."

"Don't you hear it, Robert?" She was sitting up in the bed, staring at the same window. The tenseness in her voice was mirrored in her posture.

"Hear what?" Then his senses were roused to full awareness as the noise outside answered the question for him.

Confused voices, an excited babble of many people speaking all at once. Not quite simultaneous shouting, but not normal conversation either. Fumbling with matches, he lit the lamp that sat on his end table. His pocket watch lay there and he squinted at it. Two in the morning. Too late for drunken revelry, too early for a riot.

By now he could make out individual voices in the street below the house. And there was something else, distant, echoing: a church bell ringing. No, several church bells.

Fire, he thought instinctively. The greatest danger the growing community faced and one which would bring every citizen running from his bed. But as he stumbled clear of the sheets and over to the window he saw no sign of glowing flames from any part of the city. At the same time there was a pounding on the bedroom door. Decorous, but loud enough to wake.

"Mr. Coffin, sir? Mr. Coffin!"

Samuel's voice. The din outside must have been loud indeed to rouse the old servant from his sound sleep. He started for the door.

"Robert!" Holly was gesturing anxiously.

Coffin glanced down at himself, grinned back toward the bed. "A naked pakeha's no different from a naked Maori, Holly."

She made a face and pulled the covers up to her chin as he opened the door. The old man was out of breath from his rapid ascent of the stairs.

"Men outside, sir. Many men. They want to see you. Sorry to disturb." He glanced past Coffin. "Sorry, missus."

"It's all right, Samuel."

He nodded once, looked back up at Coffin. "They say you come down quick, Mr. Coffin sir."

"What is it, Samuel? What's going on?"

"I don't know, sir. They don't tell me. They just say, you go and get Mr. Coffin quick! I tell them Mr. Coffin sir, he sound asleep. They say nobody get any sleep tonight. Mr. McQuade, he say that, sir."

"McQuade's here?"

"Yes sir. And Mr. Halworthy and your other friends."

If there was a fire they would've told Samuel right away. Therefore it was something else. He couldn't imagine what crisis would bring someone like John Halworthy running at two o'clock in the morning.

"Tell them I'll be right down."

"Yes sir!" Samuel vanished down the hallway.

Striding over to the huge French armoire that dominated one wall, Coffin flung the doors wide and dragged out his old sailor's best: heavy pants, cotton shirt. Holly watched from the bed.

"Surely you're not putting out to sea?"

"I don't know where I'm going. Don't know what's going on." He slid into the pants.

"Well I'm coming down with you," she told him suddenly.

"All right, but get a move on. If Angus says hurry, he *means* hurry."

He was already half dressed when she began fumbling with her own clothes, and he listened a moment outside Christopher's door. No suggestions of movement from inside. The boy was a deep sleeper and it was evident the clamor outside hadn't woken him yet. Down the stairs he flew, racing past the pictures from Europe that lined the stairwell, each a colorful testament both of Holly Coffin's taste as well as their rapidly increasing fortune.

His visitors had crowded through the front door. Light came from lanterns and torches just outside. The smell of many horses mixed thickly with the odor of burning oil and wood. It took him a moment to locate Angus McQuade, the one man he could count on to provide clear, concise answers to his questions.

"Hurry, Robert! We've a long ride ahead of us and you're the last we've come to get."

"Ride? Where? What's this all about, Angus?"

"First see to your weapons, Robert."

Coffin frowned. McQuade was dead serious. This was no elaborate practical joke. He turned to Samuel.

"Get the good rifle and my pistols from the den."

"Yes sir!" Wide-eyed, Samuel hurried to comply.

"It's Kororareka, Robert," Angus explained. "It's under attack even as we stand here talking."

"Under attack?" Coffin shook his head. He couldn't be hearing right. Not fully awake yet. "That's insane. We have a treaty with the Maori."

"You can't make a treaty with heathens!" This comment from somewhere in the middle of the assembled men was echoed by shouts of agreement.

Though obviously tired, McQuade took the time to explain. "Fellow came pounding into town an hour or so ago, he and his animal both rode near to death. Clear across the island he'd come, like Pheidippides at Marathon, to bring us the news."

John Halworthy stepped forward. "He's in my house, resting, with a doctor attending him. Jonas Cooper. One of my own people from Kororareka. The man could barely speak but talked long enough to tell the story. Told me to rouse every able-bodied man and bring every gun in Auckland and come as fast as we could, for the Maoris were razing the town. That if we didn't ride like the wind there'd be a terrible massacre."

"Massacre?" Coffin was trying to make sense of the

impossible. "There'll be no massacre even if this Cooper's words be true. The people can always take refuge on the ships in the harbor."

"If they have the time and the Maoris don't cut them off," Halworthy pointed out grimly.

Samuel came running with Coffin's guns. "Good, Samuel. Now see to my horse." The servant nodded, disappeared beyond the stairway.

"I can't believe any of this. That treaty was sound. I personally can vouch for half the chiefs who put their names on it."

Halworthy sniffed disdainfully. "And what of the other half? We've argued this many times, Robert, you and I. You don't know the Maori. You just fool yourself into thinking that you do. It suits your vanity."

Coffin bristled and McQuade hastened to intercede. "It may be that whoever is attacking Kororareka didn't sign the blasted treaty at all. We can't say for certain until we get there."

"Heaven help any ariki who signed that treaty only to break it," Coffin muttered intently. But his mind was on the cryptic message that had prompted him to sell his property in Kororareka some months before.

McQuade put a hand on Coffin's shoulder. "Come then, Robert. If this man Cooper's wrong I'll wring his neck meself. But if he be but half right we've not another moment to lose!"

4

"Mother, I'm frightened!"

Mary Kinnegad clutched her daughter tightly as they huddled together on the iron bed. "I am too, child."

"Don't worry, Mother, Sally. It'll be okay." Young Flynn Kinnegad held the loaded pistol in both hands. He could barely lift it from the floor, but when he did finally raise it he held it aimed steady and true on the front door.

Thus far the conflagration sweeping Kororareka had spared them, though Mary was convinced it was only a matter of time until the Maoris found the little house on the hillside. The natives had come pouring down out of the hills, gesticulating and howling. There'd been no talk and no warning. It was clear they intended utter destruction from the beginning. Now the fires that illuminated the town came not from the reducing cauldrons aboard the whalers in the harbor but from the buildings themselves.

She knew that for one of the first times in her life she'd been lucky, fortunate not to have been at work down at the tavern when the Maoris had struck. She watched the defiant Flynn aiming at the door, wondering if the old pistol would even fire. It was all they had.

From the window she could see that more than half the town was already ablaze. The attack had slowed as the Maoris broke into the taverns, making first for the biggest ones like the Fife and Drum or the Broken Anchor. Now they were rampaging through the ruins, their whoops and war cries interspersed with the sounds of crashing mirrors and breaking bottles as they helped themselves to the town's liquor supply. This time they would not settle for the cheap wine and watered rum their flax and corn usually bought.

An explosion split the sky nearby. A yellow spear of fire like a flare shot from Hell lit the low clouds. Sally tried to press

closer to her mother's breast while Flynn flinched at the sound
but kept his grip on the pistol.

They would come through the door, she knew. She closed
her eyes, rocking the sobbing Sally in her arms. Prayer had
never been a part of her life, was something outside her
experience, but she struggled with it now. The butcher knife
she'd taken from the kitchen bumped coldly against her thigh.
If necessary she would use it on herself and her daughter.

Something began pounding on the door, anxious but not
insistent. There was a quaver in Flynn's voice as he raised the
pistol a little higher.

"Stop there or—I'll fire! I will!"

The pounding came again. The boy closed his eyes and
turned his head slightly as he squeezed on the trigger with two
fingers.

A thunderous *boom* echoed around the interior of the room.
The recoil knocked the eleven-year-old to the floor, the butt of
the gun striking him in the nose and starting the blood flowing.
The pounding outside ceased. For an instant Mary dared to
breathe again.

Then her ears were filled with the sound of splintering wood
as the door was kicked in. She screamed and buried her head in
Sally's hair.

A towering figure stood in the broken doorway, silhouetted
against the glow of the burning town. His eyes were wild and
his face was smeared with blood from the two parallel knife
wounds that gashed his cheek. A ragged Maori war club had
ripped his shirt and shoulder. As he staggered into the room
Mary started to rise from the bed.

"Shaun Connaught, as I live and breathe!"

He tried to smile but the expression twisted as he grabbed at
his side. There was no blood there. "Club," he muttered.
"The bastards are strong and quick. The one that surprised me
won't be botherin' anyone else this night, though." He
gestured slightly with the old naval cutlass he carried in one
massive paw. It was stained red from point to haft.

"How be you and the little ones, Mary?"

"Well enough, though I thought when you came hammering
on our door that it was the end."

" 'Twas almost so, for me. That shot missed me by barely an
inch. You always could take care of yourself."

"It wasn't me. It was the boy." She nodded toward Flynn,

who was getting to his feet with blood streaming down his face. Gently she set Sally aside and began ripping at the bedsheets.

"Here now, lad." She pushed the wad of cotton against his nostrils and tilted his head back. He nodded understanding and put his hand against the absorbent linen.

Meanwhile Connaught was moving from window to door and back again. "We've got to leave this place. They're checking every building before firing it."

"Get out? To where, Shaun? The Maoris are everywhere."

"Aye. I hadn't thought the country counted so many of the heathen, and it seems every one of them is here this night."

"Where are the rest of the men? Why aren't they fighting back?"

"Men?" Connaught snorted. "There be no men in Kororareka, Mary. Only fishbait! Good enough for killing whales, but they've little stomach for fighting other men. A few stand their ground—those that ain't too drunk to do so."

"Here, let me see." She pulled the cloth from Flynn's face and bade him lean forward. The bleeding had nearly stopped.

Connaught was talking nonstop. "A few of the boys from one American ship put up something of a fight but most just ran when they saw the Maoris coming running at 'em, waving their bleedin' clubs and rolling their eyes and stickin' out their tongues the way they do. Instead of fighting back they ran for the woods like frightened rabbits, watching while the Maoris steal their goods and burn their homes."

"It won't do them any good," she told him. "The natives will hunt them down."

"Perhaps not, Mary. I've seen them ignore townsfolk, run right past them intent instead on this store or pub. They seem more inclined to looting than to murder. Oh, they'll cut you down if you cross them, but run the other way and they'll go right past. Might be they came planning to kill everyone, but I think their thoughts have changed. I think those who came last are afraid the first will make off with everything worth stealing." Satisfied with what he saw outside, he moved to take her hand.

"Come. There are whaleboats waiting at the piers where defense is easy. I'll see you and the little ones safely out to sea."

She helped Sally off the bed. Flynn didn't need to take her

hand as he crowded close to Connaught. She paused for a last look at the cabin but Connaught was already urging her out the shattered doorway.

"There's no time, Mary. Leave everything. Perhaps they'll spare this small building and you can come back for your things when this is done."

"No," she said with unexpected finality. "No. I'll never come back to this house. I should have left here long ago."

Sally's small hand was bunched inside her right fingers. She reached out and took Flynn's in her left, gazing down into solemn blue eyes as she bent toward him.

"You remember this night, Flynn. Remember it always. Remember who caused us to be here when this happened. Don't ever forget who is responsible for your condition." Aware she was hurting him she relaxed her grip and straightened. The boy nodded without speaking, but his eyes were fierce.

Fire surrounded them on all sides. Maoris were running everywhere, yelling and leaping into the air and waving their dreadful war clubs. In the light of the burning buildings their tattooed faces were frightful. Howling, a group of them scattered frantically as the warehouse and store across the way collapsed in a geyser of embers which filled the night air like burning snowflakes. Connaught led them in a different direction, working a path toward the docks while striving to stay as far from The Beach as possible.

Halfway to the shore they were confronted by a pair of warriors who posed no threat: both were unable to stand, much less fight. Bottles from the pillaged taverns lay in a pile nearby, flashing like cabachons in the light from burning buildings. Further on they encountered a Maori not half so inebriated who challenged them and demanded money for safe passage. Instead he caught the blunt edge of Connaught's cutlass across his forehead.

"Hurry now, before any more of the heathens espy us!" He took Mary's hand and pulled her along.

He was limping noticeably now, his free hand clutching more often at his side.

"Broken rib, I think," he replied to Mary's anxious query. "Maybe two. Don't fret, lass. I'll make it."

"Bless you, Shaun! I should've married you years ago."

He rewarded her with an embarrassed smile. "Nay, Irish Mary. Neither of us are the marryin' kind, though I'm damned if I didn't come near asking you a time or two. I count meself a better man for havin' known you and the children, and a worse one for what I once thought of you."

"Don't be too hard on yourself for your thoughts, Shaun Connaught," she told him between gasps. Stored powder erupted somewhere off to their left and they ducked instinctively, but the explosion was too far away to propel any burning debris toward them. "I'm no innocent flower and never have been."

So great was the heat from burning storehouses that they were forced to turn down the fiery tunnel that had been Market Street. A Maori came staggering out of one of the burning shops, his arms loaded down with looted goods, while his companion's quarreled over a bottle of expensive sherry.

Given the size and ferocity of the attacking war party, Mary was surprised how few actual bodies they encountered during their desperate flight. The majority of the Maoris they found lying in the streets were drunk and not dead. A man she knew as Caleb, a fine sailmaker, was not drunk, however. The back of his skull had been smashed by a war club. He lay in a pool of liquid much thicker than liquor.

The Maoris were too busy with their looting to attend to their own dead and wounded. Connaught gave the latter as wide a berth as their healthy relations.

"They're like snakes: still dangerous until they're dead." His voice was grim. "By Heaven, one of these days we'll come back here with a proper army and clean out this bleedin' island from one end to the other!"

"Isn't that what they're trying to do to us, Shaun?"

He glanced sharply down at her but said nothing. He needed his remaining strength to stay erect and keep moving. His ribs were on fire.

They could see the harborfront now, through billowing smoke. The docks had either been left untouched or had been well defended because numerous structures still stood unscathed by the Maori attackers. Whaleboats crammed with refugees could be glimpsed rowing for anchored ships.

Two piers were still defended. Four men stood near the end of one, five on the other. All held muskets at the ready. It was not a defense to make Wellington proud, but the whalers made

up in determination what they lacked in military acumen.
Clusters of Maoris had gathered at a safe distance, well out of
musket range. From time to time a warrior would suddenly
rush nearly within musket range, then pause to turn, bend, and
make appropriately grotesque faces at his enemies from
between his legs, a gesture which meant precisely the same
among the natives as it did among the Europeans. Then the
warrior would stumble back to rejoin his compatriots, usually
amidst much laughter. In this way the Maoris demonstrated
their superiority over their opponents, who gritted their teeth
and held their ground.

"They're all over on the far side of the landing," Mary said
excitedly. "We'll make it, Shaun!"

"Yes," he said weakly. He nearly fell and she had to support
him for a moment. "Blast this rib! We'll get her set. Then we'll
see about organizing a troop of seamen to come back here with
proper weapons."

Mary shook her head decisively. "That you'll never manage,
Shaun. You and I, we settled here. Those men on the piers are
doing their civilized duty, but their interests extend no farther
than the wood on which they're standing. Their homes are on
their ships and across the ocean, not here. They'll not risk their
lives for this property, you'll see."

"That we will."

Those were the last words he ever spoke.

Something *cracked* louder than a collapsing timber. It was
too brief, too unimpressive to bring down a man the size of
Shaun Connaught, a single distinct pop amidst pistols firing
and wood exploding from heat pressure. Connaught dropped to
his knees and skidded forward several inches before stopping.
Then he fell over on his face and chest not twenty yards from
the head of one of the defended piers.

Mary knelt next to him and pulled angrily at his shoulders,
trying to rouse a spirit already on its way to a better world. She
tried to cry, found she was unable to. The ability to cry had left
her years before. Sally had no such problem. She stood
sobbing nearby while Flynn clutched handfuls of his mother's
dress and pulled madly. Tattooed faces were clearly visible
through the smoke. Not all of them were concentrating on the
sailors protecting the two piers.

"Mother, Mother, please come! We can't stay here. We have
to get to the boats, Mother."

Afterwards she didn't know if she rose of her own accord or if Flynn had dragged her away bodily. All she remembered was Connaught lying face down in the sand and gravel. He never looked up, never opened his eyes to bid her farewell.

Later she imagined she'd seen a tall, gangling Maori standing thirty yards away by a burning shed, calmly reloading a brand new musket. How much reality and how much dream she would never know, though she was certain not all was attributable to imagination.

She never learned the name of the brave sailor who broke away from the group of men defending the nearest pier to put his arm protectively around her waist and escort her and her children to safety. So overwhelmed by grief and sorrow was she that it never occurred to her to thank him. But to the last of her days she knew she would remember his face. It was the face of a man with a wife and children elsewhere, safe in some sound, civilized city like Boston or Liverpool.

Secure behind the line of musket-wielding seamen she found herself being lowered into a waiting boat. She had the company of several other refugees. One man wore a makeshift bandage around his head. A young woman sat off by herself, ignoring the revealing rips in her skirt and blouse as she stared vacantly into the distance. She appeared unhurt, but Mary knew there were many types of injury that were not immediately visible.

The lettering on the whaleboat read JOHN B. ADAMS and she found herself wondering who John Adams might be. Anything to blot out the image of Shaun Connaught lying dead on the sand. Silent men pushed away from the pier. As the boat moved out onto the cool, dark water of the bay the noise of drunken carousing and burning buildings receded gradually behind her. She held Sally tightly, rocking her in her arms even as she wished she could blot the horrors of this night from the girl's impressionable young mind. She would have done the same for Flynn but he was nowhere close at hand. Instead he sat in the back of the boat hard by the steersman, staring intently back toward the burning shore.

Good, she thought angrily. Let him see. Let him remember.

The sailors who pulled silently at the oars were exhausted and streaked with soot and grime. Behind them the entire harborfront now burned brightly. The hoots and cries of the triumphant Maoris faded, swallowed by the night.

They had to haul her on board the whaler. The men who took her arms and waist handled her far more courteously and respectfully than they would have on land, but she ignored them, as she ignored the devastation still clearly visible on shore. That didn't matter now. The loss of their few pitiful, personal possessions didn't matter. All that mattered was Flynn and little Sally.

Only when the children had been taken below, to be given hot soup and blankets, did she try to talk to any more of her fellow refugees. No one inquired whither the whaler was bound now that she'd weighed anchor. It didn't matter. Wherever she was headed had to be an improvement over what they'd left behind. Mary noticed she was heavy with oil. Her Captain wouldn't sail far with a full load and his deck awash in refugees. He'd done his duty. The sooner he put his orphans ashore the happier he'd be.

Perhaps if they'd organized their forces sooner they might have counterattacked and driven the Maoris away, but she couldn't find it in her heart to condemn men she didn't know. Brave sailors they might be, but they had not signed on for soldiering. They came to Kororareka for drink, amusement and a good time. Their roots and responsibilities lay elsewhere.

She leaned over the railing, over the sea and out into the night, staring back at the angry ember that had been the wildest town in the Pacific. The Beach was a pulsing furnace. The Maoris' surprise had been complete. All the panic and destruction had been on the so-called superior side.

Perhaps if the Maoris had been treated differently, with more respect, this night could have been avoided. Or perhaps it wouldn't have mattered how they'd been treated. Many of them lived for battle. She could see the small church that had dominated the far end of town beginning to burn. She fancied she could hear the bell ringing in the flaming steeple, though it was more likely the iron reducing cauldrons banging against one another on the deck below. The whaler stank of grease and varnish, whale oil and men. Amidst that effluvia the new odor of blood was lost.

Already some of the refugees were beginning to talk of lives still to be lived. They were making plans. As for herself, she had none beyond what she'd told poor, brave Shaun Connaught: whatever else happened, she would never return to this place. Let the innkeepers and shop owners shake their fists and hurl insults at the burning shore. They were the gestures of defeated men attempting to salve an overwhelming feeling of futility.

Kororareka was dead, Shaun Connaught was dead, and a part of her had perished with both of them.

5

They rode like the Devil's honorguard, but the road between Auckland and Kororareka was little more than a country trail. Like the rest of the country the terrain was difficult, besides which they had to be constantly alert for possible Maori attack. It would have been far easier if not faster to travel by ship, but there'd been no vessel berthed in Auckland harbor ready to transport men and horses. In any event it would have taken too long to load.

While still several miles from Kororareka the armed pakehas slowed. Their leaders gathered at the head of the trail to decide strategy. Angus McQuade stared into the dawning light, listening intently.

"I hear no shouting, no gunshots."

" 'Tis strangely silent for The Beach." Halworthy's face was a study in concern.

"Could the attack have been beaten off already, by the townsfolk?"

"Not impossible," said Ainsworth. "Where one man can panic others can stand their ground. Remember, these are only natives we're dealing with, after all."

"Not quite," Coffin reminded them. "They're Maori."

"A false alarm." Angry muttering came from the men gathered behind the leading citizens. "A bloody false alarm!"

"We don't know that yet!" McQuade said sharply. The muttering subsided without disappearing entirely.

"I wish to God it were." Halworthy was straining to see even though they were still too far from the town for a good view of anything but ocean and trees. "I know the man who brought the warning. He's not the type to ride himself and good horse into the ground to perpetuate a cruel hoax."

"We know that, John," Ainsworth told him, "but if this be war it's the quietest I've heard tell of."

"See to your arms," Coffin advised. "Whatever's happened down there we don't want to go in with powder damp and swords sheathed. We'll find out soon enough what's taken place this night."

"Nay, gentlemen, if you'll pardon me."

All eyes turned as another man joined the group. He was taller than any of them save Coffin, with thick arms and voice, and eyebrows that loomed like ledges over small dark pupils.

"I know you," said McQuade. "You're Brixton, the northside smithy."

"Aye, Mr. McQuade, but before I settled in Auckland I was a number of years in the King's Grenadiers. You, sir," and he stared unflinchingly at Coffin, "you know how to fight on water. You know nothing of fighting on land." He nodded toward the hills that blocked their view of Kororareka. "This be no place to go charging blindly. If you'll allow me, I'll take command and see we give a proper account of ourselves."

Coffin saw that his colleagues were waiting for him to make the decision. He nodded deferentially to the newcomer. "We'll be glad of your advice, Mr. Brixton, and follow your suggestions readily. I'll be the first to confess my ignorance of matters military. I'm glad you're with us."

There were a few protests from men who didn't wish to take orders from a commoner like Brixton, but they were overruled by practical considerations. Better to follow a live peasant than a dead gentleman.

Brixton took no undue pleasure in this show of support. "Very well then. Gather 'round. We'll split our forces now. Half of us will ride on the town from the main road. The rest will work their way through the woods to approach from behind. If you would be so good, Mr. Coffin, as to assume command of that body?"

Coffin nodded briskly, instantly divining the blacksmith's intentions.

"This way if we're attacked coming up the main road, Mr. Coffin and the others can fall upon our assailants from behind. If our arrival is not challenged we'll be able to take the enemy from two directions."

"A good and simple plan, och. My congratulations, Mr. Brixton," said McQuade.

"Thank you, sir. I've friends in Kororareka myself and am

anxious to see what fate has befallen them. Let's move now, while darkness still provides us with some cover."

With some confusion the relief party divided into two ragged, undisciplined columns. Coffin studied his own troop uneasily, wondering if the motley and tired collection of craftsmen, traders and common citizens could be depended on to stand and fight. There wasn't a uniform among them. A few were armed with nothing more deadly than farm implements. The several members of Auckland's rudimentary police force were no more impressive than the citizens whose activities they were appointed to regulate.

He checked his watch. He and Brixton had coordinated a time for both groups to begin advancing on the town. It was a sensible idea doomed to failure, for as soon as the first men caught sight of the smoking ruins ahead there was no holding them back. Coffin and Halworthy and the others tried to restrain their people and maintain some semblance of military order, to no avail. They quickly gave up and joined their fellow citizens in riding at full speed into the community. Coffin could not bring himself to yell at his neighbors. It was unreasonable to ask discipline of exhausted farmers and shopkeepers.

No one really knew what to expect. People running in the streets cleaning up after the attack, perhaps. A few deaths and injuries, maybe a looted store or two. So the utter devastation revealed by the light of the moon came as a considerable shock to the most pessimistic of the relief party.

It was worse for McQuade and Coffin and the men who'd lived in Kororareka in younger days than for the newcomers to Auckland, most of whom had never set eyes on the whaling town before this morning. The older men arrived with memories of the Kororareka that had been, most of them good. Now the Hell of the Pacific lay strangely silent beneath a waning moon.

No laughter and drunken cries rose from the line of burned-out hulks that had constituted The Beach. No shouts and ecstatic screams from the cribs that had risen flimsily behind the stouter taverns. Instead there was something else, something new and yet familiar: a sound Coffin had rarely heard in all the years he'd spent in Kororareka. It was the soft sound of the sea washing the sand, the whispery greetings of the early morning tide.

McQuade reined his mare to a stop next to Coffin. "Good God, mon! There's nothin' left."

"The survivors'll be out in the harbor, on the ships." Coffin dismounted, secured his animal to a still-standing rail. "Let's make sure no one's been left behind."

"Robert, are you sure 'tis safe?"

"Any Maoris still around won't be in any condition to trouble us. Come on, Angus. There may be wounded who were overlooked in the confusion."

A few of the ruined structures were recognizable from their scorched stone foundations. They served as guideposts to the streets. Most of the buildings in Kororareka had been fashioned from pine unsuitable for masts and spars. Kauri burned readily. Now nothing remained but blackened, smoking stumps.

As the men rode or walked through the silent streets they began to split up to better search the ruins. They said little, the stink of death and charcoal thick in their nostrils. The horses shied and whinnied.

There were fewer corpses than expected. Some Maori, some European, but no indication of the awful massacre that might have been expected to accompany such total destruction.

"See, Angus." Coffin indicated the gutted interior of a tavern with brick walls. "They came to loot and plunder, not slaughter the population." The rising sun somehow softened the charred remains.

Walking was too slow. He remounted his horse, headed up a familiar road. Off to his left came the sharp sounds of a man screaming. It was John Halworthy. Elegant, proper John Halworthy. Coffin could see him standing in the center of what had been Kororareka's largest tavern. His hat was gone and his fine silk shirt torn and blackened as he raved at the indifferent sky. He'd kept his money in the whaling town, expanding while men like Ainsworth and McQuade gradually pulled out. Now his entire fortune was lost.

He urged his horse up the slight rise leading away from The Beach, leaving Halworthy to his misery. Coffin had concerns of his own to attend to.

"Where's he off to?" asked one of the men accompanying McQuade on a slow inspection of the ruins. "He shouldn't be going off by himself. Might still be a heathen or two about."

"He'll be fine." McQuade still couldn't believe the evidence of his eyes. There was literally nothing left of what had once been a thriving, active community. It had been wiped from the face of the Earth. "Don't worry about Robert Coffin. Worry instead about the men and women who were here when the natives attacked."

"But how, how could they do something like this?" the younger man persisted. "They're just. . . ."

"Just what?" said McQuade, cutting him off. "Just Maoris? Just natives? How long have you been in New Zealand colony, friend?"

The man sounded defensive. "Six months."

McQuade just nodded. "Och, six months, is it? You won't understand aboot the Maoris in six months, my friend. You won't understand in six years. Just because many have turned to the church for salvation doesn't mean they like us any the better for it. And finer fightin' men you won't find anywhere."

"Come now, sir. A company of British regulars could pacify this whole island inside a year."

"You think so, do you? Look what they've done here in a single night."

The younger man wasn't convinced. "Drunken sailors, barkeeps and whores hardly constitute a proper fighting force. Besides which it's clear they were caught by surprise."

"Aye, that much is true. Still you'd think they would have been able to put up more resistance." McQuade shook his head sadly. "Come along. We've missed helping in the fight. If we're lucky we'll find some poor soul still clinging to life. Those are the ones who'll need our help now."

6

The half-cellar had been constructed of loosely mortared stone. It was intact, but the little house which had stood atop the rocks was completely gone, razed to the bottom timbers. Even the floor was missing, having collapsed into the cellar when its underlying trusses had burned through.

Coffin stared at the ruin for a long moment before dismounting. Purposefully he climbed the slight rise to enter from above, shoving his way past fragmented posts and beams. Some were still warm.

The first thing he looked for was the iron bed. When he couldn't find it he assumed the Maoris had carted it away. But it was there, bent and blackened where it had fallen through to the cellar. There were no bodies, no signs of close-quarter combat. No blood staining the wood. It took but a few minutes to complete a thorough inspection. Satisfied, he remounted and rode shoreward.

A small group of men had gathered to watch a whaleboat as it pulled up to a pier. The sailors confirmed what the would-be rescuers had both suspected and prayed for: almost the entire population had been evacuated safely to waiting ships out in the bay. As for the Maoris, they'd completed their burning and looting and had vanished back into the hills, their victorious retreat observed by several Captains in possession of good spyglasses.

Coffin shaded his gaze against the rising sun as he stared out to sea. Only fifteen ships standing at anchor. Not long ago there would have been ten times as many sheltering the bay. The Maoris had done no more than accelerate a natural process. Kororareka had come into existence solely to serve the needs of whaling ships and men, and as the whaling industry declined it was inevitable the town should follow. In another decade it would have ceased to exist as a viable commercial enterprise.

He dismounted to join Brixton, McQuade and the others.
The First Mate who stepped out of the boat to greet them was
weary but unharmed. His oarsmen waited patiently on their
rowing benches, chatting among themselves. Coffin knew such
men well. Brave, but not foolhardy. Sailors and not soldiers.

The mate confirmed that the Maoris' surprise had been
complete. When it became clear the natives were attacking in
force only sporadic attempts at resistance had been mounted.
Most of the populace immediately ran for the safety of the piers
and the boats arriving to take them off. A few brave souls
sacrificed themselves to protect the women and children until
armed sailors arrived.

The ships holding the refugees were already on their way to
Auckland. The other whalers remained in the harbor because
they didn't know what else to do.

"You might as well all come 'round to Auckland," Coffin
suggested. "You'll be able to get supplies there, though I'm
afraid not the entertainments you've become accustomed to."

He turned to study the ruins. Kororareka was memory now.
The Pacific would never see its like again. Halworthy and a
few others might entertain thoughts of rebuilding, but anyone
could see such efforts would come to naught. There wasn't
anything to salvage. The only structures still intact were the
pier they were standing on and the one next to it. The sailors
sensed it too, though the sentiment went unvoiced. Already
their thoughts were turning to visions of landfall in Sydney and
Macau. No one would rebuild an entire community to service a
dozen ships a month.

For a while Kororareka had been the wildest, most lawless
place on Earth. Now it was ashes and history. Coffin smiled
slightly. He knew what Father Methune's opinion would be.
This was God's way of punishing his sinners, using the Maori
to send Kororareka down the path taken by Sodom and
Gomorrah.

"There's nothing to do here," the dispirited Brixton declared. His anticipated military glory was not to be. "Rode all
the way from Auckland for nothing, we did."

"Not for nothing." Coffin was looking back toward the
devastated town. "People will need to be told what
happened."

"There will be many who won't believe, Robert," said

McQuade. "Neither that the town's been burnt nor that the Maoris could've done it by themselves."

"You and I know better, Angus, but you're right. Anyone who refuses to believe can come and see for themselves. Some good will come of this if those who've been living in a fool's paradise will now realize we need a regular army and police force. As she stands, not even Auckland's safe." He lowered his voice. "Time to make plans so this can never happen again."

"I just had a bad thought." All turned back to Brixton, who suddenly looked worried. "What if this was just a feint, a deliberate attempt to draw the city's armed strength clear across the island away from Auckland? What if that's the heathen's real objective?"

It was enough to give Coffin pause and set his companions to muttering nervously. Now was not the time for panic. He took it upon himself to calm the others.

"I think not. I'll wager the ariki who did this deed was not one of those who signed the treaty, nor is he among those who've been selling us land. I should think he and his warriors acted alone."

"How can you be certain, Coffin?" Ainsworth pressed him. "How do we know the savages aren't in league with each other throughout North Island?"

"Come now, William. You've lived here as long as I. You know the Maoris and their blood feuds. It's unusual when two villages cooperate. Three would be extraordinary. More than that I cannot countenance."

"That's right. Coffin's right," said another man. He wasn't the only one obviously relieved.

"Auckland's better defended with all of us here than Kororareka ever was," Coffin went on. "Though I wager all of us will feel safer once we're back in our own homes."

It was a sentiment shared by all, but it was absurd to think of turning right around and starting for the Gulf that morning. Men and horses alike were exhausted. The expeditionary force would have to spend at least a day recovering from the arduous all-night ride. With most of the important merchants in the colony present it wasn't difficult to talk several of the Captains into providing supplies on the assurance they would be repaid in kind whenever they berthed at Auckland.

Given the temper of the moment, Coffin and the moderates

among the group feared the frustrated riders might turn their fury on any native they happened to encounter. Guards were posted not to watch for a Maori attack as much as to keep the men in camp.

Despite what he'd said, Coffin worried about what it would mean for the colony's future if any of the chiefs who had signed the treaty had participated in the attack. Surely his initial instincts were correct! This had to be the work of a few disgruntled local chiefs. If that proved to be the case then the peace would hold around the new farms and towns springing up throughout the colony. In another twenty years at the present rate of growth the colony would become too strong, too independent for the Maoris to threaten it seriously. But for now there was ample reason for concern.

Perhaps Te Ohine would have information about the identities of the attackers. And there were questions for the ship's mate who'd come ashore to greet them and explain what had taken place. In particular Coffin needed to know if a large red-haired woman with two children had escaped with the other refugees. But he could hardly bring the matter up before his friends and colleagues.

It was vital to find out what the victorious war chief who'd sacked the town planned to do next. Certainly he would be emboldened by the scope of his triumph. Much *mana*, or prestige, would accrue to him because of his success.

Coffin was hopeful they could still isolate this ariki, whoever he was. Most of the chiefs wanted peace and trade, not war. Te Ohine had assured him of this on several occasions. It would be harder keeping a rein on the young bloods who'd want to kill any Maori they could find. Somehow that, too, would be managed. They were merchants and traders and shopkeepers. Once back among the comforts of Auckland their bloodlust would fade.

Keep them calm and sensible and we might still come out of this with minimal damage to future prospects, he thought rapidly. The one thing they could not afford to do, especially on the heels of this shocking disaster, was to antagonize any friendly chiefs. It wasn't going to be easy. The citizens would want someone to hang. That made it imperative to find and bring to justice the ariki who'd perpetrated the outrage.

There was little that could be done and less worth salvaging. They had to drag the shrieking, wild-eyed John Halworthy out

of the ruins of the Crippled Raven. He was broken both
financially and in spirit. It grieved Coffin to see him reduced to
such circumstances. Halworthy said not a word during the long
ride back to Auckland the next morning, sitting forlornly
astride his horse mumbling to himself, the final victim of the
disaster of Kororareka.

7

The return to Auckland was not the triumph they had pictured when they set out. Having arrived well after the battle had been decided, few had been given the opportunity to fire a shot. They struggled to form a column, as they stumbled back into the city. The townsfolk who'd turned out to cheer the returning heroes soon drifted away as they saw the dejection on the faces of the tired riders. A few stayed to listen in disbelief to the story of the old whaling town's destruction.

Not all were upset by the revelation, especially when it was learned that loss of life had been minimal. The more devout Jesuits and a few others believed a kind of rough justice had been dealt, though they were careful to couch such reactions in properly sympathetic tones. As far as they were concerned, the existence of Kororareka had always been a black mark against the growing colony.

Many had worked hard to ensure that Auckland would not travel the path taken by its wild, wide-open northern relative. To some extent they'd been successful. True, there were still a few hotels in town most of whose residents seemed to be unattached young women with a marked propensity for dating visiting sailors, but these were the exception instead of the norm. In any event, they were more decorously managed than their now ruined Kororareka equivalents. There were also establishments where a man could drink himself into a stupor if he so chose. Unlike in Kororareka, however, there were also public rooms with bars on the windows and doors where he could recover his sanity without inflicting himself on his more genteel neighbors.

Coffin rode into town surrounded by tired, filthy, sweating men. Limits, he mused. Always limits. On the number of whales in the sea, on the amount of arable land. On everything but the ambition of a determined man. Aware he was half dreaming he shook himself awake and sat straighter in the saddle, working to get his bearings.

Yes, he knew where he was now. Turn left and he'd soon be back home. A relieved Holly would be waiting at the door to greet him. Samuel would draw him a hot bath. He could spend the morning soaking before returning to matters of business.

If he kept riding straight he'd end up at the docks. Having received word of Kororareka's destruction, many citizens were already heading that way. Some would be searching for word of friends or relatives, others would be going to help the refugees, and a few would go simply out of curiosity. Coffin thought he could help. The refugees from Kororareka would need all the assistance that could be provided.

He was saved the necessity of making a decision by the arrival of a young man on horseback. He was well turned out and clearly taken aback by the ragged appearance presented by the returning expeditionary force. Having located the leaders, he urged his mount in among them.

"Which of you is Robert Coffin?"

"I am," Coffin replied tiredly.

The messenger looked dubious. Clearly he expected someone more impressive in appearance. He continued nonetheless.

"Robert Coffin, I am to escort you immediately to George Gray's residence."

Coffin's gaze narrowed. "What does the Governor want with me? If it's a report on our journey, that will be forthcoming from people better prepared than I."

"The Governor already knows what happened at Kororareka. It's you he wants to see."

"Go on, Robert." McQuade drew close. "Gray's a good chap. He must know how worn out we all are. If he needs to see you now he must have a reason."

"Go see what he has to say," Brixton called out. "At least he's a man of common sense. Not like FitzRoy."

"We are in agreement on that. Why now?"

"I don't know, sir," the rider said regretfully. "I was only told to find you and convey the message."

Coffin tried to find a comfortable position in his saddle and failed. Gray's home was nearby. "Let's go, then. Angus, after you've talked with your own family would you do me the kindness of sending someone to inform Holly that I'm all right, and where I've gone?"

"Certainly, Robert. And when you've finished meeting with Gray I'd verra much like to know what's so important that he needs to see you now."

Coffin nodded. McQuade didn't have to ask. Of all his fellow entrepreneurs, McQuade was the nearest in temperament and outlook to Coffin himself, the closest thing he had to a friend among his competitors.

"Governor or no Governor, this had best be important," he told the rider.

There were many among the settlers who considered George Gray a saint. Coffin knew better. Gray was simply a decent human being in a place and time where such men were in short supply.

The reaction of most officials upon learning of Kororareka's destruction would be to order the construction of a protective palisade around all of Auckland, within which everyone from the countryside could be brought until the regular army managed to exterminate every Maori on North Island. Gray would realize yesterday's outrage was likely the work of a few native extremists and would act accordingly. He had demonstrated patience in dealing with the Maori in the past. He could also be understanding.

Coffin knew how understanding the Governor would have to be if he was to deal properly with the events at Kororareka. The burning of some isolated sheep ranch was one thing, the destruction of an entire town something else again. Perhaps that was why he was so anxious to see Coffin: not to ask how to deal with the natives but to seek his opinion on how to handle the settlers. As soon as knowledge of the disaster became widespread, the citizenry would be howling for Maori blood.

The house was less impressive than Coffin's own, though by no means inappropriate. He felt the eyes of his escort on his back as he slipped from the saddle, and his pride kept his exhausted body erect as he marched purposefully if painfully into the building.

He was admitted by a servant who favored him with the same disbelieving stare as his young escort.

"Robert Coffin to see Governor Gray, and be quick about it, man, or I'll fall asleep right here in your doorway. That'd do neither my reputation nor your job any good at all."

The servant gaped at him a moment longer, then turned to lead Coffin down a hallway and into a small sitting room near the back of the house. It overlooked a well-tended garden. Books brought over at great expense from England and America lined the walls. There was a simple, straightforward desk, a cold fireplace and several large, comfortable chairs.

Gray was working at the desk when Coffin entered. He rose immediately to greet his visitor, and expressed no surprise at Coffin's appearance as he shook his hand.

"I've been given a preliminary report. Terrible news. Sit down, Coffin." He directed his visitor to a chair facing the desk, resumed his own seat. "Can I get you anything? Whiskey, brandy?"

Coffin surprised himself with his reply. "Tea. With sugar, if you have any."

Gray nodded toward the silently waiting servant. "See to it, Thomas. I'll have some as well." The man vanished and Gray settled back in his chair. "I know what happened up the coast. There was nothing you could do?"

"We might as well have saved ourselves the effort and stayed here. The only Maoris we saw were already dead."

"I'm told the whole town was destroyed."

"Leveled. Burned to the ground. Every building. It would cost more to rebuild it than it would ever be worth."

"My thoughts as well." Gray was rolling a pen between his fingers of one hand as he spoke. "I would have asked your companions to come with you but did not wish to inconvenience more than one of you at this difficult time."

Coffin repressed a smile. "I'm flattered by your confidence."

"Do not misunderstand me, Coffin. I'm sorry to have brought you here so quickly. But of all our leading citizens it's rumored you know the Maori best. I don't need to listen to raving war-mongers: I need sound, unemotional advice. You're the man to provide that."

Coffin said nothing.

"What do you think's going to happen now?"

"By this afternoon," Coffin said thoughtfully, "you'll be besieged by people wanting to organize an expedition to punish the Maoris for what they've done."

"I know." Gray sighed, rubbed at his forehead. "I also know the tribes of the interior had nothing to do with this tragedy. It's this Hone Heke fellow."

Coffin nodded. "And a few younger chiefs he's managed to recruit."

"Ah, here's our tea."

They waited silently while the servant poured tea from a silver pot into china cups from Canton. "Tell me something, Coffin," Gray inquired as he stirred sugar into his cup, "even if directed against the right villains, what in your opinion would be the chances of successfully hunting down this Heke with a force composed of armed Aucklanders?"

Coffin sipped. "The Maoris would know we were on our way before we left. A party of the sort you propose would be butchered to the last man. We've got to raise regular militia or import professional soldiers. You can't fight Maoris with farmers."

"Eventually we'll do exactly as you say. Right now we can't afford it. We're still too small. Furthermore, as you well know I can do nothing without concurrence from Sydney." He shook his head in disgust. "One of these days we'll be an independent colony, separate from New South Wales. Self-rule will allow us to raise the army we want.

"I quite agree with you. It would be suicide to send volunteers after this Heke. While it displeases me, this is what I think we must do now." He put his cup down as he leaned forward.

"Insofar as we are able, we will pretend that the loss of Kororareka is not important. We'll shrug it off, say it was dying anyway, and let the local Maoris know we hold none of them responsible. Meanwhile we'll try to reach this Heke's supporters with emissaries. Not his warriors, but the tribes most likely to supply him with food and shelter. We'll promise them more if they agree not to support him in any way. I know the Maoris love to see a good fight but I think they love profit more."

"I see." Coffin approved. "Take away his base of operations."

"Quite. Without local support he'll find himself isolated despite his triumph. I hope his warriors will desert him, if only by ones and twos, until he no longer poses a threat. I know this is only a holding action, not a solution. When we have regular troops here we'll be able to put a stop to such outrages.

"I must first maintain the general peace. Then we'll worry about punishing Heke. The Maoris who don't take up arms alongside him will prosper. The others will see this and decide it's not in their best interests to make war on the pakeha."

"Sounds like a good policy to me." Coffin put his cup aside and moved as if to leave. Gray hastily put up a hand to forestall him.

"Stay a moment longer, Coffin. I know you're worn out, but there's something more." Gray rose and began pacing back and forth in front of the bookshelves behind his desk. "I'm going to try and establish a Crown monopoly on the sale of Maori land. What do you think?"

The proposal came as a complete surprise. Nothing of the sort had ever been mentioned previously in government circles. It took Coffin a couple of minutes to consider. When he finally replied, the doubt was sharp in his voice.

"I'm not sure that would work, sir. The Maoris know the value of an open market. They knew it before we arrived here and our trade with them these past years will have done nothing to discourage such thinking. What you're saying is that prices for land will be set and Crown agents will oversee all sales."

"That's right." Gray was nodding enthusiastically.

"The Maoris will never agree. They know they can get more for their land in a free market."

"That much is true, but a Crown monopoly will put an end to the fraud and misrepresentation in land sales that's been angering the Maoris for years. It's the principal bone of contention between native and settler. This could bring peace."

"The land dealers won't like it," Coffin warned him. "They've made a fortune selling and reselling the same plots to different people."

Gray was not always as even-tempered as people believed. Now he paused and raised his voice as he pounded on his desk with a fist, sending paper and pens flying.

"It's got to stop, Coffin! It's got to stop or it'll ruin the colony! That's why I asked you here in the wake of what you've just seen. Not just to listen to me but to carry word of my decision to the Maori. Because, you see, I've decided to go ahead with this come what may."

"All right. But why choose me to carry the bad tidings? I've no tie to the government."

"No," Gray said with a grunt, "but you've plenty of land and you've better ties to the Maori than any other merchant in the colony. I can't think of a better emissary."

"For whom? Colonist, or Maori?"

Gray smiled at that. "I can't compel you. As you say, you're not a member of the government. But I'm pleading with you to accept. Look here, Coffin: what is needed is an end to these exorbitant and unjustified profits these speculators are making. The Maoris need to know that if they sell so many acres they'll receive so many pounds, that they'll get an honest if not excessive price, and that it will be guaranteed by the government. Settlers and new colonists need to know they can come here and purchase a plot of land for a predetermined price without having to worry about being defrauded by unlicensed, unscrupulous traders. There will remain ample opportunity for profit, but not at the cost of stability."

"Put that strongly to the populace, sir, and if backed by the force of law, I suppose it's possible—just possible, mind—that the Maoris might agree to abide by it."

"They *have* to agree! It's in their own best interests to do so. Already there's been too much fighting over land sales. I know this isn't the perfect solution. There will always be individuals who will try to take advantage of native peoples."

"The Maoris are not easily taken advantage of."

"True enough, but they tend to respond to theft not with court briefs but with bullets and spears. That's the sort of thing a Crown monopoly would prevent."

"Provided we can assure them their complaints will be listened to."

"We'll make it work," Gray promised him. "We must. We'll get troops in here somehow if that's what it's going to take. We have to prove to the Maori they can trust us, trust the colonial government. Once we've done that, dissidents like this Hone Heke will find it impossible to recruit warriors for raiding."

Coffin found himself being persuaded by Gray. "It's difficult to wage war when everyone's making money. Plenty of Maoris are making fortunes off land sales as well as supplying the colony with food."

"That's something else." Gray resumed his seat and folded his hands atop the desk. "We can't go on like this, depending on the Maoris not just for the food we consume but for much of what we export. We have to start growing more of our own. Running sheep and cattle isn't enough. I think we can make a start by. . . ."

Coffin tried to pay attention as Gray droned on, but he found his attention slipping. The monopoly ought to satisfy the sensible Maoris. While regretting the loss of the free market in which they'd made so much money they would at the same time welcome the injection of law and stability. The older chiefs would be particularly pleased; the younger rangatira, the new Christianized chiefs, would prove hardest to win over.

He thought of how he would frame the Governor's proposal, how he could best make the case, as he strolled through an unnamed landscape composed largely of gigantic ferns. They looked the sort of growths one might expect to find filling the Royal Botanic Gardens in Kew, back in England. Orchids and other exquisite flowers grew in wild profusion while strange little flightless birds skittered through the undergrowth.

So entranced was he that he failed to see the rock. He tripped, threw out his hands to break his fall. But the ground was so dense with moss and smallers ferns that it was like landing face down on a vast green pillow.

Rolling over, he looked back only to find to his amazement that the rock he'd stumbled over was round and a pale cream color. He crawled back and tapped it with one hand. It didn't sound like stone. Nor did it feel like one, having a smooth, almost greasy feel. When he lifted it he found it was heavy, but not as heavy as one might have expected.

Then it slipped from his fingers to strike the ground with a crack. A thick, viscous fluid emerged from the break to stain the earth.

Instinctively he started to back away, then hesitated, sniffing the air. The odor from the object was familiar. Moving closer once more he made out the yellow of the yolk pouring out. An egg, then, the size of a milk pail. What sort of creature could lay such an egg?

When he'd first come to Aotearoa the old Maoris had told many stories of the birds their ancestors had hunted. None of the settlers had believed them, until they began to find the bones. Not fossils like those that had been unearthed in England and Germany, but real bones. Elephant birds, the Europeans called them.

The bushes were rustling off to his right. He rose warily, backing away from the broken egg. Then the bush itself appeared to rise on two immense splayed feet. From the top of the bush a neck extended that ended in an absurdly tiny skull. It towered over him, twice his height.

The elephant bird blinked at the ruined egg. Then its tiny hot eyes returned to the man standing close by. It let out a screech and trundled towards him, its weight shaking the ground, each clawed foot capable of crushing a man to death.

Coffin turned to run, but the ferns which had struck him as so fragile and delicate at first conspired to restrain him. Even so he forced his way past, flailing frantically at the branches, the *whoom* of immense feet and that antediluvian screeching close on his heels. He thought he could feel its rancid breath on his neck. Those claws would tear him to shreds.

Suddenly he spotted another figure directly in front of him. Tall, but not nearly as tall as the pursuing elephant bird. It was the slim figure of an aged Maori, and it was beckoning to him.

He called out the Maori's name. The figure did not respond. Instead it continued to beckon, a sorrowful expression on the wrinkled, tattooed face. As the gesturing hand moved more slowly so did Coffin, vines and creepers and ferns twisting about his legs and holding him back. The screeching was near now.

Then it had him, its beak digging painfully into his shoulder as it twisted him 'round to bring him within reach of one enormous raised foot. The claws glistened in the moist light of the ancient forest, each the size of a man's fist . . .

"Coffin! Coffin, wake up, man!"

He started, blinking. The Governor was standing over him, his kindly face staring anxiously down at his own. One hand held him by the shoulder, shaking him. Coffin was surrounded by the sight and smell of lukewarm tea, leatherbound books, varnished wood.

"I'm sorry, I. . . ."

Gray released his shoulder, stepped back. "You dozed off. Not the first time I've done that to people. And I've kept you unforgiveably long, given how tired you must be. Will you do what I asked of you?"

"What?" Coffin fought to regain control of his consciousness. The angry elephant bird, the shattered egg, the distant beckoning Maori were all receding rapidly from memory.

"Convey my sentiments on this land business to the Maoris. Get their reaction and report personally back to me."

"Yes. Yes, I'll do that for you, Governor. Later. First there's my own family and business to attend to."

"Of course, naturally." Gray returned to his desk and arranged pen, ink and paper. "I'll have the necessary documents drawn up appointing you my official envoy. You must convince the chiefs that this way is best, Coffin. We're in a period of crisis. If the Maoris' grievances are not addressed they may be tempted to listen to this Hone Heke and his ilk. If by some miracle they were to unify their forces they could overrun all the small towns on the island and threaten Auckland itself. We must have stability! We must buy time."

"I couldn't agree with you more, sir."

"Good! You attend to the Maori. I will undertake the more difficult task of persuading our leading citizens to restrain their desire for revenge, not to mention mollifying the land speculators. Now get you home." Gray looked up from his work. "You're certain you're feeling all right?"

Coffin saw the Governor through a dim haze as he rose. "Just tired, sir. That's all. I'd far rather stand on the deck of a ship in storm than spend days in the saddle. Whoever said a horse rolls just like a ship was no seafaring man."

"Let me see you out."

Gray escorted his visitor to the front door, stood watching as Coffin's horse was brought around and the man remounted to depart. A future Governor, perhaps. Someone to lift the burden of office from tired old men like himself. Possible, possible.

Coffin had been mumbling in his sleep, strange things. He considered questioning Coffin about some of them but hesitated. There was much to do that needed doing immediately. Besides, a man's dreams were his private business, be he merchant, beggar, or Governor.

The hot-heads would have to be pacified. That came first. Then he and his legal advisors would have to attend to the precise wording of the proposed Crown monopoly for land sales. Sydney shouldn't give him any trouble. As for the colonial office in London, by the time they learned of the monopoly's establishment and returned any objections the system would already have been working and in place for more than a year. Operating so far from the motherland was not always a disadvantage, he reflected.

He let his butler close the door and headed back toward his office. A peculiar speciman, this Robert Coffin. Resourceful certainly. Intelligent enough though unschooled. A rough sailor come to money. He could be useful to the colony or dangerous to it. For that matter he could easily harm himself if he didn't take care. With success he'd gained enemies in the city's business community.

Well, Robert Coffin would have to take care of himself, and Gray didn't doubt for an instant he could do exactly that.

As he sat back down at his desk he wondered if he was obligated to tell Coffin what he'd been mumbling in his sleep. He shrugged. A physician's task, not a politician's. He knew that Coffin had spent time among the natives. But he had never heard of a colonist dreaming aloud in Maori.

8

He really ought to go home, Coffin knew, in his daze of exhaustion. Tell Holly what had happened and reassure Christopher. Of course, she probably knew all the details already. Auckland wasn't that big. News traveled rapidly from house to house, mouth to mouth. No doubt she also knew he'd been called to see the Governor.

All he wanted now was to fall into a familiar bed to catch up on two days of shortened sleep. He needed rest even as he feared it, feared the nightmares that might rise to haunt him. The episode in the Governor's home had frightened him more than he cared to admit. Bad enough to toss and moan in one's sleep without having to worry about the nightmares extending their grip into his waking hours, and his dream seemed more than a simple product of exhaustion.

It was all fuzzy around the edges now, fading from his memory. But he'd seen an elephant bird. There were no elephant birds. Only their bones, all that the first Maoris had left to tease their descendants. Yet it had seemed so real to him. He shrugged. He'd seen the bones and an active mind had raised them up and dressed them in exotic plumage. The coloring was all in his head. Surely that didn't indicate he was unbalanced!

It meant nothing. The elephant bird, the old Maori beckoning from a distance were components of an illusion. Not so surprising for Tuhoto to appear in a dream. The old tohunga had made a lasting impression on the young Coffin.

What was important was not to dwell on the incident. How could he control an ever-expanding business empire if he couldn't keep control of himself? Now there was this additional matter of convincing the Maori to go along with Gray's proposed Crown monopoly on land sales. Given so many

things to account for it was hardly surprising he should suffer
an occasional bizarre daydream.

Nothing prevented him from surrendering some of his
business responsibilities. Elias could run the paper part of
Coffin House better than anyone, though he was no leader of
men. Coffin had wealth. Respect would soon follow. How
better to gain that than by acting as the Governor's personal
representative? There was more than one reason for accepting
Gray's appointment.

He'd done a full day's work already, but he felt too restless to
go home yet. He urged his mount through the center of town,
past the reasonably decorous taverns of Auckland—so different
from ruined Kororareka. As he turned a corner he heard Father
Methune hail him.

"You look worn out, Robert. You should be at home." His
expression turned very serious. "I heard you were called to see
the Governor."

"There are no secrets in this city. Yes, it's true. Gray wants
to establish a Crown monopoly on land sales. He asked me to
put the proposal to the rangatira, the council of chiefs."

Methune's eyebrows rose. "There will be trouble over
that."

"He knows, but in the end I think everyone will go along
with him." Coffin squinted as he looked toward the harbor.
"Myself, I'll be sorry when Gray leaves his post here. We'll
never find another Governor as understanding of the situation,
much less the native point of view."

He was unaware Methune was staring at him appraisingly.
"We might have a local person appointed to the position."

Coffin looked down at him, surprised. "I didn't think you
paid much attention to secular politics, Father."

"There are many roads to salvation, Robert. In order for the
church to succeed in its mission here we must see to it that
commerce and trade succeed as well." Suddenly he frowned.
"Are you feeling well?"

Coffin was swaying slightly and blinking. Now he forced
himself to straighten. "It's nothing. Fatigue. I haven't been to
sleep yet."

"Yes, I imagine Auckland is full of exhausted men this day.
You'd best get yourself home and to bed. This is a bad
business."

"You should read your history, Father. It'll be the same here in New Zealand as it's been elsewhere. The natives will be subdued and will learn their place. I've hopes it can be done more peacefully than in the other colonies."

"I don't know that the Maoris will take to the place most of the colonists have reserved for them. Good day to you, Robert Coffin."

"And to you, Father."

"And take care," Methune added as Coffin swung himself back onto his mount. "You truly do not look well."

Just tired, Coffin thought as he waved once before turning up the street that would take him into the finest residential section of the city. Too much responsibility. Too much to do in too short a time. But the dream weighed upon him, as the strange warning letter had months before.

9

The long, covered porch encircled most of the house like a wide belt. Holly and Robert Coffin sat in opposing chairs, he reading, she finishing a complex piece of tatting. Christopher played with his friends in the big yard.

As Gray had hoped, the initial flush of outrage at the destruction of Kororareka had been soothed. No more such attacks had been forthcoming. Except for the occasional isolated raid on an outlying farm or outpost, the Maoris had been quiet. Hone Heke's warrior band proved unable to assault communities that had been forewarned and his power faded as fast as it had ascended. Evaporating with it was the threat he'd posed in the minds of the colonists.

Somewhat to Coffin's surprise but to Gray's considerable satisfaction, the Maoris had readily agreed to the Crown monopoly regulating land sales. With government agents overseeing the business instead of unscrupulous speculators, peace and stability had returned to the country. The Maoris were not getting rich quite as rapidly as they'd been in the days of unregulation, but neither were they being cheated. It followed that such cheaters were not being hung in the middle of Maori stockades. Gray had been right all along.

Coffin and his wife were not alone on the porch. An older man was peering over the tops of his spectacles at the children playing in the garden. Holly put her tatting aside, let her own gaze travel across the yard.

"He seems much improved." There was no question Christopher was starting to hold his own among boys his own age, she decided.

Bainbridge nodded somberly. Coffin said nothing. He had yet to meet a trustworthy physician. At best Bainbridge was less of a quack than his colleagues. He had the virtue of admitting ignorance when he had no answers, unlike his associates who would cling to any lie rather than tell the truth. By now they knew him well. Bainbridge was a frequent visitor to the Coffin manse.

Christopher and another boy collided. In an instant the other child was up and laughing as he ran to rejoin the game. Christopher got up more slowly.

As Holly started to rise from her chair Coffin leaned across to grab her wrist. "Leave the boy be, woman."

"But he's hurt, Robert. Can't you see?"

"He'll be fine. Just leave him alone." He stared at her and maintained his grip until she sat back down.

In truth Christopher looked reluctant to participate in the continuing horseplay, but eventually he returned to the rough-housing. Bainbridge was disapproving.

"Such contact is not good for the child."

"He's a boy," Coffin growled as he resolutely returned to his reading. "I'll not dress him in pinafore and pigtails. So long as he can survive among boys his own age I'll let him do so."

At this Bainbridge exchanged a look with Holly. Coffin wasn't supposed to see it, but see it he did.

"What have you two been hatching behind my back?"

"I don't follow your inference, sir." The doctor did a poor job of masking his unease.

"Come on, out with it."

"Not when you're in a mood like this, Robert."

He eyed her irritably. "I'm not in a 'mood.'"

"You're being difficult. You tell him, Dr. Bainbridge."

Coffin glared sharply up at the physician. "Aye, tell me, Doctor."

Bainbridge was starting to sweat under that cold stare. Then he remembered who he was. He had a reputation to maintain.

"Very well. Mrs. Coffin and I have discussed it more than once. I don't believe the climate here is the best for the child."

"That's odd," replied Coffin without pause. "It seems to me I once heard you say that damp air was beneficial to his constitution."

"Damp air, yes, but not the damp sea air of winter, with its burdensome impurities and chill. Warm moisture would be much better for Christopher's weak lungs. He has shown much improvement recently, but when winter comes his body seems to revert to its previous feeble condition."

That didn't sound like quackery. It almost sounded like it

made sense. "What do you expect me to do? Move my entire enterprise to the tip of the North Cape where we can wave at passing ships?"

"Such extreme measures should not be necessary. Besides, moving to the Cape would continue exposing him to salt air."

"Salt air's good for a man," Coffin protested. "The boy likes the sea." Holly was glaring at him now but he ignored her, concentrating on Bainbridge instead.

"Perhaps he does, Mr. Coffin, but I do not think the sea likes him." The doctor removed his glasses and made a show of cleaning them. "I believe you must give some thought to what the boy *can* be, not what you want him to be."

It took Coffin aback. The last thing he expected from a crate of lugubrious lard like Bainbridge was penetrating observation.

"By God, sir, I believe you are overstepping the bounds of your profession."

"I am only interested in what is best for my patient, Christopher. I do not think you will disagree when I say that what is best for him is best also for his family."

Coffin took a deep breath. Holly looked gratified. "Right then. What do you think *is* best for the boy—and for his family."

Having gained the forensic high ground, Bainbridge was able to relax a little. "It is of course unreasonable to expect you to move your business out of Auckland since it has become the colony's center of commerce."

"Glad you recognize the fact."

"There's no need to be sarcastic, husband." Holly primly picked up her tatting. "Dr. Bainbridge is only doing his job."

"I'm listening to him. What more do you want? I'm not saying I know more than him in matters medicinal. I'm not one of those people who thinks he knows everything. Continue, sir."

Bainbridge pressed the tips of his fingers against each other as he spoke, tensing and then relaxing them. To Coffin they suggested a pair of mating crabs.

"I think the boy's lungs would benefit from warmer moisture. I know that you have followed my instructions to provide steam to his room, particularly in the wintertime."

Coffin nodded. Under Holly's supervision the servants often placed several kettles of boiling water in Christopher's room. The hot air and steam seemed to break up the phlegm that tended to collect in his lungs. By the time the steam stopped the boy's breathing was usually easier.

"Perhaps you know the Rotorua District? The area is alive with hot springs and mud pools. I am told it is beautiful country, as well as the sort of steamy, misty terrain that might well benefit your son."

Coffin shrugged. "Fine. So we don't move to North Cape. Instead we plunge into the interior to live in the mist."

"No, no, Robert! You're being obtuse." Holly sounded more than hopeful. She was excited. "We keep our home here but we build another in the interior. A winter place we can use as a refuge from Auckland's cold storms."

"I've never been to this Rotorua country." Coffin's mind was working. "I know it's a goodly distance from any town."

Holly had abandoned her chair to stand beside him. Her hands rested on his shoulders. "We could manage. These past years have been kind to us, Robert. You could take some time off. It would do you good. I don't ask that you do it here because I know how you feel about society life."

That much was true. Wealthy families now staged elaborate dinners and dances. Coffin could dance a fine hornpipe, but he was useless when it came to the fancy steps currently in vogue among his peers. He had no ear for the new music either, nor did he enjoy conversation for its own sake, believing that talk should be used for communication, not for amusement. If they were living hundreds of miles away during the social season it would be much harder to badger him with invitations.

He turned a wary eye on the complacent Bainbridge. "You really think the change would be good for Christopher?"

"I'm sure of it."

"You think it might help him improve to the point where he could go to sea some day?"

Bainbridge hesitated at that. "It's far too early to make such predictions. The child is still young. But if his constitution continues to strengthen, who is to say what might or might not become possible?"

"Good enough, sir. Next week I'll travel to this country and have a look at it for myself."

The doctor was smiling now. "You may not find it as isolated or uncivilized as you think. When you get there, ask for the parson with the umbrella."

Coffin half laughed. "What?"

"That is what I understand the local natives call him. His name is Seymour Spencer. An American missionary. Has a small church at a place he calls Galilee. The Maoris there call it Kariri, that being the nearest they can come to the English pronunciation. I'm told it stands on a small peninsula that juts out into the largest of the local lakes, which is named Tarawera after the most prominent mountain in the area. It should be easy for you to find."

"Thanks for the information. I'll make it a point to look this Spencer up." At least, he thought, he wasn't going to have to sleep on the ground or on a flax mat in a Maori pa.

Holly threw her arms around him from behind. "I knew you'd understand Robert, once Dr. Bainbridge explained it all to you."

He twisted in her grasp. "I haven't said I've agreed to anything. I'm just going to ride out for a look, that's all."

Bainbridge blushed and turned away as she began kissing her husband effusively. The affectionate assault weakened Coffin's lingering reserve.

It *would* be good to have another place, a refuge from the winter storms that lashed the coast. Not to mention a refuge from his wife's society friends. Nor would it hurt to have a base of operations nearer the center of the island. The move could be a practical one irrespective of how it might benefit Christopher.

10

If anything, Bainbridge had understated the extraordinary character of the country. It was alive with the most alien and unique formations, an exotic geology that delighted Coffin even as it amazed him. Spencer was pleased to show him everything in detail. In addition to the countless hot springs and pools there were the Blue and Green Lakes and expansive Tarawera, a veritable inland ocean. Not the sea, but beautiful and comforting in its own fashion.

The local Maoris might not be able to pronounce Galilee, but they had advanced to the point of growing their own tobacco so they would not have to depend on visiting traders to fill their pipes. They were civilized, friendly, and peaceable. No prospective Hone Hekes in Kariri. Mrs. Spencer was an industrious woman who was glad to watch over Christopher while her husband showed the tall visitor the wonders of the region. When Coffin and the Reverend Spencer returned from their day-long ride Christopher was already playing like a member of the junior community with the Spencers' daughters and their young Maori friends. Although it was hard to believe, the local climate seemed to have had a salutary effect on the boy already.

"Wait and see." Mrs. Spencer watched the children at play along with her husband and guest. "It's not just the air here. There are mineral pools of every size and description. Bathing in them has been said to restore the sickly to health. The Maoris have known it for years."

"Understand, sir," Spencer added, "this is not a place of miracles. But such results are claimed for the famous spas of Europe. I believe these pools have similar curative qualities the nature of which we are only just beginning to explore. There is no reason to assume they cannot be of help to your son." He smiled warmly. "As you travel through this country you cannot help but believe God has both cursed and blessed it."

"The ground itself is lively, I'll grant you that." Coffin felt wonderful as he watched the children at play. He couldn't remember the last time he'd seen Christopher run so much without stopping several times to bend over in one of his familiar hacking fits. For the prospect of restoring the boy to complete health Coffin would have sacrificed anything. To think that a mere change of air and water for part of the year might accomplish what legions of doctors had failed to do lifted his spirits higher than they'd been in years.

He turned to draw Spencer aside. The two men, one of commerce, the other of God, gazed out across the broad blue sheet of water that was Lake Tarawera. The gray bluffs of the same-named mountain formed a wall against the sky, rising from the far side of the lake.

"I've decided, Reverend. But where shall I build?" He gestured with a wide sweep of one arm. "Most of the land here is occupied by Maori farms."

"We both have the same thing on our minds."

Coffin eyed him in surprise.

"I've been thinking of moving the mission, establishing a real community here. It won't be long before the Maoris have used up the land they currently farm. They'll have to move on. When they resettle here I want to start them growing not just tobacco but maize and wheat. Several of them have discussed the possibility of constructing a flour mill."

"A flour mill?"

"It's becoming a matter of prestige among the Maoris for each village to have its own mill. You must know how quickly these people take to European invention, Mr. Coffin."

"Indeed, Reverend, I think I know better than most men what the Maori are capable of achieving. But you haven't answered my question."

Spencer acknowledged with a nod, turned to his right. "There's good land down the shore that way, enough for a large modern village. I'm going to call it Te Wairoa. With the cooperation of the local rangitira we can make a model community. In addition to the good soil there's a narrow bay extending inland. A fine place for fishermen to tie their boats." As Coffin opened his mouth to protest again Spencer hastened to quiet him.

"Patience, sir: I've not forgotten your query. Not far from this bay but with privacy of its own is a place where the land rises gradually from the lakeshore. A lovely location for a nice house, with a commanding view of the surrounding country yet close to the water's edge. A fine place to build. I would be pleased to help you with the negotiations for the land."

"I'd appreciate that, Reverend. I'm used to dealing with the Maori but I don't know anyone locally, and that's always a help." He stood breathing in the fine, fresh air. This was a place a man could come to love, not to mention what it might do for his son's well-being. "We'll start on the house as soon as possible."

"Excellent! Let's tell Mrs. Spencer. She'll be delighted at the prospect of having company, if only for part of the year."

Holly's reaction upon learning of his enthusiasm when he returned home was as joyful as Coffin had anticipated. Christopher was equally pleased. During the brief visit he and his father had made, the boy had quickly made friends among the locals. Already he was looking forward to returning to the land of steam and lakes. Perhaps the boy never would make a seaman, but when it came to dealing with people, whether pakeha or Maori, he demonstrated an ability to make people like him. That would be a valuable asset when he reached manhood and began to assume some of the responsibilities of running Coffin House.

It was more than a month before Coffin was able to take the time to return to the district. Spencer helped him to hire only the best available Maori labor and the two men saw to the laying out of the great house's foundation. The building would dominate the small hillside overlooking the lake and the dark mountain beyond.

By now the local Maoris knew him and it was easier to bargain with their chiefs. Coffin brought Samuel along to supervise and intercede for him. The old man was not well, but his mind was sound. He thrived on the responsibility Coffin gave him. With Samuel in charge Coffin knew the locals wouldn't be able to cheat him, which of course they would do given the slightest opportunity. That was business.

Purchasing the land itself proved less of a problem than he'd anticipated. With so few pakehas in this part of North Island the local Maoris had plenty of land to sell. The hillside Coffin

desired was not good for large-scale farming. The tribe it
belonged to all but gave it to him.

They sealed the bargain over pipes made of highly polished
wood, smoking local tobacco as fine as anything imported
from America.

11

Rose Hull came to a halt halfway down the hall. Her father was drunk again. She knew even though she couldn't see him. She didn't have to. It was enough to hear the sounds of things breaking, the way he was slurring his speech, the certain words he used only when he'd lost control of himself.

If she wasn't careful he'd see her and then she'd never slip out of the house. Mrs. Pertwee, her governess, slept too near the second floor balcony, so Rose couldn't use that exit. The ground floor windows were always kept locked to discourage burglars. The only door that could easily be opened from the inside by a young girl was the front door. In order to reach it she had to go down the main hall. The main hall opened onto the parlor. That's where her father was now, breaking things and using the words.

There was only one thing that made her father worse than being drunk, and that was for someone to see him drunk. He drank freely but carefully among his friends. That he would get falling-down drunk by himself in the privacy of his own home was something no one knew but herself and the household staff. Hull didn't worry about any of them gossiping. Nor were they tempted to try their master's temper by whispering his weaknesses.

She pressed her back against the wall and waited. She considered giving up and going back to the bed in her small, spare room, but only for a moment. She wasn't sleepy and she fully intended to go out tonight. Joby and Edward would be waiting for her. They wouldn't wait forever, she knew.

Joby was the netmaker's son and Edward his best friend. Nobody knew who Edward's parents were, but he was always well-dressed and had a few coins in his pocket. He refused to show Joby and Rose his home. She suspected this was because he didn't have one, but neither she nor Joby ever challenged him on it.

She was dressed in the boys' clothing her father favored, which suited her purposes well. It made her less conspicuous as she scurried around the harborfront with her friends. The heavy cap fell over her forehead. She made sure it was secure. It was damp outside and there was talk of more rain. It rained often in Auckland this time of year. Unhealthy weather for an eleven-year-old girl to be taking nocturnal strolls in.

She'd been caught once or twice but that only made her more determined to continue. Mrs. Pertwee had lectured her ad nauseum about the dangers she was risking. Why, any man might catch her and turn her over to the police, or worse. The governess had gone on at length about "other men." Not just people like themselves, good God-fearing Christian white people, but Chinamen and Malays and worse who made Auckland a temporary port-of-call. They'd like nothing better, Mrs. Pertwee assured her charge, than the chance to abduct a mildly pretty little colonist and carry her off to slavery in some sadistic sultan's harem.

It didn't take Rose long to realize that Mrs. Pertwee enjoyed giving such lessons. As a result it made it impossible for the girl to take her instructor seriously.

She knew how to run, where to hide. With the clothes she wore and the cap pulled down over her face no one could tell her from a boy. When they found out she was a girl Joby and Edward had turned leery of her, but soon accepted her into their company when they discovered she was as reckless and daring as either of them. Rose wasn't much interested in the girlish pursuits Mrs. Pertwee inflicted on her. How much more interesting to sneak into the waterfront taverns to listen to talk of pirates and whaling!

The governess protested to Tobias Hull.

"Let the whelp run where she will. If she gets killed, that's her loss."

Mrs. Pertwee never mentioned it thereafter.

Her father paid little attention to Rose at all, except to yell at her or hit her. At such times Mrs. Pertwee and the rest of the household staff would retreat to their rooms and close their doors, not coming out until the sobbing had subsided. They would walk quickly past the beaten girl, studiously avoiding her eyes. Rose didn't blame them. All of them were terrified of her father.

At least Mrs. Pertwee strove for neutrality, favoring neither Tobias Hull nor abused daughter. Her job was to teach and instruct and she resolutely did that and no more. Rose was convinced the governess didn't like her. What she didn't realize was that Mrs. Pertwee's heart often went out to her charge but that she was frightened of establishing any emotional bond that might interfere with her ability to do her work. It might induce her to intercede on Rose's behalf one day. That would only get her fired. But Rose wasn't mature enough to understand that, so she saw only the coldly formal woman who presided over her lessons every day.

She continued to listen motionlessly, standing on the thick rug which had come all the way from Persia and which her father had purchased far too cheaply. The house surrounding her was immaculate. Not because Hull was a particularly fastidious man but because he could afford to keep it that way and it impressed his occasional visitor. Every morning a cluster of Maoris and colonists appeared as if by magic to sweep and polish and wax and buff the entire cavernous edifice, only to vanish by lunchtime and reappear like clockwork the next day.

Besides Mrs. Pertwee there was Miss Tournier, the portly old Frenchwoman who did the cooking and had a room of her own at the back of the house. Miss Tournier talked to herself a lot. Tobias Hull found this amusing, especially as it unnerved the proper Mrs. Pertwee. It didn't bother Rose at all.

Her left leg itched and she crossed her right foot over to scratch. She'd have to move soon. Joby and Edward would get tired and go off without her, assuming quite naturally that the third member of the little club had been unable to gain her freedom.

A new ship had just docked at Pier Six, stuffed with cargo from both the Americas. There was no telling what it might contain, what stories its crew would have to tell. Adventure! That was something sorely lacking in the stultified, prim lives of Rose's society equals. Girls her age seemed obsessed with sewing and cooking, with frilly dresses and jewelry. They were just beginning to notice the older boys, giggling as they whispered about which was the most handsome, or the strongest, or the most polite.

None of it interested Rose. She already had boyfriends: Joby and Edward. Friends who regarded her their equal. She'd proved her worth on numerous occasions and they had long since ceased disputing whether to take her along on their riskier excursions. There were even times when they deferred to her judgement, realizing that there were areas where she was smarter than they. Neither boy was too old to take directions from a girl.

Her father had stopped shouting and was crying now. That was a good sign. Usually when he started crying he wasn't far from falling unconscious. She checked the big clock at the end of the hall. Still time. She would wait.

His mumbling drifted out of the parlor, the only other sound in the house the tick-tick of the grandfather clock. Mrs. Pertwee would be cowering in her room, Rose knew, pretending she didn't hear anything. Miss Tournier would be oblivious, muttering in her sleep.

Flora, he was moaning. Rose knew that was her mother's name. The woman who'd died giving birth to her. She knew her father blamed her for her mother's death. That had always struck her as strange, seeing as how she hadn't existed at the time. How could she have done anything? She was sorry her mother had died, at least as sorry as her father. All the other children she knew had both mothers and fathers. There was one girl her age, Clara Felling, whose mother had died when her daughter turned six, but at least she'd had a mother for a few years. At least she knew what it was like. There were good memories.

Rose had no memories at all. There was only her father and Mrs. Pertwee and dotty Miss Tournier. Sometimes when she saw the other girls playing or walking with their mothers and fathers Rose would cry. That had stopped a long time ago. In fact, she couldn't remember the last time she'd cried.

Of course she did have a father, though on more than one occasion she realized she'd be better off with him dead. She didn't wish for that. There was ample reason for her to do so but she wasn't that kind of person. It was even possible for her to empathize with her father's distress. Apparently he'd loved her mother very much, though why he felt it necessary to take out his anger and frustration on his only child she would never understand.

The English clock chimed. Was it half past the hour or one o'clock already? If one, she would have missed the boys for sure and might as well return to bed.

She couldn't linger here any longer. Go one way or the

other, she told herself, but go. It wasn't far to the door, a few feet past the parlor entrance. Surely her father was so drunk by now that he wouldn't see her tiptoe past, wouldn't hear the slight creak of the door as she slipped the latch and opened it enough to slip through. Even if he did hear, by then she'd be gone like a shot down the dark street.

She took a couple of tentative steps, already feeling the latch in her hand, the cool night air on her face.

"Girl? Stop."

Her heart rose into her throat. She took another step.

"Damn you, you stop right there, you little bitch!"

Unable to breathe, unable to swallow, she turned. Her father was standing nearby, still inside the parlor, a near empty bottle dangling loosely from his left hand. He was swaying but still erect.

"Thought you could sneak out on me, didn't you?" He raised the bottle, made several attempts to find his lips before succeeding. Whiskey trickled out of his mouth and down his chin to join the heavy stains on his shirt front.

She watched motionless, gauging the distance to the door. No good. He could move quickly when he was angry, the liquor notwithstanding.

"Flora," he mumbled. He turned back to her and his expression twisted into something so ugly anyone else would have run away instantly. Except there was nowhere for Rose to run but back to her room and she knew that wouldn't save her. Once she'd locked the door on him only to find it enraged him all the more. After breaking down the door he'd beaten her until even poor old Miss Tournier had started to cry.

She'd been unable to walk for two days after that beating. Finally a frightened Mrs. Pertwee had dared to summon the doctor. Like everyone else the doctor was scared of Tobias Hull, but perhaps not as much as some other people because he'd talked silently and steadily to her father and for a change her father had listened. Not that he cared if she lived or died, she knew, but he was worried about what the circumstances of her death might do to his standing in the business community. There might be some men in New Zealand who would do business with a child-killer, but most would not.

After that he was more careful, more calculating. He made sure he stopped beating her before he did any serious damage. But when he was this drunk it was hard for him to keep control.

He took a step toward her, hesitated and frowned as though unsure of his intentions. At such times she couldn't tell if he was looking at her, past her, or through her. Sometimes she thought he was looking not at her but at her dead mother, whom she'd been told she much resembled. She was grateful for the confusion, needing all the protection she could get.

That's when he said it again, spitting it out as he had so many times before. "Why couldn't it have been a *boy*? If you had to take my Flora from me why couldn't you at least have given me a son!"

As always, God didn't answer. He never did, despite the priest's assurances in church that he sometimes would. Perhaps her father pleaded too hard, or was too drunk for God to understand.

One time she'd tried to talk to him about it and he'd beaten her as hard as he ever had. She learned fast and never mentioned it again. When her father was like this it was best to say as little as possible. He wasn't asking the question of her anyway.

If her father was known to God, she'd long ago decided, it was only in the most fleeting manner.

"I'm not going to put up with it anymore." He was bawling now, babbling to himself and his private demons. "I'm sick of it! Sick of paying for your room and board, you useless little whore. Don't you think I know about you and your boy-friends?" He laughed, a mean-spirited, sniggering little noise as his eyes seemed to draw closer together. "Do you let them play with you? Do they give you money?"

He straightened and his eyes swept over the parlor. Two massive claymore swords hung crossed above the fireplace mantle, brought all the way 'round to the colony by a man no longer in need of them. Hull staggered toward the fireplace, taking another swallow from the bottle as he wrenched one huge blade from its braces. At that point Rose knew she should have run no matter what the risk, but she was too terrified, paralyzed by the sight of the enormous sword in her father's hand. Then it was too late to bolt toward the door or the stairs.

"Put an end to it," Hull grunted as he struggled to balance bottle and weapon. "Finish the game once and for all." He took another step toward her, very near now, then slipped two steps sideways as he momentarily lost his balance.

Her eyes were fastened on the sword. The blade was taller

than she was. "I'll tell Mrs. Pertwee," she found herself
saying in a voice so soft she didn't know if he heard.

He heard, all right. His head went back and he roared with
amusement.

"I'll tell Mr. Riggins."

"That useless twit? Wouldn't do you any good if you got the
chance, bitch." John Riggins was a local magistrate whose
children Rose sometimes played with, they being less stuck-up
than most of the children in her neighborhood. Their father had
once smiled at her. Rose remembered every kindly smile she'd
ever received in her life, easy enough since they were so
infrequent.

"He won't save you. Nobody's going to save you." Once
more his expression changed, became that of an animal instead
of a man.

He tried to take another swallow from the bottle only to find
it empty. With a roar he heaved it at her. She flinched as it
missed her by a foot to shatter against the floor behind. If not
Miss Tournier maybe the sound would bring Mrs. Pertwee.
Then she reminded herself that the governess had probably
been awake all this time, listening as she cowered in her bed
like a frightened mouse, pretending she didn't hear.

"Useless little runt." He took another step toward her, a
man trying to cross a chasm on a shaky rope bridge. A second
step.

He was gesturing weakly with the claymore when his eyes
rolled back and he toppled forward. There was always the
chance, she thought emotionlessly as he fell, that he might fall
on the sword. It was big enough to kill him instantly. She could
see it happening in her mind's eye as he seemed to fall in slow
motion: the heavy point piercing his chest, sliding through the
meat and skin to punch its way free from the back of his fine,
whiskey-sodden English jacket.

The sword simply fell from his hand, bouncing a few feet to
roll to a stop. Sword and man lay on the carpet, equally
motionless.

She started to breathe again. Then she walked over to stare
down at him. His chest was moving slowly. Once he snorted
but didn't roll over.

Her gaze shifted until she located the handle of the huge
blade. Bending, she found that her small hands would just fit
around the metal grip. It took all of her strength to raise the end

off the floor, dragging the tip across the carpet. It would be difficult to lift further but she thought she could manage it, and it was so heavy it would penetrate of its own weight. All she had to do was place it on the back of the unconscious man's neck and lean forward and it would all be over in an instant. All the torture, all the pain and fear. She would finally be safe. No one would blame her or even think of her. An accident, they would call it, or the act of a desperate intruder surprised in the middle of his thievery. The police would not even think to question a solemn-faced, quiet little girl.

She wouldn't be destitute, wouldn't be forced to roam the alleys and docks like Edward. Friendly families would vie to take her in. With Tobias Hull gone Mrs. Pertwee would leap to her defense quick enough to describe what the poor child had undergone since infancy.

Her arms were trembling from the effort of supporting the steel. Slowly she let the blade down. Having faced it so many times she knew well what death was, but she could face it again easier than she could cause it. She left the claymore by her father's side as she backed out of the parlor.

The latch on the heavy glass and wood door lifted easily. She made sure it was shut behind her, then turned to face the night. Outside the horrible house the air was rich with damp Auckland. She could smell the distant docks, other houses, the sea. A dog howled nearby and a cat flicked across her vision as it darted between two homes. Near the safety of a tree it paused briefly to stare across at her. It blinked once, its eyes flashing like tiny lights in the darkness.

The heavily swaddled shape it had been watching on the porch opposite had vanished. The cat blinked again, though this time there was no one to witness it, and vanished into the bushes.

It was starting to rain. Time for all creatures of the night to seek shelter.

BOOK THREE

1858

1

The General Thomas was not in the same class as the famed gentlemen's clubs of London like the St. James and similar establishments, but it was certainly the fanciest private watering hole Auckland had yet seen. Its comfortable sitting rooms reeked of fine tobacco and wine, were furnished with chairs and lounges of hand-carved walnut, Kauri and mahogany. Paintings from Europe and America lined the walls while glass cases displayed English silver and the best china Cathay had to offer. London it was not, but it was a far cry from the bars of old Kororareka.

Robert Coffin handed his hat and cane to the doorman. There was just time enough for a cup of tea and a quick perusal of the morning paper before he had to attend the completion of the new warehouse, the company's third. He was heading toward his favorite chair, the one by the window, when he spotted Angus McQuade, Ainsworth, Walter Ransom and a number of Auckland's other leading citizens deep in animated conversation. They'd drawn their chairs into a semicircle facing the slate-faced fireplace. He hesitated until he was certain Tobias Hull wasn't among them before changing direction.

He knew McQuade was present without seeing him. Young Angus had become addicted to expensive imported cigars and there was always a private cloud following him wherever he went. Like those of his fireside companions, McQuade's business had thrived during the past decade. The wealthy burghers of Auckland could now afford some of the finer things of life. They were catching up for years of hard work and privation with a vengeance. Coffin shook his head knowingly. They spent most of their time in ornately decorated offices these days, ordering flunkies about instead of overseeing their various enterprises in person.

Not Coffin. He delegated certain responsibilities because he

173

had to, but when trouble appeared he was always there to solve it himself. His people appreciated that kind of personal attention—not to mention that it kept them honest and alert.

Pity he couldn't have kept Hull out of the General Thomas altogether. He scanned the room but his old enemy was nowhere to be seen. Some said Hull had mellowed over the years. Coffin knew better. Hull might or might not be the wealthiest man in New Zealand but that wouldn't slow him down. When greed faltered, rage would keep him going. No matter how much success the man achieved he'd always be dangerous.

A hand dissipated smoke and Angus McQuade beamed up at him through the swirling gray wisps. "Robert! You're just in time to settle an argument."

"I hope it's not about food." Coffin grinned down at his friend. McQuade was starting to resemble poor old Titus Abelmare. Cigars weren't the only luxury the Scotsman had become addicted to. Coffin or Hull or Ainsworth or any one of half a dozen others might be the wealthiest, but no one denied the McQuades had the finest cook. Angus had long since abandoned the regimen of his ancestors in favor of a diet more suitable to a sybaritic Belgian.

Now McQuade and his expanding waistline leaned toward him. "Have you seen the paper?"

"Not yet. Just got here."

"Have a look, then." McQuade handed him a copy of the front sheet.

Everyone's attention was on him as he studied the headline and accompanying article. Finally he tossed it on a nearby table. "This is nothing new. The Americans have been arguing over slavery for decades."

Cooper Marley chewed his pipe as he spoke. "This fellow Lincoln, though: he sounds as if he means to do something about it. Leastwise the southern Americans seem to think he does."

"I wish he would, but he won't." Coffin looked thoughtful. "From what I've read about him he strikes me as too shrewd a politician to throw away a promising career for a bunch of Africans. But you're right about one thing, Cooper: the slavery issue appears to be coming to a head in America."

"The great question, then, Robert," said McQuade. "D'ye think there'll be a war?"

"Civil war?" Coffin shook his head. "The Americans are too sensible for that, just like this Lincoln is. Still, where Americans are involved, all sorts of crazy things are possible."

"Pity sheep don't grow cotton instead of wool," said Ainsworth. Several of his friends laughed politely.

"If war was to come, do you think the Crown would recognize the southern states as an independent country?" Marley wondered aloud.

"Hard to say, Cooper. Doing so would ensure a steady supply of cotton for the Birmingham and Manchester mills, but from what I hear the Egyptians are starting to grow quite a bit of the stuff themselves. Parliament might decide it's more important to keep the friendship of the free states. Whatever decision the government makes won't have anything to do with moral issues like slavery. It'll be all business, you'll see."

"Will it now, Robert?" Marley was rubbing his whiskers as he stared up at the big man. "Is everything a matter of business to you, then?"

"That's right, Cooper. Everything. Now if only we had a way to preserve our beef and mutton during a long ocean crossing. If war comes to America there'll be need for meat everywhere."

"Och, we'd be richer than Croesus. What took you so long, Robert?"

Coffin sat down in an empty chair next to McQuade and gave his order to a passing servant. "I tell you, gentlemen, if I hadn't lived here myself since the founding of this city I wouldn't believe how much it's grown." He looked at McQuade. "I was late, Angus, because I was delayed by street congestion. Can you believe it? Traffic, in Auckland of all places!"

"You've my sympathy, Coffin," said Rum Baxter. His real name was Romulus, but finding that far too patrician everyone called him Rum. "The other day my carriage was stuck on the street for two hours. Two hours, mind you! All because some fool deliveryman had run his wagon into a farmer's cart. The whole business was beyond belief." He chuckled at the memory of it.

"At least our police have settled down. They actually went about the business of trying to ascertain who was responsible for the accident instead of pulling their sticks to beat up everyone in sight."

"A lot of new people in town." Everyone knew what McQuade meant. Seven years ago gold had been discovered in Australia. Now that the initial rush was panning out many who'd left New Zealand in search of easy riches were returning, sadder and usually poorer, to try and pick up the threads of lives hastily abandoned. Joining them were other gold-seekers from farther afield. Having missed out on the great strikes to the northwest, they decided to try their luck among the green fields of Aotearoa.

"That's not news." Cooper shifted in his chair. "Now what I heard the other day you'd find truly remarkable."

"Go on, Cooper," said Ainsworth irritably. "Amaze us."

"I will do precisely that, William." He lowered his voice and made a dramatic show of looking around to ensure no one else was listening. Baxter chuckled, sipped at his drink. "I'm serious, now, gentlemen. The sloop *Malay Dandy* just put to sea for Dunedin with as eager a party of wild-eyed adventurers as ever this part of the world has seen, and I'd wager none of you know why."

There was silence among the gathered. Cooper let it hang as long as he dared before declaring with quiet triumph, "They're bound of South Island because they've heard there's gold to be found there!"

Several of his colleagues gawked openly at him.

"Gold in New Zealand. Now that's an amazin' thought, for sure," agreed McQuade with a smile.

"Come now, Marley," Ainsworth said with a huff, "everyone knows there are no minerals worth digging in this country. If this be El Dorado it's only a one for sheep."

Everyone laughed at that, Cooper included. "I don't subscribe to their madness, gentlemen. I only report on it."

"If I may bring to your attention a more pressing matter," said Sandifer. Coffin knew little about the thin, sallow-faced rancher. He spent most of his time out in his beloved hills and mountains, supervising the growth of his herds. He was a newcomer to the circle of the important, unsure of himself much of the time, laughing reluctantly at their jokes and gibes. A man more at home in the company of four-legged individuals.

"This isn't about moving the capital down to Wellington again, is it, Winston?" Baxter made a rude noise. "Give them credit though: ever since people started moving to South Island they've been demanding a more centrally located capital. Well, Wellington's not a bad place, if you can stand the cold."

"It's not about moving the capital, Mr. Baxter." Cool sort of chap, Coffin found himself musing. Not unfriendly, not cold—just different. "It's the Maoris. There's been some talk."

There was some uncertain muttering. A couple of the men exchanged puzzled glances. "What sort of talk, Sandifer?" Ainsworth finally asked.

"The Maoris are always talking. They're very good at that." Cooper leaned back in his high-backed chair. Within the warm, civilized confines of the Club it was difficult to admit the existence of any sort of problems beyond the thick, reassuring walls.

"Aye, what are they complainin' about this time?" McQuade inquired.

Sandifer seemed to shrink from the attention he'd suddenly focused on himself. His reply was barely audible. "Land sales."

"What, that again?" McQuade waved his cigar, conducting his words with wreathing smoke. "That was all settled years ago with the establishment of the Crown monopoly."

"It's not that. It's, well, some of the Maoris are complaining that they're losing their culture."

"What culture?" Baxter quipped.

Sandifer didn't take kindly to sarcasm. He sat a little straighter and his voice strengthened. "They're being swamped by European ideas. Many of their young people are giving up Maori ways in favor of ours."

"Can we be blamed if they choose how they want to live?" Baxter commented.

"Rum's right," Cooper agreed. "Nobody's forcing them."

"Christianity has been pushed on them by the missionaries," Sandifer argued.

"Hogwash!" Ainsworth sniffed derisively. "Nobody pushed flour mills or irrigation or smoking or drinking on them. They choose, and rightly so, I might add."

"Right," said Baxter. "Some of them are not unintelligent. They're smart enough to recognize the superiority of the white man's way." Murmurs of agreement came from around the circle.

"As for the land sales," Sandifer continued, refusing to be dissuaded by their attitude, "many of the rangitira feel too much of their ancestral land is being sold to the pakehas. Each time they sell a plot they tell themselves it will be the last, and next week someone else shows up with a pack of new immigrants in tow wanting to buy another hundred acres. The agents cajole individual Maoris into putting their signature on paper, or in the event none of the local natives will sell, the new settlers simply squat and start building houses and fences."

"A shame," said Marley, "but what can we do about it?" He smiled disarmingly at his companions. "Settlers will be settlers. People need room to live."

"It's not what we can do about it," Sandifer said almost loudly, "it's what the Maoris can do about it."

"Let 'em try," Baxter snorted. "If they're thinking of trying a repeat of what happened at Kororareka years ago, it'll go the worse for them."

"Well said!" Cooper was nodding vigorously.

"We're much better armed and organized than we were in the '40's," Ainsworth pointed out. "Let them try something. Any Maoris who dared attack Auckland or Wellington or even someplace like Russell would soon find themselves hunted down and annihilated. Besides which Kororareka was an isolated anomaly and that reprehensible Hone Heke an isolated leader."

"In any event," McQuade pointed out, "if the Maoris tried to assemble enough strength to threaten a town they'd soon fall to slaughtering each other before they began to march. They may dislike some of us but they hate each other far more. They've feuds goin' back centuries. No, the Maoris are too disorganized and fratricidal to give us any serious trouble anymore."

Coffin had been sipping quietly at his tea. Now he put his cup and saucer carefully aside. "Don't be too sure of that, gentlemen."

"Don't be too sure of what, Coffin?" Baxter challenged him. "That the Maoris won't form a regular army, maybe with generals and captains and," he had to work hard to keep from bursting out laughing, "perhaps even a flag?"

"Yes, that's it," said Cooper excitedly. "A maiden's flaxen skirt waving in the breeze." Even Sandifer had to grin at that.

"Just because a thing's never been done before doesn't mean it can't be done," Coffin said quietly when the laughter had faded.

Ainsworth pursed his lips as he stared across at Coffin. "You worry too much, Robert. You've always worried too much. We go back to Kororareka, you and I, and you worried too much when you were a sprout in your twenties. It's put lines on your face."

"That it has, William, and sovereigns in my pocket." Had it also brought him happiness, he suddenly found himself wondering? He shook the discomfiting thought aside. "It may be that you're all correct." He looked at Sandifer. "Keep us up-to-date, Winston. We'll depend on you for regular intelligence reports on enemy movements."

This time the laughter was so strong that Sandifer subsided and even though the conversation turned to more pleasant mundanities he did not speak again.

2

Te Rawana was speaking. He was neither the oldest of the chiefs in the meeting room nor was he the youngest, but he was among the most eloquent and forceful speakers. Recognizing his intelligence and good sense, the more senior chiefs let him ramble on. After all, he was not the first of them to speak at extraordinary length today. Never in living memory had so many of the important ariki gathered in one place—in peace.

Te Rawana was articulating not only what was in his heart but what was in their minds and hearts.

"When the pakeha first came to Aotearoa they were few. They bartered for flax and potatoes and then they went away. But more of them came in the great ships every year. They asked to be allowed to stay. Since we had land, we sold them land. Now they have brought all their relatives and more come each day. Soon there will be no more land to sell. What will the Maori do then? Live upon the ocean?"

"It is not so bad as you say." Raroaki spoke without rising. "It is true there are more pakeha than ever before and that they come in an endless stream, but most of them stay in the cities, the big pas they make from wood and stone. They do not take much land."

"But those who settle in the pas must be fed," Te Rawana reminded him. "For that they need land." His gaze swept around the circle of assembled chiefs. "They grow like children. When they were small we could talk to them. Now that they are big they do not listen to us. They take the land we will not sell."

"Very little," said Omatuto, looking satisfied. He was known for his extensive and profitable land dealings with the citizens of expanding Auckland. His tribe had grown rich selling land in small parcels. "I have no quarrel with the pakeha. Life for us is better, not worse, since they came."

180

"For how long? They spread across the land like waves before a storm. How long, Omatuto, before they insist on buying the land of your forefathers, the land on which your own pa stands? What will you do then? Go live in Auckland?"

Omatuto clearly had not considered the possible ultimate end of his own self-satisfied reasoning. His smug smile evaporated as he pondered this heretofore unconsidered possibility.

Te Rawana turned to Te Haraki, who was burnished rather than worn by age. "Did I not hear of the trouble your people had but days ago with the devouring pakeha?"

The tall old ariki nodded. "It is so." He raised his head to regard his brethren. "The pakeha came to me saying they wished to make a farm. I offered them land, good land. Land that had belonged to my tribe since the Maori came to Aotearoa. It was not enough." He shook his head at the memory of it. "They wanted still more. I would not have it, but the younger chiefs all voted against me. They see only the gold in the present and nothing of the future." His final words were tinged with shock. "You would have thought I was their enemy instead of the pakeha.

"They sold the settlers all the land they wanted, all the land lying between the river and the mountains. Not the best land but very good land. When I argued with them they said we did not use this land, that we did not grow food upon it or hunt in its brush. The white men assured them our people could still fish the river. But it is not our land any longer. Now it belongs to the pakeha." He took a long breath.

"Each day this story is repeated elsewhere. Each day the pakeha takes another piece of the land. I will not end my life living on the beach eating only fish, gazing at the land that was once mine!"

"And those are the decent pakeha," said Apatu. "There are others, the men who come with pieces of paper and big smiles to tell us that they, not we, own our own land. They say it has been sold to them by another clan. Quickly they build their houses and fences and load their guns to keep us off 'their' land.

"When we who are the real owners go to the pakeha police to complain they tell us they have seen these papers that say the land is no longer ours. They tell us to argue with the other clan. But when we go to talk to our clan brothers they have gone themselves, to spend the gold they have received for signing these papers. This is pakeha justice."

There was much murmuring among the ariki before Te Haraki spoke again. "We must do something, but what can we do? We have agreed to sell the pakeha land to keep the peace. Not all pakeha are bad. Many have traded fairly with us and respect our traditions and customs. I myself have joined their religion."

"Many of us are Christian," said Apatu. "I am beginning to wonder if it is possible to be both Christian and Maori."

"At least they have not asked you to become white," Te Rawana said dryly. Many of the chiefs laughed, but not all.

"The pakeha is greedy." Apatu had not laughed. "He wants all the land. Well, he will not have ours! I will fight him."

"You cannot fight. Not anymore," said Te Rawana somberly. "There are too many pakeha abroad in the land now and they have too many guns. We should not have allowed them to settle here but they are here and it is too late to do as Hone Heke once did. For this we must blame our fathers."

"Then what can we do?" wondered Omatuto.

"Perhaps we cannot drive the pakeha away, but we may be able to save what remains of our land."

"If the land sales stop," Te Haraki pointed out, "soldiers will come."

"I am not sure that is so. I have studied the pakeha's language. I can read his 'papers.' That is why Te Rawana's tribe has not been cheated. We have sold them only the worst land and kept the best for ourselves. The Crown monopoly which protects them protects us as well, if you know how to interpret it."

"But this selling of land that belongs to a whole tribe by one small clan must stop. That is the wedge the pakeha is using to split us apart."

"You will never get the clans to agree to that," said Raroaki. "The clans hold the tribal land in common."

"We must!"

A chief who had not yet spoken struggled to his feet. He was impressive in his massiveness and he spoke with assurance as well as dignity.

"Te Rawana is right. The best way is to learn how to use the pakeha's papers against him. There are those who will help us in this. I myself have good friends among the pakeha."

"Everyone knows how you love the pakeha, Te Ohine." Apatu glanced significantly around the assemblage. "Te Ohine talks with the pakeha all the time."

"There is no reason to fight. I agree with Te Rawana that something must be done, but war is not the way. It is true we have sold much land, but we still have more than the pakeha, much more. Not only do we sell land but the pakeha buys all we can grow. If we war with them there will be no business.

"What we must do is stop fighting among ourselves. Not just between clans, but between the tribes. The time has come to forget the old feuds." At the murmuring this induced Te Ohine raised his voice. "If we do this thing then the pakeha will respect us. If he respects us as one people he will not try to use soldiers."

"Let him send his soldiers," Apatu said angrily. "Why are you all so afraid of these soldiers? Te Ohine is right. We must forget the blood feuds and stand together so we can *fight* together. We have guns of our own and there are pakeha who will sell us more. For 'hunting.'" He snickered aloud and a few of the chiefs joined him. "Guns are what the white man respects. They are his true god, not this Christ. Guns and gold. The same god will serve us as well."

"There must not be any fighting." Te Ohine was troubled. "You do not know the pakeha as I do, Apatu. I have heard him talk of other people not unlike ourselves whom they have encountered in other lands. Each time the pakeha settled among them they soon found themselves fighting these people. They have won every time. Every time! Because these people always fought more among themselves than they did against the pakeha.

"That is why he always wins. Not because he is a better warrior."

"Certainly not because he is a better warrior," said an unidentified voice.

"His enemies fight among themselves," Te Ohine continued, "until they are too weak to stand against him. Then he makes them do as he wishes."

"The clans will never forget their feuds," insisted Te Haraki.

"They must!"

"I do not understand," said Apatu softly. "You argue for unity but not for war."

"That is so. There is a better way than fighting. If we make peace between ourselves we can do as the pakeha do. They are strong because they fight for one ariki, one King." His eyes swept the gathering. "We must be able to deal with them equally. We must show them we are as strong as they are. We must also have a King."

This time there was no discursive muttering. The rest of the chiefs were rendered speechless by Te Ohine's remarkable and utterly unexpected declaration. Then as they found their voices the meeting room was filled with excited conversation. Only when it subsided was Te Rawana able to speak.

"A King? There has never been such a thing among the Maori."

"You will never persuade all the tribes to accept such a phenomenon," Raroaki said with assurance.

"We need not persuade all the tribes," Te Ohine pointed out. "Only a majority. The pakeha respect strength and unity. If we can unite enough to choose a King it will make the cheaters and the greedy ones afraid and we will be able to deal with the pakeha Governor as one people."

"What an extraordinary idea." Te Haraki's eyes were shining. "Just extraordinary enough to work?"

Apatu was muttering to himself. "My clan holds blood feuds with three others who sit in this very room. If we were not meeting under the sign of peace we would be trying to split each other's skulls. Yet what Te Ohine says makes sense. I still think," he said, raising his voice, "we will have to fight, but it would be better to fight side by side. I will try this new thing, yes, I Apatu say I will try it. But," and he glared up at Te Ohine, "there is one thing yet I am not sure of. If this fails and we have to fight, can I be sure Te Ohine would fight alongside me like a brother? You have many friends among the pakeha. You do so much business with them. Can I be sure of my brother? Can I know he is thinking more of me than his light-skinned friends?"

Te Ohine replied with remarkable aplomb. "I am not a white Maori. It is true I have friends among the settlers, but I have more friends in this room."

"Enemies too," Apatu reminded him. "Your tribe is not feud free."

"That is so. Yet I will put them aside so that we may confront the pakeha as equals."

Apatu leaned back. "I am satisfied."

"We must have a King, then," said Omatuto. "But who?"

"Not I," said Te Ohine quickly.

"Nor I," Te Rawana added. "I have not the wisdom nor the manner."

"Then we must seek answers at the House of Learning." Te Ohine and Te Rawana had by now formed an unspoken alliance despite the difference in their ages.

A delegation was chosen to put the question before the assembly of tohungas. To no one's surprise, the spiritual masters were as stunned by the concept as the ariki had been.

"This is not a matter to be decided in haste," the senior tohunga told the chiefs in a quavering voice.

"We agree, but it must be done quickly." Te Ohine saw Te Rawana nod in agreement. "Do not take too long. The pakeha are constantly on the move. The sooner this is decided the easier it will be to deal with them."

The tohunga retired to consider. Meanwhile the chiefs discussed the question among themselves, though they did not put forth their favored candidates. It was a matter for the tohunga to decide.

At last the wise ones achieved a consensus and reported to the council. The tohunga who addressed the ariki was pleased. "If this thing can be made to happen we believe the spirits will look on it favorably."

"The spirits, yes, but what of the Christian god?" Raroaki inquired.

"I have studied the white man's scripture," the tohunga replied, "and I find nothing in it that would object to a Maori King."

"This man will still be only a man, an ariki, one of us," Omatuto reminded them all. "He will not rule as the English King rules. That would not be possible."

"We all know that," said Te Ohine. "We are Maori still, not pakeha. But the pakeha will not know this. They will only see that we have a King whom most of us stand behind."

There was more debate but the course had been chosen. The ariki selected was one of the most dignified and respected of all the chiefs, senior but still a powerful warrior. In the manner of Kings, Te Whereowhereo chose a new name, calling himself Potatu the First.

When all was done the chiefs themselves were dazed, unable to believe what they'd accomplished in so short a time. Yet they did not celebrate. It had been a difficult and controversial decision and those who disagreed left the meeting with bitterness in their mouths.

Te Ohine and Te Rawana found themselves alone off to one side, watching as the ariki made preparations to return with the news to their respective villages.

"This has been a great day," Te Ohine murmured.

"Yes. Te Whercowhereo—excuse me, Potatu—will deal forcefully with the pakeha Governor." He went silent for a while, considering, then spoke softly so none could overhear.

"Now you must tell me what you truly believe, Te Ohine. You know the pakeha better than most of us. How will they react to this announcement of a Maori King?"

"It is difficult to say. The pakeha are unpredictable."

"Even your friends among them?"

"Especially my friends among them. Some will consider it a provocation and argue for war. Others will think it a fine thing that we have decided to be like them in this fashion." He grinned ruefully. "Most will be so busy trying to make money they will ignore it.

"Meanwhile we must work hard to get as many tribes as possible to acknowledge Potatu, if only as their representative in dealing with the pakeha government."

"You ask much." Te Rawana was doubtful. "From what I have seen of our brothers it will be all we can do to get those who agreed here to continue their support. One can speak of forgetting feuds that go back through generations. Getting the ariki involved to actually do so is another business."

"Even so, we must try. While I have many friends among the settlers and no desire to go to war with them, I fear their numbers." Te Rawana looked startled and Te Ohine smiled back at him. "Just because I argue in council against hotheads like Apatu does not mean I disregard his arguments. The pakeha breed like rats. Their roots sink deep into our land. We cannot pull them out, but we can slow them down. We must, or as Te Haraki said there will be no room left in Aotearoa for the Maori.

"Yes, I have many pakeha friends, but I will not end my days sleeping on the beach either!"

There was a celebration for those chiefs who had not left by nightfall. After consultation with his personal spiritual advisor, John Mathis, one of the Christianized chiefs, agreed to submit to the ancient ritual of facial tattooing. Many of the Christianized Maori had given up tattooing in order to look more like the pakeha, who regarded facial scarring as barbaric.

But Mathis was caught up in the fervor surrounding the selection of a Maori King. Older ariki sat and watched him with quiet approval as the tattooing was begun, nodding and smiling to themselves as the first elaborate whorl appeared on one cheek.

"I have read the pakeha scriptures," John Mathis told them, speaking to take his mind off the pain, "and there is nothing in it that speaks against tattooing one's face or body. There are pakeha priests who insist it is not a Christian thing to do, but I cannot see how this makes me less of a Christian in God's eyes."

"They will continue to call it barbaric," said Te Haraki. "That is the pakeha way. Our carvings are barbaric. Our dress is barbaric. Everything about us is barbaric."

"Except our land and the food we sell them," Omatuto pointed out.

"Let them say what they will." Mathis flinched as the tattooer's needle went in deeply. "I will show them a man can be Christian and Maori at the same time. Besides, do not their women decorate their faces? They punch holes in their ears and hang rings from them. How can tattooing be barbaric and ear punching not?"

"Even to those who know him well the pakeha can be difficult to understand." Te Ohine knew whereof he spoke.

Abruptly and without making proper obeisance a *tutua*, a commoner, burst into the room. He glanced excitedly from one ariki to the other until his gaze fell on Te Rawana.

"You must come quickly, great sir!"

"What is it?"

"Apatu and Waraki are fighting. I fear one will kill the other."

"Waraki?"

Te Ohine was struggling to rise. "I know him. He and Apatu's tribe have a blood feud that goes back three grandfathers. I told you it would be difficult, but we must do better than this. Our King is not yet a day on his throne and already his followers are fighting among themselves."

They hurried from the house. "If we cannot stand together for even a day," Raroaki was saying, "how can we stand together when the pakeha traders offer gold to any willing to set their mark to paper?"

"I do not know," Te Ohine replied as he huffed to keep pace with the younger Te Rawana, "but I know only that we must. For if we fail then what Apatu declared will surely come to pass."

"You think there will be war?"

"I do not wish to say that." They could hear the sounds of fighting coming from behind one of the elaborately carved granaries that were found in every Maori village. "But I have seen that gold can be a more deadly weapon than the finest greenstone war club. I have never feared the pakeha would push us off Aotearoa, as Te Haraki does. But I have always been concerned that they would buy it out from under us." They were almost to the granary. Omatuto was drawing his knife and Te Ohine moved to stop him.

"No. This must be ended without bloodshed. If an ariki is slain under the sign of peace then Potatu will be King in name only."

Omatuto stared hard at the other chief. "Apatu is my kinsman. I am bound to aid him."

"We are all your kinsmen now, Omatuto. It is true you must go to Apatu's aid—but his enemy here is not Waraki. It is the pakeha who has no name and no face."

Omatuto considered this as he stood there panting heavily. At last he nodded and resheathed his blade.

Together the ariki rushed to separate their brothers.

3

Hull studied the men clustered around him. They weren't a very dignified lot and he knew it, but they were enough to impress the Governor. They'd have to do. He'd had a tough enough time getting this bunch to back him. He'd almost managed to persuade young McQuade to join them—he still thought of McQuade as young despite the Scotsman's wealth—but at the last minute he'd decided against coming.

"What's wrong with you?" Hull had pressed him. "Where's your backbone, man? Are you going to be like the rest of these fops and let the Maori push you around?"

"I'm not aware any Maoris are pushin' us around, Tobias," McQuade had replied.

"No? What about the Hamptons, then, ay? What about them?"

William Hampton had seen his farm burned, his livestock slaughtered and his crops stolen by Maoris up near Mt. Egmont not three days previous. Everyone in Auckland knew about it by now and while there had been plenty of angry murmuring and talk of seeking vengeance no one was quite sure what to do about it.

Entreaties had been made to the Governor's office. The matter would be taken under advisement, the supplicants were informed. They were mollified but not pleased. The Hamptons weren't the first. McQuade knew that as well as anyone. But the Maoris had been careful—or perhaps they simply knew how reluctant pakeha officialdom was to use force. A farm burned here, a timber operation halted there, a wagon looted while journeying northward from Wellington: these were isolated incidents. It was hard if not impossible to identify the culprits responsible for such acts. And there were instances of white highwaymen staining their skin with tobacco and dressing themselves as Maoris to mislead their victims. The

189

Governor was only being prudent in disavowing indiscriminate reprisals.

Not every man in Auckland was as sensible as the Governor, however. Hull and his friends considered all Maoris to be thieves at heart if not in fact. It was necessary, Hull knew, to teach the natives a lesson. Cut a few throats and this intermittent raiding and looting would cease immediately. He said as much to McQuade, which was a mistake. He could tell by the expression that came over the younger man's face that he'd lost him.

"Not all such incidents are entirely without reason. There are proven instances where the Maoris have been provoked."

"Provoked?" Hull could feel his face turning red. "What possible provocations could justify siding with the heathens?"

"Let me remind you, Tobias, that not all of them are heathens anymore, though that's beside the point. Each occurance must be considered separately from others of a similar nature. There is the incident, for example."

Hull turned away in disgust. "The incident! That's all you or anyone else can talk about when you try and talk sense to them about the natives."

There was no need to speak of it further. The case of the three Godwin brothers was too well known to require discussion.

They'd been prospecting for gold and silver outside New Plymouth, far down the western shore of North Island. Samuel Godwin, the youngest of the brothers, had come stumbling into the town one evening, dripping blood, missing an eye, and nearly dead from starvation. To those who found him he told a rambling, half-coherent story of how Maoris had come down out of the hills to trade with him and his brothers. Of how the Godwins had traded fairly with them only to be set upon one night and slaughtered in cold blood, their goods stolen, their gold spirited away.

Samuel told of how his brothers had been cut to pieces a little at a time until they'd died in agony. He'd escaped only because the Maoris had discovered the brothers' cache of liquor. He'd bided his time until they'd fallen into a drunken stupor, then loosened the bonds and slipped away into the woods. Only a beneficent God had preserved him long enough to tell the tale.

The resultant outcry was such that every able-bodied man in New Plymouth promptly armed himself and joined in an

expedition to deal the bloodthirsty savages a lesson they'd
never forget. Shopkeepers and farmers marched into the
interior with death in their eyes.

Only the determined intercession of a local merchant who
frequently dealt with the local tribes prevented the men of New
Plymouth from massacring the first family of Maori they
happened upon.

This family told a tale different from Samuel Godwin's.
There were still many in the expedition who would have
murdered them out of hand anyway. Fortunately, their leaders
were men of common, if not good, sense. After much talk and
not a little violent disagreement it was decided to send a small
party of volunteers, in the company of the insistent merchant,
to the nearest village of unrepentant savages. Despite the
urgings and entreaties of Sam Godwin it was determined that
there would be no shooting until this brave group concluded
their parley.

The chief of the village knew the Godwin brothers well and
readily admitted to the murder of the two elder brothers. Quite
taken aback by this guileless and unprovoked confession, the
leaders of the punitive expedition found themselves listening to
a portion of the story Sam Godwin had neglected to include in
his impassioned recitation. By way of conclusion the chief
sorrowfully showed his visitors the still unburied bodies of the
two young women the Godwins had abducted, repeatedly
raped, and subsequently strangled. He then apologized if he
had offended the pakeha's sense of justice.

The men of New Plymouth quietly told him they were not
offended.

Upon returning to the main body of the expedition it was
discovered that Samuel Godwin was nowhere to be found.
Seeing that his deceptive attempt to gain revenge for his dead
kin was bound to fail once his companions commenced talking
with the Maori instead of shooting at them, he had prudently
absented himself. Though his former neighbors searched
diligently he was never seen again in New Plymouth province
or anywhere else in New Zealand. It was surmised he'd fled to
Australia. He was not missed.

Hull listened as McQuade rambled on, finally shrugged the
story off. "I agree there are a few bad apples in any barrel, but
the Godwins were an exception. Don't tell me that justifies the
burning of Hampton Farm."

"Nay. All I'm sayin' is that you kinna blame all the Maoris for the acts of a few. You've no proof these scattered malefactors are even Kingites."

That concluded Hull's attempt to bring the redoubtable Angus McQuade into the activists' camp. At least Harrington Pettit was with him. And there were others present who would carry some weight with the Governor. Hull felt confident. They'd persuade him if it took all day. Then there would finally be some action, action that should have been taken years ago. Long overdue it was, but not too late.

Pettit and the rest were talking among themselves when a well-dressed assistant returned to interrupt them. "The Governor will see you now, gentlemen."

"About time," Hull grumbled. With a backward glance to insure that his supporters did not back out at the crucial moment he followed the flunky into the Governor's office.

That worthy was receptive to their complaints and suggestions but clearly hesitant to implement any of them. At least you could talk sense to him, Hull thought. Not like that damn Maori-lover George Gray. Gray had finally gone back to England and this Browne had taken his place. A reasonable man, Gore Browne. One who seemed to understand the proper relationship of Maori to white man.

He listened, but would he act? Hull let Pettit add his own complaints to the steady litany, then waited to see how Browne would respond.

"You argue very plausibly, gentlemen." Hull was pleased to see that the Governor was speaking to him instead of Pettit or any of the others. Browne was enough of a politician to know who held the reins of power here. "But what would you have me do? Call out troops to slaughter whatever natives they happen to encounter?"

"And why not?" Pettit replied. "Teach them some manners."

"No one is really suggesting any such thing, sir." Browne looked gratefully at Hull, which was the idea. He and Harrington had planned it this way. Pettit would be challenging and provocative, which would enable Hull to appear the voice of sweet reason.

"We're not really suggesting anything so arbitrary. We'd rather avoid war if we can." As if on cue his backers murmured their agreement.

Browne looked relieved. "Then what is it you do want?"

Reasonable and sensible, yes, but not especially quick-witted. Not that unusual intelligence was a requirement for a good Governor, Hull knew. Gray, now Gray would have seen past these subterfuges and gone right to the heart of the matter, complicating the issue with discussions of personal vendettas, personalities and other inconsequentialities. Not Browne. Browne was a man other men could deal with.

"We're starting to face some real pressure on our resources, sir, as I'm sure you're aware."

"I know there have been complaints," Browne admitted.

"More than a few, sir. The colony is growing by leaps and bounds, but always under restraint. Unnecessary restraint, to our way of thinking. We're doing well. We can do better. But not the way the system is currently operating. It's too restrictive, sir. Confining, if you know what I mean."

Browne's fingers were twisting. "You're suggesting a breakup of the Crown monopoly on land sales, I believe."

"Among other things. That would certainly help. It's only a few tribes who are being unreasonable, sir. These damned Kingites and their allies."

"Yes, yes, the Kingites, the Kingites." Browne leaned back in his chair, sounding tired. "I'm sick of hearing about this Maori King. It's tiresome and aggravating. Still, they have committed no atrocities, attacked no towns. What am I supposed to do?"

"I know how you worry about the problem, Governor Browne. We all do." His supporters made appropriately sympathetic sounds behind him. "But we have to do something, and soon. We can't continue to expand without land. Land for sheep, for cattle, for growing grain and other foodstuffs, land for people to live on."

"The Maori representatives claim they've already sold us more land than they intended to."

"The Maoris say!" Hull's voice dripped contempt. "Liars all. Why, they've hardly sold us any land to speak of. They've vast tracts they lay claim to that they haven't set foot on in years. They don't farm it, don't fish in the rivers. Yet they refuse to sell it to decent, hard-working settlers who'd make something of it, who'd turn it into useful, productive country. They're just mean-spirited, sir, if I may say so. Their constant raids and harassment of honest folk is proof enough of that. Put an end to this King foolishness and the raiding will stop."

"I must disagree with you there, Mr. Hull. We've no evidence the Kingites are responsible for these incidents."

Hull smiled knowingly and tried to inject a confidential tone into the discussion. "Ah, but don't you see, sir, that's just how they've planned it. These Maori have a certain savage cunning. The declared Kingites stand aloof and insist they've nothing to do with thievery and assault. They tell us a few rogues and criminals are responsible. The fact of that matter is that the very existence of a so-called Maori 'King' lends others the courage to commit these outrages. They're confident their King will shield them, as we believe he does. Disband the Kingites, declare their self-appointed King subject to the Crown, and we'll see an end to this banditry as well as a proper increase in land sales. The Maori must be taught his destiny does not lie in defiance but in cooperation. If he will not cooperate voluntarily, he must be instructed on how to behave.

"We must have an end to these raids, sir, and we must have land. Putting an end to this sham of a King will accomplish both ends at a stroke."

"That's the way of it, sir," Pettit put in quickly. "It's the way it's been everywhere the British flag has gone. New Zealand mustn't be any different."

"I don't know. . . ."

Hull pressed him relentlessly, sensing his hesitation. "We have to show them who's in charge here, sir. The presence of this King undermines your authority and we can't have that."

Browne sighed. "I ask again, gentlemen: what would you have me do?"

"Let us buy whatever land the people wish to buy. We don't want war. We don't want conflict of any kind. Bad for business. All we want is a chance to buy—not take, but purchase for an honest price—land for new settlers and expanding farms that the Maoris themselves are not even using. If they won't sell this land voluntarily then they must be compelled to sell. Once we've forced some to do so the others will see how powerless the Kingites really are. They'll see how they've been duped by their own chiefs. It won't take much to do so, sir. One or two such sales will put an end to this dangerous organization permanently."

Browne was nodding to himself now. "I've heard reports of fighting and dissension among the Kingites."

"Exactly, sir." Hull leaned over the Governor's desk. "By compelling one or two tribes to sell land they're not using anyway it will show every Maori they must obey *our* laws. This Potatu I will be laughed off the island. Once the Kingites have been disbanded the Maoris will become cooperative and peaceful. It can all be accomplished without anyone firing a shot."

"You hope," said Browne with unexpected sharpness.

"Really, sir." Hull smiled broadly. "You've just pointed out how feebly this Potatu holds his realm together. If the Maoris can't stop fighting among themselves how can they present any real danger to us? These aren't the old days, when one renegade chief could march into a town and burn it to the ground." He gestured to his left. "I could walk out on the street and raise a thousand militia in a few minutes, and more in Wellington. The Maoris may think they still control North Island, but in reality it is we who have them surrounded."

"You might indeed raise your regiments," said Browne, "but the Maoris have guns too."

"Which they use to slaughter each other to our eventual benefit." Hull turned to regard his companions. "In fact, if it was up to me I'd sell them all the guns they'd buy." There was some nervous, uncertain laughter. Hull looked back at Browne.

"That way they'd kill each other off all the sooner. Give a Maori a gun and the first thing he'll do with it is turn on his neighbor, not on a farmer or stockman.

"We all know this Kingite organization is a farce. But it's a dangerous farce, sir, because it gives all the Maoris a false sense of invulnerability. It encourages their young men to raid and steal and burn. Compel them to sell us the land we need anyway and you'll shatter this illusion for all time. Then and only then will we have a lasting and practical peace."

No one applauded but Hull knew he'd done well. Pettit and the others had done their part. Now it was left to Browne.

They could see him wrestling with their arguments. Hull couldn't understand the delay. It was a simple question that brooked only one possible answer. He held his patience, however. Let Browne have a decent interval in which to make it look like he was really pondering nonexistent complexities.

When he finally looked back up at them he spoke with assurance. "You're right, gentlemen." Hull relaxed for the first time in weeks. "We must have more land, and these Kingites must be shown their place. It's not right for good land to lie fallow merely because a few natives choose to be obstinate.''

"Then we're in agreement, sir." Hull moved to the side of the desk and extracted a map from one pocket. He spread it out so Browne could see it clearly. "If I may be so bold, Governor, we've already taken the liberty of marking certain tracts of land which could be put to immediate use. Not by those of us here today, but by other settlers and new colonists. These are the areas we feel should be opened to immediate development.''

Browne's brows drew together. "Immediate? I'm not sure that's such a good idea. We are agreed in this matter, I admit, but it might be best now that we are decided to move with some caution.''

"I must differ with you, sir," said Hull firmly. "The Maoris grow more confident by the day. We must move quickly and decisively to stabilize the situation.''

"If necessary we can bring regular troops in to see that it *stays* stabilized," one of the other men added emphatically.

Browne looked up narrowly. "I thought you said this would mean no fighting.''

"It will, it will, sir." Hull glared at the individual who'd spoken. "I think what Mr. Howard meant was that the presence of some of His Majesty's soldiers will be a sign to the Maori chiefs that we are serious in this. We should not miss any opportunity to awe the natives. The mere presence of regular army would indicate to them that all further resistance is futile. Call it an inducement to peace.''

"An inducement to peace." Browne was obviously pleased. "Yes, I like that. And I suppose it would be a good precaution." He looked down with renewed interest at the map spread out before him. "These new lands you wish to compel the Maori to open to settlement—this portion here, for example." He tapped the map with a finger. "I always thought this region was too mountainous for farming.''

"For farming, yes, but not for sheep. As you can see by the presence of these streams here, and here," and Hull moved to stand at the Governor's side while the rest of the supplicants crowded eagerly around the desk, completely blocking it from sight.

4

Sumner paused with the heavy axe in mid-swing as Gould came up behind him.

"Excuse me, sir. Something's up."

Sumner let the axe fall carefully, surveyed the tree that was only a quarter cut through, then turned to regard his field hand. "What is it, man?"

"I don't quite know how to tell you, sir. There's a Maori here to see you."

"A Maori?" Sumner wiped sweat from his forehead with the back of his arm, leaned on the axe. "What does he want? Can't you or one of the other boys deal with it? What about Fieldston?"

"We tried that, Mr. Sumner, sir. He insists on seeing the owner."

Sumner let the axe fall, the handle bouncing off a log, and turned to shout into the woods. "Harkin! Keep the men working. I have to go an' talk to some bloody Maori!" The foreman's reply was faint but audible, masked as it was by the sound of cutting and chopping that rang through this portion of the forest.

Auckland and Wellington and the new towns springing up everywhere needed lumber. Sumner and men like him stood ready to provide it. The owner of the logging operation shook his head sadly as he followed Gould down the slope toward the bunkhouses and newly erected sawmill. Not for Sumner an office and lackeys. That was no way to keep watch over a man's business. Besides, he liked getting his hands dirty, liked the smell of fresh sap and sawdust. Hardly enough hours in the day for cutting trees as it was and now some dumb native had the gall to interrupt him.

"Did anyone think to ask the beggar what the emergency is?" He made no effort to disguise his impatience and displeasure.

"No sir." Gould sounded as if he didn't believe the entire business. "This fellow shows up at the front gate and demands to talk—demands, mind, doesn't ask—to talk to the big boss. So I tell him that's impossible and can someone else help him? Me for instance? And he looks at me and says that's impossible. He mentioned you by name, Mr. Sumner, sir, so I couldn't very well say I was you. He seems to know quite a lot about our operation here."

"We haven't exactly made a secret of it, Jack. Bloody Maoris. Be better for everybody if Browne would send a company down here to push 'em out." They were inside the compound now, striding toward the main gate. "Right! We'll soon have this settled and the fellow sent on his way."

Since none of the men would let him inside the perimeter the Maori was waiting patiently outside the gate. If this offended the native he gave no sign of it. He turned to face Sumner and Gould as they approached.

Newly tattooed, Sumner noted with interest as he studied the native's face. There'd been quite a revival of interest in the ancient arts since this ridiculous Potatu chap had set himself up as King. Well, they could tattoo themselves to blazes for all Sumner cared, so long as they stayed clear of his mill and men.

"What do you want?" Sumner had no time to waste on formal greetings for savages who couldn't appreciate them anyway.

"My name is Alexander Gibson," the Maori replied.

Sumner grinned and behind him Gould stifled a chuckle. "Gibson, eh? Thought you looked too good to be all native."

The visitor's expression did not change. "My father was Irish."

Sumner just nodded. There'd been quite a lot of intermarriage between settler and native the past half-century. Dark meat wasn't to Sumner's taste but he knew plenty of men who were not as discriminating. Certainly the Maori women were willing and comely enough.

"That's very interesting, friend Gibson, but I'm right busy now. If it's a job you want there's plenty of hauling to be done." He gestured behind him. "This is Jack Gould, one of my foremen. He can tell you where to start. We can always use another strong back."

"I am not here to help you cut the forest." Gibson spoke

softly, without a hint of an accent. "I am here to tell you to stop."

Sumner gaped at him for a moment, then grinned back at Gould. "Oh, are you now? Well then, Mr. Gould, I guess we might as well break early today. We'll just put down our saws and axes, shut down the mill, pack up our things and hurry back to Auckland."

"That would be good," said Gibson calmly.

"Speaks nice for a native boy, don't he?" Gould said.

"You see," Gibson continued, "this is not your land."

The two white men exchanged a glance. When Sumner spoke again it was slowly, as though addressing a child. "Maybe you'd like to see the deed? You know what a deed is?"

"I know. It is the paper you used to cheat the tribe out of this land. I know how you got the rangitira from Maware drunk and then had him put his name on your paper."

"*I* didn't get him drunk." Sumner was grinning knowingly. "He managed all by himself. I've noticed you boys are always ready to top off a few pints."

"This land was acquired fraudulently. It is not yours. Therefore you must take your belongings and go."

"Who says so?" said Sumner belligerently. He was convinced he'd wasted enough time on this impertinent native.

"I say so. My ariki says so."

"You tell your ariki he's full of shit. That's what *I* say." He turned to his foreman. "I don't have time for this foolishness."

"The land must be returned."

"Sure, we'll return it. As soon as we've logged every marketable tree. That shouldn't take more than a year or two. Then you can have it back. See, I'm a reasonable man."

"No." Gibson shook his head slowly. "You must leave *now*."

"And if we don't?" Sumner asked tiredly.

"Then you will be moved forcibly. We will move you."

"Will you now? You just bloody well try, me bucko." He gestured for Gould to head toward the office. "Enough. I've real business to attend to." They turned their backs on their solemn visitor and unconcernedly strolled away.

"You think he's serious, sir?" Gould wondered.

"No, but we won't take any chances. Have Harkin set out a night guard. I don't want anybody sneaking up on me when

I'm asleep. All the raids in this region have been minor. If fifty or a hundred Maoris want to try and push us off this land, let 'em. That'll mean fifty or a hundred fewer Maoris we'll have to argue with in the future.'' The foreman nodded understandingly.

After checking in at the office Sumner returned to the tree he'd been cutting, but he never did finish felling it. Gould was turning to leave to report back to his own crew when they heard the first shot. Both men turned to stare into the woods.

''Wonder what the boys are firing at?'' Sumner mused aloud.

''Maybe the Maoris are making some trouble after all.'' Gould shivered slightly. It was one thing for the boss to talk about fighting Maoris from behind the shelter of wooden fences and walls, quite another to have to deal with them out in the open. He moved to stand alongside Sumner.

''Maybe we better get back, sir.''

Sumner shook his head. ''Worried? It'll be over in a minute or two. These Maoris fight pretty well for heathen but there's no way they can break a line of well-armed white men.''

The instant he finished, a dozen loggers burst out of the woods. They were running at top speed, throwing aside axes, saws, chains and everything else that might lighten them. Several of them fell, skinning themselves badly on the rough ground. Instantly they scrambled back to their feet to continue their headlong flight, heedless of cuts and bruises.

Sumner didn't react until the first few had raced past him without stopping. Then he tried to intercept a member of the remaining group.

''Wait there—you, stop—stop, I say!'' Finally he stepped into another man's path and grabbed him bodily.

He recognized a logger named Johannsen. A big man, stout and powerful. His eyes were wild and his face streaked with grime and blood. A deep cut ran from his chin around the side of his jaw. Raw flesh showed where the beard had been slashed away.

''What is it, man? What's happening?''

Johannsen didn't take kindly to being held up and struggled violently as he looked back into the forest. ''The Maoris! Jesus, Mr. Sumner, let me go! They're killing everybody!'' He ripped his way out of Sumner's grasp and plunged down the hill in pursuit of his friends.

Gould was already starting to retreat, keeping a wary eye on the trees. "I think we'd better go too, Mr. Sumner, sir. I think we'd best take cover behind the stockade."

"Shots." A dazed Sumner allowed himself to be pulled along by his foreman. "We heard shots. It should be over by now." He was staring blankly at the forest and shaking his head.

They heard the yelling then: a high-pitched ululation. When howled by a few Maori it was sufficient to chill the blood of even a brave man. When the same sound was produced by more than a hundred throats wise men took shelter and primed their rifles.

Then they were coming out of the woods, a line of tattooed, heavily armed warriors. Their feathers bobbed against their black hair and their weapons glistened in the bright sunlight. They waved shark-tooth-edged spears and greenstone clubs above their heads and gestured with shiny new muskets.

Gould was all but dragging his employer now. "Mr. Sumner, for God's sake, move your damn legs! Run for it!" At last he released his grip and turned to race for the camp buildings, legs raised high, arms pumping.

Sumner's lethargy left him and he turned to follow. He was a fast runner, always had been, and he soon passed Gould and then several others. A moment later the air shook to the thunder of dozens of muskets discharging. It was an echo of the gunfire he'd heard before. That's when it dawned on him that those first shots had come not from weapons wielded by his own men but from guns carried by the attacking Maori. Decades of practice had made them expert in the use of European firearms.

Several bullets whistled past his head. Half a dozen loggers pitched forward or back almost simultaneously. Sumner fought to lengthen his stride. His heart pounded and his legs ached each time a foot struck the ground. By the time he reached the stockade, the last survivor to do so, he was completely out of breath.

But he'd made it. Now he could relax. It would be all right. The Maoris had been known to raid farms and rural villages but never to attack a fortified position. They would prance about outside for an hour or so, firing their guns into the air and hurling insults before slinking back into the woods.

Even so, he didn't have time to catch his breath because he saw Martin Carroll, his second-in-charge, beckoning to him from atop the stockade rampart. Sumner climbed up alongside him and stared. Carroll pointed, a thoroughly unnecessary gesture.

The ground beyond the stockade was brown, but not with the color of earth. The Maori army covered the cleared area all the way back into the first trees.

"God help us, Mr. Sumner, there must be a thousand of 'em."

"Easy, Martin. We'll get out of this yet." Sumner hoped his assistant couldn't smell the fear sweat staining his attire. "What the hell's that?"

Two dozen Maori warriors had advanced to take up a position ahead of the main body of fighters. Now they paused atop a low hillock. As methodical as any platoon of grenadiers they raised their loaded muskets and fired in unison.

Just before the guns went off someone yelled to take cover. Sumner didn't hear the warning clearly because he was too dazed to listen. *They really are going to attack*, he mumbled to himself. The muskets roared and he felt something strike his left shoulder. Staggered, he glanced down and was surprised to see blood welling from a hole in his shirt half an inch in diameter. Then he was falling.

They carried him off the wall, but by the time they reached the ground he could look up and see Maoris coming over the top. They'd brought scaling ladders with them. Very well made ladders, too. They really knew how to work wood and flax, he thought weakly.

His bearers had to put him down to defend themselves. Men engaged in that peculiarly jerky, unsteady dance called hand-to-hand combat all around him, screaming and bleeding and dying as the loggers tried to beat back the overwhelming assault. Some of them fought bravely, but there were too many Maoris. Far too many.

He rolled over and tried to crawl towards the main building. Halfway there he stopped as a masklike face materialized in front of his own, staring down at him. The warrior's eyes were bulged and his tongue darted in and out in the traditional war challenge.

Sumner raised a hand, but it did nothing to slow the descent of the heavy club. The carved whorls and designs on the jade matched those tattooed on the native's face. That thought was Sumner's last as the sharpened edge of the war club sliced

through skin and nerves, halting only when it cut into the upper
vertebrae near the base of his neck. He died instantly.

The man who'd killed him extracted his club from the
pakeha's neck and hurried off in search of combat elsewhere.
Soon the only screams and cries to be heard the length and
breadth of the camp were those of Maori warriors disappointed
there was no one left to fight.

Tobias Hull rode out of Auckland several days after the
logging camp massacre in the company of four hundred armed
men. They brought along not only guns and ammunition but
supplies and a dozen heavily laden wagons. The latter would
slow them down but permit them to pursue the offending
natives all the way to their home pas. This time there would be
more than "lessons." The members of the expedition vowed to
continue the hunt 'til the last Kingite had been exterminated.

Nor was the massacre at the logging camp the only incident
of its kind. Everywhere on North Island the Maoris were
making their frustrations and anger known. Meanwhile Governor Browne sat in his office, consulted the provincial councils,
and dithered over how to respond.

While politicians debated, men decided. Determined men,
who would take action to resolve the crisis as it ought to have
been resolved years before.

Harrington Pettit rode his favorite sorrel next to Hull. The
attention of both men lay on the road ahead as they watched for
any sign from the scouts who'd ridden out in advance of the
main body. The brush through which they rode appeared
undisturbed, but that was not reason enough to relax vigilance.
The Maori could stand motionless as trees until the time came
to attack.

"I'm still not sure we shouldn't have waited for the
Governor's blessing, Tobias, if not for an official empower-
ment."

Hull spat into the bushes. "If we stand around waiting for
Browne to make up his mind the Kingites will devastate the
whole interior. We must nip this rebellion in the bud."

His companion looked resigned. "I suppose so. I just wish
we hadn't left in such an all-fired rush. I've had to leave
important business unattended."

"As have we all. So the sooner we flush these Kingites and
put paid to them the faster we'll be able to get back to normal
commerce."

"That's so."

It was a startlingly clear day, devoid of cloud. Men had to be restrained from dashing into the woods after the slightest sound or suggestion of movement, so anxious were they to cut a few Kingite throats. Hull turned to examine the column behind him approvingly. Let the Maoris attack now! They wouldn't find well-armed militia as easy as farmers and loggers.

Pettit was not quite as confident. "I hope we're ready, Tobias. Some reports claim these Kingites have fifteen hundred warriors in their war party."

"We may find ourselves outnumbered, but our firepower will carry any battle." Every man in the column carried a rifle. Some had more than one, and there were pistols and cutlasses as well. "I doubt these Kingites have a hundred muskets among them. Nor will they have the advantage of surprise this time."

"Still, I worry."

"Thinking of turning back?" Hull knew it was a risky question. Pettit had paid for a hundred of these men out of his own copious pockets. If he lost his nerve now and took his people back to Auckland, the expedition's strength would be severely reduced. Pettit considered a moment, then shrugged.

"Of course not. We must put an end to this devilish business now or more Maoris will flock to align themselves with the Kingites."

"Exactly." Hull masked his relief. "And I wish I could get you and everyone else to quit referring to them as 'Kingites.' I realize the label is convenient, but it gives their cause a ring of legitimacy it does not deserve. I would not ennoble this Potatu. We're after heathen bandits and no more."

That night they camped on the southern shore of a river too deep and wide to ford. Though none in the expedition called soldiering a profession, many had served twenty years and more with various European armies before emigrating to New Zealand. Their advice gave the expedition the air of a real military campaign.

By camping against the river they protected the column's rear. Supply wagons were arranged in a circle to make a corral for the horses and mules. Rifles were properly tripoded in front of tents. While the tired marchers set up tents or put out sleeping bags, a line of pickets was established to watch for Maori thieves.

Meanwhile the expedition's leaders met to discuss forthcoming operations. As the sun dropped behind the tree-fringed horizon lanterns were produced and lit.

Pettit drew on smooth ground with a pointed stick. "The village of Avakerere lies three days' march from here. It is known the tribe consists largely of Kingite sympathizers, though the chief still wavers. It's almost certain some of them participated in the attack on the Sumner settlement. If nothing else we can be certain they viewed the outrage with approval. We must press them to tell us which way the Kingite army has gone."

"And if they refuse?" asked one of the onlookers.

Pettit rose. "We must convince them it is in their best interests to be frank with us."

"Even if they did not participate in the actual fighting they probably provided supplies and support." Hull didn't smile. "If we threaten to burn their granaries and homes I think they'll be forthcoming with the information we need."

"And if they still prove reluctant to talk," Major Williamson put in, "there are other ways to persuade them."

Williamson had served thirty years in His Majesty's forces. His claimed rank of Major was open to debate, but none disputed his knowledge of military matters. So despite the fact that Pettit and his genteel associates looked down on the commoner, his actual combat experience resulted in him being named the expedition's battlefield commander. His language was blunt, his attitude unsophisticated, and his approach to war not for the gentlemanly or the squeamish.

Hull did not belong in either classification in spite of the wealth and status he had acquired over the years. Men like Williamson had their uses. This was one of those times. After all, it wasn't as if they were going to war with real human beings. Noncombatants were inevitably drawn into the conflict and would have to be dealt with. Hadn't some of the Kingites already demonstrated callous disregard for the rules of civilized warfare?

Pettit and the others could stand aloof if they wished. While they pontificated, he and Williamson and other men of action would put a speedy end to this rebellion, in such a way as to insure that no Maori would ever again raise a gun or spear in defiance of English law.

5

Sleep inspires contentment but not confidence, so Hull was as startled as his less militant colleagues when the shot roused him to wakefulness. The sun was barely peeping over the horizon when he scrambled out of his tent, fighting with his trousers. An excited, out-of-breath guard nearly ran him down.

"Maoris! A whole army of 'em!"

"Easy, man. Where?" Looking past the wheezing guard, Hull could see frantic men running back and forth, loading muskets and waving swords dangerously about while Williamson and his subordinates yelled and cursed.

The guard turned and pointed, almost too excited to talk. "Downstream, Mr. Hull sir. Came sneaking up on Matthew and me. Matthew, he and I we work at the mill up on the. . . ."

"Spare me the details of your domestic life. What happened?"

"Tried to surprise us, they did, but Matthew spotted 'em right off. We both fired. The Maoris fired back and missed, so soon as we saw we were outnumbered we came running for the rest of the boys." He took a deep breath, grinning hugely beneath his floppy-brimmed hat. "Before they can get away we'll wipe 'em clean off the face of this Earth."

Hull was checking his pistols. "How many are there?"

"Hard to say, sir. We didn't have time to count 'em. A hundred, maybe two. Wiremu Kingi's men for sure!"

"I hope you're right, man. If it is and we can trap him we'll put paid to this nonsense once and for all."

Both men looked downstream as a series of distant *pops* reached them, toy guns going off in the distance.

"Major Williamson's already started after them, sounds like. I heard an officer say they're gonna try to get two lines of men up on the high ground so we can pin the buggers down against

206

the river." But Hull was already running in the direction of the fighting.

Mull Cosgrove joined him, his smooth-cheeked face full of excitement. Cosgrove owned several large general stores. He wasn't used to hard physical exertion but seemed to be bearing up manfully.

"Did you hear?"

"Hear what?" More gunshots, louder and more frequent, could be heard as they neared the battlefield.

"They thought to surprise us by sneaking up the river and using the sound of rushing water to muffle their movements, but some of our people caught them out. Williamson says if we can hold them here he'll send a hundred men around their flank. If they try to retreat then we'll wipe them out, and if they stand their ground we'll push them into the river."

It sounded like a good plan to Hull, simple and thorough. They were close enough now to smell blood and powder. Men milled about in front of him and he recognized many of the anxious faces. Williamson and his officers moved through the ranks, trying to organize a formal military battle line. It took Hull several minutes to catch up with him.

"Where are they?"

Williamson turned to growl, took note of who his questioner was and stopped long enough to point. "Over there, back against the river. Tried to break away a couple of times. Each time, our boys threw 'em back. My only worry now is that they'll spot our reinforcements coming up and decide to make a dash for it before we can cut them off entire."

Hull nodded his understanding. With the roar of pistols and muskets filling the air he'd barely been able to make out Williamson's words. Dense smoke began to obscure the river and the brush clinging to its banks.

When the firing subsided slightly, he pressed close to Williamson. "What are our prospects?"

"Prospects, sir?" The old soldier looked composed and confident. "Well Mr. Hull, it's my considered opinion we'll have every surviving man-jack among this lot hangin' from the Kauris before suppertime."

Nodding, Hull tried to find a place from which to watch the battle. It should be simplicity itself. The Maoris had tried to sneak into camp only to run afoul of Williamson's well-positioned sentries. Now the attackers found themselves pinned down. If they held their ground a while longer the flanking troops would cut them off completely. That would spell an end to at least a few of Wiremu Kingi's outlaws. The execution of several dozen should take some of the fight out of the others, when word reached them. They'd think long and hard before attacking another defenseless village or farm. With luck they might disperse altogether. Why, the war could be ended here and now, today, in this place.

Williamson had finally managed to cajole, threaten, and whip his undisciplined fighters into two battle lines. They were ragged and uneven, but they held.

"Ready? Fire!" Hull heard him shout, whereupon the front line of militia unleashed an impressive mass volley of shot. As they fell back to reload, the second line was brought forward a dozen paces before Williamson called for them to halt and fire. The first line had advanced beyond the second again when Hull hurried up to join the Major, a pistol in one hand and saber in the other.

"Just a moment, Mr. Williamson."

The old soldier turned to glare at him. "What do you mean, just a moment, sir? Who is giving the orders here?"

"You are, Major, but while I defer to you in most of this I think you'll agree in matters of war it's best not to waste shot and powder. Who are your people shooting at?"

Williamson started to say something, hesitated, then turned and squinted toward the brush lining the river. There was no longer any return fire emanating from the spot where their quarry was supposed to be trapped. Faces turned toward them as the line of ready men awaited the order to unleash the next broadside. The only sounds at all came from a few isolated groups of militia firing on their own without discipline or direction.

"Hold your fire!" Williamson abruptly bellowed. One more lone shot rang out. It did not come from the bushes in front of them. "Hold your fire, I say!"

As the men stood poised and alert the smoke surrounding them began to dissipate. "By God," Williamson rumbled, "they've gone and run off! I knew we should've advanced faster." He glanced into the hills off to their left, where his flanking force was moving. "The others won't be in position yet."

Hull was frowning as he stared at the bushes and the river

beyond. "Something's wrong here, Mr. Williamson. This isn't right. Maoris don't run away from a fight. They're heathens but they're not cowards."

"You know them that well then, sir."

"Well enough to say that this battleground suddenly smells of more than powder, Mr. Williamson. I've dealt with the natives here longer than just about any other man on North Island."

"Then if they've not run away, where are they?"

Hull had no answer for that. One was, however, forthcoming.

The sound of musketry made both men turn, not to where their opponents ought to be but back toward camp. Williamson looked across to a thin man attired in sailor's garb.

"Merrick! Did you leave anybody in camp?"

"No sir," the subordinate shouted back. "You said to bring every available gun."

"By damn!" Williamson threw his hat to the ground and kicked it. Hull ignored it as it went sailing into the bushes. "Get back to camp, everybody!" Behind him the twin lines of riflemen were gaping at him, at one another. "Back to camp I said, on the double!"

Williamson took off. The lines broke as men began to follow, suddenly panicked. Hull tried to keep up with the Major. When he found he couldn't handle the pace he slowed and let the rest of the expeditionary force race past him.

There was no fear of losing his way. The smoke insured that. Smoke rising from burning tents and food bales. By the time Williamson and the first militia men stumbled into camp most of the horses were gone along with every last one of the supply wagons. While they'd been off hunting down a supposedly trapped and demoralized enemy, other Maoris had slipped into camp to hitch up the dray horses. Then they'd simply driven away, untouched and unseen.

The distraught returnees organized in an attempt to put out the fires and save what goods and supplies the Maoris hadn't made off with. It did not take long because the Maoris had missed very little.

Cosgrove was standing alone in the road the natives had taken, dust settling on his boots. "We have to go after them," he was mumbling.

"What, on foot?" It was Harrington Pettit.

"Unless you can fly, sir." The two men glared at each other.

"Stop it, the both of you." Hull sat down on a nearby rock, tired and worn out but not as dispirited as his companions. Not only had they been duped, they'd been duped by a bunch of ignorant natives. Obviously they were going to have to rethink this campaign and all subsequent ones. Their opponent was cunning and deceitful in ways they had not imagined.

Pettit articulated what everyone was feeling at that moment. "This is no way to have a war! Don't they intend to fight? This is nothing more than theft on a large scale."

"Your pardon, Harrington," Hull said, "but let me remind you that the Maoris are not civilized. So don't expect them to act that way in war any more than in times of peace. They're interested only in winning. At this point we should be thinking similarly. In any event, Mr. Cosgrove, Harrington is right. We can't go after them. Not through that." He raised his untested blade to gesture into the woods where the wagon tracks turned off the road.

"And why not, sir?" the store owner wondered. "Our best and most fleet of foot should be able to overtake them, slowed as they are by their booty."

"Suppose they do manage that? What then?"

Cosgrove made a face. "I do not understand you, sir."

Hull sighed. "If you somehow manage to overtake them on foot you'll be too tired to fight. Isn't one lesson a day enough? There are easier ways of committing suicide."

Cosgrove stiffened. "Are you suggesting that in battle a Maori is the equal of a white man, Mr. Hull?"

"I'm saying you don't track a lion to his lair unless you're damn well sure you've got him outmatched ten to one. I'll wager you haven't watched Maoris hunt. I have. A Maori can stand still as a tree all day without moving a finger until his prey steps within range.

"And that's not all." Hull looked back downriver toward where the brief battle had been waged. "You think they missed all those shots because they don't know how to handle guns? Some certainly, but not that many. That bothered me right off but everything was happening so fast I didn't have time to think on it. They were missing us deliberately, leading us on to think we'd have an easy time of it." He nodded at the woods.

"The way I see it, gentlemen, we should be thinking about survival instead of revenge. It's a long trek back to Auckland on foot. All our supplies are in the hands of our enemies. They must know how badly they've hurt us. Eventually they're going to start trying to exploit that fact. I'd rather not be around when they do." He pushed himself off the warm rock. "Best we get moving immediately."

At first Williamson resisted. Like Cosgrove, he wanted to pursue. Hull was a man of little patience. He had to employ all of it to hold his temper.

"The men are tired and they haven't had any breakfast," Williamson argued.

"Breakfast? Most of our supplies are in the hands of the Maoris, or have you forgotten that already? If they're hungry, let them eat greens and berries. It's a diet they might as well get used to. There won't be more than that between here and the nearest farm. You wanted to trap them between high ground and the river. Hasn't it occurred to you yet that that's just where we're sitting right now?"

Williamson blinked at him, then glanced toward the hills off to the right, suddenly nervous. "That's right. By God, you are right, sir. We must move." He hurried off in search of his lieutenants.

So instead of pursuing the Kingites to their lair the disgruntled members of the glorious punitive expedition found themselves trudging listlessly homeward, glancing uneasily over their shoulders all the way. Nor did the Kingites let them retreat in peace. Without warning, shots would come from between the trees to fell several men. The whole column would fire back in unsupervised, erratic fashion until by dint of word and the occasional blow to the head their leaders succeeded in getting them to stop. By the time a rational defense could be organized, the Maoris responsible for inspiring it had inevitably vanished from sight. Loud challenges quickly gave way to cursing and muttering as the men picked up their dead and wounded and resumed the long march.

These hit-and-run tactics devastated the column's morale. It was an uncivilized, unorthodox way to fight. It was also ruinously effective.

"Had an uncle fought in America back in the '90's," one of the marchers was telling his companions. "Remember him tellin' me this was the way the Red Indians used to fight. They'd just sneak up on you and pick you off one at a time, and if you chased 'em they'd ride off and hide until you gave up."

"They're spirits, these Maoris," the man next to him whispered. He'd acquired a severe limp thanks to a native musketball that had grazed his thigh. "Bleeding spirits. This is their land and they know the countryside. Never should have been a war anyway. Damned land speculators."

"You ain't sayin' you're afraid of 'em, are you?" a man walking behind challenged.

The limper looked back sharply. "You're bloody well right I'm afraid of 'em!"

As if the random attacks weren't bad enough, the Maoris eventually grew bold enough to taunt the column from the safety of the forest. In some ways these verbal barbs were worse than the musket fire because they struck everyone simultaneously. Only shots from the column's best marksmen sufficed to drive them away.

Williamson quickly put a stop to that waste of lead and powder. The Maori pursuit continued, forcing the men to bear the laughter and insults all the way to the outskirts of Auckland. Every imprecation was delivered in impeccable, if slightly accented, English.

They were a sorry sight as they reentered the city. The wounded were convoyed to the hospital, the dead to various graveyards. There was no formal mustering out. The column simply dispersed with nary a word, men making their own way back to homes and shops, farms and ships. They'd lost more than a quarter of their force killed or wounded, while many of the survivors were sick and weak from lack of food and sleep.

It was a sobering, disheartening experience for every man in the expedition, and for none more so than Tobias Hull.

6

Several days later he found himself walking slowly but without hesitation toward the one house in Auckland he'd sworn never to set foot inside. It was easily the grandest such structure in the city, fashioned of wood and stone and imported glass. He mounted the wide steps leading to a porch that encircled the entire house and rapped for attention. The lion's head brass knocker boomed within.

Instead of the aged Maori servant he half expected to see he found himself greeted by a sprightly young Irishwoman clad in a green and white uniform. She eyed the gentleman visitor curiously, glancing past him briefly to observe the elaborate carriage waiting across the street. For his part Hull tried not to stare past her. The hall beyond was pungent with the smell of fine carpets and oiled furniture.

"Sir? Was there something?"

"Tell. . . ." He swallowed, had to begin again. "Tell Mr. Coffin that Tobias Hull is here and begs the pleasure of his company for a few moments."

The maid nodded slowly and vanished within. Hull watched the perky switch of her derriere and wondered if perhaps Coffin might be spreading his interests around. He could certainly afford it now. But no, Hull decided. Coffin was too staid, too restrained for that. He'd been something of a hellion in his younger days, but now he was a respectable family man. Hull nearly laughed aloud at the thought.

All he could do now was wait.

As the years had gone by Robert Coffin had acquired something he'd once vowed to have no trick with: a taste for luxury. As a result the houses in Auckland and Te Wairoa had been filled with the finest furnishings Coffin's Captains could find in Europe, America and the Orient.

Original muslin curtains had been replaced by folds of

213

damask silk. The table setting of finest china that he'd bought for Holly was now flanked by finely wrought English silver. The clocks came from France. Fine paintings covered the walls. Coffin had been assured they were the work of respected artists. Respected or not, he found them pleasing to look upon: Italian ruins dappled with Mediterranean sunshine, dark English forests, horses and dogs frozen in oils.

His favorite piece was by a lesser-known artist. It held the place of honor above the marble mantlepiece in the expanded sitting room. There was a twin in the house at Te Wairoa. It depicted Holly Coffin standing alone before a garden of flowers. She was wearing the blue dress he'd given her many years earlier. The dress was all satin and lace, but both of them referred to it simply as the "blue dress." It flowed down her figure much as the sunshine filled the Italian paintings, illuminating hollows and niches, highlighting the swells and ridges of her body. It was not quite lewd.

A much smaller portrait of Christopher hung nearby. Coffin's son was almost as tall as his father now, a handsome if thin and delicate young man. A sailor he would never be and both men knew it; his constitution simply wasn't hardy enough to cope with that rigorous life.

But while he would never become a Captain, neither had he turned into a dandy as Coffin once feared. He came by his interest in the family business naturally, without his father having to push him in that direction. So adept had Christopher become at juggling orders and papers under Elias Goldman's careful direction that Coffin himself was able to spend many pleasant afternoons at home with his wife, secure in the knowledge that his son was watching after his interests.

It was hard for him to take a day off. Having worked so long to inure himself to privation and long hours, Coffin found the thought of relaxation more than a little alien.

The table in the formal dining room was long enough to seat thirty for dinner. At lunch only the seats at the north end were occupied. Coffin would sit at the head of the table with Holly on his immediate right. Christopher often sat opposite his mother, but today he remained at the office. Something about inventory control, Goldman had muttered. Coffin could have insisted, but knew better than to go against Elias's judgement. If he needed Christopher, then so be it. It was the best business schooling any young man could ask for.

The thought pleased him. After years of worry and concern it seemed certain his only son was not only going to survive but was going to do so in style as an important contributor to the ongoing success of Coffin House. Christopher would never be one to go exploring new country on horseback or sailing to San Francisco to develop new markets, but now that he'd discovered a niche where he could prove himself the equal or better of any man his age he was definitely happier than Coffin had ever seen him before. And he was in the best of hands with Goldman, who treated him like his own son.

Few people knew that Goldman had married Kamine, his Maori mistress, and that they had two fine healthy girls of their own to raise. Coffin often wondered what the members of Kamine's whanau, or extended family, made of Goldman's Jewish beliefs as they struggled to sort out the various Christian doctrines vying for their souls.

Like everything else in Auckland, the quality of the city's medical community improved a little each year. Yes, with good doctors to care for his body and Goldman to look after his mind, Christopher was going to survive to take control of Coffin House completely one day. Then Coffin would allow himself to retire to the life of ease to which he was reluctantly becoming accustomed.

There was little, he mused, that a man could have that he didn't. Why *not* learn to enjoy some of life's finer things? He could afford the time to appreciate them. He pushed a forkful of fresh venison into his mouth and chewed slowly.

"This is excellent," he said expansively. "Be sure and tell Cook."

Holly put down her knife and fork and gaped at him. "What's this? A compliment from Robert Coffin? You can be sure I'll tell Cook, husband, though it would be best to have a doctor standing by to rouse her from the fainting spell she'll surely suffer as a result."

"Now Holly," Coffin said, chiding her, "you know I'm not that bad. I always give credit for good work done."

"In business, yes. Credit to one of your Captains, congratulations to a master of fields, compliments to a clerk—but never to a member of your household. Nevertheless, I'll take care to break it to her gently." She grinned as he took a playful swipe at her, ducking back out of his reach.

She was so beautiful when she smiled like that, he reflected.

Holly had hardly aged at all. The woman was a wonderment. Somehow she had stopped time, still looked almost as she had when he'd courted her back in London. Nor was he the only one to remark on her unmarred beauty. She doesn't change at all, they whispered enviously. She's as beautiful as ever she was.

No one said that about Robert Coffin, nor would he have cared one way or the other. There was no vanity in him. Lines and wrinkles gave him character while his hair could turn no grayer than it had been on his twentieth birthday. His developing taste for fine food had not made him fat, but it couldn't be denied that he was not as lean and muscular as he'd been when he'd spent half a voyage standing on the bowsprit of the *Resolute* or weeks fighting his way through previously unexplored bush country. He patted his waist appraisingly. A slight increase in girth was nothing more than an indication of prosperity, to be admired as such.

Emily, the day girl, came in from the main hall. Coffin reflected that some day soon he would have to see to engaging a proper butler to supervise the household staff. There were two full-time maids now, as well as Cook and the groom, Wallace, who saw to the livery, and a housekeeper on watch at Te Wairoa. Coffin could have done with less but Holly enjoyed the luxury of servants and there was no dearth of destitute new immigrants ready to work hard for modest wages. A butler would be a help to her.

Emily curtseyed adequately. "Excuse me, sir, but there's a gentleman here and most anxious he is to see you, sir."

Coffin put his linen napkin on the table, pushed back his chair. "Always when I'm having lunch."

"Now don't bark at him, whoever he is, husband," Holly admonished him. "Midday is the only time anyone can catch you."

He bent to bestow a quick peck on her forehead. "I'll be right back. I wouldn't want to miss whatever Cook has conjured up for dessert."

"Perhaps you should." She gave him a mischievous poke in the middle.

Though Coffin had seen much in his life it still never failed to astonish him how rapidly a human being could travel from the heights of contentment to the depths of disappointment. It wasn't Emily's fault, of course. How could she have known who it was she'd politely permitted to enter?

Hull sat on a couch in the parlor, openly admiring the crystal and other furnishings. Coffin halted in the portal.

"You've got a lot of nerve, Hull. You always did. Look all you want to. It'll do you no good. The good silver's put up and my wife's jewelry is in a safe."

Hull flashed his famous crooked smile. As always he appeared to be laughing at some particularly nasty private amusement.

"I've no need of either, thank you, Coffin. I've plenty of my own."

"How's your daughter getting along, Hull?"

Each man had known the other long enough to know exactly the wrong thing to say. On the other hand, certain insults and provocation were growing old. In any event Hull's expression didn't change.

"I wouldn't know. I don't pay any attention to her comings and goings."

"She'd be a grown woman by now."

"It's not something I concern myself with."

"I'm not surprised. And now that we've exchanged pleasantries and you've seen the interior of my home perhaps you'd care to leave through the same door by which you entered." Coffin stepped aside and gestured with one hand.

Hull didn't move. "I'm not here for idle chatter nor to inspect your architecture. If you'd cool your blood a moment, Coffin, you might well wonder why I've taken a step which I assure you is no more pleasant for me than it can be for you. I must ask that you oblige me on a matter that concerns both of us. I promise I will take as little time as possible."

Coffin considered as he regarded the man on the couch narrowly. At last he nodded. "Little time let it be, then." He entered the parlor. "May I offer you something to drink?"

Hull's answer was surprising. "No."

Coffin sat down in the chair closest to the couch, gestured at a humidor. "Smoke?"

"Again, no."

"Have you changed that much?" Coffin leaned back in the chair.

"I think not, though I've recently undergone a sobering experience. Surely you've heard."

It would have been easy to smile knowingly, to gloat. As was clear from the resigned expression on Hull's face his old rival expected him to do exactly that. Coffin did not. Whatever personal embarrassment Hull had suffered was nothing compared to that of the rest of the militia. Wiremu Kingi's men had killed too many for anyone to smile about it. As more warriors were attracted to his army the country was laid waste. Neutral Maoris were more inclined to offer surreptitious support in the form of weapons and food. It was a bad time for New Zealand. Coffin couldn't smile about it.

"Sobering is a mild enough description. You're lucky the Kingites didn't massacre the lot of you."

"I think they could have done so had they been sufficiently inclined." Hull made a sign of disgust. "That's what comes of trying to put down a rebellion with untrained militia led by military rejects. It's a mistake we won't make again. Though I'm not so sure regular troops would have been any more effective. Imagine trying to fight people who shoot at you from behind trees! And when you do confront them, they run away. I ask you, Coffin, can people who do such things claim to be civilized?"

"According to the tenets of Maori civilization they can. Tell me: if you think they could have slaughtered you to the last man, why didn't they?"

Hull fought to form the words. "I think it gave them more pleasure to taunt us all the way back to the city."

Still Coffin didn't smile and although Hull was grateful for the understanding, he would never have admitted it. "Yes, that sounds like the Maoris." He lowered his gaze. "But surely you didn't come here for sympathy."

Hull laughed sharply at that. It was such an extraordinary sight that Coffin committed it to memory on the spot, certain it was something that might never be seen again: Tobias Hull laughing at something other than another's misfortune.

"Think of me what you will, you know me for a realist, Coffin. There have been numerous discussions among the leading citizens of Auckland, Wellington, Napier and the rest of the colony about the feasibility of financing another expedition to fight the Kingites. A proper one this time, with the right sort of equipment and better leaders. We must put an end to this rebellion before it can spread any farther!" He calmed himself with an effort. "You have excellent sources. I'm sure you're aware of these meetings and their aim."

"Just as I'm aware that it's a foolish man who throws good money after bad."

Hull couldn't restrain himself any longer. "Then what the Devil do you expect us to do? Hole up in the towns and cities and surrender the rest of the country to the natives?"

"I'll thank you," said Coffin coolly, "to compose yourself while you're a guest in this house." Hull glared at him a moment longer, then took a deep breath and crossed his arms across his chest, waiting. "Better. I would lend my name and resources to such a compaign if it was professionally led and manned. Indeed, under such circumstances I'd join myself. You know what I'm talking about, Hull, and so do the others. Professional soldiers. Men whose business is war."

"Even McQuade's contributing," Hull muttered. "So are Cosgrove, Pettit and many more. They make no stipulations."

"Which means they didn't learn their lesson well enough the first time." Both men were silent for a minute before Coffin continued. "Much as it pains me to admit it, we do agree on one thing. Something must be done about this Wiremu Kingi and his army, at the least. The smaller war parties we can deal with ourselves, but this Kingi's successes raise the possibility of a Maori nation united for war beneath a single standard. Frankly I thought that an impossibility until only recently. You're right that we must stop it now."

"I've spoken to the Governor. He'll give us his personal support and that of the treasury. As for our recent debacle, it may do more good than harm in the long run insofar as it's frightened many who did not previously take the Kingite threat seriously. It's been too easy lately in the towns. Cityfolk sit back and insist the rebellion will never endanger them. Our latest defeat puts the lie to that.

"The Governor has thrown in the full colonial militia. This time we'll put a thousand men under arms. Scouts have been paid to seek out the Kingite's headquarters.

"As to your qualification, you'll be interested to learn, Coffin, that a full contingent of British regulars commanded by regular army officers will arrive shortly in Auckland to take charge of the campaign."

Coffin's eyebrows lifted. "I hadn't heard that."

Again Hull favored him with that lopsided grin. "You don't know everything that's going on in the government, you know.

There are some who still know how to keep information to themselves."

"I never doubted that for a moment." Throughout the conversation neither man's eyes had wavered from the other's. It was as if an invisible barrier set up between them permitted only this tenuous visual contest to continue. While they spoke of cooperation their wills fought on.

"If what you say about the arriving troops is true then you'll have my support, though I can ill afford the time away from business."

"In that you're not alone, Coffin. Rest assured the army will be here in a few days at most. I don't know their number, though it's in the hundreds. Combined with our militia and secondary volunteers we should muster more than enough to exterminate this Kingi and his followers forever. Then we'll at last have an honest peace in this country."

"There are those," Coffin murmured, "who'd say we've always had peace in this country and if not for the machinations of certain unsavory land dealers that we'd enjoy it still."

Hull shrugged it off. "The Maoris love war. They loved it before we came and they'll continue to do so until we reform them. We must show them that if they want to fight it'd best be among themselves." Abruptly he rose. "You spoke of business. I have my own to look after. I'm sure you'll not be offended if I choose not to linger," he finished sarcastically.

Coffin also stood. As he passed, Hull extended his right hand. "If you would, I'd shake hands on this, Coffin."

"There's no need." Coffin made no move to grip the proffered hand.

Hull let it fall to his side. "Good. I've endured enough unpleasantness for one day. It was necessary to discuss this or I wouldn't have come."

Only the maid, Emily, saw the two men part.

7

If it had been left to Coffin he would have chosen to slip quietly and in small groups out of the city, so as to give the Kingites as little warning as possible. Alas, there was nothing for it but to have a parade, complete to gaudily waving handkerchiefs and brass band. The army regulars insisted on it. Coffin consoled himself with the knowledge that they couldn't have concealed their intentions anyway. The quietly observant Maoris would surely have noticed the movement of so many men and animals, even in small groups. But if given the choice he would have opted for secrecy.

As it was, the regulars looked proud, resplendent and invincible in their bright uniforms. Their appearance induced the colonial militia to push and shove themselves into something resembling a military line of order, while the rag-tag band of volunteers comprising the rear of the column managed to look halfway respectable as they streamed out of city.

Nearly three thousand strong, the army marched out through well-kept farms and fields. There was reason to hope that when confronted by such a show of strength and determination, the Kingites would simply break up into arguing family groups and the rebellion would melt away without anyone having to fire a shot.

Robert Coffin did not believe this, nor did Tobias Hull, but it was a thought much in vogue among the newly arrived troops.

Coffin and Hull saw each other rarely, which pleased both men. In such a large group there was no need for them to suffer each other's company.

They'd already met Colonel Gold, the commander of the regular troops and by extension the entire expeditionary force. Coffin thought him unnecessarily contemptuous of colonials and Maoris alike, as well as a bit vain, but there was no denying his professionalism. There were Captains and lieutenants whose skills Coffin admired more, but though he'd done plenty of fighting in his time he was not a military man by trade, so for the sake of harmony he kept his qualms over the choice of leadership to himself. He'd had previous encounters with individuals who, while unpleasant on a personal level, had proven themselves masters of their respective professions. Colonel Gold might well be kin to such men.

While there were those who doubted the natives would dare to confront such an overwhelming force, the majority felt the rebels would have to make a stand somewhere lest suspicions of cowardice lose them the support they had so painstakingly cultivated among neutral Maoris. It was simply a matter of forcing them into smaller and smaller areas until they would have no choice but to fight or surrender. They were not by nature a nomadic people. Nor was this Australia, with its thousands of square miles in which to hide.

Even so, when scouts brought them news of the location of the Kingite's camp, Coffin and his fellow colonials weren't the only ones who tried to dissuade Gold from making a frontal attack. A couple of his own officers tried to remonstrate with their commander, to no avail. The arguments persisted as the expedition's leaders gathered on a low hill to study the nearby pa in to which the enemy had retreated.

"Come now, gentlemen, you can't mean what you say," said Gold as he lowered his spyglass. "However brave you think they are, these are still savages we are dealing with here. They've never had to face an attack by regular troops. I can assure you from experience that these Maoris will break and run as soon as we begin our advance."

"You can break a Maori, but you can't make him run," said one of the colonial officers. "They're not your usual heathen."

"All heathen are alike." Gold's confidence was unshakable.

A small party of soldiers had been sent to test the Maori's will. Halfway to the pa they'd been turned back by a fusillade of rifle fire, clear indication those inside were ready and willing to resist. Meeting armed Maoris out in the open was dangerous enough, but taking a fortified pa was not something the experienced colonials were anxious to attempt.

Kingi's village was protected by an encircling stockade of stout Kauri pine. It sat atop a hill, which meant that any attackers would have to struggle uphill against whatever fire the village defenders could bring to bear. At least the rocky terrain had prevented the Maoris from adding a deep moat to their defenses. As the expedition's officers looked on, smoke could be seen rising from several cook fires. Of the defenders themselves there was no sign. They wisely chose to keep their heads down lest some English sharpshooter pick them off. But neither Coffin nor any other militiaman doubted for a moment that they were being watched closely from at least a dozen spy holes in the wooden palisade.

"If you would not have me attack, then what would you have me do?" Gold protested. "Return to Auckland?"

"Of course not, sir." The officer who had the courage to speak was one Captain Stoke, a man Coffin had already come to know and respect. As the men of the militia had learned during the long march, while Gold was senior among the soldiers he was by no means the most experienced in combat. In that regard he was outstripped by several Captains and not a few lieutenants. Like too many fellow officers in His Majesty's armed forces, Gold owed his position more to social status and contacts than actual skills, although his knowledge of classical tactics gleaned from study was impressive.

The only problem was, the Maoris were anything but classical opponents.

To Gold's credit, he was willing to listen to suggestions instead of slapping down those like Stoke who offered them.

"I say we encircle the entire village," said Stoke. "Taking especial care to station a large contingent by the stream that runs behind it. That will cut them off from their water supply and force them to use only what they've stored within the stockade. Then we wait them out."

"A siege?" Gold frowned unhappily. "I'm in no mood for a long campaign, Captain. It would be bad for the morale of the men."

"Bullets are worse," someone muttered, but Gold didn't hear him.

"In case you have forgotten, gentlemen, we were sent here to put an end to this rebellion as expeditiously as possible. That is what I intend to do. These natives are to be taught a lesson in the superiority of European arms and tactics. We'll teach them nothing by squatting around campfires and exchanging harsh words. The lesson is as important as victory.

"I want the regiment ready to make a frontal attack on the main gate of this village tomorrow morning. Regulars in front

backed by militia. The irregular volunteers will remain in the
rear until they are called, by which time the village should be
secured. I anticipate no difficulties, gentlemen. Once they see
that we are determined to finish this and find themselves
exposed to real soldiers I'm confident many if not all of them
will lay down their arms and surrender. You see, we need only
convince the commoners that their cause is hopeless and they
will abandon their chiefs and leaders, who can then be rounded
up and escorted back to Auckland for trial. Any questions?''

Coffin studied the faces of the other officers. Clearly there
were uncertainties, which no one chose to voice. Just as clearly
Gold had his mind made up. They were going to attack in the
morning. Coffin could see their hesitation. Gold just might be
right. Confronted by professional troops some of the Maoris
might indeed decide to surrender.

Most of them, however, would be delighted at the prospect
of doing battle with the best the pakehas had to offer. Coffin
didn't venture that opinion because he could imagine Gold's
reaction. Instead he contented himself with hoping the Colonel
was right.

As the meeting broke up and the officers returned to their
tents, discussing details of the forthcoming attack among
themselves, Coffin found a vantage point where he could see
the cookfire smoke rising from inside the fortified pa. He
missed Holly terribly. The older he grew the more indispens-
able she became to him. She was his anchor, his reassurance,
the one who comforted him when things grew difficult. While
that gratified him it also bothered him. He'd never intended to
sacrifice so much of his emotional independence to any
woman. But that was what he'd done.

I've become domesticated, he realized with a start. Like a
dog or a parrot. I, Robert Coffin, a man to be feared and
respected. I've become the head of a family.

And why not, he told himself? Why not ease back, relax,
and enjoy the fruits of his labors? That he could look forward
to sharing that with the company of a woman who loved him
true ought to be reassuring, not troubling.

Of course, no one would or could relax until the campaign
concluded. If Gold was right, it would all be over tomorrow.

Heavy cloud cover at sunrise forced even the determined
Colonel to postpone the assault. All night rain had turned the
slopes leading to the base of the Maori stockade into thick

mud. In addition to complicating the loading of muskets and pistols it made any thought of a rapid, concerted rush up the hill impossible. Meanwhile the Maoris could wait and keep dry until it was time to open fire on the attackers.

Gold was impetuous but he was no fool. They waited all that morning until the last of the low-lying fog lifted and an hour more for the sun to dry the saturated earth. Only then was the order given to advance.

From his position at the head of a company of militia Coffin had to admit it was a grand sight. Nothing like it had ever been seen in New Zealand before. Helmets gleaming in the sun, buckles and buttons flashing, the brightly clad soldiers followed their officers across a small dry gully and up the hillside opposite. Bugles blew and drums rolled, the latter reminding Coffin of a chorus of keas startled from their tree. Waving impressively in the breeze above all was the Union Jack.

His gaze rose to Wiremu Kingi's pa. The cookfires still smouldered but of the stockade's defenders there was no sign. Why didn't they mount the wall? Either they were afraid of army sharpshooters or else Gold was right and they were huddling fearfully within. Much as he wanted to believe in that scenario he could not. It wasn't Maori. But then, the Maoris had never faced anything like Gold's experienced, disciplined troops. They'd always fought badly organized farmers and shopkeepers. If all the spit and polish, the bugle blasts and drum rolls impressed Coffin, what effect must it be having on the natives?''

The fanfare ceased and everyone heard Captain Stoke's voice ring out sharp in the late morning air. Like a machine the first line of troops dropped to one knee and raised their weapons. They fired and the ground shook as several hundred muskets discharged simultaneously.

Smoke obscured the front lines, cleared long enough to reveal the second line advancing to fire. Thunder ripped the air for a second time and a new smoke cloud formed in the wake of the first. Still the Maoris did not respond.

A man on horseback rode over to greet him: Angus McQuade taking a moment's leave from his own company. Both men stared at the silent pa.

"What kinna be happenin', Robert? What are they up to in there?"

"Either they're arguing among themselves what to do next,

or they're waiting out of sight until Gold's men are well within range before responding." He shook his head. "If they let Stoke's men get too close to the wall they won't have a chance of driving them off."

"Which means the battle will be won."

Coffin nodded. "I don't understand, Angus. I know Maoris who could shoot as well as any European."

"Perhaps no such marksmen have joined the Kingites."

The first line of regulars continued their steady advance. They paused only once and then briefly to fix bayonets. It was possible that the massed fire had driven the defending Maoris away from the stockade wall. If so then fighting would break out furiously once the soldiers broke through the main gate. Meanwhile Coffin knew that a large body of troops waited alertly on the other side of the pa, ready to cut off any retreat should the Kingites attempt it.

Buglers blew the charge and the soldiers, yelling and whooping, rushed the gate. They spread out, slipping their own muskets through the gunports that had been cut in the stockade. Others brought up scaling ladders and scrambled up the rungs while their comrades covered their ascent. Rifles slung, they went up with pistols and swords drawn.

Musket smoke continued to obscure much of the scene, fading gradually along with the now irregular firing.

"Kinna you see anythin', Robert?"

"No. I wish I'd brought my old seaman's spyglass. In the rush to get off I forgot to pack it."

"Nay, see!" McQuade fought to control his excited mount. "There's the flag already, at the top of the wall!"

The militia and irregulars saw it at the same time and a great cheer arose from the waiting men.

"All that fire must have driven them back to the main houses," McQuade opined. "Once we got over the wall they had no choice but to surrender."

"I wonder." The assault had gone like a textbook exercise: too smooth, too efficient. They had participated in a parade not a battle. Yet—there was the Union Jack waving over the Kingite's pa, a sure sign of victory. Moments later it was replaced with signal flags as the troops inside communicated with their commander. Looking to his left Coffin could see Gold and his orderlies riding up the trail that lead to the main gate.

Both Coffin and McQuade watched as the last of the smoke lifted. They expected to see at least a few bodies strewn about the hillside below the wall. There wasn't a one.

"Something's wrong," Coffin muttered uneasily. He turned to Rollins, the young banker who was his second-in-command. "Keep the men alert and ready, Will. We're going down to see what's happening."

"Yes sir."

"Come on, Angus."

Together they rode toward the pa, following in Gold's wake.

The pa had been captured: of that there was no doubt. But there were no bodies inside either. Coffin located Gold and his officers, Stoke among them, inspecting a line of Maori granaries. Eyes formed of bright paua shell stared down from garishly carved tikis and other heathen symbols.

Of the Maoris there was no sign.

Coffin thought he heard something different then, drew McQuade off to one side. "You hear that, Angus?"

"I dinna think—wait, yes. There's somethin'."

They climbed one of the ladders that would have enabled the pa's defenders to reach a platform running along the inside of the wall near the top. From this height one could see the whole battlefield. Off to the left were the reinforcements that would not be needed. Far off to the right could be seen the mass of troops defending the stream.

They could hear it clearly now, even though it was already beginning to fade. Laughter.

"Damn them!" McQuade was so angry he was shaking. When he saw that Coffin was hard put to restrain his own laughter his eyes widened. "Robert! You canna be laughin' with them?"

"I'm sorry, Angus. It's just that, well, see what they did. They left a few warriors behind, just enough to make us think the pa was defended when we first arrived. They fired a few shots to keep us busy and spent the rest of their time tending all these cook fires. Kingi hasn't set foot inside this pa for no telling how long." McQuade shook his head slowly, numb at the discovery that the entire army had been badly fooled.

"You realize what Kingi's done, Angus? Not only has he bought himself more time, but his scouts have had the chance to see regular troops in action. They'll not only know what to expect from now on, they'll have a good idea of our strength and disposition."

"Then," McQuade looked over at him, "where are Kingi and his people now?"

"Probably holed up in another pa somewhere." He turned, could see by the way Gold was haranguing his officers below that the Colonel had finally realized they'd been duped. "I hope Gold doesn't take this personally. We'll all need clear heads when the time comes for the real fight. At least he had the sense to let someone like Stoke lead the actual attack." He turned away from the noisy cluster of frustrated soldiers, let his eyes sweep across the country that the Maoris had refused to sell to the settlers.

"I'm sure Kingi will fight next time. He's learned what he wanted to learn. Once is amusing, but if he runs a second time it will smack of retreat. He can't afford that."

"Dinna worry, Robert. We'll catch up with 'em."

"I know we will Angus. That's what's always worried me."

8

It took the scouts weeks to finally locate the pa where Kingi intended to make his stand. The hill on which the village sat was not high, but it was surrounded by a deep ditch which would slow any attack. Scaling ladders would have to be used to span this wide moat. Worse, there was a small lake nearby. This meant the pa's defenders had wells inside the wall. No matter how long the battle took there would be no shortage of water for cleaning and cooking.

As the soldiers formed their lines they were greeted not with silence but with gesticulations and insults from the Maoris who lined the stockade wall. They bugged their eyes at the troops, jumped up and down, gestured obscenely with their weapons and flicked their tongues rapidly in and out in the traditional form of challenge. Gold and his officers merely sniffed at the barbaric demonstration and went about their business, but it riled the average soldier. Men clutched their muskets tightly and glared at their half-naked opponents, eager to engage them in combat.

As he heard them talk of what they would do to the pa's defenders, Coffin reflected that barbarism was all a matter of perspective.

He and McQuade and Tobias Hull and several other militia officers tried their best to persuade Gold not to repeat his strategy of marching troops straight up to the stockade as he had the previous time, now that the Maoris were aware of the tactic. Gold held his ground. Even Captain Stoke, whom Coffin had come to respect, was convinced that such an attack would scatter the pa's defenders.

"If there's trouble we'll hit them with the militia and the volunteers," Stoke argued. "They'll be overwhelmed, sir."

Coffin shook his head impatiently. "It won't work. They're ready for us this time, Stoke."

McQuade spoke up. "I've men who won't march against Maoris over open ground."

"Then they'll be shot," Gold said evenly. "Need I remind any of you, gentlemen, that this is a formal military expedition operating under military law. You'd best tell that to the faint-hearted among your people. I will not tolerate desertion in time of battle, not even from volunteers. Besides, you worry needlessly. Once they see how the battle progresses your people will be eager to follow my troops into this village. I suggest you steady your men as best you're able, have confidence, and leave the conduct and manner of the actual assault to those of us who are trained to manage it."

Coffin departed trying to convince himself Gold was right. True, the Kingites had had the chance to observe British troops in action, but against an empty pa. Some of Gold's men were veterans of the Crimean War. They might just be able to awe the Kingites into surrender.

Once again the lines were formed, the bugles blew and the drums rolled. Muskets at the ready, brass gleaming, the regulars commenced their assault. This time they were met halfway up the hill not by a cryptic silence but by a steady barrage of musket and rifle fire from within the stockade. Thick smoke soon obscured the battlefield.

Out of the noise and acrid cloud came the order for the militia to advance. Shouts and curses stood in for bugles as the colonials began to move. Some of the men held back but, mindful of McQuade's concerns, officers had been stationed in the rear of the column to drive the recalcitrant forward.

Musket balls were soon whizzing through the smoke around them. It was impossible to see anything directly ahead and almost as difficult to hear due to the steady firing on both sides. The smoke was a sulfurous fog that obscured their vision. Only the fact that they were advancing uphill told them they were moving in the right direction.

Soon they were able to see more than the earth underfoot. Men began tripping over the twisted bodies of dead and wounded soldiers lying where they'd fallen. Coffin couldn't remember a great deal of what happened after that. His own men were falling around him. They couldn't shoot through the damnable smoke lest they hit the regular troops in front of them, while the Maoris had only to aim and fire in the general direction of their assailants.

The nearer they drew to the stockade itself, the thicker the bodies became. Angus McQuade had his horse shot out from under him. Seeing their commander go down, his men panicked and began to retreat.

Ignoring the shots whizzing about his ears, Coffin rode through the pall of blue-tinged smoke and fairly flung himself from the saddle. McQuade lay on the ground, his face contorted with pain.

"My leg," he whispered agonizingly, "it's my leg, Robert."

Looking down, Coffin saw that his friend's left leg was pinned beneath the dead horse. Blood streamed from the animal's neck and its eye bulged hugely.

"Here, over here, you cowardly buggers!" Coffin waved angrily at a cluster of men. At his shout they hesitated, uncertain whether to advance or retreat. Their eyes were full of fear. With a curse Coffin yanked a pistol from his belt and pointed it at them.

"Get your worthless carcasses over here now or I'll shoot you down where you stand! This man needs your help!"

It was enough to shock them out of their paralysis. They hurried over. Coffin put his pistol away and directed them. Several grabbed the saddle strap while two more helped Coffin.

"Together now, on three. One, two—lift!"

As they dragged McQuade from beneath the horse Coffin thought he recognized one of the men leaning on the saddle strap. Hodgkins, yes, that was his name. A miller from just outside the city. He called him over and together they bent to examine McQuade's injuries.

"Broken, certainly," Hodgkins commented worriedly.

Coffin used his knife to slit his friend's trousers. There was no blood, no bone protruding whitely. He breathed a little easier.

"How bad?" McQuade had his eyes shut against the pain.

"Not as bad as it feels, Angus. The bone hasn't come through." Both men knew that meant there would be no need to amputate the leg, provided it healed without infection. Coffin rose, gave orders.

"You men make a litter with your muskets." When this was done and McQuade lifted from the ground he turned to Hodgkins. "Get him back to camp and to a doctor. And don't abandon him until he's safe or you'll hear from me."

Hodgkins nodded reassuringly. "Don't worry, sir." Coffin's

calmness under fire and his cool words had restored the man's
confidence if not his courage. "We'll see him back safely. But
what are we to do then? Do you know how the battle's going?"

Visibility had improved to perhaps ten feet. "No more than
you, sir."

One of the other men spoke up. "They would have sounded
the bugle if they'd taken the gate."

"Never mind the fighting. Get this man to camp." He
watched until they'd vanished into the smoke. Then he hefted
his saber and moved sideways along the hillside until he'd
rejoined his own men.

They were milling around confusedly. As he tried to
organize them one man pointed. "There, look there!"

Shapes were materializing out of the mist: Gold's soldiers.
They were not walking in neat, disciplined rows now. Many
had lost caps and helmets. Blood showed on torn shirts and
trousers and their faces were streaked with powder and soot.
Shots continued to fill the air around them like drunken
hornets.

Coffin watched as one man bent double and went down, his
body arching like a bowstring as a musketball struck him in the
spine. A mustachioed sergeant bent over the man briefly, then
rose and fought to rally his ragged troops.

"Form up, boys, form up! Keep your line!"

They weren't listening to him and you could hardly blame
them. The soldiers were being asked to assault a well-protected
enemy they couldn't even see. Bodies continued to fall,
shadows in the smoke. The volume of fire was beginning to
decrease. Visibility improved but little else. Dozens of figures
were crawling, limping down the hillside. None was advancing. Coffin reached a decision.

Recovering his horse he mounted and rode among his own
militia. "Keep firing, keep firing!" Regular troops continued
to retreat all around. "Aim high for your targets!"

"What targets, sir?" a colonial sergeant asked plaintively.
"I can't see a bloody thing!"

Coffin bit his lower lip, then swung his sword decisively.
"Then get back! Get clear!" This order was not met with
cheers, but it was obeyed with alacrity. Coffin was damned if
he was going to wait for instructions to retreat when the attack
had obviously collapsed. He would not stand by while these
men, many of whom he knew personally, were cut down by the
withering fire the Maoris continued to pour down the hillside.

"Back to camp, get out of range! Make sure you take the wounded with you!"

A semblance of order returned to the colonials as they commenced a measured retreat. Coffin rode back and forth among them, quietly urging them on, trying to raise their spirits. Ironic that they should be more easily rallied in retreat than when on the attack, he thought.

He saw Tobias Hull once as he rode past in the smoke. Hull was trying to urge his men onward but they were breaking, retreating in small groups. Not even Hull's threats were strong enough to maintain determination in the face of defeat.

What was important now was to minimize the disaster and prevent panic, keep the colonials and volunteers from running all the way back to Auckland. With the help of the regulars, Coffin and his colleagues succeeded in reforming their units in front of the camp. Panic subsided as soon as the exhausted men realized they were out of musket range and therefore out of danger. The Maoris had won, but they were not strong enough to abandon their fortress to give chase. Shouts and screams gave way to the moans of the wounded and dying.

Those who had escaped unhurt moved to aid the injured. Militia worked alongside regular army to carry the wounded to waiting beds.

As the firing ceased, the true extent of the defeat could be ascertained. There was no way of telling how many Maori had been hit since those who'd been shot had fallen inside the stockade, but the gentle slope outside the pa was littered with corpses. Losses were heaviest among the regular troops, though the colonials had suffered their share.

As the survivors counted the cost, the hooting challenges of the Maoris still safe inside the pa resumed. Certainly the Kingites had been hurt, but they had not been defeated and their tone indicated they were anything but intimidated.

Gold tried again that afternoon, still again the next day. Each time the result was the same. While the soldiers advanced in predetermined formation the Maoris greeted them with devastating fire. They spent powder and shot as though they had enough to last for a hundred such confrontations. Militia and volunteers backed up the troops with increasing reluctance.

A few men actually managed to reach the stockade and put up scaling ladders. They were promptly cut to bits by the defending Maoris. In close-quarter fighting shark-toothed clubs, spears, and greenstone axes proved the equal of bayonets.

The mood in Gold's tent that night bordered on the funereal. The Colonel's face was gaunt and his eyes hollow. He'd aged visibly in only a few days. But his determination had not weakened.

"Tomorrow," he told his subordinates. "Tomorrow we'll overwhelm them." He looked up. "Captain Rogers, you'll take your men up the south side this time. Then we'll. . . ."

"With your permission, Colonel." It was Stoke who interrupted. Coffin held his breath. He'd expected the Captain to speak up earlier. His silence had cost another hundred men. "We can't fight this war that way."

Gold stiffened. "I beg to differ with you, Captain. I know my tactics. We must show them we can't be discouraged, that we won't give up. In a war of attrition the professional will always emerge triumphant."

"Which professional?" someone whispered.

"Colonel, traditional tactics don't apply here. We're not fighting a traditional opponent. They make up their own rules as they go along." Stoke leaned forward. "I'd like to speak bluntly, sir."

Gold looked at the anxious faces filling his tent, then seemed to slump. He waved an indifferent hand. "If you must, Captain."

"Colonel, it's been a shooting gallery out there. You've seen it for yourself. If we keep marching men up that hill the regulation twenty-five inches apart they'll continue cutting us down the way they have in every previous assault."

As if to punctuate Stoke's comments the tent was filled with the whine of a single rifle shot. Everyone flinched instinctively. That was another unpleasant surprise. Several officers and men had been hit at extreme range. It developed that several of the chiefs supporting Kingi owned superb hunting rifles. When the frontal assaults ended they mounted the stockade and amused themselves by picking off unwary soldiers who believed themselves safely out of range. As a result the entire camp had been forced to move back another hundred and fifty yards.

"We can't keep this up, sir," Stoke concluded.

"As long as I'm in command here this war will be carried out according to approved tactics."

"Colonel Gold, sir, we've close to one third of our entire

complement killed or wounded." The man who'd spoken
unexpectedly was a sallow-faced elderly veteran named Colville. "Over a thousand men. If we keep trying regulation
frontal assaults not only will we be wiped out but there'll be no
armed force of any size to stop these natives from overrunning
the whole country."

At first Coffin thought Gold would hew to his original
intentions, but finding himself assailed from all sides he at least
had the common sense not to resist to the point of absurdity.
His voice fell to a murmur and he stared at the oil lamp hanging
from the centerpole.

"What do you suggest, gentlemen? Captain Stoke? Since
you find my strategy not to your liking you must have
something to offer in its place."

"It's not your strategy, sir. I've heard you say myself a good
officer needs to improvise in the field." Gold nodded, looked
away from the lamp. Coffin eyed the Captain approvingly. A
good soldier was also a good diplomat.

"I'd like permission to begin sapping operations. We'll start
digging from the closest point where there's tree cover. When
the sap is within twenty yards of the wall we'll split right and
left as well as continuing forward. It will take more time but
I'd rather do that and be able to blow the stockade simultaneously at three points. That way there's no chance they'll be
able to repair the gap before we break through. With adequate
covering fire we should be able to do that.

"Once inside we should be able to carry the day by virtue of
superior weaponry if naught else. Surely they've suffered
substantial losses of their own. He didn't plead, but there was
no denying the earnestness in his voice.

"It's the only way, Colonel. This isn't the Crimea or
Belgium. We have to modify our tactics to suit local conditions. I'm sorry if that goes against the niceties of traditional
warfare."

It was silent in the tent for a long moment. Gold nodded
slowly. "We're not here to maintain traditions, gentlemen.
We're here to win a war." Murmurs of approval rose from the
listening officers. "Mr. Coffin, Mr. Hull, can you guarantee
your support?"

Coffin replied first. "There are men in my group who've
talked openly of desertion. They have crops to get in, shops to

run. But I think they'll stay, especially if they think they've a chance to win."

"He's right," said Hull. "Pains me to admit it, but the heathen have given us a hiding. It's a foolish man who doesn't learn from experience. My men will fight on, never fear."

"Right, then. Captain Stoke, get your engineers started. Coopt as many men as you need. Lieutenant Colville, I want the sentries doubled. We don't want these bastards sneaking away from us the way they did at the last village." He rose. "Now we'd best to sleep. I'll see you all in the morning, gentlemen."

As they were leaving Coffin heard two junior officers conversing. "Why the bloody hell would they try and sneak out? They're winning."

It was a measure of how far the army's confidence had fallen—and how much they'd learned—that two professional soldiers could speak such words.

9

It was hard to be patient while the army engineers began the slow, arduous task of digging a deep trench toward the pa. The men had enlisted to fight, not sit and listen to taunts. They busied themselves as best they could, but the colonial militia and irregulars still lost a number of men to boredom and impatience.

It began to rain again. The trench collapsed in several places, necessitating the installation of complicated and painstaking shoring to protect the diggers. But the work went on. When the rain stopped, thick shielding was built by carpenters and metalworkers to form a bullet-proof ceiling over the lengthening trench.

They were two-thirds of the way to the stockade wall when one of Coffin's own people, a blacksmith named Hawkins, brought him the latest in a succession of bad news.

"I've just come from the quartermaster, Mr. Coffin, sir. Says we've only enough food left for a few days."

"Thank you, Mr. Hawkins. I'll see to it." The blacksmith hesitated as if he wanted to add something more, reconsidered and left with a nod.

Coffin had been expecting the news earlier. Soldiers and civilians alike had marched confidently out of Auckland expecting a quick campaign. A few dozen armed men could forage successfully for themselves, but an army of thousands needed extensive support facilities. These had not been provided for.

Gold, Stoke and the regulars were no better off. Colville proposed keeping a small force in camp to protect the engineers and diggers while the rest returned to the city for supplies. Gold ruled it out immediately. Any substantial reduction in strength would tempt the Maoris to sally from the pa in hopes of destroying those who remained behind to continue to work. There seemed no choice but to abandon the field to the Maoris while the army returned to Auckland to regroup and perhaps await the arrival of additional regiments.

"Artillery!" said Colville through clenched teeth. "That's what we bloody well need here."

Big guns would have made a big difference. None had been brought along because no one gave a thought to their necessity. Artillery would only slow down any expeditionary force, and why would British regulars need cannon to subdue a few rebellious natives?

Packing had begun when a loud cry rang through the dispirited camp. Coffin emerged from his own tent, frowned as he saw men moving en masse in one direction, and ran to join them.

Soon he could see the soldier who was the focus of all the attention. It was one of the sentries, running toward headquarters with others dogging his heels excitedly.

"What is it? What's going on?" He intercepted a private, out of breath.

"White flag!" the man gasped. "They're coming out with a white flag!"

Coffin let the man go, looked sharply toward the impregnable pa. The front gate so many men had died to reach stood open. A line of Maoris was emerging, marching down the path toward the camp. He turned and ran to tell McQuade.

Angus was lying on a hospital cot, his leg heavily bandaged, awaiting evacuation. He would not be participating in any future battles, Coffin knew, and would likely walk with a limp the rest of his life—but the doctors had saved the leg.

"The Maoris are coming out with a white flag, Angus!"

"Be damned you say." McQuade let his head fall back on the pillow. "Providence has delivered victory to us!"

Coffin hesitated. "It's delivered something. As to victory, we'll see."

He left the hospital on the run to join Gold and the other officers. They were forming up to meet the Maori delegation.

As they drew near everyone could see that the *tutua* in the back of the column were carrying large bundles between them.

"What do you suppose that's all about?" Stoke inquired.

"Gifts maybe," said Coffin uncertainly.

"Maybe they think they can buy us off without having to make a formal surrender." Hull leaned out for a better look.

It was an impressive procession, the chiefs in front handsomely decked out in feathered capes that shone iridescent in the sun. There was no sign of Wiremu Kingi, however. He prudently remained behind, in the pa.

"We should move to meet them."

"No," said Gold. "Let them approach us. If they're here to negotiate a surrender we'll choose the spot for discussion."

But as the column slowed Coffin wasn't so sure surrender was what the Maoris had in mind. The long line of warriors began dumping their burdens, huge sacks and bundles bound with rope. A lower chief supervised this unloading before walking over to confront the Europeans. He was well over six feet and was tattooed from face to shoulders.

"I am Atuawhera. I bring greetings from Wiremu Kingi. Which of you is the Golden Colonel?"

Gold took a step forward. Somehow he'd regained the air of confidence and soldierly dignity the past weeks had beaten out of him. It was an impressive recovery considering how little time he'd been given to prepare for this meeting. Gold had his best dress uniform on and his back was straight as a board. You couldn't tell by looking at him that he was a man whose entire outlook on his profession had been given a rattling good shaking these past few weeks.

Atuawhera turned to gesture at the massive pile of bundles his warriors had brought with them. "We know that you are running out of food."

A couple of the officers flinched but there was no point in reprimanding them. It hadn't been framed as a question. Nevertheless, Gold struggled to maintain the fiction.

"We have ample provisions, thank you."

"Then why are you preparing to leave?" When no one replied the chief continued. "It would be bad if you had to leave. This is a good fight, the best. So that you will not have to leave just to find food," and again he indicated the mountain of bundles, "we have brought food for you so that you can stay and keep fighting. The land has been good to us for several years. We have plenty to eat and drink. We would share with our brave opponents. There is flour for making bread, also potatoes, mutton, and vegetables. Give this food to your cooks, since you have no women to cook for you, and eat well this night." He grinned broadly, showing brilliant white teeth. "Tomorrow we will fight some more!"

With that he turned and barked orders to his warriors. Still under the white flag they retraced their steps back along the path leading up to the pa. Gold and his officers looked after them, speechless. Leastwise they remained speechless until several of the warriors paused to bend over, stare back between their legs and make faces at them.

"What does that mean?" a thoroughly stupefied Gold asked.

"Means the same in Maori as it does in English, Colonel," Tobias Hull informed him. He walked over and put his sword to the binding of the nearest sack. It was full of baskets of finely milled flour. Hull picked up a handful, let it trickle back into the expertly woven container.

One of the younger officers was shaking his head as he stared admiringly up at the pa. "They're all insane. Instead of surrendering they give us food so we can keep fighting them? What kind of people are these?"

"Maori." Coffin dropped his gaze from the pa to the pile of supplies. There was more than enough food to keep the remaining troops fed for weeks, albeit on short rations. Enough to allow small mounted parties to go scavenging the surrounding countryside for more.

Muttering to himself, Gold retreated to his tent, leaving supervision of the on-going engineering work to Stoke and Colville.

The Maoris tried several times to flood or otherwise destroy the lengthening sap. Each time they failed. When the three-pronged trench had undermined the wall the engineers set mines, lit fuses, and hurriedly retreated beneath their protective wooden roof. A great cheer arose from the assembled and waiting soldiers and militia when the mines went off, blowing apart a long stretch of stockade.

There was no holding any of them back now, not even the ragged volunteers. They charged up the hill and burst through the hastily formed line of Maori defenders, only to discover that while the pa was full of bodies, most of the warriors had managed to slip away in twos and threes. Wiremu Kingi and all his principal chiefs had got away clean. It was the army's second Pyrrhic victory in as many tries.

"They'll recruit new warriors to replace those they lost here." Coffin stood within the pa, looking on as the militia torched the houses and granaries. Captain Stoke stood nearby, sword drawn and bloodied, shielding his eyes as he watched the flames take hold.

"Don't worry, sir. They may have learned something of our tactics from this battle, but so have we learned about theirs. We won't make the same mistakes again. No more frontal attacks in the traditional manner. No more attacking high walls with bayonets. We'll try and catch them outside their pas. We'll prepare for long sieges. And by Heaven, next time we'll have artillery if I have to requisition it from the Tower itself!"

"I think I can help there." Coffin looked thoughtful. "We can buy big guns from the Dutch at Batavia."

Stoke stared at him, extended his hand. "You should have been a soldier, sir."

Coffin shook his head. "I prefer commerce to combat, Mr. Stoke. It's a matter of self-defense, you see. I won't expose any more of my people to heavy musket fire until we're better able to respond."

"I understand." Stoke wiped his sword clean on a leg, sheathed it. "It may take a while to get the cannon, but when we do it'll put an end to this business of sapping and mining. You'll see, sir. We'll put paid to this rebellion of yours in a few months."

They both turned back to watch the destruction. As Coffin stared at the burning storehouses the faces of the Maori gods carved thereon seemed to twist and dance, paua shell eyes shining in the orange light, toothy jaw alive with laughter.

It had been a long time since he'd suffered from his recurring nightmares, but he had one that night. He could have sworn that one of the faces he'd seen burning atop the chief's house belonged to someone known to him, but he couldn't quite place it or put a name to it. The face hadn't been carved into a grimace like the others. It simply stared down at him, fire licking at its edges, until it was consumed. At the last it threatened to consume Coffin too.

As he lay back down, trying to will himself back to sleep, he knew that despite his confidence and competence Stoke was wrong. All of them were wrong. Artillery would help, but it would not end the Maori war in a matter of weeks, or even months. The war would go on and on. There would be no peace in New Zealand until the last Maori warrior had been killed or pacified. And how could such a people be pacified without being defeated?

Once they were certain they had Kingi himself trapped, but he slipped from their grasp again. Coffin noted that in the intervening months Gold and the rest of the British regulars had stopped referring to the Maoris as heathen, had started calling them the enemy soldiers. Neither he nor Hull nor any of the other colonials bothered to point out that it didn't really matter whether they caught Kingi or not. There would always be another ariki, another Kingi ready to put on the mantle of Kingite leader.

Nor could they concentrate exclusively on Kingi's band. Pockets of armed resistance had erupted all over North Island, which diluted the resources available to Gold. Farms and villages had to be protected from Maori raids. The army and militia simply couldn't spend all its time chasing around the country after one particular enemy band.

The Maoris never attacked any of the larger communities, nor did they attempt to confront the army in open combat. They fought best from behind their strong-walled pas or out in dense forest, striking hard and retreating when they encountered determined resistance. Travel of any kind, much less ordinary commerce, became more and more difficult except by ship as the Maoris ambushed one wagon after another.

Extremists called for laying waste to every Maori village and town, believing that even those who denied supporting the Kingites secretly aided them with food and information. They wanted to burn all the Maori fields to deny the Kingites supplies.

Coffin and the calmer heads among the colony's leaders prevailed. A few such acts of unprovoked destruction and violence would surely have driven all the Maoris into the Kingite camp. As it was, a great many managed to maintain their neutrality despite provocation from both sides, and some actually fought alongside the colonials.

Fresh troops arrived regularly from Australia, rotating with exhausted veterans. Men came from England and India and other outposts of the Empire. They always arrived brimming with self-assurance, confident they would bring the war to an end in a matter of weeks. The new officers were the worst. They were unable to understand how a few natives had managed to battle His Majesty's regiments to a standstill. Why, India alone contained hundreds of times as many heathen, and India was firmly under control. Impossible to believe this petty rebellion of Polynesians had continued for so long.

Soon such men got their first taste of Maori fighting, and as quickly they came to understand that Te Ika-a-maui, as North Island was called, was not the Punjab. Cockiness gave way to wariness, and men talked of survival instead of quick victory.

Stoke got his artillery. Though they could now reduce the walls of a pa from a safe distance it in no way brought the rebellion to a close. If anything, the Maoris thrived on this greater challenge. The more they lost, the harder they fought. Instead of trying to defend their pas, when the army unlimbered its cannon they simply melted away into the woods to attack and harry the besieging troops. Soldiers cursed and died as they hunted for an enemy that refused to stand still and be defeated.

The regulars weren't the only ones who rotated combat duty. Coffin managed his militia assignments better than most of his colleagues thanks to the dedication of Elias Goldman and the increasing responsibility Christopher took for the day-to-day operations of Coffin House. Even Holly was supportive. She reluctantly accepted the fact that as one of the community's most influential citizens, Coffin could hardly sit back and live in luxury while everyone else took their turn fighting the rebels. But she didn't like it.

In truth, he missed her as much or more than she missed him. He spent too many lonely nights out on the road with the cold wind battering at his tent.

There seemed no end to it. Many members of the militia and volunteers took to bringing their wives or sweethearts along with them. The regulars had their camp followers. The expeditionary forces were like large animals that surged back and forth across the countryside, striking at tormenting Maoris, killing some, extracting pledges of neutrality or allegiance from the rest only to find that once they'd passed, a hitherto peaceful tribe would suddenly choose to join the revolt. Such unpredictable actions prevented any region from becoming permanently pacified.

They were bound to win, Stoke assured everyone repeatedly. It was only a question of time. The war had become a part of daily life, with men moving on a regular basis between home and combat. Though devoid of gaiety and ease, life continued much as before. They might not be able to kill every Kingite, but eventually they would wear the rebels down.

Indeed, the Maoris had already lost, though not even their own gods could have convinced them of it.

BOOK FOUR

1861

1

He was thinking of Holly. Of her bright eyes and smooth skin, of the cool breezes that blew off the lake at Tarawera. Of how the summer house at Te Wairoa was going to look when at last it was finished to his satisfaction.

A shout from ahead and the column halted. Men chatted softly behind him, on foot or horseback, as one of his outriders pulled up before him. Almost, he turned to say something to Angus, but McQuade no longer rode with the militia. His injured leg prevented him from joining in the fighting.

"Major Stoke's respects, sir, and would you ride on up to join him?"

"What is it, Corporal?"

"Maoris ahead, sir."

Coffin rose in his stirrups but could barely see the end of the column of regulars the militia had been following. "Any fighting yet?"

"No sir." The messenger turned his horse about. "None expected, either. These natives are neutrals, or so they claim." It was clear from his tone that this soldier had no use for neutrals.

"Then why has the column stopped? Why not just march around them?"

"Major Stoke has decided to bivouac here for the night, sir. Also, I was told that one of the Maoris wishes to speak with you personally."

Coffin frowned. Several of his subordinates eyed him curiously. "We'll soon straighten this out. Lead on, Corporal."

"Yes sir."

The messenger wheeled about and Coffin followed. Already the regular troops were unpacking tents and cook pots from the supply train. They rode on past until his guide turned off the main road and led him down a slight incline.

Camped against the near shore of a narrow stream was a small group of traveling Maoris. Even if they'd been hostile they would have posed no danger to the heavily armed troop. Experience had taught the soldiers to keep pickets moving constantly on both flanks of a marching column.

Being in no way opposed to the adoption of the best of European culture, these traveling Maoris stayed in tents the equal of any officer's. There was no mistaking the chief's tent. The entrance was decorated with carved wood, which had been erected to give the tent the look of a Maori house. When he recognized several of the carven images Coffin smiled.

"It's all right, Corporal," he told his guide. "You can return to your unit."

The younger man eyed him uncertainly. "You sure you'll be okay here, Mr. Coffin, sir?" He was obviously uneasy at leaving an officer alone among a number of armed natives, no matter how strenuously they protested their neutrality.

"I'll be safe, Corporal. Do as I say."

"It's your neck, sir." The soldier turned and spurred his mount up the bank leading to the road.

Coffin dismounted and approached the chief's tent. An expressionless old woman pulled the rain flap aside and bade him enter. He bent, then straightened once inside.

"I thought it might be you, old friend," he said to the tent's only other inhabitant.

Te Ohine had lost some of his imposing girth. His hair was now as gray as Coffin's, a change not entirely induced by advancing years. The conflicts of the past several years had aged many men, Maori and pakeha alike. The chief sat on a small carved wooden chair, gestured to Coffin to sit on a nearby woven mat.

"A bad time, Coffin. A very bad time it's been."

"I know. Too many good men dead on both sides." Silence for a moment, then, "Do not the Kingites see they cannot beat us? Why do they not give this wastefulness up and make a treaty with us?"

Te Ohine sighed heavily. "Many treaties have been made between the Maori and the pakeha. They seem to mean more to us than to you."

"Not to me," Coffin protested quickly. "Are there not good and bad men among the Maori? I know there have been problems with land dealing. All this can be worked out without the loss of more lives. There's no need for men to die."

"If men cannot die for their land what else is there worth dying for?"

"And yet, you do not fight."

"No, I do not fight. I am a Christian."

"There are many Christian Maoris with the Kingites."

"I know, and that is sad. Such people listen to the fathers' teachings, but they hear only what they want to hear."

"That is true for the pakeha as well, I'm afraid."

"Many Kingites are not Christian. They believe the Old Gods will rise up and help them." He looked down at Coffin. "Help them to throw all the pakehas into the sea."

"That's not going to happen." Coffin spoke softly. "I know it's not and so do you."

Te Ohine nodded. "Yes, I know this. So we must find a way to live here together, in peace."

"We will, but for those who persist in fighting, peace will come only in one way."

For the first time the old chief grinned. "You are a wise man, Robert Coffin, but you do not see everything. It is true the Kingites cannot push you into the sea, but neither can you defeat the Kingites. Not as long as there is a cave to hide in or a tree to stand behind. They will hide from you until you think you have finished them and then they will come out to attack you anew. You will never have peace."

"We *will* have peace," Coffin insisted. "It may take a little longer than first thought, maybe another year or two, but the Kingites will be beaten."

Te Ohine sat on his chair shaking his head. "Have you learned so little about us? The Maori love to fight. So long as you fight the Kingites they will fight back for the pure joy of it, even if they think they cannot win."

"That's stupid." Coffin couldn't keep the brusqueness out of his voice. "If a man knows he cannot win he should lay down his arms."

"Ah, that is how a pakeha would think." Te Ohine chuckled gently. "It is not the way of the Maori."

"We'll see." He nodded toward the tent's entrance. "You know, there are any number of men in that column who would gladly fall on you and kill you all, just because you're Maori."

"I know that. If I were to be killed and not reach my

destination, all my tribe and all the clans bonded to it would no longer be neutral. They would rise up as one and join the Kingites. That is what protects me, more so than the flag of truce I travel under." He leaned forward and put his hands on his knees. "Enough of war. What of your life, my old friend? You are older than when last I saw you but you stand straight and look well."

"No thanks to this bloody conflict."

"Will you have something to eat and drink?"

Coffin smiled. "When did I ever refuse to break bread with a friend? There's more of the road in my throat than on my horse's hooves."

Te Ohine laughed. The tenseness Coffin had sensed when he'd entered was gone, each man once more sure of the other. Outside, war and rebellion might dominate relations between Maori and pakeha, but in here, in this one small place, peace and understanding reigned. The chief turned and shouted toward the back of the tent.

A woman entered. She carried a carved wooden tray laden with cakes and bottles. The instant he set eyes on her Coffin forgot about the war, forgot about politics, forgot how tired and sore he was.

Forgot everything.

At first sight he wasn't sure she was pure Maori. Her features were too delicate, almost oriental; her body from shoulders to hips too svelte and trim. The rest of her was not in question, from the lustrous dark hair that fell in waves and curls to her waist to the obsidian eyes.

Conscious of his stare, she set down the tray and looked straight back into his eyes with a boldness that matched his own. She wore a light, filmy top that might once have comprised a portion of some wealthy white woman's nightgown set. It looked incongruous against the flaxen skirt below.

He could no more look away from her than he could suspend time, though he tried to do both. She poured drinks into silver cups, the Maoris having acquired a taste for many pakeha luxuries. Te Ohine traveled in the style befitting a great chief. Only then did she subject Coffin to a second shock. Instead of retiring the way she'd come, she crossed her legs and sat down on the map between the two men. That was unheard of.

He waited as long as he thought proper before glancing curiously at his host. "Aren't you going to order her to leave?"

Te Ohine's expression twisted as he turned to regard the young woman. She couldn't have been more than nineteen or twenty. "Some fathers are blessed with children. This one is a curse. Her name is Merita." He tapped his forehead. "She is not right up here."

"Not right." Coffin looked back at the girl. She continued to sit quietly, staring at him with astonishing intensity. Would she speak, or would she at least show enough respect for tradition to keep silent? He found himself hoping she would speak, if only so he could hear her voice. It occurred to him that her actions were as outlandish as her attire. There was nothing in that bright, penetrating stare that hinted of idiocy.

"She listens to no one," Te Ohine was saying, "but instead does just as she pleases. Sometimes it pleases her to obey me. Sometimes not." He shrugged. "I keep her with me because I am too embarrassed to offer her in marriage to a reputable warrior. None would have her."

At that the girl glanced challengingly up at her father. "I will choose my own man." Her English, like her voice, was beautifully modulated, sweet as a flute.

"Your daughter is the most beautiful woman I've ever set eyes on."

If he expected her to turn modestly away or to blush he was disappointed. Instead, she just smiled back at him. He was so tense he hurt.

Te Ohine sounded indifferent. "Oh, yes, I suppose she is pretty. But who wants a crazy woman for a wife, no matter how attractive?"

"I do as I please," she said, throwing back her head. The black waterfall rippled. She was daring her father to contradict her. Evidently the old man knew better. She continued to stare at Coffin with a hint of shame. He wondered if anything could intimidate her.

"It is good to meet you, Makawe Rino. My father has spoken of you before."

"Thank you," said Coffin. "Your English is excellent for one so young."

"Of course—and I am not so young!" Dark eyes flashed. "I can learn any language I wish. I can do anything."

"There, you see?" said an exasperated Te Ohine. "Not a bit of modesty or restraint in her. I don't know what I am going

to do with her. As she grows older she becomes more of
a burden."

"Not as much of a burden as Opotiki," she said, finally
shifting her gaze back to her father.

Opotiki. The name resonated in Coffin's mind, coalescing
out of the past. Earlier, happier times. Plump Maori children
playing around a village maypole. One boy in particular.

"Your son."

"Yes, my son."

"Your favorite son," Merita added, not satisfied with her
father's reply.

"Opotiki, yes, I remember him," Coffin said thoughtfully.
"Husky little fellow. I'd enjoy seeing him again. He must be
all grown up by now."

"He is grown, but you would not like to see him." Te
Ohine's tone was full of sadness. "More and more it is painful
to be a man of peace in these times. Opotiki is with Alexander
Rui."

That was a name Coffin knew immediately. Rui was one of
Wiremu Kingi's most bloodthirsty war chiefs. A year ago he'd
split away from Kingi to form his own raiding party. Despite
his Christian first name he'd proved himself among the most
ruthless of the rebels. Unlike many, he had no compunction
about murdering women and children.

And Te Ohine's son fought alongside him.

He tried to sympathize but the old chief was not easily
mollified. The pain this admission cost him was plain to see.
"None of my children will obey me," he moaned. "I am
cursed in my old age."

"That is not so," Merita argued. "Only Opotiki fights the
pakehas. All your other children, even I, follow your lead in
this."

Te Ohine looked down at her. "I wish you were as
reasonable in all things."

She laughed and her laughter became shivers that slid down
Coffin's spine. There was a wildness here he hadn't encountered since his days at sea.

"I'm sorry about that," he heard himself saying. "I hope we
do not have to fight Alexander Rui's men."

"It does not matter," said Te Ohine. "You would not
recognize Opotiki. It might be that he would kill you first." He

shook his head, old before his time. "Too much killing. Friends slaying friends."

They talked awhile longer, Merita sitting silently nearby. It was an effort for Coffin to address himself to his old friend. They discussed the weather as well as the war, what the future might hold for both of them, how the crops were doing. To everything Merita listened intently, as though she were incapable of relaxing.

It struck Coffin that in spite of what she'd said she might well be a spy for the Kingites, relaying information on troop movements while traveling under her father's banner of neutrality. Hadn't she admitted her brother was a rebel? No, he decided. Subterfuge was not this woman's way. If she wanted to oppose the pakehas she would have picked up a gun and joined Rui's band herself. She was not in any way—domestic.

As Coffin prepared to leave they shared a final drink and toast.

"It was good to see you again, old friend." Te Ohine shook Coffin's hand. The conversation and visit, remembrance of better times, had rejuvenated him. His voice had deepened, his expression improved.

"Very good." Merita had risen with them. "I will be ready in a moment."

"Ready?" Coffin smiled ingenuously at her. "Ready for what?"

Again that hungry stare. He was more than half a foot taller than her but felt as though he was gazing into the eyes of an equal. "I am going with you. Since it seems I am not to be married to anyone worthwhile, I have determined to seek my fortune among the pakehas. With what better pakeha than the famous Makawe Rino?"

"Hold on, girl. I haven't said anything about. . . ."

"You were not asked." She favored him with a taunting, teasing smile. "I made the decision."

"Did you? Suppose I refuse to have you along?"

"Then I will follow behind your army until you change your mind. I will haunt you until your guilt demands you take me into your service."

"I do not suffer from guilt."

"Do you not, Makawe Rino?" She was teasing him with more than her smile. Had she already sensed the weakness he wasn't prepared to admit?

As if that weren't enough, Te Ohine spoke up eagerly. "Yes, yes, take her into your household, old friend. Give her work to do, teach her obedience if you can. She is useless to me. Perhaps she will take orders from you."

"Who knows?" she said coquettishly.

"Make a proper daughter of her and you will forever have my gratitude," Te Ohine went on. "If she disobeys you, you must beat her. But be warned: she is fast and hard to catch."

"No." Coffin felt as if he were standing outside himself watching characters performing in a play, unable to affect the course of action. Drama, he mused, or farce? "No, I won't beat her."

"There, you see?" She turned a quick little circle. The strands of her skirt went flying, revealing slices of smooth brown flesh between. "I've learned something already. I have little to bring with me." Quick as a butterfly she vanished through the rear flaps of the tent.

Te Ohine watched her, turned back to Coffin. "Teach her pakeha ways, old friend, and forgive me for keeping my intentions secret. What she learns from you will help her if we lose this war."

"You still think Kingi and the others have a real chance to throw the pakeha out of Aotearoa?"

"My mind knows this cannot happen, but," and he hesitated out of deference to a good friend, "my heart tells me all is possible for a Maori warrior. Bear that always in mind, my friend. It may preserve you when those around you are dying."

"I'll take care." He struggled not to stare at the canvas portal through which Merita had disappeared. "I'm not one of those ignorant pakehas who underestimates the fighting ability of the Maori. Not many of the soldiers do either. Not anymore. Most of those who did are dead. I thought this would be a short war."

Te Ohine shook his head. "As I have told you, it will go on as long as there are those who would rather fight than farm. If you have learned anything about my people you must know there are thousands of warriors so inclined."

"I know it all too well."

The old chief turned to regard the back of the tent. "She is very strange, my daughter. You will have to be patient with her, though it is hard sometimes. She will not have her face tattooed but neither does she accept the Christian god. I do not know what she is, my friend, whether pakeha or Maori or something of her own choosing. Do not let her deceive you with her appearance."

"What?" Coffin was startled.

"You see she is beautiful. Do not let that prevent you from making her work. She said she can do anything. This I have come to believe. She can sew and wash and cook and till a field. All these things she does well, but only if she wants to. It is good when marching to war to have a woman to look after such things."

"Yes. Yes, that's so." Any man, be he soldier, volunteer, or Oxford-educated officer would take one look at Te Ohine's panther of a daughter and make his own inferences about the services she would provide. But that was all she was going to do, Coffin told himself firmly. He would take her along because everyone seemed powerless to prevent it, but only as a favor to Te Ohine. As for himself, he had a wonderful wife waiting for him back home. There would be rumors, inevitably. Robert Coffin of Coffin House could stand aloof from such gossip. He knew exactly how he was going to handle it.

The only thing he could not be sure of was how Merita was going to handle it.

2

There was plenty of whispering at first, as expected. Not because Coffin had chosen to take on a servant but because that servant was a young woman of extraordinary beauty. But as the campaign continued and Coffin's friends saw Merita doing only cleaning and cooking and washing, the talk died down and the insinuating speculation along with it.

Te Ohine had been right: Merita was efficient, clean, and thorough. She always seemed to be the first one in camp to awake and would not go to sleep no matter how tired until she had polished the last of his clothing. There was only one problem. He tried to ignore it and, finally failing, decided to confront it head on.

She was washing out socks when he found her. Bending over the wash basin thrust her backside up and out toward him, as smooth and perfect a curve as a mathematician's proof of some higher theorem. He swallowed and moved around in front of her. As he did so she looked up and smiled. The thin top she wore was soaked with soap and water and clung to her breasts.

"Merita, you're going to have to change your clothing."

"My clothing?" She looked down at herself, wringing out a sock. Water trickled into the basin. "What's wrong with my clothing?"

"Nothing's wrong with it." He offered what he hoped was a paternal smile. "It's just that there isn't enough of it."

"Isn't—ah, I understand." She looked at him sideways. "Don't you like to look at me?"

"Damnation, girl, are you always so direct?"

"So father tells me."

His voice fell farther than he intended. "Of course I like to look at you. There isn't a man alive who wouldn't want to look at you. That's the problem. You're distracting half the army,

256

parading around like that. If I didn't know better I'd think you were a secret weapon planted by the Kingites, to keep our pickets from watching the forest and hills." She giggled and rose. Her breasts thrust out at him from behind their thin cotton covering.

"But I like to wear this!" She executed a quick pirouette which sent the strands of dried reed she wore for a skirt swirling up as high as her waist.

Coffin deliberately looked away, anywhere else but at her. "I know you enjoy the freedom, but if you're going to stay in my service you've got to learn to wear European clothes."

"Pui!" She was pouting now. "All that clothing!"

"You'll get used to it, and when winter comes you'll be glad of it. We're going through Pemberton tomorrow. There'll be a store there and we'll find you some dresses or something."

"If you insist." Her eyes flashed defiantly. "But I will not wear any of those ridiculous undergarments the pakeha women bind themselves with. I'd rather you tied me up."

"That won't be necessary." What he didn't add was that if he insisted she wear a corset, he would be forced to show her how to put it on and take it off, and he knew any lingering physical contact would be more than dangerous.

With the aid of a saleswoman they found Merita a couple of plain print dresses. Coffin breathed easier until he saw her returning from a stream where she'd gone to get water. In filling her bucket she'd managed to get half again as much water on herself, with the result that the dress clung stickily to every curve of her body. The result was twice as tantalizing as what she'd worn previously. Coffin could only sigh and turn away, and hope his men would do the same.

Months into the campaign, Coffin found a surprise waiting in his tent. As he entered, a tall, slim young man turned to greet him with a familiar shy smile.

"Hello, Father."

"Christopher!" Coffin embraced his son affectionately, hugging him hard before standing at arm's length to look him up and down. "You still don't eat enough, boy."

"Father, I'm twenty-four and you're still calling me 'boy.'"

"You're right, you're right." He gave his son a last hug, then directed him to the small folding table that was set up in the center of the tent. "I won't do it again. Sit here. Will you have a drink? A little brandy would be good. There's a chill in the air already."

Christopher took the indicated seat. "I'd like that. It's going to be an early winter, Mr. Goldman says. Will that be good or bad?"

"Both. Good because the fighting will slow. Bad because we haven't caught Rui or Kingi or any of the other important Kingite leaders." He yelled to his right. "Merita! Company! Bring the brandy!"

"It's not going well then? Back in Auckland you're afraid to believe what you hear."

"Then believe half. That much is usually true." Coffin grinned, overwhelmed with delight at the unexpected visit. "Maybe Rui and the rest are still free, but we're wearing them down, Son, we're wearing them down. Took a bunch of the dirty buggers just the other day. Stoke thinks we're closing in on Rui's main force. Of course, he's been saying that for weeks. Just when you think you've got them trapped, you wake up to find they're burning fields in the next province over." He shook his head. "There's never been a war like this, Christopher. But we'll hold on, press 'em hard. So long as we do that the rest of the Maoris will refuse to join the rebellion. Eventually they'll lose heart."

"How long is eventually, Father?"

Coffin sat back in his seat. "I don't know. No one knows. You can't make predictions when your tactics and strategies change from day to day. The Maoris don't stand still. They're always probing us, looking for a weakness." He leaned forward again and lowered his voice. "I'll tell you one thing you keep to yourself. If Gold hadn't brought in artillery I'm not sure it wouldn't be the Maoris pressing the attack now instead of us." He straightened and shouted a second time.

"Merita, dammit! Where's that brandy?"

She entered carrying a tray with bottle and glasses. Christopher's eyes locked on her, following every step. It neither surprised nor troubled Coffin. She had that effect on every man seeing her for the first time. She wore no jewelry and her rippling black hair was combed and bound in back. Beneath the thin dress her body moved fluidly.

"Merita, meet my son, Christopher."

Christopher rose half out of his chair, nodded awkwardly.

Merita replied with a curtsey. She'd been practicing, Coffin noted approvingly. This time she didn't stumble.

She put the tray on the table and stepped back. "Will there be anything else, Mr. Coffin sir?"

"No, Merita. You can retire for now."

"Yes sir." She was trying to be utterly formal and failing utterly. Her mischievous eyes burned into him as she curtsied again. She flashed her smile at Christopher and turned to sweep out of the tent.

"Who," said Christopher, still dazed, "was *that*?"

"A servant girl. She was given to me by chief Te Ohine, an old friend from my Kororareka days."

"I remember you speaking of him."

Coffin nodded toward the back of the tent. "His daughter. She's a hard worker." Christopher nodded. "And rather attractive."

"Attractive! Father, she's—I wish I was better with words."

Coffin poured until both glasses were half full. "She does have an effect on people, doesn't she? She does all my cleaning and cooking, looks after my gear very efficiently." His gaze came up sharply. "That's *all* she does. Her father wanted her to enter pakeha service in the hope she'd learn some discipline. She's very independent. If she wanted to I've no doubt she'd up and leave tomorrow and nothing I or her father or anyone else could do or say would make her stay. She's not as pretty as some, though. Your mother when she was the same age, for example," he half-lied.

"At least you're being well looked after." Christopher sipped at the brandy. "Mother worries about you being so long on the march. I do too, you know."

"Do I look ill? I'm fine, son, just fine. Never felt better. How goes Coffin House?"

Christopher sounded slightly embarrassed. "Well enough, I should say."

Coffin knew his son was being unduly modest. "More than that, according to the reports I receive." He chuckled. "Poor old Tobias frets that his employees will steal him blind while he's off fighting Kingites, while I can relax in the knowledge that you and Elias are looking after things as well as I could myself. Hull can't leave to check on his commerce because he'd risk accusations of cowardice. I've seen him rant and rave when some messenger brings him news of doings in Wellington or Auckland. His face fairly crawls with frustration."

"You shouldn't enjoy another's misery so much, Father," Christopher chided him. "I know you and Tobias Hull were never friends, but don't you think this feud's lasted long enough?"

"You can't make up and be friends with a man like Hull." Coffin knocked back the rest of his brandy, refilled his glass. "Oh, you could try, fake the appearance of it. The old devil's an expert at grinning and fawning. Ten years later you'd discover he'd bought you out or sold you blind. No, it's better this way. Each of us knows where the other man stands. It's an honest relationship, even if it is founded on something other than love and kisses."

"I'll be damned, Father, if I don't think you two *enjoy* hating one another."

"Hate?" Coffin was surprised. "There's no hate involved. An active dislike, surely. Hate involves a lack of rationality, and neither Tobias Hull nor myself is an irrational man." The warm imported brandy left a trail of fire as it slid down his throat. "It's the spirit of competition that keeps Hull and me apart. Because we know that we're the best, the cleverest. If Hull wasn't around to keep my wits sharp, life would lose its edge. If we truly hated each other in the way you think, we wouldn't be able to fight together against the Kingites, though it's true we have our little disagreements on tactics. Hull, for example, would rather treat the rebels much as Alexander Rui treats his captives. He has to be watched constantly or we'd never take any prisoners.

"Enough of Hull. What of yourself and your mother? What of home? Tell me everything." He leaned forward eagerly.

Christopher talked on, of friends and gossip, of the good life in the city. When his father finally steered the conversation around to matters of business, Christopher produced detailed reports written in Elias Goldman's methodical hand. Goldman's figures were as near to print quality as human fingers could produce.

"Wonderful, excellent." Coffin finally put the sheaf of reports aside. "I hesitate to say it, but this endless war's been good to us."

Christopher nodded. "We've certainly made money these

past few years. People have needed to import more, since they can't trade with the natives."

Coffin nodded admiringly. "You've learned fast and well, Christopher. I can't tell you what a blessing and joy you've been to me. Your work frees me to pursue these rebels with a clear mind."

"We still miss your judgement and shrewdness, Father."

"No, no." Coffin waved a hand. "You and Elias have done as well as if I'd been there or not."

"Well—I *have* learned a lot. Mr. Goldman's a marvelous teacher."

"Yes. I don't know what I'd have done without Elias these past years. He's been my strong left arm. And now you're to be my right one."

"So you find that the business has been well looked after?"

"How could anyone think otherwise after looking at these?" Coffin held up the pile of reports.

"And that Elias has done properly in your absence?"

Coffin eyed his son uncertainly. "Haven't I been saying that all along?"

"Good. Because, Father, I need to help with the war. It's time. It's more than time. If my presence would make you uncomfortable I'll join one of the other regiments. Major Thierry has already offered me a commission."

It grew cold in the tent. "Christopher, I don't. . . ."

"Listen to me, Father!" Christopher rose and began pacing the narrow confines of the canvas shelter. "Every man of my age and station strolls about Auckland in uniform. All the girls fawn over them."

"If it's women you want, son, of any status—you have money, position, power, and you're not unattractive to look upon."

"It's not that, Father. It's what they say, the way they talk about me." He was almost pleading.

"What do you mean?" Coffin asked darkly.

Christopher took a deep breath. "I mean that I'm the only man of my position and age who hasn't participated in at least one expedition. There's talk—there are people who say I'm a coward."

"No Coffin is a coward!" Aware how absurd it was to be shouting when only he and Christopher were present to hear, Coffin hastily calmed himself. "It's ridiculous! Everyone knows that in my absence you've taken charge of Coffin House."

"But don't you see, Father? That's just it." Christopher leaned forward, resting both hands on the table as he stared down at the older man. "I don't *have* to run it. Mr. Goldman is there. He knows more about the business than I ever will, and he has men of his own to help him. I need to fight, Father. I don't feel right riding home every night in that fancy carriage, taking tea with Mother's friends while everyone I know is off helping. Look at me, Father." He straightened proudly.

"For the first time in my life I'm completely healthy. Even the doctors say so, and you know how they vacillate over such things. Of course, Mother still persists in treating me like an invalid, but I haven't had a spell or attack in over a year and a half. I have to participate, Father. I *have* to. Otherwise I'll have no friends left when this war is over."

Coffin couldn't meet the younger man's gaze. "You're no soldier, Christopher."

"Who was, before this war began? I'm not good with a sword, but I'm an excellent shot and a decent horseman." He lowered his voice. "You know what else they say?"

"No, what?" Still Coffin didn't look up.

"They say that the presence of another Coffin would be good for the morale of the colonial troops."

Coffin couldn't keep himself from smiling. "I've no doubt it would, but I can't give my approval, Christopher. You're too valuable where you are. You must understand that. I know it's difficult for you."

"It isn't fair, Father. I can't stand aside while my friends are fighting and dying. Besides, I can speak Maori, which makes me doubly valuable. Yet I spend my time sitting home drinking tea and listening to the pianoforte, when I'm not behind a desk totaling figures. It isn't right."

"Of course it is." Coffin rose and came around the table to put his arm around his son's narrow shoulders. "The future of the colony depends as much on keeping commerce going, on maintaining the flow of supplies and war material, as it does on the actual fighting. We need generals in logistics as badly as we do in the field. We're more in danger of being starved out by the Maoris than we are of being beaten by them in combat. Business must be kept going, lines of communication kept open. If the colony's commerce is left to men like Hull, we'll have little to return to when the war is over.

"Don't you see? This way we wage a war on two fronts. You're sort of a quartermaster general, seeing to the health and well-being of the colony, protecting their interests against raptors like Hull. That's vital, Christopher. Absolutely vital." He stood back, studied his son earnestly. "Can you understand that?"

Christopher was clearly confused. He'd gone over what he intended to say to his father numerous times, until he was confident of his reasoning. As always, his father had out-maneuvered him. He'd been so sure of what he wanted before he'd arrived. Now he no longer was.

"I don't know. I hadn't considered it that way."

"It isn't easy because it isn't obvious. That's the way war really is, son. Confusing as it is complex. Keep to your work in Auckland. Only you can do that. There are plenty of others to wave sabers and pistols at the rebels but none to take your position."

"Maybe you're right, Father. Maybe."

"Of course I'm right!" Coffin fought to conceal his relief. "You'll stay the night. Merita's a fine cook and she's learning how to use spices and pakeha utensils. I'll tell her there'll be two for supper. Tomorrow you can accompany us awhile, get a taste of what life on the march is really like. There's no glamor in it, son, you'll see. No glory. Just cold and fear and dirt. As soon as you see what it's like I think you'll be glad to rid yourself of these unreasonable thoughts. Though you will," he added with a twinkle in his eyes, "have the consolation of looking at Merita for another day."

Christopher managed to smile at that. Thanks to the brandy, father and son were soon laughing steadily and easily. Their conversation on the road the following day was relaxed and inconsequential. Christopher made no further mention of wanting to join the militia. Coffin plied him with additional liquor later that evening. When the two men parted, it was respectfully and with affection. Christopher continued waving to his father until at last the night swallowed him up.

Robert Coffin had always been able to hold his liquor against any man, but when he finally retired he found he was having trouble removing his boots. He'd enjoyed Christopher's company so much he'd overindulged in his private stock of spirits.

Ah, well. It was good to celebrate something. Been a long time since he'd relaxed so completely. If his old sailing mates could see him now, weaving unsteadily on his feet like a tidewater rum-besotted bum, they'd split their sides laughing.

Taking a deep, deliberate breath he focused intently on his feet, managed to remove the first boot. The second he kicked clear across the tent. He removed his jacket and shirt and let them fall indifferently to the ground. With a sigh he slid beneath the blankets that covered his field bed.

His fellow officers perferred to sleep in undergarments or dressing gowns, not only to ward off the night chill but in the event the Maoris were to attack after sundown. The cool air invigorated Coffin, and in all the time he'd been battling the Kingites they had yet to attack at night. Didn't anyone realize the rebels had to sleep as well? Besides, in the event they proved him wrong he had no compunctions about fighting in the nude.

The heavy blankets were a luxury reserved for officers, who could afford to have baggage carried. He lay wondering what time it was. The moon cast its diffuse light through the material of the tent, but not enough for him to read the face of his pocket watch. No matter. An orderly would wake him in time to dress for the march, or Merita would.

As he tossed and turned beneath the blankets, unable to get comfortable, it seemed he saw her close by. Saw her not as she was but as he always imagined her to be. She was clad only in a filmy robe of lace, a gift from him to keep her modesty intact at night. As he'd learned right away, she had no inhibitions whatsoever. If he'd let her move about at night or in the early morning hours stark naked there would have been riots among the troops.

She seemed to be staring down at him, silent, her form silhouetted by the pale moonlight shining through the tent's ceiling. Then the robe was slipping from her shoulders, down her arms, her upper body, her hips, to form a silver-tinged lace puddle around her feet, a swirling base for the statue she'd become. He was breathing hard, painfully, even though he knew it was but a dream. Knew it was a dream because there was another figure in the tent with her. A tall, elderly shape that stared expressionlessly at him as it leaned on a carved wooden staff.

He ignored the other figure and as he did so it dissolved. The dream-shape of Merita had moved closer and he could see nothing else beyond her. But he could think, and he could compare.

Holly. Holly had a fine figure, but she was not Merita. No one was, for a body like this was not of this Earth. It belonged on Olympus among the other gods. Merita was perfect, an ideal made flesh. As he stared fixedly at the vision she presented he felt both lust and fear, fear to touch such beauty lest it too dissolve and go the way of the old man.

Sheets and blankets were eased aside. Cold night air shocked his exposed skin. Then a torch was pressed against him, burning. Arms slid around him like pythons to hold and grasp him tightly. Wet heat covered his mouth as she moved atop him. She took one of his hands and pressed it hard between her legs.

After that he could think no more. All the rest of that night he remembered, and yet none of it.

3

Neither of them spoke when morning woke them together. There was no need to speak, not when expressions and sideways glances spoke more eloquently than could any mere words. From then on she came to him every night. Sometimes only to sleep, warm and soft against him. More often to make love in explosive yet silent passion. Auckland suddenly seemed as far from this war-torn country with its dense forests and smoking ground as Sydney or London.

When they encountered Kingites there was fighting, usually brief and inconsequential. The Maoris would attack, do what damage they could, and then retreat before the army could inflict a fatal blow. The column crisscrossed the central highlands, skirting brilliant blue lakes and somber mountains until winter began to set in in earnest and heavy rains made roads impassable to wagons. The Maoris retreated to their secret pas as the militia returned to their homes, leaving the pursuit of the Kingites to the regular army. Coffin lingered as long as he dared, until the new problem which now dominated his life could no longer be put off.

They stood together on the outskirts of the town of Taurangi, overlooking the vast freshwater sea known as Lake Taupo, and time refused to stand still for them.

"I could come back to Auckland with you." Merita took his hand in hers and leaned against him, staring out across the water. "I will not go back to my father."

Coffin gazed down at her. Save for hair the color of night and her coffee-colored skin she could have been the most beautiful debutante at any royal ball. Any of these past days could have brought death at the point of spear or musket, yet they were the most relaxed and contented he'd ever known. Now it was at an end. He could no longer put off returning to Auckland through the gray clouds and haze that lay to the

266

north. Already he'd stayed too long, risking pointed questions from friends and fellow officers.

"I could live in your house as your maid. I know the rich pakehas do such things. Your wife need not know."

He smiled fondly. "You don't understand the effect you have on men. Women are aware of such things too, even pakeha women. My wife would see immediately. Every time you passed me: in the parlor, helping with dinner, making a bed, the truth would show in my eyes. I might as well walk about wearing a written confession."

"Then what will become of us?"

"I've been thinking on that. I won't ask you to go back to your father. I can no more give you up than I can give up breathing." He stretched out one arm toward the lake.

"You know where Tarawera is?" She nodded. "I have a large home there, on the shore of the lake. It's not as big as the house in Auckland but it's large enough. We don't live there. We only visit sometimes when the weather is bad in the city. A big place like that needs constant attention. I've been hiring local people to look after it. I don't need to any longer." He turned her around to face him.

"From now on it'll be your house, Merita. Our house."

She clapped her hands together like a child. "A house of my own! What a wonderful idea!" She threw her arms around his shoulders and jumped on him, her legs wrapping around his hips. "Our house, Robert, yes, our house!"

"Easy, easy." He couldn't keep himself from putting his arms around her in return while simultaneously glancing over a shoulder to make sure no one else was watching. "There's a man there, a priest named Spencer. He's a good friend. He's married and has children. I don't think you'll overwhelm him quite as easily as you would some others. If you need any help, ask him. I'll set up an account for you to draw upon for household expenses and you'll be able to spend all the money you want without attracting attention. I'm afraid that to maintain the fiction you'll actually have to do some house-work."

"But I would do that in any case. I'm very good at it, you know."

"So I've noticed. You'll be mistress of the house."

"Not only of the house," she reminded him with a low growl.

"No; not only of the house." He pressed his lips to hers, feeling her whole being respond as passionately as it had that first time months earlier.

It would work. There'd be no trouble. Far from Auckland and its gossip they would be safe. What more natural, after all, than that out of the goodness of his heart he should agree to take a young Maori maiden into his service in order to please her father, his old friend?

He glanced skyward. "Maybe the weather will clear a little. I have to start back. You know that."

"I know, Robert." She slid away from him. "I would not be the one to keep you from your life's work."

He put his hand under her chin and lifted her face so he could look into her eyes. "I think that my life's work is going to require many trips into the interior."

Her lips split in a wide grin, teeth bright against her dark skin. "I will live for such visits. In your company I will be forever young. Whenever you come you will find me ready and waiting for you. I will be there whenever you need me, Robert." She looked down and patted her belly. "We both will."

"You're sure?"

She nodded. "Soon I will get big and ugly."

He laughed. "Merita, ugliness flees from you like mullet from a shark. You couldn't be ugly if you tried." He hugged her again—gently this time. "Our child will grow up in our house."

"What shall I tell him of his father, when he is old enough to want to know?"

Coffin frowned. "Nothing of his father. That cannot be, for the foreseeable future anyway. I will be his 'uncle' until such time as he can be told."

"I understand."

"I knew you would. I'll be as much a father to him as I can, Merita. Or to her."

"It will be a boy. It was foretold."

"Foretold?" he said idly. "By whom? A relative?"

"No. When I was very young, it was said my firstborn would be a boy. I do not know who foretold it for my mother and father. A tohunga, I suppose."

"Yes. It would be a tohunga."

Of course it would, he mused. That was part of a tohunga's

job. Natural and to be expected. So why then was he suddenly so cold?

"I'll visit every chance I get," he told her, suddenly anxious to be on his way. It was said spirits dwelt in Lake Taupo. "And if this damnable war ends soon I'll come more often than that."

4

But the war did not end soon. Though he visited as frequently as he could, Coffin's brief stays could not fill all of Merita's lonely hours, all of her empty nights.

There was the baby to busy her, when he came. A boy, as she'd known it would be. And the house. It was bigger than any building she'd ever seen, though Mrs. Spencer told her stories of much larger structures, and showed her pictures in books. Not a cobweb, not a speck of dust escaped Merita's lethal broom.

It was spring again and still Alexander Rui and Wiremu Kingi hid from the vengeful pakeha army, striking when and where they pleased. She'd just finished cleaning the downstairs when she noticed the singular pakeha standing by the front gate. He was staring at the house, only partly concealed by the newly planted rose bushes.

This young man should be in the fighting, she thought as she studied him. Certainly he looked strong and healthy enough. He appeared to be about her own age, though he might have been older. With pakehas it was hard to tell. There were lines in his face that hinted at knowledge beyond his years, but there were many such young men traveling in Aotearoa these days. War aged them quickly.

She thought she heard a sound from upstairs, turned to listen, then looked back toward the fence. Andrew slept soundly, as usual. He was almost a year old now. None of the pakehas in Te Wairoa knew who his father was, of course. As for the Maoris, they did not press such questions, it being none of their business. How fortunate she was, without a father for the child, to have such a fine position in so important a household!

She returned to her work and only later thought to look again at the fence. To her surprise the young man was still there. He hadn't moved. She found herself admiring his lean muscularity, hastily shut down that line of thought lest it carry her in dangerous directions. It was only her loneliness. It had been quite a while since Robert's last visit.

If he stood there much longer, though, he was going to make her nervous. Deserters from both the Maori and pakeha armies wandered the countryside, committing the occasional theft or murder.

What was this? Was she not Merita, daughter of the great Te Ohine? How could she be afraid of one lone pakeha? Straining, she could see he carried neither rifle or sword. True, the big house was isolated, alone atop its hill overlooking the lake, but she still thought she could make enough noise to be heard by the Maori fisherman whose family had a small house not far up the shore.

In any event, she wasn't going to spend the rest of the day with him standing there, mooning at her house.

Putting aside her dustmop she went into the den and took Robert's lightest hunting rifle from the gun cabinet. She loaded and checked it the way he'd shown her to, then headed for the front door. Halfway down the porch steps outside she stopped, holding the rifle firmly in both hands.

"All right! You've seen the house. You've been looking long enough to memorize every board and nail. If you've a place to go I think you better go there." She gestured down the road with the rifle's muzzle.

The young stranger looked back and smiled, tipping the large wide-brimmed hat he wore. The pack on his back didn't look like the type normally carried by displaced persons. When he replied she noted his tone was educated without being formal.

"Sorry, miss. Didn't mean to upset you. Do me a favor and put the gun aside? I've seen too many guns these past years. I assure you I intend no harm." He looked up and past her. He certainly was fascinated with the house, she thought. "Can you tell me if this is the house of Robert Coffin?"

"It might be," she replied guardedly.

Once more he lapsed into staring silence. She began to wonder if he might be sick in the head. Not all the injuries suffered in the war damaged only arms and legs. He walked toward the front gate, his attention still fixed on the house.

His preoccupation with the building bothered her. She was

more beautiful in her maturity than she'd been when Coffin had first met her, or so she'd been told. It was said there wasn't a man in New Zealand who could pass her without turning to stare. Yet this young man was ignoring her. Initial fears gave way to piqued vanity.

As if suddenly realizing he was being impolite, the stranger looked back at her. One hand rested on the gate, toying idly with the latch. He stood there framed in the wooden archway, flanked by pink and yellow roses.

"I'm terribly sorry. I don't mean to upset you."

"What makes you think you upset me?"

Instead of answering, he rambled on. "I've been on the road for some time. As you can see, I've no horse, though my purse is full. I was traveling to the west and thought to pass by Tarawera." He nodded at the house. "Architecture interests me and I'd heard about this place. It equals its reputation." He sighed and took his hand off the latch. "I guess I've lingered too long."

He seemed to debate with himself, then looked back up at her. "Could I trouble you for a bit of food and water? I've had nothing to eat for a day."

Again she gestured with the rifle. "There's a mission in Te Wairoa. The Reverend Spencer will feed you."

The young man looked in the direction she was pointing. "How far?"

A ways, she almost said. How fatigued was he? If he hadn't eaten in that long—what if he collapsed before reaching the mission? She tried to see behind deep blue eyes.

"Never mind. I can give you something to drink, at least. Come in. But I warn you, the Reverend is due here any minute now, and if you've anything more than food or drink in mind. . . ."

He laughed as he opened the gate and stepped onto the gravel path, which led through her meticulously kept garden. "I'm not one to abuse another's hospitality. Besides, you have a gun."

"Just remember that." She retreated to the porch. He was a shade under six feet tall, she noted, and those eyes were so blue they were almost purple.

"What might your name be, miss?"

"Merita. I'm the caretaker here for Mr. Coffin when he's living in Auckland. He's a very important man."

Her visitor nodded. "Everyone's heard of Coffin House."

He was closer than she intended him to get, she suddenly realized, just as it struck her she'd been doing some staring of her own. The broad hat had shaded much of his face, masking his true handsomeness. Up close there was a fierceness about him not evident from a distance, but she wasn't afraid. His smile was genuine. She moved toward the open door, lowering the rifle but not putting it aside.

"I think we can find you some cold mutton, and bread. There may be some sausage as well."

"I'd appreciate that more than I can say, miss. I'll pay, of course."

"Nonsense! Reverend Spencer would never forgive me."

"As you will. I'd wager you're as good at cooking as you are at defending your master's property."

She winced slightly at the word. "Master" was a pakeha term she'd barely learned to tolerate in the presence of Coffin's guests. Leaving the front door ajar she watched him as he studied the crystal chandelier, the broad stairway that led to the second floor, the woodwork and the paintings on the walls.

"A fine house," he was murmuring to himself. "Befits a man like Robert Coffin."

She brushed past him. "The kitchen's back this way." She deliberately passed close enough so that he could have made a grab for the rifle, but he made no move of any kind. The lingering tenseness went out of her. "What's your name, traveler?"

He smiled again; an open, disarming smile. "Kinnegad. Flynn Kinnegad."

Such an intense young man, she thought as she watched him. Too intense, too direct for a thief. As intense as his interest in architecture, for as they made their way back to the kitchen he noted every bit of ornamentation, every piece of furniture and scrollwork. Surely he would relax in the kitchen, but to her surprise he seemed as interested in the common furnishings and utensils as he'd been in the expensive vases and watercolors.

"Over there." She pointed to the small wooden table where the servants ate. Taking a seat, he doffed his pack and set it down carefully.

Eventually he'd inspected everything in the kitchen. Only

then did his attention return to her. And about time, too, she mused crossly.

She was used to men staring at her, but the longer he did so the more she grew aware this was different. It was unsettling: not threatening, but disquieting in a manner she couldn't identify. She set food and drink before him, expecting him to dive into it with all the grace of a hog at the trough. Again he surprised her. Hungry he obviously was, but he ate slowly and with good, if not elegant, manners, chewing slowly for someone who hadn't eaten in a day.

"I suppose you've come to the Tarawera District to see the Pink and White Terraces." These were, she'd been told by European visitors, the two most spectacular hot spring formations in the whole world, unsurpassed in their size and beauty. Across the lake, water that ranged from tepid to boiling tumbled in magnificently colored cascades down pure limestone, leaving behind frozen waterfalls and mirror-like travertine pools, until at last seeping into the cool blue water of the lake itself.

"I've heard of them," he said around a mouthful of bread. "I would like to see them, but that's not really why I've come this way."

"You said you were traveling west. What's your ultimate destination?"

He had a maddening habit of not replying directly to her questions, instead poured himself another glass of well water. "What are you journeying for?"

He shrugged. "I'm just seeing the country. I've been all over North Island and much of South. Been to Australia, too."

"I've heard of Australia. There are no Maoris there."

"That's right. Just slim people black as the button on your dress."

She glanced down at the button in question, then back up at him. "Not really? Black?"

He nodded somberly. "With hair like sheep's wool and broad flat noses. Some say they can talk to the Earth. Their music makes men shiver and they run about more naked than the first Maoris. They live in the middle of a land so dry it never rains there, a place where you or I would die in a few days." He looked down at his glass, suddenly troubled. "The pakehas there treat them very badly."

"Are the pakehas everywhere? We Maoris have only

Aotearoa. If the pakehas would only understand that, this war would stop."

"I agree with you."

"But you are a pakeha."

He looked up sharply. "Not all pakehas are bad. You work for one, don't you?" She had to nod at that. "One of the sad things is that there are a lot of Maoris and pakehas who just like to fight."

Such a strange man, she thought. One moment he appears rough and crude, the next educated and experienced. Then the import of what he'd mentioned so casually finally sank home.

"You mean you have been walking all around the islands for a long time?"

"Several years now."

She gazed at him in astonishment. "You should be dead. Shot by Maoris or by pakehas who would consider you a deserter."

"I keep to myself and I like the woods. I'm as at home in the forest as the city. I've sold the location of Maori hide-outs to pakeha scouts. I've watched the pakeha army on the march and given knowledge of its course to Maori warriors."

"I do not understand. Who do you support?"

"Both. Neither. I view the whole stupid confrontation with sublime indifference." For an instant his expression darkened so terribly that she was frightened. It vanished as abruptly as it had appeared. "You see, I have my own wars to fight. I can't be bothered with the foolish concerns of settlers and chiefs." He smiled at her again, that wonderful reassuring smile, and she relaxed.

"Too much talk of war when there's so little peace," she finished.

She found work to occupy her hands if not her mind, standing at the sink. "I do not understand you. You've been many places. Where is your home?"

She thought that fury so briefly glimpsed might return, but he calmed himself. "My home is wherever I happen to be at the moment."

"Well, where is your family, then? Your mother and father?"

"My mother died six years ago. Syphilis. A white man's disease. Not a pretty death."

Merita had seen people die of that dreaded affliction and shuddered for him. "I am sorry."

"Thank you," he replied with dignity. "My sister was killed at the battle for Haore. As for my father, he died a long time ago."

Merita was saddened. The Maori sense of family was stronger than that of the pakeha because in addition to close relatives every Maori child was also part of a whanau, an extended family grouping. The pakehas did not have whanaus, which meant this young traveler was denied even that little comfort.

He noticed her expression. "Don't sorrow for me. I've learned to live with my fate. In these times I'm not the only one without family left."

"That is so." She scrubbed harder at the pan she was cleaning. "I do wish this war would stop! But who cares what someone like me says."

"I care," he said quietly.

She smiled back at him. "That's very kind of you."

Most of the meat, bread and cheese she'd placed on the table had vanished. He leaned back and sipped at his water. "This Coffin must be rich."

"Oh yes!" She was delighted to shift the conversation to more pleasant topics. "He's the richest man in New Zealand, I think."

"When I entered I thought I heard a child upstairs. His?" He'd risen from his chair and was walking around the kitchen, studying details again.

Merita hesitated at the unexpected question. "Of course not," she finally lied. "It's mine. The father is—a soldier. An officer. A good man."

"Everyone's a soldier these days." But he didn't inquire further. It would not have been polite.

Instead he asked casual questions about the house and grounds. She followed him and answered as best she was able, until quite unexpectedly he turned sharply on her. During the conversation they'd moved closer and closer, until she was barely inches from him. Now his face was very near, those bottomless eyes locked onto hers.

"This Coffin—is he good to you?"

"Good? To me?" She was so shocked by his impertinence

she could hardly reply. "I just look after his house. If you mean does he pay me well, I am comfortable here."

"I'm glad to hear that." His hand was on her shoulder and she felt it through her dress, searing into her skin. "It's obvious you're not starving."

She pulled away from him, wondering even as she did so why she didn't strike him. "If you've had enough to eat and drink you'd best be on your way. The Reverend Spencer will be here soon and he might find your presence awkward." She was breathing hard and fast suddenly, not entirely from nervousness.

Slowly, deliberately, he put his glass aside. "Come now," he said challengingly, "surely you're not frightened of me? I doubt anything could frighten you."

"That's right." She spun back to face him, trying to remember where she'd left the rifle. There, in the far corner. But she didn't make a dash for it. He hadn't done anything, had he? "I'm not frightened of anything." She was closer to the rifle than he. A moment later she had it in her grasp.

He stopped. "Are you going to shoot me, then?"

"If I have to. If you make me."

He resumed his slow advance. "I hope I won't." He was close again and she had to look up to see his face.

"Who are you?" she whispered. "What do you want?"

"I'm just a visitor, a friend." His voice was so low she had to strain to make out the words. "One with no home, no family, no place to go and no hurry to get there."

She could have avoided his hand. She could have stepped aside, or moved back, or slapped at it. Instead she stood staring up at him as it brushed her cheek.

"The question, Merita, is what is it you want? This is a big house, an empty house, and if your child's father is a soldier then he's away far more than he's here. Are you married to him?"

"No," she said truthfully even as she wondered why she was answering his questions. "No, we're not married."

"Well then." He moved closer still. Her fingers still gripped the rifle but she no longer thought of raising and aiming it. "As a good guest it behooves me to do my best to repay your hospitality—the only way I can."

Both hands were on her now, one on her cheek, the other

falling to a shoulder. She was breathing so hard she thought her lungs would explode.

"I'll scream."

He grinned slyly at her. "I expect you will. I may myself."

"Kinnegad," she whispered. "You're a devil."

"No." He brought his face down toward hers. "I'm no devil, though if it means anything to you, I'm related to one."

The first time they made love Kinnegad did so out of a desire for revenge. The second time it was to compound the satisfaction.

The third time, later that night in Merita's bed in the maid's room off the kitchen, a maid's room decorated far more lavishly than any maid's room should have been, everything changed.

At first he was furious with himself. This wasn't quite the way it was supposed to be, not the way it was supposed to be at all. He wasn't supposed to get involved in any way, wasn't supposed to feel anything. He had determined long ago not to care. Nothing was supposed to matter. Just as it didn't matter to the bastard sharing Merita's bed whether the bastard upstairs was his father's or not.

He'd been told his father's mistress was beautiful, but the reality was almost too much to bear. His first glimpse of her, standing on the porch with the rifle in her hand, had almost turned him away from the gate, from all his plans. Almost.

Now that he'd achieved his initial goal nothing else seemed to matter as much. He'd anticipated satisfaction and had experienced it, only to find that something new and unexpected had presented itself. Something he hadn't been able to plan for.

It wasn't hard to learn the truth. Not for one as adept with questions as Flynn Kinnegad. He was good at drawing information out of people without them even realizing they were telling him things they'd never tell anyone else. He could both question and listen well.

As he lay contentedly on the bed with Merita sleeping by his side the sun began to peer over the horizon. Everything had changed. His plans, the future, himself. Gently he touched the side of her face. She shifted slightly but did not awake. She'd changed him.

He would deal with it somehow. All his life had been spent in coping with the unexpected, from the time his father had abandoned his mother. He wasn't going to weaken now.

Coffin, he thought. Coffin hadn't been there to see him and his sister Sally cowering in the back of their mother's hovel while drunken seamen did unmentionable things to her. Hadn't been there to see his children growing up in rags, begging in the streets. Hadn't been there when Mary Kinnegad had died writhing in pain from the slow sickness that ravaged her mind and soul as thoroughly as it had her body.

For years Flynn had considered simply confronting Coffin in a public street and shoving a pistol against his heart. As he grew older he realized such a death was far too easy, too quick for such a man. The debt had to be repaid gradually, thoughtfully.

He'd long ago ceased thinking of Robert Coffin as his father. He was simply Coffin. Better that way. Only now did he think of him again, because it made this first small triumph better. Sleeping with his father's mistress was only the beginning.

Merita opened her eyes and gazed up at him. She was open, inviting, enticing and utterly irresistible. Flynn's thirst for revenge remained, but it no longer included this woman. She had seen to that. He had come planning to take her, only to find that he himself had been taken. Whatever there was about her was powerful enough to overcome the hatred that had burned inside him all his life.

She reached for him then and he jerked away. "Good God, woman, have you no shame?"

"None at all." She was grinning wickedly.

"Well, then, at least have some pity." Her hand was moving again.

"All right." She laughed and it filled the room in concert with the rising sun. Then her smile faded and she stared at him meaningfully. "Flynn, my Flynn, what are we to do? Something has happened between us. It will not go away as easily as it happened."

"Do you want it to go away?"

"No, I do not."

"Nor do I." He felt safe in moving to embrace her again. Holding her close brought a warmth and contentment he'd never known. His revenge was important, but it would not spoil this new thing. It was all so confusing. What had seemed simple had become complex. Once so certain of everything, he was suddenly sure of nothing. In a single night Merita had shattered the plans of years.

As always, he thought bitterly, his father had excellent taste.

"You could stay here," she murmured.

"What?" He was so startled he almost let go of her.

"I could create a job for you. The gardening and landscaping has become almost too much for me to take care of by myself, especially with Andrew to look after. Coffin always hires extra help when he's staying here. I am sure I could talk him into taking you on."

"No!" She looked at him in surprise. "I mean," he went on quietly, "there's a better way. I'll get a job, but elsewhere. Somewhere close by. I'm good at a number of things. If I can't find anything in Te Wairoa I know I can in Rotorua."

There was no reason why his father should recognize him, Flynn knew. The last time he'd seen his son Flynn had been an infant. But if they spent time under the same roof Flynn knew there was no way he could keep his identity a secret, anymore than he could control his emotions.

"Rotorua's not that far," he added.

"Too far. Anywhere but here is too far." She kissed him passionately.

"You could come away with me," he suggested when he could finally breathe again.

She sat back and looked uncomfortable. "I almost would, my Flynn. But I've only known you a night and a morning. Nor could I ever find a position as satisfying and well-paying as this one. I make enough to support both of us, if need be."

"I'll take care of myself. If you must stay on here, I'll understand. And it's good to have such a fine place to play in, a grander house than I could ever afford for you. Though perhaps someday. . . ." He stared intently at her. "Maybe someday a house just like this one will be yours in name as well as everything else. A house where others clean and wash for you, where you can receive whomever you please whenever you wish."

"That does not matter. What matters is that you came to me."

"Then I'm content, Merita." He reached for her and she came to him readily, without hesitation. As before when she was in his arms all thoughts of revenge, of his long-held plans, of the future, faded and died.

But only while she was in his arms.

5

Three years, Tobias Hull thought. Three years it had taken to run Alexander Rui to ground, but the hounds had finally cornered the fox. Three long years of traipsing back and forth across North Island, following rumors and fading trails from east to west, north to south. Fighting in dense forests and up mountain slopes, along gray beaches and through bush country hidden by the mists of hot springs. Three years.

This time he wasn't going to get away.

The pa he and his warriors defended backed against a sheer cliff overlooking the sea. While it made his position unapproachable from the east, it also eliminated any possibility of retreat. There was nowhere for the rebels to run.

It'll go differently now, Hull reflected. Not this time would they storm a fortified village at great cost only to discover upon taking it that their quarry had slipped away to freedom yet again. It was true Rui could concentrate all his warriors on the west side of the pa, but if they could take it, the settlers and the army would at last have a real victory.

Other Kingites commanded deeper allegiance among the tribes. Great ariki led larger bands. But none embodied the darkest fears of the colonists like Alexander Rui. There were no Christianized Maoris in his army, though some like himself had taken Christian names. Rui's men worhsiped their old heathen gods and tattooed their faces in the traditional manner. The delight with which they engaged in wholesale butchery and slaughter set them apart from their other war-loving but less brutal kinsmen.

So vile were some of the incidents Rui's men had perpetrated in the three years of war that even many of his fellow Kingites shunned him. Others whispered that Rui wasn't pure Maori, that in fact he was largely Melanesian, child of a family that had drifted to the south from other islands. That the barbarities

281

and cruelties he practiced on those unlucky enough to fall into
his hands were learned from his cannibal ancestors.

Now he'd been cornered, not by Stoke or Gold but by a
young, unassuming Captain called Philip Marker. In his life
Hull had met few men wholly without ego. Marker was among
them. Furthermore, he'd accomplished the rare feat of rising to
his current position from the ranks of the enlisted. He hardly
ever raised his voice, in fact spoke infrequently. He was one of
those men who let their deeds do their talking for them.

His bravery and skill were such that commissioned officers
had no choice but to promote him. Though slight of build and
plain of appearance he could march for days while stronger,
more boastful men fell by the wayside. In his pursuit of the
rebels he proved relentless. This brought him the unqualified
support of Hull and the other members of the militia who'd
been attached to his regiment. Unlike their regular army
counterparts, the colonials were not interested in parades,
decorations and medals or fancy uniforms. They wished only
to return New Zealand to peace as rapidly as possible.

It had become a stranger war than anyone could have
imagined. Though it had gone on for years, the countryside
was not in flames. Isolated groups of rebels would appear
unexpectedly, sometimes to perish of internal discord before
troops could even arrive to confront them. It was more like
malaria than a real war, Hull mused. Just when you believed
you had it beaten it would pop up abruptly when and where
least expected.

The death of Rui would not cure the disease of Kingism, but
it would make life much easier for the farmers and ranchers of
the central highlands. They would go to their beds knowing
that the most murderous of the Kingites had met his end.

Some still spoke of capturing him. Hull thought this an
unlikely eventuality. There were too many men who would
take pleasure from personally putting an end to Alexander
Rui's life. Still, Hull and many others argued for taking him
alive so he could be carried back to Auckland where, after a
fair trial, he would be hung by the harborfront as an object
lesson to would-be rebels. It was going to be difficult to
restrain anyone from putting a bullet through Rui's head.

No one spoke of failure. Similar pas had been assaulted with
heavy loss of life and eventual retreat the result. Everyone was
confident the outcome would be different this time. Philip

Marker commanded them, an officer more interested in victory than in looking good on a reviewing stand. He paid less attention to how his troops wore their uniforms than to how they fought.

Hull didn't mind taking orders from Marker, who was younger and much poorer than himself, because he recognized Marker's military genius. Unlike some of his fellow colonials, Tobias Hull did not fancy himself a great general. He was comfortable with mere competency in command, preferring to take orders from someone more knowledgeable than himself. These he could pass on to his own subordinates, subsequently taking credit for any successful maneuver.

They would have to make do without artillery, as Colonel Gold kept the big guns for his own use. That would make this particular pa doubly difficult to take. The stockade was high and reinforced by supporting logs. Furthermore, the rocky ground on which the village stood prevented Marker's engineers from digging a sap. They were not going to be able to mine the wall and blow it up.

Alexander Rui's pa was going to have to be taken by frontal assault. Or so it appeared. Hull and the other officers waited for their orders in confidence, knowing young Marker had set his brilliant military mind to work on a solution.

In the meantime they surrounded the village and settled in for a long siege. By now there were no complaints, no questions. Everyone knew his job, including the colonials. Pickets were stationed well out of range of Maori sharpshooters. Meanwhile army snipers tried to find protected positions from which to fire at the village. This constant sniping by both sides was important. It let the enemy know he was being watched and that his opponent was on his guard.

Still, there was little fighting, beyond exchanges of curses and obscene gestures by men on both sides. The Maoris waited for the pakehas to attack, and the pakehas waited for Captain Marker to invent something unexpected.

They'd already tried a night attack on the northern curve of the pa. It had been driven off by the Maoris, but not before the militiamen who'd carried out the assault had inflicted substantial casualties. The Maori, Hull mused as he readied himself for the upcoming meeting in Marker's tent, weren't the only ones who could utilize hit-and-run tactics. The British regulars felt such maneuvers were beneath them. That didn't stop the colonials from learning to use the rebels' own strategems against them. Unfortunately it was the sort of thing that could only be used once. From now on the pa's defenders would be alert for any future nighttime attacks.

Hull buckled on his saber and then picked up his umbrella, wondering as he walked out into the rain what was happening to Hull House and in particular to its newly opened facilities in Christchurch. He should be there to oversee, to supervise and make decisions. Instead he was stuck on the eastern side of North Island, far from Auckland or Wellington and real civilization.

He knew he was obligated to this tour of duty. It was a responsibility he couldn't avoid. Somehow his innumerable commercial concerns succeeded in muddling along without him. Hull House wasn't growing and dominating the way it ought to, but neither was he losing any important commercial ground. From time to time he would unbend enough to write grudging letters of approval to his immediate subordinates and managers. By rights he should have suffered failure and setback. It just proved that with the right kind of discipline you could accomplish anything.

His subordinates knew that he could return at any moment to pass judgement on their decisions, that they could be dismissed with a casual wave of the great man's hand. So they worked hard and overachieved. It was a good thing to rule through fear, Hull believed. A man would work longer hours to keep his job than to gain a bonus. For those who performed well, the rare compliment and reward was thus thrice valued.

Keep them anxious, keep them hungry: that was Hull's motto. It had worked well for many years. If they could put an end to Rui this time he could return home a military hero. That would be good for business, even though everyone knew full well Rui's death would not put an end to the Kingites. The war would most likely go on, though in a more civilized fashion with Rui out of the picture.

As he collapsed his umbrella and entered he murmured greetings to those officers already assembled in Marker's tent. It was raining harder than ever now, violent droplets which assailed the roof and pounded the earth outside like massed drumming. The officers chatted fitfully among themselves, anxious to hear what Marker had to say so they could return to their own sanctuaries.

As it developed, those individual islands of warmth and comfort were not to be enjoyed for some time yet.

Marker's soft voice bade them all turn. "Gentlemen, ready your troops. We will make a full-scale attack on the pa within the hour."

Stunned silence greeted this pronouncement. "Within the *hour*?" one of the regular officers finally exclaimed.

"Sir," another lieutenant hastened to point out, "some of the men have just settled in for the night. Soon it'll be pitch dark out. Even if there was a moon, you won't be able to see your hand in front of your face in this rain."

"Precisely, Lieutenant Kneally. Consider: as the war has progressed the Maoris have become expert riflemen. We cannot mine their stockade and I will not have my men advancing over open ground towards a wall as well-built and as heavily defended as this one. Therefore we must find some other way of negating Rui's advantageous defensive position.

"He has chosen to make his stand here because he is unassailable from behind. But since he cannot retreat, we are spared the necessity of attacking on several fronts simultaneously. Because they cannot retreat, the Maoris will fight more determinedly than ever.

"In the dark, however, they will not be able to aim."

"Neither will we," someone else pointed out unnecessarily.

"True enough. But once we gain the wall the advantage will be ours. We shall attack in three columns several minutes apart. With luck the Maoris may assume all our forces are concentrated in the initial assault. They will respond by unbalancing their defense accordingly. Under the cover of rain and darkness, one or both of the other columns may be able to scale the stockade and get inside the village before the enemy realizes what is happening.

"I want every man to carry a waterproof container of hot coals with which to set the Maori buildings on fire. That will spread confusion and panic among the villagers while providing us with light to shoot by."

"Nothing will burn for long in this rain," Hull observed.

"Long burns will not be necessary. Our objective is to destroy Rui's fighters, not burn his houses. In any event, we're not interested in a lengthy battle, are we, gentlemen?"

A chorus of "nos" resounded through the tent.

"Everyone must take care to move quietly. Instruct the men

to wrap their weapons so their powder will be dry when finally they have targets to aim at. The initial assault will be made with sabers and swords only." He smiled thinly. "The Maoris will not expect the silence. In the past we've always attacked with all guns blazing. In the panic that will hopefully ensue their natural reaction will be to utilize their own weapons, with the result that they will become well soaked by the rain while ours remain ready and dry."

"I don't know, begging your pardon, Captain, that it's possible to panic Maoris," Hull said thoughtfully.

The young Captain didn't back down. "There is always a first time, Mr. Hull. The Maoris are tough fighters, but they are still human."

"Well then, sir, that aside, I think it's a good plan." A quick survey indicated his fellow militia leaders were in agreement. "Anything new's worth a try."

"It's not proper strategy," Lieutenant Kneally protested.

"I'm aware of that, Lieutenant." Marker was unruffled. "And this isn't Sandringham. The only thing that concerns me is winning this battle with as few casualties as possible."

There was silence in the tent. A couple of the junior officers eyed one another uneasily, but no one else spoke. Marker waited patiently, giving them a last chance. When no one took it, he gave the order.

"Let's go, then. We'll attack as soon as every unit is ready, and for Heaven's Sake caution them to keep their grumbling down. I know it will be impossible, under these conditions, to shut them up entirely." A couple of the more senior lieutenants chuckled at that.

"The Maoris have had ample time to observe us settling in for the evening. It was to preserve that illusion I kept my intentions secret from you all until now. Hopefully our enemy is also relaxing. Our surprise could be complete, though I am not counting on it."

"The militia will be ready, Captain. They'll gripe more than most, but they'll be ready." The more he thought about the plan the more excited Hull became. Marker was right. If they could divert most of the defenders and get another column over the wall and into the pa proper, it would be the beginning of the end for Rui's warriors. Once they got inside there was no way on Earth the Kingites were going to drive them out.

On the other hand, if they didn't achieve at least partial

surprise, if the Maoris were waiting for them as they attacked, the Kingites would slaughter the men trying to scale the stockade, picking them off with ease since those behind would not be able to provide any covering fire in the pouring rain. Everything depended on surprise and speed, qualities the British army was not noted for. But Marker had enough experienced men to give the attack a good chance of success, men who no longer cared about following rules or looking impressive on the battlefield. Men who would do what was necessary to win.

He squinted at the sky as he left the tent, unfolding his umbrella as he hurried to give the news to his own troops.

6

The full moon was masked by the clouded sky. If the storm broke, the Maoris would surely detect the three columns of pakehas advancing toward them. That would put paid to Marker's plan. Dangerous it was, Hull knew. Dangerous and daring. He supported it as strongly now as he had when the Captain had proposed it. Those unwilling to take risks inevitably failed, whether in commerce or in war.

Initial worries faded as the men silently struggled up the slight slope toward the fortified pa. If anything, the storm intensified and the sky grew darker. It was incongruous to see hardened troops smiling as the weather became steadily more miserable, but on this night everyone new the rain and darkness were their allies.

It was a most methodical storm, the water falling straight down. There was no wind. The raindrops pounding the earth helped to muffle the noise of the advance. Hull saw grizzled, scarred veterans trying to tiptoe through ankle-deep mud. Fortunately, the same underlying rock that made the digging of saps impossible restricted the mud to a depth of a couple of inches. It did not slow them down.

Regulars and militia alike clutched their muskets and pistols close to their bodies. Every gun had been wrapped with whatever material was at hand: dirty socks, shirts, extra coats, even nightwear. Anything to protect powder from the downpour. The Maoris would not be able to prepare. They would respond instinctively and their weapons would quickly become waterlogged.

Hull tried and failed to make out the tall rampart of the stockade. He had to rely on the movement of the men ahead of him. Behind him someone bumped someone else with the end of a scaling ladder. The brief exchange of curses was hastily shushed by other men. Still there was no response from within the pa. Soldiers breathed sighs of relief and continued their advance.

They trudged upward for what seemed like hours. Hull began to wonder if his column had wandered completely off course. That could be dangerous in itself, with a sheer cliff plunging into the sea not far away. He listened but couldn't hear the booming of surf against stone.

Then one of his lieutenants appeared, to whisper they were barely a ladder's length from the wall. Ten feet and still you couldn't see the stockade logs. Only the sound of the rain and the shuffling of anxious feet proved he hadn't wandered off the face of the planet.

The men began to spread out to the left and right, noncoms whispering orders to the regulars, officers moving nervously back and forth among them. Ladders were placed against the walls. Their tops had been padded with coats and strips of linen. They made no noise as they were positioned. Hull tried to check his pocket watch but couldn't make out the numerals in the dark and rain. He put the watch away and stared to his left. His group was part of the righthand column. Marker had taken the middle for himself.

It was important that all three columns commence scaling the wall at the predetermined times. Hull could only hope his people weren't early. They certainly were not late because it was silent as the grave on the other side of the stockade. Where were the Maori defenders? Around him men began to show signs of excitement as they started up the ladders unopposed, following close on the heels of the regulars who were leading the way. Marker's plan was working better than anyone dared hope.

Then Hull heard a startled oath in Maori, followed by the sound of a pistol being fired. Someone inside the pa had made contact with Marker's column. Hull went up the nearest ladder fast, shoving another man out of the way. Erratically at first, then with rapidly increasing frequency other shouts and yells sounded from inside the pa as the startled Maoris awoke to the realization they were being attacked.

Hull dropped to the ground on the other side of the pa, his knees protesting at the impact. He took two steps forward and nearly tripped over the body of a Maori sentry lying on the sodden ground with his skull split wide. A shape materialized out of the rain and he readied his saber, then lowered it as he recognized one of Marker's scouts. His breath was coming in short gasps and the sounds of rising battle had begun to fill the night air. Sharp echoes of steel on greenstone, of musketry and pistols, overwhelmed the noise of falling rain. Brief flashes of light momentarily illuminated the darkness, then vanished.

The scout slowed, glanced backward as Hull moved toward him.

"How goes it, man?" Hull pressed him.

The man was wheezing. "At least half the regiment's already inside the wall, sir. Don't know about Lieutenant Schale's column yet. Seems your people are almost all in. I was sent to check on that." He was already backing away. "Excuse me, sir. Got to get back to my unit."

Hull watched him go, eagerly led his own men forward. The rain was subsiding slightly, the clouds parting to let a suggestion of moonlight through. He saw a dozen Maoris running to his left, tried to direct the men following him in their direction. The Kingites were naked and lightly armed, still stunned by the unexpected attack.

Marker had achieved all the surprise he'd hoped for, but the battle's outcome was far from preordained. Hull knew that when the Kingites began fighting in earnest they would fight grimly and until they dropped. He bellowed orders, hoping some might be heard above the noise and confusion. Officers tried to keep control of the fighting, but with men from all three columns mixing in the darkness that quickly proved impossible.

The Maoris were fully awake and alerted now, pouring from their houses. The initial success achieved by surprise was muted by the ferocity of a desperate counterattack. In hand-to-hand combat the Kingites could more than hold their own, but now the invading pakehas brought out their dry muskets and pistols. When the Maoris tried to respond in kind they found their drenched weapons useful only as clubs.

Something massive and shadowy flashed past in the darkness. Hull ducked to his left and the enormous greenstone war club smashed into the mud nearby. He slashed sideways with his saber. Blood mixed with rain as the stocky form that held the club slumped to the ground. He moved forward, feeling the comforting press of his men around him, using his saber whenever there seemed something to strike at while holding his pistol secure and dry in case he needed it later.

Screams and shouts, curses and war cries in both English and Maori mixed with the falling rain as the battle continued. The Maoris had sacrificed too much already. They were falling back under the relentless if undisciplined pakeha assault. By the time they managed to mount an organized defense, their numbers had been severely reduced.

The battle degenerated into the sort of massacre Marker and his officers had feared. In the rain there was no controlling the troops, much less the militia. The officers did their best to save women and children, with only partial success. These were Alexander Rui's supporters, and there was no sympathy to be found for them among the colonials.

The Maori resistance collapsed, broke up into isolated pockets of warriors. Some tried to escape, only to be cut down in front of their own still securely fastened gate.

The largest group still resisting had been forced to the very back of the village. They'd formed a defensive semicircle where the men could hear the surf booming against the rocks far below them. A few had managed to dry their muskets sufficiently to load and fire at their attackers. Others had heaped up sacks of grain and a few loose logs to create a crude barricade.

The invaders slowed, content with picking off those Kingites who exposed themselves. It was only a matter of time now. So Hull thought until a tiny older colonial came rushing up to him. The man couldn't have been more than five feet tall, but he gripped his sword as tightly as any corporal.

"Captain Hull? That be you, sir?"

Hull found himself staring down into a whiskery face streaked with blood. The rain was washing it away.

"We got to go at 'em, sir! We can't hold here."

"Easy there, man. We'll have them all soon enough."

"No sir, you don't understand." He was so excited he was hopping up and down, nodding toward the Kingite barricade. "I saw, I got a look. They got a ladder back there."

Hull frowned. "What?"

"A ladder, sir. Flax. I'd say it's a good fifty feet long. See, I went over to the edge and looked 'round. There's Maoris climbin' down it right now. They got a big boat in the water, big sea-goin' canoe or somethin'. They. . . ."

Hull was pushing past him, shouting orders, shoving and hitting startled men out of his way. From the little man's description of what he'd observed the Kingite's intentions were strikingly clear.

Even now they were trying to snatch victory from defeat. If he hadn't already escaped to the waiting boat below, Alexander Rui was doubtless preparing to do so. The pakehas weren't the only ones who could spring a surprise. The hated ariki would use ladder and boat to escape by sea. He and his most respected warriors would land somewhere far away. There he could bide his time and rebuild his forces until again ready to commence his swift, horrible attacks, just when everyone believed he'd been finished.

It had to be prevented.

Hull gathered a group of militia about him and ordered them to ready their weapons. When he explained the reason for the urgency, not a dissenting voice was raised. All had suffered, even if only indirectly, from Alexander Rui's depredations.

"Lead us to 'im, Captain," one of the men shouted.

"Aye sir! We're with you!"

As Hull turned to study the makeshift barricade that was concealing Rui's flight it struck him that this was the first time in his life he'd led a group of people who respected instead of feared him. He felt oddly exhilarated and out of place.

"At them men!" he heard himself screaming. "Down with the Kingites! Down with Rui!"

The twenty men surrounding him roared as they rushed the barricade. Several discharged their muskets, drawing answering fire from the defending Maoris. The distance was not great and in an instant they swarmed over the barrier, rifle butts and swords and sabers slashing at anything that moved.

Hull brought his own blade down across the face of a startled warrior, saw the man's expression contort as he fell away clutching at his eyes. A small cluster of Maoris materialized out of the rain, running towards him. Maybe half a dozen, he determined quickly. In their midst was a tall warrior clad in the splendid battlefield attire of an ariki.

When they saw Hull they turned, and the tall chief glared straight at him. In the darkness their eyes met for a moment, and Hull felt his heart leap. Rui had yet to make it to the boat waiting for him below.

The sounds of burning wood reached him as houses and granaries were torched. They burned furiously against the rain.

The battle was good as won, except that their principal quarry was about to escape.

Then Hull was in among the chief's bodyguard, clutching his saber tight with both hands and swinging with a strength he hadn't felt in twenty years. Around him all was chaos and confusion. For a terrible instant he feared he'd outrun his comrades, that he was taking on Rui's soldiers all by himself.

As he ran one warrior through he caught a glimpse of Rui's face disappearing over the edge of the cliff. Suddenly someone was battling alongside him, a young colonial officer he didn't recognize. As he stared he saw the man break away and rush to the cliff to start hacking with his sword at the top of the rope ladder.

"That's it, that's it! Go to it, man!" Hull tried to defend himself and lend encouragement as he divined the other man's purpose. With the ladder cut away Rui would be well and truly trapped.

So intent was he on cutting the ladder that the officer didn't see the warrior who snuck up behind him. Even as he realized it would come too late, Hull tried to scream a warning.

The warrior was over six feet tall and broad in proportion. The spear he wielded came down fast to slam into the young colonial's back. He arched in pain as he fell, his own sword falling to the ground. Even as Hull let out a cry and rushed forward the warrior was withdrawing his weapon and turning to meet the threat.

Rui's bodyguard was regrouping as the surviving Maoris, desperate to help their leader escape, rallied around them. Hull ignored them all, seeing only the young officer slumped near the top of the ladder.

The warrior who'd struck him down let out a yell, jumped forward and thrust with his bloody spear. Hull ducked under it. His saber flashed. He felt it bend slightly as it hit rib. Then it straightened, slid forward, and pierced the heart. Clutching himself, the Kingite staggered backward and raised his spear as if to throw. Suddenly he was gone, over the edge of the cliff. Hull knew he wouldn't be able to hear the other man strike the water.

He dropped to hands and knees at the top of the rope ladder and wiped rain from his eyes as he stared down. Rui was less than a fifth of the way to the bottom because the ladder was full of warriors. Frantically Hull started sawing at the thick ropes

with his own saber. The fine Italian blade hadn't been intended
for work like this.

The young officer whose life was bleeding away close by
had almost cut through the first rope. Hull finished it and saw
the ladder sway, heard Maoris below yelling in surprise. Now
he could see the war canoe clearly, even as he saw Rui and his
companions try to hurry their descent. Once more the rain was
an ally, making the rope slippery and dangerous.

When half the remaining rope had been cut Hull raised the
saber over his head and brought it down with all his strength.
More screams from below, this time fading rapidly. As he
sprawled exhausted on his chest and belly he could see the dark
shapes falling, falling, the rope ladder coiling about them like
an accompanying snake. Seconds passed. Then a few dull
thuds as objects struck the rocks which protruded from the cliff
base.

Good-bye, you rotten stinking bastard, Hull whispered into
the wind. Hell take you and all your murdering kind.

Ignoring the noise of the intense fighting raging around him
he glanced to his right, saw an arm move weakly. The officer
was still alive. Hull crawled over and pulled the man onto his
back. Innocent eyes in a smooth face stared up at him. A quick
check revealed that the wound was severe. No physician, Hull
couldn't tell if any vital organs had been pierced. There didn't
seem to be too much blood.

Laying his saber aside he worked both arms beneath the
younger man's arms. Though much taller, he was no heavier
than Hull and the merchant was able to drag him through the
mud.

"Easy there, young sir. We'll get you to a doctor. It'll be all
right, you'll see." The injured man didn't respond.

Someone was calling his name. It sounded like Marker but
Hull couldn't be sure. Then something slammed into his back,
a dull hammer blow. There didn't seem to be much force
behind it. It wasn't even painful, but all his strength left him
like water spilling from a shattered crock. His hands still under
the other man's arms, Hull dropped to his knees. His vision
was blurring rapidly.

Tired. So tired. Too tired to try and see what had hit him.
Instead he found himself regarding the man he'd been trying to
save. Maybe the doctors would get them both. For the first

time in a long while he sensed the rain on his back and neck, felt the chill of the damp night air.

"I'm sorry."

The last thing he expected was a response. But the young man blinked up at him, through the falling rain. "It's—all right." He was trying to smile, though you couldn't tell for certain for the mud that covered his face. "Tell my family." The eyes closed.

Hull wanted to say that he was sorry, that he wouldn't be telling anyone's family anything, including his own. Not even then did he think of his daughter, Rose. For the first time in a long while he did think of his long-departed, beloved wife Flora. That in itself was unusual. There had been a time when he was certain he would never be able to go as long as a day without thinking of her.

Well, he wouldn't be seeing her now. She'd gone one place and he hadn't the slightest doubt he was headed elsewhere. Perhaps the Lord would look kindly on his efforts this day and grant him a little leeway.

"Why?" he murmured as he had murmured on his wife's deathbed more than twenty years earlier. Then he fell over onto his side, in the mud, his eyes open and staring but no longer troubled by the rain that struck them.

The young soldier he'd been trying to rescue didn't move. His eyes remained shut, but he managed to whisper, unaware that his would-be savior could no longer hear him.

"It's all right. It'll be all right. Listen, if I don't make it will you—will you get my name to my family?" He swallowed, an ordinary action that now required an extraordinary exertion of will.

Other faces crowded around as the men of Marker's regiment finally broke the last Maori resistance. A distant voice was yelling.

"Captain Hull! Over here, quick, it's Captain Hull!"

The young officer didn't hear this. He was concentrating on the face of the sergeant who was bending over him.

"What's your name, son?" the noncom was murmuring even as he and two of his men struggled to lift the dying colonial out of the mud.

"Coffin. Chris—Christopher Coffin."

In times of battle it is not at all unusual for the last words a man utters to be among the first that are spoken after his birth.

7

Coffin was feeling good as he rode up the street toward the splendid house that dominated the cul-de-sac. It had grown over the years, he reflected. Turrets and rooms had been added and the expensive iron fence now fully enclosed the park-like grounds. A home to be proud of.

The sun shone brightly and the city seemed to expand beneath it. News of the death of Alexander Rui and the total defeat of his band had reached Auckland only a few days ago. There'd been much drinking of rum and whiskey when it became known that the worst of the rebel leaders had met his end. Not that it meant an end to the interminable rebellion, but it did allow men like Coffin to return home to see to their families and businesses.

Later today he would be able to meet with Elias, but Holly came first. She would listen enthralled to his stories, they would have breakfast on the porch, and then tonight he would once more be able to sleep in his own bed. After several months of marching and fighting, rain and mud, that seemed like the greatest reward of all.

The war would drag on for a while longer, though. While the number and frequency of attacks had been reduced, they had not been eliminated. Not even Rui's death would ensure that. The Kingites had only been stalemated.

They would bring over more soldiers, more artillery to reduce the remaining rebel pas. Surely one more year of fighting would see an end at last to the revolt. The war had gone on far too long as it was.

He rode in the back way, wanting to surprise Holly. The stableman came out to see who had brazenly entered through the rear gate. A smile came over his face as he recognized the intruder.

"Mr. Coffin, sir! It's good to have you back."

"Thanks, Jack." Coffin dismounted as the stableman took the horse's reins. "How are things up at the house?"

"Just fine, sir, just fine."

"And Mrs. Coffin?"

"Well enough. She's been visiting this morning, but she's back now. They went off in Mrs. Abigail's carriage and I didn't see them return, but I think I heard wheels on the front drive not long ago. You're looking well yourself, sir."

Coffin acknowledged the compliment with a nod. He was staring at the house, suddenly conscious of how deeply tired he was. Years of riding back and forth across North Island hadn't made him any more comfortable in the saddle. He much preferred the rolling deck of a good ship.

"There's a gentleman here to see you, sir. Been waiting some time. He was here yesterday as well but I told him you weren't expected until today. 'I'll come back,' he said, and sure enough he did."

A family friend? Perhaps word of Coffin's return had preceded him.

"Who is he?"

"He was reluctant to give his name to anyone but you, sir. I thought it strange but didn't question him. Didn't strike me as the sort of chap who'd talk if he didn't want to. I don't know him. He said it was important, sir."

Coffin nodded thoughtfully. The stableman was a tall, lanky Dutchman. He'd been with the Coffins for several years now. He wasn't much on people but he was wonderful with horses. In his care Coffin's tired mount would be properly cooled down.

"He's in the tack room, sir. Wouldn't go up to the house. Insisted on waiting here."

"It's all right, Jack. I'll see him."

Coffin intended to make the irritating detour as brief as possible. Probably some small business matter, vital to the visitor. Something to be disposed of quickly.

His guest didn't have the look of a small businessman. A big, burly, dark-haired individual, he looked more like a blacksmith. He sat, well-groomed and silent, on a back bench surrounded by gleaming tack. He was engrossed in a book, which struck Coffin as out of character. As Coffin entered, the man put the volume up without showing the title.

"Robert Coffin?" His voice was deep, the words hesitant.

"I am." Coffin's grip was easily matched by the other.

"I would've guessed, sir, though we've never met. I'm Alfred Cobb. Sergeant Cobb much of the time." He smiled slightly, almost apologetically. "Of the New Plymouth Irregulars."

Coffin nodded. New Plymouth was a town on the west coast of North Island. It was far from Auckland, but then so was just about every other settlement in New Zealand.

"How goes the Taranaki War in your district?"

"Well enough. You heard about our little punch-up with Alexander Rui?"

"Who hasn't? So you were with Marker? My congratulations."

"Thank you."

"We're doing well everywhere these days. My group's had a success or two itself, though nothing so grand as the triumph over Rui. What can I do for you, Mr. Cobb?"

"Well sir." The sergeant's fingers moved unceasingly over his book. "First I'd best explain what I'm about. See, I've been serving as a sort of courier much of the time. I know the back country pretty well and I'm good at living off the land. So the various commanders, they've been using me to carry messages back and forth."

"I was about to say you're a long way from New Plymouth."

"I'd been given a number of communications to deliver. This here's the last one." He nodded toward the house. "I was told by your man that you were expected soon, so I thought best to wait and give you the news first."

Coffin's expression changed. This wasn't what he expected.

"What news? And why me first?"

The big man wanted to look everywhere but at his host. He kept fiddling ceaselessly with his book. "Mr. Coffin, sir, I'm not much good at expressing myself. I've had a lot of practice but it never seems to help much."

"What are you driving at, man?" Coffin was getting angry. He hadn't been gone these many months, hadn't ridden all this way home to spend precious time locked in cryptic conversation with a total stranger.

"It has to do with Rui's defeat, sir."

"Hmph. It's good news then, whatever it is. Anything having to do with that bloody bastard's demise is good news.

The Maoris are well rid of him too, though they don't realize it yet."

"Yes sir. Everyone's agreed on that. You heard how his last pa was taken?"

"Only the barest details. I know this young Captain, Marker, was promoted to Major as a result. That's the sort of army man we need. Not these over-decorated popinjays who acquire their commissions through political connections."

"I couldn't agree more, sir. Well sir, it wasn't an easy fight. None of us who were there expected Rui to give up easily, and he didn't. When they were finally cornered his people fought harder than ever. But we took 'em anyway. It's just that. . . ." Cobb paused, then seemed to draw strength from some inner source. "Well sir, I'm afraid your son's among the dead, sir."

Coffin's face went completely blank for a moment. Then he half smiled, a crooked, lopsided sort of grin, as though his brain had temporarily lost control of his facial muscles.

"Christopher?"

Cobb nodded slowly. "Yes, that's the name I was given, sir. Christopher Coffin. He was your son, wasn't he?"

Was your son. Was. Trembling, Coffin leaned against a large sink for support. "Can't be." He swallowed, raised his voice. "It can't be. My son's here, in Auckland. He's working in my offices. He's not a soldier. He wasn't with a reserve unit, even."

"I'm truly sorry, sir. He was attached to the Third Northern Militia. The identification was positive, I'm told."

Coffin turned away, staring at nothing. "We talked about it. We talked about it. He agreed with me. He said he wasn't going to do any fighting." That was what Christopher had said. But what had he felt, that last time they'd talked in Coffin's tent? What had he really meant to do? Hadn't he gone on about how badly he'd felt? Hadn't he said he felt he was shirking his duty? He hadn't really agreed with anything his father had said. Coffin had just assumed his son would do as he was told. People always did what Robert Coffin told them to do.

"I'm sorry, sir. I didn't realize you didn't know of his participation. It was something the young man did on his own?"

Coffin could only nod. The disbelief was giving way to acceptance, to horrid reality. He knew why the army used a man like Cobb. You couldn't wish him away. The fellow simply stood before you, grave and commiserating, as substantial as a mountain. He was a man you had to believe. All the delight, all the happiness and relief Coffin had been feeling as he'd ridden the final mile homeward this morning, it had vanished. Only a vast emptiness remained to take its place.

Cobb wasn't through. Would the man never shut up? "I understand he fought bravely, sir." As if suddenly remembering something half forgotten, Cobb hunted through his shoulder bag to extract a small packet bound with dirty twine. "I was told to give this to you."

Coffin accepted the package without looking at it. "Thank— thank you, Sergeant Cobb. You've come a long way on a difficult mission and I know you must be anxious to be on your way home."

"That I am, sir." Cobb headed for the doorway, paused to glance back. Coffin had not moved, stood staring at the far wall. "Sir, I've done this many times. Too many, thinks I. They keep asking it of me. I'd rather they didn't. He was your only son, sir?"

"My only child, yes." Coffin's voice was raspy, quiet. He'd absorbed the news now, as he absorbed everything sooner or later. "He was a fine young man."

Cobb nodded understandingly. "So the report led me to believe, sir. A pity you didn't know about him joining up. Might've made it easier. Hard to tell these days where anyone is or what they're doing with their lives." He adjusted his hat, tugging the brim snugly over his forehead. "I won't intrude on you any longer, sir. At least he didn't die for naught, picked off by a sniper while cooking supper. He helped put an end to Rui."

"Yes, of course." Coffin sat down on one of the wooden work benches, convulsively clutching the unopened package as he stared across the room.

Cobb was about to close the door when Coffin looked up sharply. "I want the body."

"There's a soldier cemetery near the site of the battle, sir. Having been on many campaigns yourself, I'm sure you know we've no means for transporting the dead. Barely make do by the living. I'm sure his grave's marked. If you want to disinter the casket and bring it all the way back to Auckland I'd say you need to take a proper mortician with you."

"I know. Was there anything more, Mr. Cobb?"

"No, not really, sir. Oh, there was a senior militia officer tried to save him. Got himself killed too for his trouble. They buried him next to your son because of that. Him being a senior officer and all, he'll have a slightly larger marker. Might help you find your son's site."

"Tried to save him, you say? What was his name?"

"Just a moment, if you will, sir." Cobb opened the book again, the same one he'd been reading when Coffin had entered the tack room. He flipped through half the pages until he found the one he wanted. "A militia Captain. Also from Auckland, I believe. Yes. Tobias Hull."

"Hull?" Coffin rose so quickly from the bench that Cobb flinched. "What do you mean?"

"Well sir, the story as I got it, and you've got to understand I didn't see it for myself, is that this Captain Hull risked his life trying to pull your son to safety and was cut down while doing so. They say it was a gallant thing."

Coffin looked past his visitor. "Can't be. It can't be."

"Did they know each other, sir? This Captain Hull and your son?"

"No!" Cobb eyed him askance. Noting the sergeant's reaction Coffin forced himself to lower his voice. "No, they didn't know each other, Mr. Cobb. I'm sure of that. He died trying to save Christopher?"

Cobb nodded. "That's the story they tell, sir. That sort of thing goes on all the time. Not so much of a coincidence really, when you think about it. Most of the colonials who took part in the assault were from this area." He looked sideways at his host. "You okay, sir? Should I send for your man?"

"No, thank you. I'll be fine."

"Again, I don't enjoy being the bearer of bad tidings, but some poor sod's got to do it and they keep picking on me. I've already informed Mr. Hull's family, in case you're curious."

"What?"

"Mr. Hull's family. I went there first. Seems he has a daughter."

"Yes, yes, that's right. Rose her name was. She would be the only surviving relative. I would imagine she took the news quite well."

Cobb looked genuinely surprised. "That she did, sir. Now how would you know that?"

"I know the girl. Enough to guess how she'd react."

"Handled it calmly she did, sir." Cobb opened the door of the tack room preparatory to departing. "Though I wouldn't call her a girl, quite."

"No, that's so." Coffin's brows drew together. "She'd be in her twenties now. Like Christopher."

The sergeant looked thoughtful. "Hardly blinked when I gave her the news. Not a tear. That's one strong young woman, Mr. Coffin. Well, I'd best take my leave. Listen, sir. I've lost one of my own boys in this stinking war. So when I say I know what you're feeling, I do so honestly, from the heart."

He backed out, closing the door behind him.

Coffin stood motionless. He happened to be staring at a pile of old leather, worn-out bridles and straps Jack had stacked in a corner. They were a dirty, tangled mass, the leather black with age and horse sweat. He was shaking his head as he stared even though none were present to observe the gesture. There was no hope or joy in the room. Only darkness.

Why had Christopher done it? And if he was that determined why hadn't he insisted on being assigned to his father's unit? Coffin could have watched over him, protected him, shielded him. Which was why, he knew, his son hadn't come to him. He'd done that once, only to have Coffin all but order him back to Auckland, back to Elias Goldman's side. Christopher knew his father well enough not to try a second time. So he'd run off to join another regiment without his father's knowledge. Was it without his mother's knowledge as well?

Coffin moved to the single window and gazed up at the big house atop the manicured hill. Did Holly know? He doubted it. Christopher would have told her he was going off on business. He knew how his mother felt about her son exerting himself physically, much less about soldiering. No, he wouldn't have told her because she would have been more vehement in her refusals than Coffin had been.

As he exited the tack room he passed the stableman. "Sir? Are you feeling unwell, Mr. Coffin, sir?" Coffin didn't acknowledge the query, didn't look in his direction. Suddenly he was more tired than he'd ever been in his life.

As he forced himself up the stone steps that led to the back entrance of the main house he thought he caught a glimpse of a shape off to one side, a tall figure clad in flax and a simple shirt who carried a long wooden staff. But when he paused to look behind the tree where he'd seen it there was nothing but neatly pruned bushes and flowers.

The door was unlocked. He entered the empty kitchen. It was mid-morning now and Cook would be occupied elsewhere, but the downstairs maid saw him.

"Mr. Coffin! It's good to . . . ," she broke off as he trudged past her. Then she put a hand to her mouth and rushed up the servant's stairs. He could hear her yelling as she ascended. "Mrs. Coffin, Mrs. Coffin!"

Having no actual destination in mind, he stopped when he entered the library, sat down on a small couch. The walls were lined with books, thick leatherbound volumes he would never have the time to read, books he'd bought because a gentleman's library was supposed to be filled with such things. The room was awash with the trappings of wealth and success: finely wrought furniture, Persian carpets, Italian crystal and hand-painted lamps. A meaningless blur of ostentation.

The sound of feet running sounded in the hall. Then a voice: "Robert? Robert!" The joy of it was like a sword in his side. Was that how Christopher had died, he wondered?

"Robert, it's so wonderful to. . . ." She stopped, the smile vanishing from her face.

Still beautiful, he thought as he stared back at her. She doesn't age.

"Robert, what's the matter?"

Maybe if he'd been given more time, if he'd received the news a day earlier, then perhaps he would have had time to prepare. Subtlety had never been his forte. Though he could be diplomatic at times, now he was too consumed by grief to think of tact.

"Christopher's dead."

She stared at him, then leaned on the nearest chair. She didn't look like she was going to faint, for which he was grateful. As with him it took time for the real shock to set in.

"He was with the regiment that killed Alexander Rui and destroyed his pa."

He sensed dampness on his cheeks, was astonished to find that for the first time since he was a boy he was crying. Silently, steadily. It was strange. The tears fell of their own accord. Otherwise he felt no different. His chest didn't heave, he had no trouble breathing. The water simply dripped from his eyes.

"They told me Tobias Hull died trying to save him. Can you believe that? Tobias Hull."

She strode over to him and her palm slammed across his face. He looked startled. "You should have been with him! *You*! Not Tobias Hull!"

"I know. I know. But I didn't even know he'd joined up to fight. God, Holly, I didn't know!" He rose to embrace her but she skipped back out of his reach like a frightened water bug.

"Don't touch me," she whispered, eyes wide and staring. "I don't want anybody to touch me!"

He spread his hands helplessly. "Holly, I didn't know. We talked once, briefly, on the road. I told him not to join up. Told him to stay with Elias and concentrate on the business. He—he seemed to agree with me. He didn't tell you either?"

"No. No, he didn't tell me." She looked up at him, her face agonized. "It should have been you, Robert. Why was Tobias Hull there and not you? Why?" Her tone was shrill, unstable, and it worried him.

"I told you. I thought he'd agreed to stay here, at work." He advanced slowly toward her. She kept backing up until she bumped into the reading table. Both hands were cupped over her face now, hiding everything except wide, frightened eyes.

"It can't be. It's a mistake."

"It's not a mistake. I wish to God it were but it's not. The man who told me didn't seem the sort to make those kinds of mistakes."

"Then it's a lie. He lied." Suddenly she was furious. "It's got to be a lie!"

She kept repeating it, over and over, as he finally grabbed her in his arms. She began pounding both fists against his chest and he let her flail away, holding her as tightly as he dared. Gradually her fury and her strength ebbed. She sagged against him, sobbing uncontrollably. He didn't know how long they stood there like that. Eventually she pushed away. The blank look she wore scared him.

"I—I've got to go now. I've got to tell Cook." She turned and walked halfway to the door before she crumpled like a doll made of straw.

"Holly!" He rushed to her side, turned her over. She stared back, but not at him. Not at anything. He screamed into the hall. "Mary! Mary, get in here!"

He picked her up. She'd always been slight but now she

seemed lighter than ever. The downstairs maid arrived and gasped at the non-expression on her mistress's face.

"Get Jack. Tell him to take the best horse and ride to Dr. Hamilcar's. Get him back here *fast*."

"Yes sir." She turned and ran without remembering to curtsey.

"Tell him to hurry!"

He carried Holly up the stairs, slid back the covers on the big bed and set her down gently. The bed was an ornately carved mass of walnut that had belonged to some Portuguese duke or baron. It had been brought around the Cape in sections. Holly looked very small alone in the center of it.

He placed his hand over her breast, felt her heart beating steadily. A filled water basin stood nearby. He soaked a small towel, wrung it out and gently dampened her face. She moaned and turned away from him.

Coffin rose, staring down at her. He did not need to look heavenward as he thought.

If there is a just God you will make my wife well again.

He did not expect a reply and in this, at least, he was not surprised.

8

"She'll live."

Hamilcar was a young man, too handsome to be a doctor. Physicians should look like kindly uncles, Coffin thought. Not like heroes from Byronic poetry. A recent immigrant, Hamilcar had quickly established himself as one of the most knowledgeable men of medicine in the colony, as well as its most skillful surgeon. Like everyone else, Coffin forgave him his appearance because of his talent.

"She's had a shock, a terrible shock, and she hasn't taken it well. I've administered something that will help her to sleep comfortably. Right now that is what she needs more than anything else. I'm sorry about your son."

Coffin had explained the circumstances of his arrival and Holly's subsequent collapse. "Never mind that now." He nodded toward the bed. "It's her I'm concerned about. Are you sure she'll be all right?"

"I said she would live. Beyond that we cannot be sure of anything until she awakens. Sometimes," the young physician hesitated, "a shock like this can have lingering effects."

"I've been fighting a war for three years. Before that I fought Malay pirates on the high seas. I know what shock can do."

"Keep an eye on her after she awakens. She'll need some nourishment. Soup would be good."

Coffin spoke to the maid without looking back at her. "Mary, tell Cook."

"Yes, Mr. Coffin, sir." The girl vanished down the hall.

Hamilcar closed his bag. "I'll come back and check on her tomorrow."

"Thank you, Doctor. Thank you for your help."

Hamilcar left Coffin standing by the bed, staring down at his sleeping wife. I'm afraid she may need more help than I can

306

provide, the doctor thought, but said nothing as he exited. He might be wrong, and one could always hope he was.

Coffin spent all the rest of that day sitting by Holly's bedside, waiting, watching as she moaned in her sleep. She tossed and turned but didn't wake. Afternoon became night, then morning. He'd fallen asleep in the chair without realizing it. When he awoke she was still asleep. Well, the doctor said she would sleep.

He washed his face with water from the same basin he'd used to try and revive her, took a last look at the bed, and left the room. The house, the grounds, had become oppressive, a place of grief instead of joy, despair instead of exhilaration.

The maid saw him descend the stairs. "Mr. Coffin, sir?"

"I'm going out, Mary."

"Can you tell me where, sir, in case the Mrs. wakes up?"

"If she wakes up she'll be all right and then it won't matter where I've gone. If she does, just tell her I'll be back soon."

"Yes sir," said the maid dubiously.

Coffin disdained the riding horses, the scrupulously maintained carriages, in favor of walking. He needed to burn some frustration. He headed for the busiest part of town, wanting to surround himself with the sounds of contented people, people engaged in ordinary mundane tasks. People whom tragedy had bypassed. When he found himself instinctively angling in the direction of Coffin House he forced himself to turn onto another street. He didn't want to see Elias or anyone else he knew right now. Nor would he seek pity from his other employees. He didn't want to have to guess whether it was genuine or not.

He walked for hours. When he finally stopped he found he was standing outside Hull House. Rose might be here, he mused. Or she might be at home. Not that it much mattered. Wherever she was he doubted she'd be in mourning.

Anyway, this was where he was.

On impulse he entered. A receptionist eyed him curiously. Coffin was aware that after a night spent sleeping in a chair he might present something less than a reassuring sight.

"Can I help you, sir?"

Coffin looked past the man, into the bustling offices beyond. "Is Rose Hull here?"

"I believe so, sir. She can't see anyone. She's very busy. As you may know, the company has suffered a tragedy recently and. . . ."

"Spare me the tears. She'll see me. Tell her Robert Coffin's downstairs."

Clearly his name if not his appearance was instantly recognizable. Not only the receptionist but several nearby clerks looked up in surprise. Coffin favored the others with a hard stare and they immediately returned to their work.

"Robert Coffin. Yes sir, Mr. Coffin." The receptionist rose hastily, all but tripping over the legs of his chair. "If you'll just give me a moment, sir." The man vanished around a corner.

Coffin took the time to study what he could see. In their own way the offices were as impressive as those of Coffin House. That was to be expected. Tobias Hull had been almost as successful, almost as wealthy, almost as influential as Coffin. Almost.

He didn't know how long he'd been standing there when the breathless receptionist finally returned. "Miss Hull will see you now, sir. If you will follow me?"

The man led him up two flights of stairs. Unlike Coffin House, Hull House was still located close to the water. From the windows on the upper floors one could look out upon ships and busy crews.

There was a single desk in the middle of the office and Chinese carpets on the floor. A few drawings of ships and animals had been placed indifferently on the walls. Compared to Coffin's own luxurious facilities the place was positively Spartan.

He expected the handsome young woman seated behind the desk to rise with his entrance. What he did not expect was for her to come around to shake his hand. He knew he was staring but couldn't help himself. How old had Rose Hull been the last time he'd seen her? His mind held vague remembrances of a filthy, mistreated little waif with torn clothes and stringy hair. It was hard to match those to the tall, self-assured young woman standing before him.

"I was sorry to hear about your son," she said.

Memories broke apart like cobwebs. "How did you know? Did the sergeant tell you?"

"The sergeant? Oh, the man with the wide shoulders and long face. No, I knew before he came to me. There are other sources of information besides the official ones." She returned to her seat behind the desk. "Please, take a chair." Coffin complied, wondering what he was really doing here. It would have been more appropriate to call on her at home. But his presence did not appear to have upset her.

"I might've heard earlier myself," he mumbled, "but I was on the road."

"I understand," she said sympathetically. "Can I do anything?"

"Do? You mean, for me?" he said, startled.

"Of course. I can see how distraught you are. This must be very difficult for you."

"But not for you?"

Her expression didn't waver. "My father and I were never—close. I always admired him, but I'm afraid that admiration was never translated into affection. He wasn't an affectionate man."

"I knew him well enough to know that," Coffin replied somberly. "How are you managing?"

"Well enough."

"What will you do now?" Prodded by possibilities, his mind was beginning to function normally for the first time since that horrible moment yesterday when Cobb had given him the news. There were still lives to be lived, decisions to be made. "I presume you're going to sell the business."

"Why would I want to do that? Hull House and its myriad components are operating profitably. Why would I want to sell any of them?"

"I see. Well then, you're going to be needing advice, help. Who's going to run the business for you?"

She smiled slightly, glanced down at the desk, then folded her hands on the wooden surface in front of her as she looked back up at him. "Mr. Coffin, my father was very involved in the war, right from the start. I believe you were also. Who do you think ran Hull House in his absence?"

"Actually I never gave it a thought. I had my own concerns to worry about. I just naturally assumed his managers were handling things."

"You 'naturally assumed.' Mr. Coffin, as my father's only heir I have been seeing to the day-to-day operations of Hull House for more than two years."

"Tobias knew that?"

"I'm not sure how much he knew. When he was off fighting

the Kingites he only followed up bad reports, and there were few of those. As long as the balance sheets he received were positive, he felt free to concentrate his energies on militia work. Balance sheets weren't signed by me. When he did want details he never came to me. He rarely knew where I was and cared less, so I don't think he learned how involved I became with the business. His managers would tell him all was going well and that was usually enough to satisfy him. But when it came to making important decisions, I did that. Not his underlings."

"Well you won't have to worry about such things anymore," Coffin said reassuringly. "I can't imagine what a strain it's been for you, but what's done is done. Obviously you coped admiringly. Now that it's over, you can make proper arrangements."

"I see." She was still smiling. A very pretty smile, Coffin noted. "What sort of arrangements would you suggest, Mr. Coffin?"

"Call me Robert, please. I don't know how aware you were of the relationship between your father and myself, but we were never on what you'd call the best of terms."

"I know that much."

"A lot of people were afraid of your father."

She nodded slowly. "I'm aware of that also. I was afraid of him myself."

"I think I was one of the few who wasn't. That was one of the things that made our disagreements so extreme. It bothered him when he encountered someone he couldn't frighten. In any event, we were competitors. Coffin House and Hull House have many similar interests. Now that he's gone, along with my son, I feel I should do something to compensate for all those arguments your father and I had."

"Compensate how?"

"As I mentioned, there are many areas of duplication in our businesses. Shipping lines, stage lines, farming and manufacturing and so forth. A merger of our two grand companies, of Hull and Coffin House, would not only result in greatly improved savings of economy but also in larger profits. Consolidation would bring strength. The result would be by far the biggest company in the colony. One might go so far as to say it would be dominant."

"I'm sure you're right, Robert."

"You would be able at last to take your ease, to release the reins which I'm sure have been an intolerable burden to you these past years. No more strain, no more unnatural dealings with crude, rough businessmen. You would be able to relax and live the life of a proper English gentlewoman. A very wealthy one at that." He made a strenuous effort to mask his eagerness. "How does my proposal strike you?"

"It makes a great deal of sense."

"Then you agree?"

"Naturally. I'll start sending my people over tomorrow to attend to the structuring of the merger."

Coffin frowned slightly. "Your people?"

"Of course. If Hull House is to take over Coffin House we should begin as soon as possible, while there is a lull in the fighting."

He sat forward in his chair. "I think you misunderstand me. I was proposing to lift the burden of administering your father's diverse and far-flung enterprises from your shoulders, to set you up as an independently wealthy woman. To make up for all those years you were mistreated."

She stiffened slightly. "How I was treated as a child is not your concern. I think you're the one who misunderstands, Mr. Coffin. I think you misunderstood when you came here and I know you misunderstand now. I am already an 'independently wealthy woman,' thank you. One who intends to become wealthier. What makes you think I have the slightest interest in leading the life of a 'proper English gentlewoman'? You forget, sir, whose daughter I am."

He should have thanked her, it was such a catharsis to be able to get mad at someone else. "Are you toying with me, young woman?"

"No more than you were toying with me. Let us understand each other, *Robert*. I have enjoyed running Hull House in my father's absence. I expect to enjoy continuing to do so in the future."

Maybe he shouldn't have laughed, but it was all so absurd he couldn't help himself. "You're out of your mind. It'll fall apart around you. You'll never be able to cope with the stress."

"Why not?" Her tone was icy now. "Because I'm a woman?"

"And a young, attractive one at that. Who's going to respect your opinions now that your father's not around to back them up? Do you really think you can give orders to Captains who've sailed between here and Sydney for twenty years? Or to wagon masters whose every word is one not spoken in polite company? What makes you think for a moment they'll do anything other than laugh at you?"

"Because if they do not listen to me they'll soon find themselves looking elsewhere for employment. Then I'll find men who *will* listen to me.

"I've already taken care of my father's will. It is vague in some areas but not where matters of direct inheritance are concerned." Her smile returned. "Tobias Hull was far more generous in death than ever he was in life."

Coffin rose, glaring down at her. "You've let me talk for your private amusement."

"Not a bit of it." She looked calmly back at him. "As I recall you came here to console me over the loss of my father, not to do business. However, I've no objection to you opting for the latter. And now that you've concluded what you came to do, I think it's time for us to part. I've a great deal to do and I'm sure you do also." She hesitated, added in a less formal tone, "Only once did I have the pleasure of meeting Christopher. It was a long time ago. I understand you two were alike in some ways, different in others."

It was intended to soothe Coffin but it only made him angrier. It was good to have someone to direct his frustration at. "Have it your way then, Miss Hull. In all the years your father and I competed we gave each other no quarter. I assure you I won't change that just because you're a woman."

"I wouldn't expect you to."

"I intend to take over Hull House. If our situations were reversed I know your father wouldn't have hesitated to do the same to my family."

"I look forward to doing business, either with you or against you, Mr. Coffin."

He spun and strode toward the door. "You'll never make a go of this. You'll see. People you think are loyal are already plotting against you, waiting for the right time to ease you out of the director's chair. Men who'll throw you out in the street. You'll end up with nothing. When that happens you'll remember the offer I made you this day, but then it'll be too late. You're throwing away a life of luxury and ease, for a whim."

"I assure you, Mr. Coffin, I do nothing on a whim. Now I bid you good day."

He nodded once, brusquely, too furious to reply. He could not say what he wanted to say, not and retain his dignity. There was nothing more to be gained here, certainly not by verbally abusing this stubborn, ignorant young woman.

He let himself out, ignoring the curious glances that followed him. Let her enjoy her brief moment of triumph. His eventual takeover of Hull House was as inevitable as the rise and fall of the tides. With Tobias Hull dead nothing could stop him from merging the two concerns to form the biggest private company in the country. He'd waited this long for his final victory over Hull; he could wait a little longer. A woman's attempts to direct Hull's extensive and far-flung enterprises would quickly result in the company disintegrating of its own weight. All he needed to do was be patient and wait for it to fall into his lap.

She'd spurned his generous offer. The choice had been hers. She was young and pig-headed and one day she would come to regret her words. Nor was he the only one she was going to have to contend with. Angus McQuade and the rest of the colony's merchant barons would rapidly move in on Hull House regardless of whatever Coffin did, probing and testing like gulls picking at the corpse of a seal. She wouldn't halt such incursions with words.

The thought of her fighting to stave off the predatory thrusts of men like Angus, Ainsworth and Sanderson muted his anger. She was upset and confused, after all. Her father had only just died, leaving her with innumerable decisions to make. Let her try to deal with the situation for a month or two. Then he would make his proposal again. No need to argue. She'd soon see the light. Better if he could take over with as little fuss and trouble as possible.

As he emerged onto the busy street he found he was feeling better. He could be generous in victory—yes, generous. Keep in mind that underneath, Rose Hull was still a frightened child sneaking around the fringes of Hull's immense, gloomy mansion when she wasn't prowling the wharfs and docks. It was only natural for her to reject overtures of friendship and assistance. Only realistic for her to be suspicious.

Let the others wear her down while they enlightened her to the realities of the business world. When he made his offer anew she would be ready, nay, eager to accept. He would swallow his momentary outrage, she would swallow her false pride, and all would be well. And Holly would improve. He would see to it. Soon he would have everything he'd ever wanted.

The sun shone down brightly as he walked homeward, but it was not strong enough to penetrate the darkness that shadowed him.

9

"My sister is a whore!"

Te Ohine sighed and leaned back in his chair. It was a good, solid chair, made of English walnut, and it supported his considerable weight with ease. He had another, but his son wouldn't sit on it, preferring instead the low, carved traditional stool.

This was no day to fight, to argue. The sky was clear, there was no sign of rain, and there was enough sun to warm the blood of an old man. Outside, children ran through the village, laughing and playing. Into the midst of this contentment had come his son, an evil dark spirit, a black cloud drawing stares from everyone he passed. In his presence the very air itself took on an oppressive heaviness.

Yet Opotiki was his favorite son. He could not deny him entrance, nor could he turn away the thirty or so warriors who traveled with the young man. Te Ohine had looked on them with pity. They were a ragged, tired-looking lot, many of them carrying recent scars. A few were missing eyes or limbs. They were slowed by their heavy burden of clubs and swords, rifles and sabers. The villagers eyed them warily and whispered among themselves. At Te Ohine's bidding they had been given food and drink, a courtesy that would have been extended to any travelers regardless of their politics or the color of their skin.

The old chief had to think a moment. "Your sister is not the thing you have said."

"She is worse than a whore!" Opotiki repeated contemptuously. "She is a traitorous whore. Not only does she lie with men to whom she is not married, she lies with pakehas."

"If I know this thing rightly, a whore is one who sleeps with men for money. Your sister would never do that. So she is not what you say. She is too proud to do such a thing. If she sleeps

315

with a man it is because she wishes to. Where is the harm in that?"

"Not even with a warrior," Opotiki sneered quietly. "She sleeps with a common laborer, a workman who does not fight with the pakeha soldiers. A coward."

"You have seen this for yourself?"

"No, but it is spoken of."

"Then you cannot say it is so."

"Will you say she does not sleep in the house of your pakeha friend Robert Coffin?"

"Of course I will not. This everyone knows. She is keeper of his Tarawera house."

"You deny she sleeps with him as well as this other man?"

Te Ohine considered. "Without asking him myself I can say nothing, though I would not think it likely. Coffin did not wish to take her into his service, but I argued with him and finally he agreed. The pakehas take only one wife at a time. Do you think he sleeps with Merita with his family present?"

"Pagh! There are many times Coffin is at Tarawera without his wife."

"And if this be true, is it such a bad thing?" Te Ohine smiled condescendingly. "What will be between a man and a woman will be."

Opotiki's reply was vehement. "He is the enemy!"

"Robert Coffin is, has long been, and always will be my friend. He would be your friend too, if you would let him." Te Ohine was aging, but he could still summon the commanding tone and presence of a high ariki when necessary. Under that relentless, unblinking stare Opotiki found he could only nod dutifully.

"As you say, Father."

"That is better. Now, why the long face, why such misery? Did you not have pakeha friends of your own before the troubles?"

"I did. They are strangers to me now. All pakehas are my enemy." He gazed earnestly up at the old chief. "As they should be yours. If we do not fight together we will never defeat them. Maoris should no longer quarrel among themselves."

"I have no quarrels with you, my son."

"I know that, Father." Opotiki's tone softened. Anger having failed to move the old man, he now decided to try reason. "Surely even you can see what is happening. Each year there are more and more pakehas. They come in the great canoes and they breed like flies among sheep. Their sicknesses kill us. Every month they take more and more of the old lands for themselves. The pakeha has a hunger for land that treaties will never satisfy, and what they take they never sell back. They will not be sated until they have pushed us into the high mountains or off Te Ika-a-maui altogether. Then they will push us off Te Waipounamu as well. Where will we live then, Father? What will we do? Take to the canoes like our ancestors and sail off in search of another Aotearoa? This is the land the gods gave us. Not the pakehas. We will stay *here*."

"Of course we will stay here." Te Ohine smiled condescendingly. "An end will come to the fighting, you will see. The pakehas will tire of it, the Maori will tire of it, and there will be peace as there was before."

Opotiki shook his head violently. "It can never be as it was before, Father. Can't you see that? No matter who wins, Maori and pakeha will never be able to deal truthfully with each other again. What has been broken cannot be made whole again."

"What nonsense is that? Broken canoes can be mended, broken hands, broken friendships as well."

"I do not believe that. Now I must fight harder than ever because it is known that my sister has a pakeha lover."

"I see." Te Ohine adopted a somber mien. "You, my son, have never slept with a pakeha woman?"

"No. Nor do I have a desire to do so."

"Pity. They are pale, fragile creatures. You would think love-making would break them like eggs, but they do not break. This I can vouch for myself." He smiled down at his son.

Opotiki turned away, perhaps to conceal a smile of his own. He was a good man, Te Ohine knew. It was not his fault he still suffered from the sickness of youth. Like that of many young warriors his heart was easily filled with a lust for fighting. This had ever been so for the Maori. Before the coming of the pakeha their love of battle had been directed at each other. Now those who would fight had a common enemy. Yet even in this time of long war there were many Maori and pakeha who remained friends, who did not fight, who stood apart from the killings on both sides.

"Those who lived in peace before can do so again."

"It is not hard to live in peace with the pakeha," said Opotiki contemptuously as he turned back to face his father. "All you have to do is give them everything they want, give in to all their demands, and there will be peace. They will pat you on the head and smile and call you a good boy. That is a life for children and slaves, not for warriors."

Te Ohine took a deep breath. "You cannot defeat the pakeha. As you have just said, their number is endless. They have better guns than we have and they do not have to ration their powder and bullets. They have the big guns and the warships. The pakeha are the People of the Gun. We cannot fight their ships with our guns so we cannot keep them from coming to settle here. We cannot fight their big guns so when they bring those we have to run away."

"All that you say is so, Father." Opotiki gestured with his own rifle. "But we can shoot as well as any of them and when it comes to close fighting," he smacked his greenstone war club with an open palm, "we are better than they. Each day we learn new ways to beat them. It is true we cannot defeat them all at once, but we can keep bleeding them. The strongest man will fall if he bleeds constantly.

"Some day we will have bled them so much that they will realize it is better to make an honest peace with us on our terms then to go on bleeding. Maybe we cannot defeat them, but so long as real warriors are left neither can they beat us. This is still our land first. We know the valleys and the forest. The land is our ally, as it was Rui's, as it is the other war chiefs'. We will keep bleeding them, Father, and it may be that with the help of the gods we can even defeat them in spite of all you say."

"You speak of our gods. What of theirs? They claim their god is the greatest among gods and that he will give them the strength to defeat us."

Opotiki rose and began pacing. "I do not believe in their god, but if they are right, if he is real, if he is the greatest of all gods, then it must also be that he is the kind of god the pakeha tohungas say he is. A god of peace and not of war. The Maoris have war gods to help them. The pakeha have no war god. Only their lies and their guns." He halted suddenly and walked over to look down at his father.

"I and my warriors thank you for the shelter and food you have given us."

Te Ohine did not meet his son's gaze. "I remember Maori hospitality," he mumbled, "and you are still my favorite son."

Opotiki leaned forward and rested one hand on his father's shoulder. It was not a properly respectful gesture for a young warrior to make to a high chief, but they had seen little of each other the past three years.

"You and Mother must keep well, must stay healthy until this war is over. Then you will see that I was right. I hope you may come to see it sooner."

A very young warrior, not yet out of his teens, entered in haste and waited until Te Ohine spoke to him. "What is it?"

"Your pardon, ariki, but there are pakehas at the gate."

Opotiki was instantly on guard, grabbing up his rifle and club. "I must go."

Te Ohine indicated his son should wait. "Stay. Perhaps you will learn something." He addressed the young warrior. "What do these visitors wish?"

The adolescent hesitated. "They say they want to trade."

"There, you see?" Te Ohine looked up at his son. "You were wrong. The pakeha are not the people of the gun. They are the money people. That is what will bring this war to an end, because the Maori are money people too."

Opotiki's gaze narrowed as he regarded the messenger. "What kind of trade?"

Te Ohine indicated the youth could reply. "They say they have swords and guns to sell."

At that Opotiki's eyes lit up. "Weapons! You see, father, the war gods of the Maori help us even here. It is true the Maori still quarrel among themselves, but the pakeha do not always agree either. We cannot stand together because we always argue. The pakeha cannot unify because their lust for gold is their greatest love." He looked sharply back at the youth. "What kind of guns? Army? Sporting rifles? Old muskets?"

"The pakeha leader did not say."

"It does not matter." Te Ohine was clearly upset. "We have no need of guns here."

"Father, please!" Opotiki came around in front of the old man. "You should buy some to defend yourself. This pa is badly situated."

"Not for access to fields and water. I have no need for a great fortress around my home. I am at peace. That is the strongest stockade of all."

"At least see what he is offering, what they have brought. You know I cannot approach him in your village without your permission."

"I will not buy weapons for you, my son."

"We have gold of our own. You must at least speak to them."

Te Ohine went silent while both his son and the young messenger waited for a decision. At last the ariki looked up. "Yes, you are right. I must speak with them." Opotiki smiled broadly and Te Ohine was quick to chasten him. "But not to buy his guns! It would be impolite to turn a trader away without greeting him properly."

Te Ohine hurriedly assembled a formal retinue, including Opotiki. Then he went out to greet his visitors.

The two big wagons had already been wheeled inside the gate. There were only four pakeha, which Opotiki thought foolish even though they were well-armed. He and his warriors could have overpowered them easily. But his father's village was a "neutral" one. Though tempted, he did not give the idea serious thought. Even if such an attempt proved successful, he would have gained some guns at the expense of a father.

Besides, there was a good chance they could buy the guns without trouble. And the four pakehas were alert and well-armed. Better to pay for them without the risk of losing any more of his men. He was not surprised to see that the pakehas who sat atop the wagons, one in front and one behind, kept their own rifles close at hand. They had to be ready to defend their cargo not only against marauding Maoris but against their own people. The pakehas looked with great disfavor on other whites who sold guns to the Kingites.

On seeing the chiefly retinue approaching, one man hopped down off the nearest wagon. Opotiki frowned. Could this sorry specimen be the pakeha leader? The man looked more nervous than he ought to be considering he was inside a neutral village. He was unsteady on his feet. As he drew near the reason for this became evident: he was quite drunk. So were his companions. Opotiki sniffed in disgust, hoping they traded in a better grade of guns than they did of whiskey.

The trader focused rheumy eyes on him. "You the chief?"

It was expected such men would know little of politeness, but even among the ruder pakehas there was usually an attempt at cordiality. Opotiki detected no hint of this. Still, if their guns were good. . . .

"No." He stepped aside as his father moved forward.

"You may call me Te Ohine." The ariki did not bother to give his full name since it clearly would be wasted on these visitors.

"I'm Barber. Simon Barber." The trader did not offer his hand in friendship. Instead he retreated a couple of steps until he was standing next to the wagon he'd been riding. He patted the heavy tarp that covered the load. "Got somethin' in here oughta interest you."

"Guns, weapons. More death," Te Ohine muttered distastefully.

"Why sure. That's what you folks are interested in, ain't it? Fightin' an' killin'."

"We value the ways of the warrior," Te Ohine replied slowly, "but we do not glorify death." He made a sweeping gesture. "This pa is a peaceful one. We take no sides in the war, as any of the pakehas nearby will tell you."

"Yeh, we talked to some of 'em." Barber stroked his whiskey-sodden beard, then ran the same hand through his hair. The strands protruded like tree roots from beneath his filthy brown hat. "O' course these farmers an' sheep herders, they ain't real bright. Don't even know what's good for 'em."

"We don't need your guns here," Te Ohine said sharply. "Take them and go away."

"Father!" Opotiki stepped forward. "You said that. . . ."

"No!" Furious but obedient, Opotiki retreated. To challenge his father in front of the whole village would have been an unpardonable insult. Te Ohine turned back to face the trader. "This is a neutral village. My people are farmers. We do not fight."

"Maoris what don't fight? Ain't no such thing." Barber's cracked lips split in a wicked, unpleasant grin. "Don't you want to see what we got anyway, just to see what you're missin' out on?"

Te Ohine was unyielding. "I will look at your weapons out of politeness, but I tell you now I will not buy any of 'em."

"Oh, that's all right," said the smiling Barber as he backed closer to the wagon, "cause we didn't bring 'em here to sell 'em." He let out a whoop as he yanked hard on the canvas tarp. "Let's get 'em, boys!"

The canvas sheet was wrenched aside to reveal not crates of rifles or ammunition, but a wagon crammed with armed pakehas. Some of them were as drunk as the drivers, but it didn't much matter since at point-blank range the massed fire of more than forty rifles was enough to cut down every Maori standing in the line of fire. In the still afternoon air the thunder of so many guns going off simultaneously was deafening, shocking.

At least a dozen Maoris went down. No one had time to count and the smoke from the guns momentarily obscured the wagons and their immediate surroundings.

Opotiki didn't wait to see what would happen next. He moved fast to one side, shouting for his men to rally around him. Without waiting to see who responded he raised his greenstone club and rushed through the smoke in the direction of the pakeha leader.

Simon Barber's eyes widened as he saw Opotiki plunging through the haze toward him. He had his pistol up and ready and fired when the Maori was not more than six feet away, but in his drunken panic the shot went wild. Opotiki felt it singe his cheek, as if someone had touched him with a hot splinter. It didn't slow him down.

Barber managed to get his sword up in time to counter Opotiki's initial blow. The club shattered the cheap steel, sending fragments flying. Opotiki raised the weapon for another swing, intending to crush the pakeha's skull, but the man let out a terrified yelp and ducked beneath the wagon.

The smoke was clearing and the pakehas in the wagons had begun to reload. Opotiki hesitated. He couldn't see the pakeha's legs. Perhaps he'd burrowed into the ground. If he stayed where he was he'd surely be shot, and that would do no one any good. So he turned and ran, not pausing to stare as he raced past his father's body, a large and somehow peaceful form lying on the ground with at least three bullets in it. He was too busy screaming to his own men, trying to organize some kind of defense in his mind.

It was useless. The lightly armed villagers were in a panic, running in all directions, their chief dead. The pakehas' surprise had been complete. Now they were pouring out of the two wagons, stumbling over each other in their eagerness to get off as many shots as possible, whooping and hollering as they fired loaded pistols at any Maori within range. They did

not discriminate in their choice of targets, not bothering to
ascertain whether their victims were armed or not.

A few pakehas made for the gate, cut down the two guards
there, and flung the entrance wide to admit the rest of their
fellows who'd been hiding outside. Opotiki could see that all
of them had been drinking, perhaps to bolster their courage.

The attackers comprised the worst of pakeha society, men
too cowardly or criminal to be allowed to serve in the militia,
much less the regular army. Somehow this Barber and his
colleagues had gathered a mob of them together, scrounged
weapons, and decided to aid the war effort in their own way.
How secret could such plans be kept? Opotiki wondered how
many "respectable" pakehas had known of the attack but had
voiced no opposition.

Off to one side a woman was running toward the presumed
safety of a house when one of the pakehas cut her off. She
whirled and tried to retreat in another direction, clutching a
small child in her arms. She ran straight into another pakeha's
sword, impaling herself. The baby fell to the ground, squawl-
ing. Both men ignored it as they began arguing among
themselves, the first man screaming at the second for killing a
young woman. While they fought among themselves she bled
to death at their feet.

Other screams began to rise above the constant crackle of
gunfire, screams that had nothing to do with murder. Opotiki
ignored them too as he finally found his own warriors. Several
were using their own rifles but many didn't know what to do or
how to react. He had to hit them to get their attention.

"We cannot stay here!" he shouted. "We must leave!"

"But this is your father's village," Auruneri protested.

Opotiki gave the man a shove. "My father is dead. So is this
village. It died when it thought it had made peace with the
pakeha."

One of the other warriors was reloading his musket. "We
can still fight them!"

"Not here." Opotiki tried to see back through the smoke.
"There are too many and my father's best fighters were all
killed right away. Others are dying before they can reach their
own weapons. We must flee or we will all die here."

Another woman's scream lingered piercingly in the air.
Several of the warriors turned in its direction. One looked

pleadingly back at Opotiki, who was also staring in the direction of the heart-rending sound.

"Warriors do not abandon their women." The expression on the young man's face was pitiful to behold.

Opotiki steeled himself. "These are not our women. We have women of our own to protect elsewhere. If we die here they will die too. Quickly now, this way, go, go!" He began grabbing them by arms and shoulders, shoving, urging, cajoling them toward the rear of the pa.

Flames began to fill the sky as the pakehas set fire to the long houses and granaries. Inside the smoke it was difficult to tell pakeha from Maori. While this restrained Opotiki's men it did not seem to bother the pakehas. They fired wildly and frequently, not appearing to care if they hit their own people.

Opotiki formed his remaining warriors into a defensive semicircle as two of them began to cut at the ropes that bound several logs in place. As Te Ohine had said, his was not a strong pa. The stockade was as much for show and tradition as for actual defense. The ropes parted easily. Logs were shoved aside, creating an opening large enough for men to file through one at a time.

"We could circle around outside and get behind them." Auruneri looked hopeful. "Attack them where they do not expect it."

Opotiki spoke deliberately. "We are few, they are many. There could be a hundred or more. Besides, that is how the pakehas would like to fight us: out in the open where we can be surrounded and shot down like pigs. We must get back to the woods."

Auruneri considered this, then straightened. "Animals hunt in the woods. I am tired of hunting like an animal."

"Live animals can still bite. Dead ones are just meat."

The two warriors locked eyes for a precious moment. Then the defiant Auruneri slumped, nodded once, and vanished through the gap in the stockade.

Opotiki waited until the last of his men had gone through. He paused at the makeshift exit for a final look at the village of his youth. This was where he had spent his childhood, his happiest years, before the pakeha had swarmed over the land. Off somewhere to his right, hidden by the swirling smoke, was the maypole where he had played with his friends. His friends and his sister, who was dead to him now because she sought the affection of pakehas. Perhaps after all his father had been right about that. Perhaps she was nothing more than a servant, which was bad enough.

But if it could be proven true he would kill her pakeha lover. And if she had also slept with Robert Coffin who had been a friend to his father, he, Opotiki, would kill this Coffin as well, as they would kill every pakeha on Aotearoa.

His father had spoken of peace. There could be no peace with creatures like this, Opotiki knew. One might as well try to make peace with the shark. Like him, the pakeha knew only how to kill.

He tried to close his ears to the screams of dying women and children even as he tried to shut his mind to what he'd already witnessed, to no avail. Everything had been burned into his memory. He could never, would never, forget. At last he turned and followed his men into the trees that grew behind the village, covering the ground in long, powerful strides.

He would remember it all until the end of his days, and the worst of it wasn't the sound of men dying or of women screaming. The worst of it was the echo of drunken pakeha laughter.

10

Merita watched him dress. As it often did, her gaze went to his silvery hair. So strange. He had gone gray as a young man, he'd told her. That meant he looked older than he was. It also meant that while other men aged, Coffin seemed to stay the same. Sometimes he seemed eternally young, at other times eternally old. A contradictory man, even for a pakeha. Knowledgeable, strong, yet naive in ways even he didn't realize.

The past months had been difficult. She had done what she could to try and comfort him, but he still mourned for his son. When first she'd learned of his tragedy she feared he might not care for her anymore, might look on her differently because the death had come at Maori hands. She relaxed only when she saw this was not so.

Then word had come of the death of her father and the destruction of her village and it was his turn to comfort her. Instead of driving them apart their mutual pain only brought them closer together.

His hurt was deeper than hers, for in some ways she had given up a part of her family when she'd come to stay in a pakeha house, even though it had been partly at her father's bidding. And she still had many relatives to turn to, members of her whanau living all across North Island. Coffin had only his wife, and from what he had told her that woman was no comfort to him at all. His other relatives lived on the other side of the world, in that strange pakeha land called England. Here, now, there was only Merita, and though she tried she could not take away his sorrow.

When she'd moved away from her home she'd left behind the warmth and reassurance of her family. She'd needed him. Now he needed her.

At first he and some other pakehas had talked of revenge, of justice, but even that was a dead issue. As dead as her village. After the massacre the men who'd perpetrated it had looked on what they'd done and become ashamed. They'd drifted away, scattering to the distant corners of the colony and across the sea. Their leader, a man named Barber, had been killed soon after in a fight with warriors over in the Urewera country. Most of his men had died with him, having found armed warriors harder to deal with than women and children.

And still there were men to be found among the pakehas, even among the well-meaning ones, who shrugged it all off. It was no more than another unpleasant and regrettable incident in a long and increasingly debilitating conflict, they said. Hadn't the Maoris, under barbarians like Alexander Rui, committed similar atrocities? The line between Maori and European had grown blurred. Some of the pakehas began to wonder aloud and in public what the war was really about, and to debate which side was the more civilized.

She rolled over in the bed, the clean white sheets highlighting her coffee-colored skin. "I wish you didn't have to go, Robert."

He looked back down at her as he fastened his belt. "I don't want to go, Merita. I never want to go when I'm here with you. Sometimes I think this is the last place in the world where I can really be happy. But I have to go. You know that."

"I know it," she said softly.

His visits were growing longer and for that she was grateful. At the same time they had to be increasingly careful. Te Wairoa was still a small community, but new families kept moving into the area. Pakehas were beginning to settle in the vicinity as well. It was harder to keep their true relationship a secret.

There were times when Coffin no longer seemed to care, when he teetered on the edge of abandoning his previous life altogether. When he talked of giving up everything he'd worked for to settle here in the central highlands with her. It remained only talk and nothing more. His wife needed him more than ever, needed his care and attention. Coffin House needed him, now that his son was gone. The colony needed the military expertise he'd gained fighting the Kingites.

He would say these things to her as he reluctantly mounted his horse and rode away northward, alone, as if daring the rebels to attack him. Perhaps somewhere deep inside he hoped that they would, thereby putting an end to his personal agony.

Only a Kingite bullet could resolve his insoluble problem. It never came.

She knew as she watched him ride away that she would never truly understand him. He was too complex for her, too complex for anyone perhaps. She would have to be satisfied with loving him.

She stood on the porch and waved until he was out of sight. Once he turned to wave back at her. Then he was gone. As always she stood staring for a long time and as always he did not reappear. Only then did she turn away from the road that led northward to face the lake.

Tarawera shone in the sun, a vast blue mirror that reflected the mountain it was named after. The mountain itself climbed to its ultimate height in several gentle, surging rises, miles to the south. This was a fine place, a beautiful place, here by the great lake. She was surprised more pakehas had not chosen to settle here. Robert told her it was too remote for most. The pakehas loved their towns and cities, even as they loved the ocean. All of their largest pas were built on the coast. It was almost as if the sea provided some kind of tenuous tie to the mother colony of Australia and to distant England.

She looked away from the lake and its mountain in the direction of Te Wairoa. If she sent word Flynn would be at her side by tomorrow.

If only she could somehow combine both men in one. Now that was an intriguing thought. Merge the wealth, the confidence and experience of Robert Coffin with the fiery nature, the intensity and youthful joy of Flynn. What a man that would make! Something else that could never be, she knew.

There had been times when she was comforting Robert over the loss of his son and the indifference of his wife when she'd been tempted to tell Flynn not to come again. To tell him she was committed to serving Coffin in whatever capacity he would have her: as mistress, as second wife, or just as housekeeper and confidante. Then winter would settle in. The big house on the lakeshore would stand empty for long periods of time. She would pace the hallways and rooms until her own footsteps began to follow her and little Andrew's cries became oppressive instead of joyful.

And Flynn would come, to warm and comfort her, to work at her side keeping the house in good repair, a task he went at with a dedication that amazed her. It was almost as though he was working not for his salary, which she paid from the household account, but for himself. It was good during the cold nights to have someone else to carry the wood and keep the stove and fireplaces blazing, better still to have someone to keep her warm regardless of what burned in the stone firepits.

She felt so different when she was with Flynn. You never knew what he was going to say or do next. His very unpredictability was exciting. She stayed alert and alive in his company. He was always ready to try something new, do something different, whereas in Robert's presence there was quiet strength and reassurance, the calm power of a man who could wave his hand and accomplish anything.

I am very lucky, she thought. She had not been in the village and so had escaped the massacre that had taken the lives of most of her friends and family. And she had not one but two extraordinary lovers. Most women would never have one such in a lifetime.

She wondered how long she could maintain her dual life, how long she could keep Robert ignorant of her relationship with Flynn. It hurt her to think about it, so most of the time she did not.

11

"Hello, Holly."

She was sitting motionless in the same chair, staring out the same window. She lived there, he thought to himself. The only time she moved was when one of her friends came to visit. Only then would she show flashes of the old Holly, of the vivacious, determined, seemingly indestructible woman he'd married. Spying on her and her friends at such times his heart would jump, only for the hope such visits raised to vanish when they left and she slid back into her former apathetic state, turning again to staring silently out the window, not wanting to talk, to go out, not wanting even to eat.

At such times one of the maids would have to feed her by hand, almost as one would feed a child. Holly would eat then, chewing and swallowing, indifferent to the food itself no matter how much effort Cook devoted to the meal. "Terminal depression" the doctor called it, and nothing could shake the mood. His wife wore gloom like a second skin.

Coffin turned the Auckland house into a veritable palace, filling it with every possible amusement and diversion. For a while he tried giving gala parties, which he personally detested, in the hope it would bring Holly back to something approaching normal. They worked no better than anything else. Eventually the list of those willing to attend grew smaller and smaller until the few people who came clustered tightly around the mountains of food and drink Coffin provided, chatting in low voices and whispers as they tried not to stare at their host and silent hostess. When Coffin realized he was the only one talking, he declared that he'd thrown his last party.

Quietly he walked over toward her window. She was still beautiful sitting solemnly in her chair, a blemishless wax effigy. She wore black, as usual. Attempts to dress her in anything brighter provoked violent fits.

"Holly. Christopher's not coming back. Nothing can change that. So why do you continue to keep watching for him?"

Usually she didn't respond. Now she turned slightly in the chair to look up at him. "Because it is all I can do."

"Dammit, it's *not* all you can do." He tried and failed to make it sound important, knowing even as he spoke his words would have little effect on her.

In the beginning he'd begged, pleaded with her, abased himself as he never would before any other human being, done things he'd never thought he'd do for anyone. All this proved he still loved her. He told himself that repeatedly, but could never bring himself to admit whether he did so to convince her—or himself. It was difficult to love someone who'd voluntarily withdrawn from life, yet love her he did.

What made him keep trying were those rare, isolated instances when she would unexpectedly respond, when she would abandon the death-chair and ask to go for a ride through the country or into the city, or simply to play a quick hand of cards. At such times, though quiet as a ghost, she could look and act almost normal. Then when he dared to hope, she would revert to her somnambulist self. Those were the cruelest moments of all.

"It's not the only thing you can do," he repeated. When she didn't respond he turned away in disgust. "I have to go to the office. Elias needs me."

"I know. You go ahead, Robert. I'll be all right." She tried to smile. Once she'd had a smile brighter than the lighthouse that now lit the way for ships entering Auckland harbor. Now even that tiny suggestion of happiness was an effort for her.

He did his best to hide how he was feeling. "I'll be home as soon as I'm able."

"I know you will."

He started for the door, suddenly whirled on her, his voice tight and intense.

"Look, *I wasn't there*. I couldn't have done anything even if I had been. Hundreds of families have lost sons in this miserable war!"

She sat and stared out the window, neither smiling nor frowning, not responding at all.

Things were going to get better, he knew. George Gray, their esteemed and revered former Governor, had heard of the trouble afflicting his old command and had agreed to return from Cape Town colony to take charge. It was unheard of for a former Governor to return to a previous post but Gray was determined to do it. If anyone could find a way out of the morass New Zealand had plunged into, could make a just end to the Maori war, then Gray was the man to do so. The Maoris, the old chiefs, even those who had set their course irrevocably against that of the pakehas, would remember Gray's fairness and wisdom. They would trust him where they trusted no one else. Gray would put an end to the fighting.

"Did you have a good time at Tarawera?"

"What?" Her words unnerved him badly for a moment, then he relaxed. A perfectly natural question considering he'd spent the last two weeks at the lake house. There was nothing suggestive in her tone. Tarawera was too remote, too little visited by colonials for gossip to work its way up to Auckland. Many of their friends knew Sydney and Melbourne better than they did the Tarawera district. She couldn't know, and even if she did he doubted in her present state that she was capable of drawing conclusions.

"It was a useful stay, as always. Our sheep ranches in the region are prospering, though of course they'd do better if the war was ended." He hesitated for the barest instant. "Wouldn't you like to take a ride down there again? The weather's good. I built the place for you, you know."

"Yes." She let out an ethereal sigh. "For Christopher and me." He had to strain to hear her. "I don't know."

"We'll go sometime soon."

"Yes. Soon."

Suddenly he had to get out of the room, out of the house. Once it had been a cheerful, stately place, the finest residence in the whole city, nay, in the entire country. Now it was a gray ghost of its former self, not unlike its mistress. The darkness that had enveloped her had extended itself to the building and surrounding grounds. From home to tomb, he thought angrily. Well, he was damned if he was going to bury himself here.

For a weekday the streets were unusually quiet. There was little traffic. He walked past unattended wagons whose dray animals pawed boredly at the ground. Puzzled by the silence, he lengthened his stride. What had happened in the two weeks he'd been away? Today wasn't a holiday. Something unusual must be going on, perhaps a real fight down by the waterfront.

Serious brawls were rare these days. Anyone who wanted to fight joined the militia to do battle with the Kingites; there was no need to fight with one's neighbors.

Even Coffin House was muted, only a few people using the front doors. The normal rush and bustle was absent. He entered frowning.

A few clerks glanced up at him before resuming their work. Coffin's jaw dropped. More than half the desks were deserted. He should have stopped someone in the street and questioned him, but he'd been so caught up in his own personal problems he'd shrugged off the absence of activity. By the time he burst into Elias Goldman's office he was all but running.

It was an impressive chamber, as befitted the number-two man at Coffin House. The heavy wooden desk was piled high with papers. Of Goldman himself there was no sign.

He entered from a back closet a moment later, looking in surprise at his unexpected visitor.

"Mr. Coffin! When did you get back, sir?"

"Just this morning, Elias. Haven't had much sleep." He went silent, listening. It was much too quiet. He missed the noise of people walking the halls, the steady hum of pencils and pens on paper, the underlying murmur of men and women active at their positions.

"What's going on, Elias? Where is everybody? If our competitors get wind of this we'll be in for some real trouble."

"No we won't, Mr. Coffin, because our competitors are in as bad or worse shape than we are." Goldman moved to gaze out the window that overlooked the city's new financial district. "Everyone has the same problem."

"What are you talking about? Elias, what's been going on here?"

Goldman turned to gape at him. "You mean you haven't heard?"

"Dammit, man, I've been two weeks in the interior! You don't get much news at Te Wairoa."

"Then you really don't know." Goldman relaxed in his chair, looking thoughtful. "It's quite astonishing, really. There was of course nothing I or anyone else could do to stem the exodus. Not once the word came in."

Coffin sat down in a chair opposite, trying to stay calm. "What word might that be, Elias? You still haven't explained what's happened to everyone." Had the whole world gone completely mad in his absence, Coffin wondered? No, not the whole world. Elias was still here.

"Gone." Goldman spread his hands in a gesture of helplessness. "They've left. Most of them, at any rate."

"Left? What do you mean, 'left'? Don't they know this will cost them their jobs?"

"The ones who've gone don't care about jobs anymore. Oh, I expect some to begin trickling back in a few months, but in the meantime it's going to be difficult to run things properly. Our only consolation is that every other merchant in the country is in the same position. Or will be, once the word has spread everywhere. The situation's no better in Wellington or Christchurch, I'm sure. And Dunedin." He shook his head. "Ah, Dunedin! That's where they've all gone, you see."

"Why would anyone go to Dunedin, much less everyone?" Dunedin was a sleepy fishing port on the cold southeast coast of South Island.

"It's actually quite funny," Goldman replied. "Once you get past the fact that we're going to have trouble running things. Here good old George Gray is returning to take charge of the government, the war is gradually being won, even the Taranaki Rebellion in the west is winding down, and then this has to go and happen."

"What has to go and happen, Elias? I'm tired of trying to guess."

"Something we used to joke about. That's what's so amusing. Gold."

Coffin knew he hadn't heard right, asked again.

"Gold. Don't you remember?" Goldman prompted him. "We used to talk about the possibilities, years and years ago. Everyone always said there was nothing worth digging out of the ground in this country except greenstone and amber. Well, it seems they were wrong. It seems we were all wrong. Gold has been found in the Otago country on South Island. And there, Mr. Coffin, is where most of the able-bodied men, not to mention clerks, accountants and messengers, have run to."

Coffin absorbed this astonishing pronouncement. Then he rose and walked around Goldman's desk to stare out over the strangely empty city. Goldman swiveled to watch him.

"It can't be," he said finally. "It's got to be some kind of false alarm. There's no gold in New Zealand."

"Try telling that to the man who arrived by ship from

Dunedin just last week, sir. He had two saddlebags with him and both were filled with gold. I know. When I heard, I went to the bank to see for myself. Nuggets and dust. Thirty or forty pounds of the stuff. I was there when Longmount himself assayed it out. It's real enough, Mr. Coffin."

There was silence in the office. Finally Coffin turned back to face the desk. "Well, *we* aren't going anywhere, at least. You're not, are you, Elias?"

"Who, me?" Goldman smiled up at him. "Do I look like a gold miner, Mr. Coffin? I wouldn't last ten days in the Remarkables. Besides, I know where my fortune lies."

Coffin nodded. "Your gold's always been in your head, Elias."

"And lately in my teeth." Both men laughed.

"They'll be back," Coffin told him with assurance. "It was that way after the Australian rush and it'll be that way here."

"I agree, sir. But until they do start returning it is going to be hard to find even barely qualified people to do the most basic work."

"We'll manage. We've done so before and we'll do so again."

Coffin turned to stare out across the new buildings toward the forest of masts that dominated the harbor. Many vessels but few sailors, he suspected. Seamen would be among the first to run for the gold fields.

Having struggled and fought to build Coffin House into the dominant commercial enterprise it was, he'd expected at this point in his life to be able to relax and enjoy the fruits of his labors. Now he was going to have to plunge back into the routine of long days once more. He should have been disappointed. Instead he found himself oddly elated. Work was going to require his full attention again. There would be no time for sadness and frustration, no room for the dark malaise that had settled like a cancer on his soul. The only thing he regretted was that he would not, for a while at least, be able to make as many visits to Tarawera, or stay as long when he did. Not until he and Elias wrestled the business back onto its feet.

They would be desperately short of personnel, but as Elias had pointed out so would their competitors. If they acted correctly this debilitating discovery might even offer opportunities to gain on their opponents.

Rose Hull, he thought, would be having more trouble than

most retaining her male employees. Not long ago he'd promised to show her no quarter. Now was the time to do exactly that. One way or the other he'd get control of Hull House. Let her compete with him now, with half her best people racing wild-eyed toward the gold fields. Let her try and stop him.

Let anyone try and stop him.

BOOK FIVE

1870

1

"Gentlemen, I'm convinced the only choice left open to us is to abandon the colony now, sell out and realize what money we can, before we are all ruined forever."

The tumult which had preceded the declaration was nothing compared to that which followed it. As was his wont, Coffin sat back in his chair in banker Longmount's office and let the rest of them rave and shout. There were harsh words and several men all but came to blows. They weren't angry at each other so much as they were at fate. It did no good to curse fate, however, so they had to settle for screaming at one another.

In truth they seemed to have little choice left. Rushton had merely voiced what many of them were thinking. You had to give him credit for that much, Coffin mused. Rushton was a gambler, the sort of entrepreneur who could be broke one week and wildly wealthy the next, only to squander his new-won fortune anew on some exotic money-making scheme none of his colleagues would touch with a shaved Kauri. Coffin admired the man if not his judgement. Like Rushton he believed in taking chances. That was how he had built the commercial empire that was Coffin House.

He just didn't believe in taking as *many* chances.

"There's no denyin' things are bad." Strange to see Angus McQuade suddenly looking his age, Coffin thought. He'd always thought of Angus as so much younger than himself. Now time had caught up with the perpetually youthful Scotsman as well as with the rest of them. "But they aren't that bad."

"How can they get any worse?" That was Charpentier. He was on his third brandy. "The only thing that's keeping this economy going is the gold from Otago, and we know that's not going to last forever. Some of the first deposits are already starting to run out. When that's gone," he shrugged and bolted the last of his glass, "there'll be no credit for New Zealand at all."

The banker had put his finger square on the problem. Running a subsistence economy was one thing, but New Zealand had become much more than that. Its complex, developed business structure was centered not on farms now but on growing communities like Christchurch, Wellington, New Plymouth, Russell, Dunedin and Auckland. The colony had been drawn inexorably into the web of international commerce, and lately "international commerce" didn't think much of the colony's prospects. With the collapse of the price of wool on the London market, gold was the only thing propping up the colony's credit. Coffin was in as precarious a position as Rushton and the others. The terrible cycle of depression had become self-perpetuating.

The more the price of wool fell on the international market, the worse their credit rating became and the harder it was to find banks willing to extend new credit. Without that it grew increasingly difficult to maintain operations until the price of goods rose anew.

The real problem was that prices weren't about to rise any time soon. Nor was it hard to find reasons. Most damaging had been the end of the American Civil War several years earlier. Now cheap American cotton was once again flooding Europe, making good quality cotton garments available to everyone. New Zealand wool was still popular, but it no longer had a large chunk of the market to itself.

As for their other major export, corn, the Australians had begun to grow enough of their own. They no longer needed to import. There was little left the colony could export to raise hard cash. Too many people had expanded their flocks and fields. Coffin was as guilty as anyone else.

He longed for the shouting to be done with. They were wasting their time and many of them besides himself knew it. They knew one thing, though: until this crisis could be overcome normal competition was going to have to be put by the wayside. They were going to have to cooperate.

To his great surprise he found himself wishing Hull was present. Predatory he'd been, but at least he'd said what he believed. You could deal with such a man. Some of those seated with him, the young land speculators recently out from England in particular, you never knew which line they'd follow, which way they'd jump.

Not all of them were useless. Wallingford, for example. Twenty-five years Coffin's junior, the man was an overweight, overdressed, slick-haired dandy. He was also possessed of a sharp mind that could be counted on to listen to reason. Indifferent fop he might seem, but he was a powerful ally.

Wallingford had sunk his family fortune into New Zealand investments. Now he stood to lose it all. While the others ranted and wailed, he sat back in his chair and dabbed at his lips and nose.

"I'll tell you what it is." That was Dunleavy, Coffin saw. "It's all the fault of these blasted heathen! If we could just settle with them once and for all it would release crucial assets presently tied up in fighting this damnable war!"

Coffin couldn't help but smile at the younger man's outburst. Across the table he saw McQuade smiling as well. When in trouble, blame the Maori. When in doubt, blame the Maori. But the Maoris had nothing to do with the falling prices of corn and wool.

He could understand the young merchant's frustration, though. Wherever the British army had fought—North America, Africa, India—they'd eventually overpowered whatever native resistance was to be found. But not here. Not on an island of modest size where if anything lines of supply were easier to protect and the fighting should have been over and done with quickly.

Instead it had dragged on for more than a decade. When one pocket of rebels was wiped out another magically appeared elsewhere to resume the fighting. Based on their losses in the great battles at Ngatapa and Te Porere the previous year it was reasonable to assume the Maori would give up and agree to a treaty. Instead they continued to fight as furiously as ever under yet another mysterious new war chief, the devilish Te Kooti. For two years he and his men had been fighting to push the settlers off the east coast of North Island. They gave no indication of surrendering until they had done so.

So the war went on, unending.

With the rush to the gold fields Dunedin had rapidly become the colony's largest community. In response to the population shift Wellington, at the southernmost tip of North Island, had been made the new capital. But Auckland remained the colony's financial center. Old money and real power remained by the harbor he and Angus McQuade had surveyed so many

years before, even if the seat of government had shifted some
hundreds of miles to the south.

Yet a man still couldn't ride with impunity between these
two burgeoning cities for fear of being ambushed by Maori
rebels.

Not all was despair, however. While Te Kooti had grown
stronger, many of the Maoris were beginning to lose heart.
Though they won individual battles, they were unable to
dislodge the colonists from the cities and major towns. For
each warrior who died valiantly, five more pakehas seemed to
disembark from the great canoes. Then there was the colonials'
greatest ally—disease. Epidemics repeatedly swept through
both friendly and hostile pas, devastating a population which
had no resistance to the imported infections.

Despite all that, it now seemed as if the Maoris might win
anyway. Not on the battlefield, but in London. Rushton's
proposal was extreme but not beyond the realm of possibility.
After finally defeating them on the battlefield, the colonists
might find themselves giving the land back to the Maori
because they could no longer obtain the credit necessary to
farm it profitably. That might very well happen unless the price
of wool experienced a dramatic and unexpected rise, or unless
extensive new gold deposits were unearthed.

Somehow the colony's good credit had to be reestablished.
Fighting a protracted war with the natives while the price of
one's primary exports continued to plunge was not the way to
reassure already uneasy bankers. South Africa and Australia
were big enough to ride out such periodic depressions. New
Zealand was hardly an afterthought on Fleet Street.

The new court ruling might break the Maoris faster than the
army, Coffin knew. It had been decided that any Maori holding
title to any portion of land was qualified to sell it, even if it was
land traditionally held in common by an entire tribe. This
proved disastrous to the Maori while at the same time it
eliminated the problems of fraud and illegal land seizure by
legitimizing them. It made many neutral and friendly Maoris
sullen and bitter.

Those who continued to fight adopted a new name, the Hau
Hau, and fought on with a ferocity unknown ten years earlier.
While they could not hope to defeat the now experienced and
well-armed soldiers of the regular army and militia, they were
able to continue bleeding the country.

"What do you think we should do?"

"Yes, Coffin, what do you suggest?"

He looked up, realized they were all looking over at him. He'd been drifting. The cacophony had finally died down. They were looking to him for advice, and not for the first time. Angus was smiling encouragingly.

What did they expect from him? Miracles? He was fifty-seven, still strong and healthy, but not the harbinger of new ideas. By rights that should come from men like Wallingford and Rushton.

That wasn't why he felt so tired all the time, though. That much he could admit to himself honestly. No, it was because when this meeting was over and done with, regardless of what was decided, he knew he would have to climb into his carriage and ride home. Knew he would once more be compelled to pass into the finest private residence in Auckland only to enter a world unimaginable to the men around him. A world where the staff moved in unnatural silence, dusting and cleaning, cooking and washing, speaking only rarely among themselves and then in whispers.

Coffin sympathized with them, did not make an issue of their murmurings and sideways glances. He knew they lived for the time when they could escape that turreted, stained-glass mausoleum and return to the world of the living. He wished only that he could go with them.

He couldn't, of course. His place was in his home, beside his wife. Holly, clad in never-changing black, sometimes reduced now to moving about in a wheelchair, at other times rising to walk like a sooty spectre through empty halls and rooms.

The household staff attended to her well enough, seeing to her simple daily needs and wants. Coffin ate in the great house as infrequently as possible, pleading the press of business, unable to sit anymore at one end of the long table while she ate mechanically at the other. She'd aged rapidly, shockingly so. Though younger than he she'd taken on the aspect and appearance of an old woman.

The doctors came and examined her and went away shaking their heads dolefully. They had prescribed and treated ad infinitum. Nothing worked. Eventually Coffin gave up on them and they ceased coming. Except for Hamilcar. He at least kept her alive.

His wife had willed herself into a kind of living death, Hamilcar explained. It was the shadow of a real life. Sometimes she responded to Coffin's inquiries and comments, usually not. Why she continued to live he couldn't imagine. So he spent as little time in the vast mansion as he could while dreaming of the days and weeks when he could escape, could mount a horse and ride as fast as possible toward Tarawera and the cheery, open house which overlooked the lake. There he would throw himself into the arms of a Merita who'd grown steadily more beautiful in maturity.

Andrew would be there to greet him too. A strange, quiet little boy, healthy enough, always willing to murmur a curious "hello" to his "Uncle" Robert. It would continue to be, would have to remain "uncle" until Holly passed away. But though his wife had abandoned her spirit, her body continued on.

He didn't hate Holly. Despite everything it had never come to hate because he understood the reason for her withdrawal. He still loved her, too, though not as he'd loved her in those earlier, happier days. That time seemed little more than a dream now.

"Robert?" It was Angus, prodding him gently. Coffin was aware of nervous murmurings around him. This time he pushed back his chair and sat up straight. Damned if he was going to let them think the grand old man of colony commerce was entering into early senility!

"I don't know what we're going to do. There's nothing we can do. This I do know: our bankers in London aren't going to extend us any more money because we're such nice chaps. They want something tangible, and we don't have it to give them. All we can do is hang on."

"Hang on?" said Rushton contemptuously. "How! We have no credit, we have no money beyond what Otago brings in, and as we all know that is running dry." He looked at his colleagues. "I have four warehouses full of wool that no one wants at any price. I would let the Maoris burn it but I can't get insurance because of the war."

That set off the debate all over again. Coffin had had enough, he realized. Didn't they see that arguing and fighting among themselves wasn't going to produce any solutions? Destitution was a concept alien to most of them, and it had them panicked.

He was in better shape than some. By selling off his tangible assets he could survive. The servants would have to go, of course, and much of the jewelry and the paintings. All the accoutrements of wealth Holly had accumulated over the years. Not the house. In the midst of depression there would be no one with enough money to buy it anyway.

It was clear nothing was going to be solved at this meeting. The only alternatives were kin to those proposed by Rushton. That amounted to total surrender. It might well come to that, but not today, not today.

McQuade saw him leaving when no one else did. He left his chair and came over to help Coffin on with his cape.

"Where are you off to, Robert?"

"Not home."

"No, I dinna think that." McQuade was a bit taken aback by the vehemence of his friend's response. "Where then? To the Club?"

"No. I think I'll take a walk. Good day for a walk. City's pretty on a day like today." He took a deep breath. "At least it's still here."

"Auckland'll always be here, Robert." McQuade smiled. "Remember the day I first brought you here and showed you the harbor?"

"There was nothing here then. Trees and water."

"Aye." There weren't many ships in that wonderful harbor these days, McQuade knew. Those that called stayed just long enough to provision themselves before continuing down the coast and on through Cook Strait to the gold fields of Otago. Gold, which had given the colony a false sense of security. If they were going to survive without returning to a subsistence economy it was going to have to be on a far firmer foundation than that provided by gold dust.

"It may shrink, may become a fishing village, but it'll never disappear," he told Coffin as his friend lumbered out the door. Coffin waved briefly without turning, a hasty and casual farewell.

Though you and I might, McQuade thought, if something remarkable doesn't happen soon. He turned and reentered the noise-filled room.

2

Coffin had gone only a few blocks when a sudden thought made him turn off up a side street. It wound through and into a part of town he rarely visited.

The church was still there. He remembered it well and ought to, having paid for much of the construction including the big stained-glass windows which were the silent stone structure's sole adornment. As expected, the front door stood ajar.

No crowds shuffled about on a mid-week morning. The few worshippers present implored their savior in silence and did not look up as the tall stranger entered. Each was immersed in private grief or contemplation. Coffin did not disturb them. He'd come to find not salvation but a man.

The Vicar smiled when he saw his visitor. "Well, Robert. It's been a long time."

"It has." Coffin smiled back at the other man as he doffed his hat and cape. While most men put weight on, Methune had grown thinner over the years. The result of an ascetic life as much as work and worry.

"Come into my office, Robert. It's good to see you."

"You too, Vicar." Coffin allowed himself to be led.

"Orere, we will have tea, please. With sugar and cream."

The Maori servant bowed slightly, turned and left the room. It was a measure of Methune's stature that he allowed a Maori into his confidence in these times.

"I heard about the meeting this morning," Methune was saying.

Coffin nodded. "Just came from there."

"Was anything decided?" Methune was as grizzled and worn as an old sailor, but his voice still rang out clear and telling from the pulpit.

"What would you expect?" Coffin stirred sugar into his tea. "A great deal of noise. Not a joyful one, either." Methune nodded solemnly. "The younger ones like Rushton see the writing on the wall and they don't like what they're reading. Most of them don't know whether to put their pants on first or last in the morning. Wallingford's the best of the newcomers and he just sits there like a Buddha. If he has any brilliant ideas he hasn't chosen to share them with the rest of us.

"McQuade and myself and a few of the long established will hang on somehow, but as to the future of the colony itself," he shook his head, "I don't know. It's going to be rough. There are times when I think it was simpler in the old days, when all a man had to worry about was selling flax and pine and rum."

"I would agree they were simpler, but not better, I'm afraid."

"You and your soul-saving, Vicar." Coffin smiled.

The servant brought fresh-baked scones with butter and jam. Coffin bit into one hungrily. "Nice day but some rough weather coming. Not all the chill's in the air. How are you doing?"

"Well enough. Collections are way down, of course, but my concern is not money." He lowered his teacup from his lips. "It distresses a number of my colleagues, though."

"I'll bet. You never cared much for comforts, as I recall."

"I would go back to working out of a Maori hut if God required it of me. That is not what troubles me these days." For the first time the vicar looked distressed. "It's strange, you see, but many of the Maori converted to Christianity because they believed Christ was aiding us, the pakehas. They thought he would aid them as well, but their conversion hasn't done anything to improve their fortunes. As a result many who converted are abandoning their new faith and returning to the worship of heathen deities. But that is not the saddest part.

"Many believe both Christ and their old gods have abandoned them. As a result they have nothing to believe in. They see their world crumbling around them, their land rights being sold by drunken relatives, and they feel they have nothing to live for, either in this world or the next. I don't know what to do with such people, Robert. I don't know how to convince them they mustn't give up."

"I hope you're right, Vicar. I hope most of them have better to look forward to in the afterlife, because they're sure as hell getting buggered in this one." Suddenly he glanced over at the old servant, who'd retreated to a respectful distance and stood listening silently. "What about you?"

The old man hesitated uncertainly. "Me?"

"Yes," said Methune. "What do you think of all this, Orere? Is your faith still strong?"

"It is, Vicar. It's all I have now." He looked down at Coffin, found the Vicar's visitor staring back at him appraisingly. The Maori straightened slightly. "Some of the younger warriors, though, it's not enough for them. They must have justice, too."

"They could join the Hau Hau," Coffin suggested, his gaze unwavering.

This time the servant didn't hesitate. "The Hau Hau fight only because they do not know what else there is to do. Many of them do not care. They only want to fight the pakeha because it is what Maori warriors do. Others fight because their only choice is to move deep into the forest where one cannot farm properly or to come into the city to beg on the street. Some Maori still find more pleasure in fighting than getting drunk."

"Then the teachings of the Church aren't enough for them?" Coffin knew Methune was probably the only churchman in the country who wouldn't be offended by the asking of such a question.

Orere considered before replying. When he finally did he displayed real animation for the first time.

"Can you blame them for not believing? The pakehas point toward Heaven and while we look up other men steal our land."

"That is not God's fault," said Methune. "True Christians do not do such things."

"What is a true Christian, Father? One who believes in what he does or does what he believes?"

Methune had no answer. Coffin couldn't ever remember seeing his old friend at a loss for words, but then they were all at a loss for words these days. The economic depression had brought with it a mental one which infected every man and woman in the country. You could feel it all around you, just walking down the street. Life went on, but without the same enthusiasm and energy as before. It was like living a part in a Javanese shadow play. People worked and laughed and played while glancing over their shoulders, convinced disaster was close on their heels.

"Everyone must have faith, Robert. Why not come back to the Church?"

"Sorry, Vicar." Coffin smiled to make his refusal as palatable as possible. "I'm afraid what faith I had died with Christopher."

"Faith can also help people to live. It does so for Mrs. Coffin."

"I suppose so." It was true that the only time Holly showed much interest in getting out of the house anymore was on Sunday morning. "If you can call that living."

It hurt Methune but he didn't show it. "Things will improve, Robert. Everyone needs to believe that, especially these days."

"Some of them are already thinking of giving up, pulling out completely." He told the old priest the details of the morning meeting.

"I didn't know that feelings were running so strongly. Such a thing would be unthinkable for the Church. We could never abandon this land."

"No, but a lot of people could, Vicar. You'd better brace yourself for that possibility. If a few like Rushton sell out it's going to have a devastating effect on the middle class. We're liable to be in for a real panic, with folks trying to sell everything they've built up, everything they've worked for, only to discover there are no buyers because they're all running like hell themselves. We have to stop talking about growth and prosperity and start trying to maintain what we have left."

"It would be easier if the well-off provinces were more willing to help their hurting brethren. Otago is reluctant to support the unemployed in Auckland."

"True enough, Vicar. We need a real central government, with real powers, and we need it bad. This business of each province ruling itself and making decisions independent of and without regard for the welfare of its neighbors has got to stop. We can't afford that kind of fragmentation any longer. No wonder we haven't been able to stamp out the rebellion. But the damn provincials in the wealthier provinces don't want to surrender any of their power." He shook his head in frustration. "They don't realize that the trouble we're having up here in the north is going to sink down to Christchurch and Dunedin once the gold runs out."

"I agree that something must be done," said Methune readily, "but I confess I know not what."

"Nor do I, Vicar." Coffin and his friend finished their tea in silence, each sunk in his own thoughts. At last Coffin rose.

"Thank you, Vicar. I enjoyed the visit."

Methune stood and came around the table. "I also, as always. Something will happen soon, Robert. You'll see. Someone will think of a solution. All that's needed are some fresh ideas."

"I'd settle, Vicar, for a stale miracle."

3

Goldman was waiting for him when Coffin returned to Coffin House.

"How did it go this morning, sir? I expected you back earlier."

"I stopped off to chat with an old friend. As to the meeting, it went about as you'd expect."

Goldman was crestfallen. "That badly?"

"I'm afraid so, Elias. Frightened fools, the lot of them."

"Can you blame them, sir?"

"No, I suppose not." Coffin handed over his cape and greatcoat. "There was endless arguing. It seems no one can carry on a conversation these days without shouting. Nothing was agreed upon except the fact that the colony is in desperate financial straits. It wasn't necessary to attend the meeting to learn *that*. Everyone's known it for months. The Kingites may win their victory in the banks instead of on the battlefield. A few spoke of selling out and pulling back to Australia."

Goldman looked startled. "I hadn't realized it was so bad."

"It's not, really, but as far as some are concerned the colony's already done for, a lost cause. They're looking to their ledgers instead of to their futures."

Goldman was silent for a moment. Then, "If you'd come into my office Mr. Coffin, there's someone I'd very much like you to meet."

Coffin grimaced. "You know I don't have time for social niceties, Elias, and neither do you."

"This isn't a social call, sir. I think you should listen to this man."

It was rare for Elias Goldman to insist on anything.

"All right. But this had better be worthwhile, Elias."

As he followed Goldman down the hall Coffin was already regretting the loss of time. There was much to do and he was in no mood after this morning's indecisive gathering to meet anyone. There were preparations to make and figures to juggle, orders to commit to paper, financial defenses to be erected.

The young man in Goldman's office didn't wait for an introduction. He sprang from his chair to pump Coffin's right hand enthusiastically. Coffin was too startled to object. As the man spoke he kept bouncing in place, as though half filled with helium. Such an attitude was refreshing. Many of Coffin's friends were only filled with hot air.

"Mr. Coffin, sir, in person! I am delighted to meet you. Delighted! I've heard a great deal about you, from Elias and my own sources, and I'm certain we're going to get on well together."

Coffin took his time seating himself, spoke dryly. "You have the advantage of me, sir."

"This is Julius Vogel," Goldman explained. "He's not long here from England. He thinks he can help."

"Does he now?" Coffin regarded the young man calmly while Goldman closed the door. Vogel didn't sit down. Instead he began pacing the room like an agitated greyhound, hands and eyes in constant motion. It tired Coffin just to watch him. "So you think you can do something to help Coffin House, young fellow?"

"Not just Coffin house. What I have in mind will require the support of the entire business community if it is to have a chance of success."

"If what is to have a chance of success?" Am I getting old, Coffin asked himself, or is it simply that this chap is running at double normal speed?

"My plan for saving New Zealand Colony, of course."

"Oh. *That* plan."

The sarcasm went right past Vogel—or he chose to ignore it. "Yes." He drew himself up proudly. "I call it my 'Grand Go-Ahead Policy.'"

"This is all very interesting." The fingers of Coffin's right hand were doing a small staccato dance on the arm of his chair. He glanced at Goldman, who was nodding reassuringly and smiling. Clearly Elias believed there was something to this peripatetic visitor's ideas. So instead of simply dismissing him out of hand, Coffin said, "You must know that the colony's main financial backers have been trying to figure out a way to do exactly that for the past several years. This depression we find ourselves in is like living at the bottom of a well. Nobody has the slightest idea how to climb out.''

"Oh, I know all that," said Vogel brightly. "You all have the wrong idea how to go about it. No disrespect intended, sir.''

"No," said Coffin very quietly, "naturally not. You'll pardon me if I sound slightly skeptical, but most of us have been in business in this country for twenty, thirty years and more. What makes you think you're better qualified than we to tell us how to proceed?''

"It's not your fault, sir," Vogel replied, not in the least intimidated.

Coffin saw that Goldman was trying to warn Vogel. That in itself was amusing. Elias was worrying needlessly. Having gone this far, Coffin was prepared to let the young man have his say. But he'd better have something more to offer than enthusiasm and energy.

"Nice of you to say so. Perhaps you'd be good enough to tell me precisely where we've been going wrong?''

"Everywhere, in everything.''

Goldman sighed softly, leaned back in his chair and shut his eyes. Coffin found himself taken by the young man's complete lack of tact and diplomacy.

"Could you be more specific?''

"Certainly.'' Vogel adopted the attitude of an enthusiastic schoolmaster imparting a new lesson to a select group of pupils. "First of all, you're not borrowing enough.''

"Not borrowing enough?" Coffin nearly burst out laughing. "Are you aware that the colony is effectively broke?''

"All the more reason why you need to borrow, and borrow heavily.''

"You'll pardon me, young man, but I've been running Coffin House for a few years and it's always been our practice, as well as that of most of our competitors, to avoid debt when one is already busted. You can't spend yourself out of poverty.''

"Of course you can! That's the best way.''

Coffin stared at him in disbelief. "You're serious, aren't you?''

"Dead serious, sir.''

"I never heard of such a thing.''

"Naturally not. It's rather a new concept in economics. Quite the rage in certain circles.''

"Not in New Zealand circles it isn't."

"The only way, sir, to get an economy that's gone as stagnant as New Zealand's moving again is to pump new money into it. Lots of new money." As he spoke, Vogel gestured like a manic policeman. "Since you don't have the money here because your local resources are depleted you must seek it elsewhere."

"Now that's brilliant." Coffin sat back in his chair. "What a clever idea. Isn't it, Elias?" When Goldman didn't reply, Coffin looked back to their visitor. "It's so easy to get new money when you have no credit."

"It can be done," Vogel insisted. "It's just a matter of convincing the bankers."

"Oh, well, you must excuse me," Coffin said sardonically. "How could I have overlooked the obvious? Assuming just for the moment we could borrow a farthing, what would you have us spend it on? Improving our farms? Probing deeper into The Remarkables for more gold?"

Vogel was shaking his head. "That's private development. That's not what's needed here. I'll give you an example."

"Do," said Coffin testily.

"One of the colony's main barriers to accelerated development is its inadequate transportation system. You simply can't keep shipping most of your goods by boat. It takes too long. It's fine for transporting products between Auckland and Wellington but it does nothing for internal development. Right now the colony's like a spider's web with the whole middle missing. Not very efficient. The farms, the ranches, the inland towns—those are the areas that need help. The colony desperately needs a modern system of roads."

"Ah, but you aren't going to convince the provincial governments to spend money on roads except within their own boundaries."

"Unless," Vogel said knowingly, "they're convinced it will put an end to the Maori wars."

It took a moment for it all to sink in. Then Coffin sat up a little straighter in his chair. "You know, young man, you just might have something there. Convince them that it would benefit them all, not by improving commerce but by ending the wars. Yes."

Vogel had resumed his pacing. "If we could move large bodies of troops, not to mention artillery, into areas where they

currently have to march overland, it would make things much
harder on the Hau Hau."

"It certainly would. Trouble is, the provinces don't have the
money for that kind of development either."

"Then it must be found elsewhere," Vogel insisted. "Nor
am I just talking wagon roads, gentlemen." He looked over at
Goldman, then back to Coffin. "We need railroads. Not just
here on North Island but on South Island as well. Say,
Christchurch to Bluff. That would offer the chance to open up
all of South Island."

"That's terrible country." Coffin was shaking his head.
"You'll never get a railroad in down there. Christchurch to
Dunedin, maybe, but not as far as Bluff. That's ice country."

"It's the only way the southern provinces will agree to help,
if they're promised an equal share in the development
schemes. You've said as much yourself, sir. And it's the only
way this country is going to be developed properly."

"We've done all right with ships."

"Your pardon, Mr. Coffin, but that's an age that's passing.
Ships do nothing for development of a country's interior. The
Australians know this."

"The Australians," Coffin reminded him, "have a much
bigger country to develop than we do. They've no choice in the
matter."

"The principle is the same when applied on a smaller scale.
Please, all I ask is that you consider my ideas."

"It's not your ideas," Coffin told him. "The road network
makes sense. Railroads? Possibly. The problem is still money,
or rather the complete lack of it. London's not about to lend us
enough to build a cross-island road, much less the extensive
system you're talking about."

"Oh, they'll make the loans, you'll see."

Coffin went silent, thinking. Vogel and Goldman exchanged
a glance and held their breath. Finally Coffin looked up.

"I'll make you a deal, Vogel. If you can sell my friends,
people like Angus McQuade and Rushton and Wallingford, on
your ideas, then I'll throw my support behind you. If you can't
persuade them then it won't matter whether I back you or not."

"I need more than a promise, sir. I can give them the same
speech I gave Mr. Goldman earlier and that I've just delivered
to you, but before I confront the rest of the financial
community here en masse I need the support of at least two

merchants of stature. I can convince an audience of one without any trouble, but a group of skeptics might shout me down before I have the chance to explain myself."

Coffin nodded slowly, looked over at Goldman. "What do you think, Elias? I could probably talk Angus into it."

Vogel had the temerity to disagree. "Your pardon, Mr. Coffin, but it's widely known how close you and Mr. McQuade have been over the years. The others would suspect a collusion detrimental to their benefit. It should be one of your stronger competitors. That would lend my position real strength, if my support was seen to come from two opposing sources. Besides, I believe Mr. McQuade to be far more conservative than yourself. That is one reason why I have presented myself here first. So whomever else backs me must be someone equally receptive to new concepts and new ways of financing."

"Since you denigrate my own choice, who would you choose?" Coffin asked without rancor.

"If I may make so bold, sir, I need the support of Hull House."

That took Coffin aback. He muttered aloud. "I told that woman I'd have control of her enterprise one day. I couldn't take it from her father, but by God I'll take it from her!"

"And one day we shall, sir, one day we shall." Goldman tried to mollify his employer. "But right now she's the second most powerful force in the colony's financial community, even if people like Wallingford won't acknowledge the fact or deal with her."

"Rose Hull wasn't at the meeting today?" Vogel asked.

"Of course not, young man. You think they'd let a woman into the Club?" Coffin eyed him pityingly.

"She could buy the Club and the grounds it stands on if she so desired, even though she can't buy her way in," Goldman pointed out. "The point is, Mr. Coffin, sir, that she'd listen to you in this matter. I'm convinced of that."

"I can't believe what I'm hearing. Me go hat in hand to Rose Hull? I thought after all these years that you knew me better than that, Elias."

"You wouldn't be going begging, sir. You'd be going with a proposition that could benefit the entire colony. You've said yourself that we'll all survive this or drown together."

Coffin took a deep breath, glanced back at Vogel. "You think I'm stubborn, don't you, young man?"

"That remains to be seen, sir."

"If you think I'm stubborn, you should meet this woman.
Yes, come to think of it, you should. I'll meet with her, but
only if you come along. And you too, Elias."

"Oh now, sir, I don't think. . . ."

"I *do* think. It's about time. *If* she will agree to meet with
us."

"I think she will, sir. Difficult times make for strange
bedfellows."

4

When word got out that Robert Coffin was to meet with the daughter of his old enemy it had an unforeseen effect on the rest of the business community. Instead of jeering or whispering snide remarks, most asked, nay, demanded to be allowed to participate lest they find themselves excluded from some grand proposition. Coffin would not have thought it possible, but so unnerved and suspicious were his colleagues and competitors that they could even suspect collusion between himself and Rose Hull.

So Vogel had to change his plans and ready himself to present his proposal not only to the head of Hull House but to Wallingford and Rushton and McQuade and Lechesney and all the rest.

Since no women were allowed in the hallowed sanctuary that was the Club and since its members would not bend that policy even for the sake of the colony's future, a room was found in the back of Auckland's largest bank for the meeting to take place. Vogel repeated his entire presentation as energetically and enthusiastically as he had in Goldman's office.

Having heard it all previously, Coffin was able to concentrate instead on the reactions of his counterparts. It was amusing to see the astonishment and anger young Vogel's suggestions provoked. Rushton departed early, regarding those who remained with contempt while insisting he would not be a party to fiscal suicide. Nor would he allow his name to become a joke in the boardrooms of the Bank of England, where their outrageous proposals would surely be laughed out of existence.

But the others stayed, and listened.

Vogel was sweating when he finally concluded his presentation. As Coffin expected, it was Wallingford who commented first.

"Are we to understand, Coffin, that you and Miss Hull agreed with this young man's radical notions?"

Rose Hull nodded once. "That is correct, sir."

Wallingford shook his head and dabbed foppishly at his forehead with a hankerchief of Belgian lace. "It all sounds rather backward to me. I am not sure Rushton isn't right."

"What do we have to lose?" Coffin said quickly. "Our dignity? We've no credit now. Applying for ten times what we haven't got can't make things any worse." He looked around the table.

"That is so, Coffin. However most of us still possess hard assets of a sort." Murmurs of agreement filled the room. "If we were by some miracle to obtain this new credit and if we failed to repay any new loans, it would be the final ruin of us all. As it now stands each of us could salvage something more than just our self respect."

"Salvage what?" Coffin growled. "Defeat? Salvage and move to New South Wales to live out the rest of your lives on a pension? What kind of victory is that?"

"Victory enough for some," Wallingford argued.

"Some like Rushton." Coffin turned in surprise to Rose Hull. So did most of the others.

She was aware they listened to her opinion grudgingly if at all, barely tolerating her presence among them. They did so because they had no choice. In this place she could not be expelled by reason of her sex, if for no other reason than that she was one of the majority stockholders in the bank where they had gathered.

"We have gambled everything so far. Why not gamble one more time? Double or nothing, I believe it is called?"

Lechesney managed a smile. "Miss Hull, few of us can call upon the kind of reserves available to you. You are asking us to look for money in our socks."

"It's my money too," she said primly. "And if we fail, you men can enter into new partnerships elsewhere, begin anew. I will be a destitute and single woman."

"True enough!" Vogel gazed fearlessly around the room. "Are there only two real men in all New Zealand? Robert Coffin—and Rose Hull?"

"You impertinent young bastard!" Jason Merrill rose from his chair and started around the table. "I ought to cut your tongue out for that!"

Coffin interposed himself between Vogel and the much

larger Merrill. "Easy, Jason. This isn't a council of war and we don't do duels these days."

Merrill subsided, staring past Coffin. "All right. I'll respond to reason, but I won't be insulted into risking what's left of my holdings. Certainly not be some damn Jew."

Vogel stiffened. For the first time his perpetual smile and good humor was replaced by something else. But he responded coolly and without anger.

"Perhaps you have forgotten, Mr. Merrill, that less than two years have passed since the Prime Minister of England was a Jew."

"Yes, but for how long?" Merrill reluctantly returned to his seat, glanced around the table. "What was it? A few months?" Some snickers came from his supporters and friends.

"Mark my words," Vogel told them, "Disraeli will be Prime Minister again some day. Gladstone can't dominate Parliament for very long."

"You think not?" Merrill snapped.

"If you don't mind, gentlemen, it's not the politics of the old country that concerns us here today." Wallingford sniffed delicately. "I care not who advises the Queen so long as the colony survives." Merrill looked toward him and Wallingford simply turned away as though the other man was not present. "We are agreed, then, that we have much to gain and little, significant as it may be to us individually, to lose by requesting a substantial loan?"

"*We* can't request it," said Coffin. "No one will loan money to our respective enterprises if they believe the colony stands on the brink of collapse. Not even to Coffin House." He glanced over at Vogel. "Under such circumstances God himself couldn't pry money out of the Bank of England. It will have to be a government request."

"Never happen, never." Lechesney was adamant.

"The Governor will agree."

"Perhaps, but the Governor has no power in these matters. You know that as well as the rest of us, Coffin. He cannot request money like that on his own authority."

It was true, Coffin knew. The way the colony's government was presently structured it was the provincial councils that would have to make the formal request for additional new money. Such a request would expose them to ridicule if it failed, and to political defeat at the hands of their constituents.

"Then we'll put it to the councils individually. As you've seen, Mr. Vogel here can be damn persuasive. I for one intend to support him fully in this. Who else is with myself and Hull House?"

Wallingford heaved an ursine sigh. "As you say, Miss Hull, double or nothing."

"I'm in," mumbled an obviously unhappy Chesterton from the far end of the table.

"And I . . . I also. . . ."

Enough agreed, though it was by no means unanimous. Merrill dissented vociferously and Rushton had long since abandoned them. Even they might come around later, Coffin reflected, when they'd had time to pause and think.

As the meeting was breaking up Poole Van Kamp, the old Dutchman with extensive land holdings in the south who'd come up by ship specifically for this gathering, walked over to shake Vogel's hand. He tilted his head forward to peer at their brash would-be savior over the tops of his bifocals.

"I don't mind telling you, young man, I don't much like you. Personally I find you brash, offensive, and insulting. But I'll go along with your ideas because I don't see anybody promoting any better ones, and if you succeed I'll support you wholeheartedly in anything you choose to do in the future. Actually I think what you propose is ridiculous and probably unworkable. But if it's good enough for Robert Coffin and Rose Hull, then it's good enough for the rest of us to get behind it."

"All I ask for is your trust, Mr. Van Kamp." Vogel returned the man's handshake firmly. "I don't ask that you like me, though I hope with time to change that as well."

"We'll see about that." Van Kamp turned and headed for the door.

The private, relatively quiet gathering at the bank was a picnic compared to Vogel's presentations before the various provincial councils. The young economist tried his best, but in the spacious council halls the intimacy of his delivery was lost. He was outshouted if not outargued.

They were in New Plymouth. Coffin had gone along to lend his support. Two straight hours of shouts and accusations, counterproposals and imprecations had left him frustrated and tired. With the debate raging behind him he walked outside in search of a momentary respite.

He was not the only one who'd temporarily abandoned the fight for a little peace and quiet. Rose Hull was seated at the end of a bench not far away. Her attire was decorous, even attractive, and so was she. He looked left and right down the long hall outside the council chamber. It was empty except for the two of them.

As he approached she looked up at him. For the first time he was conscious of how closely she resembled her father. He tried to remember what her mother, Flora Hull, had looked like, but that took him back too many years.

Good God, he suddenly realized. How we've all aged.

She wasn't what he would have called "pretty." Not horsey either. Handsome, and tall. Much too tall. She was reading a book and though she saw him coming she didn't move to close it. Since he'd approached her, it was incumbent on him to initiate any conversation.

He nodded toward the book. "Interesting?"

She glanced up again and smiled politely. "Very strange. It's *Frankenstein*, by Shelley."

"That's a poem I don't know. I don't have much time to read for pleasure."

"A shame. It's not a poem, it's a novel. And it's not by Percy but by his wife, Mary." She set the page ribbon and closed the slim volume, nodded past him. "How is it going in there?"

Coffin glanced back in the direction of the doors that led to the council chamber. "Not too well, I'm afraid. This is what happens when you don't have a strong central government. The Americans seemed to manage it better when they put their thirteen provinces together in a union."

"Mr. Vogel hasn't been able to convince them?"

"I don't think that's the problem. Everyone seems willing to authorize him to seek the money. What they're all fighting about is who gets what chunk of it if he succeeds. The Otago council wants to build the southern railway first, but the Wellington people are more concerned with a proper north–south roadway on North Island. In New Plymouth they want money to expand the harbor." He shrugged.

"It's been like this everywhere. Everybody thinks Vogel's plans are fine, as long as they get to decide where the money goes. So they're all afraid to authorize him to seek the loan until they know where it's going."

"I see." She was nodding. "Everyone's afraid the province next to them will obtain the greater share."

"That's about it. Julius is a convincer, but he's no peace-maker."

"Then there's only one way to stop all this in-fighting," she said firmly. "We must go to the Governor and have Julius appointed Treasurer. That way *he'll* be the one to decide how any money's to be apportioned."

Coffin was startled. "I don't know about that. He hasn't been here that long and there are other considerations. Political ones."

"Are you referring to the fact that Mr. Vogel is not of the Christian faith?"

"There's that," he admitted.

"It won't matter. As Treasurer Julius could distribute the money to the provinces as he saw fit, without government interference. Since he is seeking this loan in the colony's name and not in that of individual provinces he should have the authority to spend it accordingly."

Coffin jerked his head in the direction of the council chamber. "They won't like this idea, you know. They'll fight it."

"Then we must take care they don't hear about it until it's a *fait accompli*."

"'A what?" He frowned at her.

"Until the appointment has been made," she explained with the slightest of smiles. Putting her book into her purse she rose and extended an elbow. "If you would care to accompany me, Mr. Coffin, I suggest we make our way to the Governor's office while the provincials continue screaming at one another. It may be that they will continue talking so loud they will fail to hear that which is truly important."

Coffin eyed the proferred arm. Thirty years he'd spent fighting everything Hull House stood for, hating the man who'd founded it. But what, after all, had it stood for except competition? Tobias Hull wasn't here now. He lay in a plain grave on the east coast after giving his life trying to save Coffin's only son. If Hull could do that, couldn't Coffin do somewhat less?

He slipped his arm through the crooked elbow. Rose Hull smiled up at him.

"There now, isn't this better than making faces at one another across a table?"

"I don't know. It doesn't feel right and I'll have to think about it. But while I'm thinking, there's no reason for us not to join forces to try and save this country."

"Well said, Mr. Coffin. Provided we *do* save the country."

He eyed her sharply as they started down the hall. "I thought you believed in what Vogel's doing?"

"I do not believe, but I see no alternative. We have to do something to try and pull the colony out of this awful depression. As someone who grew up hoarding pennies in order to have any money at all I frankly confess I find this business of borrowing still more money than we can possibly pay back not only risky but frightening. Yet in risky and frightening times are not such measures called for? I think so."

"Then we agree on that, at least."

They left the building and Coffin called for a carriage.

"And your wife," she inquired casually, "how is she?"

For a moment there was a slight crack in the hardened merchant's veneer she had adopted. Coffin hadn't expected the question but he had no difficulty responding since it was one commonly asked of him.

"The doctors tell me she is improving, but very slowly. There is still a chance she may emerge from the long depression into which she's fallen."

"I'm glad to hear that. May she and New Zealand emerge from their depression together."

"I hope so." Coffin hoped he sounded more enthusiastic than he felt.

5

Rose Hull's ploy worked. The Governor saw the sense of it and Julius Vogel was appointed Treasurer before anyone in the provinces had time to object. To prevent outraged and disgruntled provincials from forcing his removal before he had a chance to act, it was decided that their new Treasurer should be sent on his way to England as quickly as possible.

Coffin stood next to the much smaller man on the wharf as the noise and confusion of the harbor boiled around them.

"We'll be anxiously awaiting your return, Julius."

"A long journey. Halfway around the world." Vogel was blinking at the bright sunlight bouncing off the water. "I don't much care for the sea myself but it has to be done this way."

"You'd better come back with good news," Coffin advised him. "If you don't I can't say what might happen."

"Never fear." Vogel drew himself up confidently. "As you know, I can be most convincing."

"I know, but the directors of the Bank of England aren't the members of Auckland council."

"Thank heavens for that." Both men chuckled.

What Coffin didn't say was how he longed to go with him. How he wished he could forget the responsibilities of running Coffin House to feel once more the heavy roll of a ship under his feet. He knew he couldn't do that even though he could trust the daily operations of the business to Elias Goldman. Couldn't because there was still Holly to look after, Holly who actually and astonishingly was improving. And there was the other house, at Tarawera, with Merita and the boy.

So he could only shake hands a last time with the energetic little economist and watch while he boarded his ship, knowing that his chances of success were slim at best. If Vogel failed utterly they would never know the details of it. That much had been plain in the other man's face. Julius Vogel would succeed, or he'd never show himself in the South Pacific again.

There was no reason to linger. As he turned to walk back to his carriage he was surprised to see the other carriage from the house drawn up nearby. A face was staring out at him from the window. Still dressed in black, but now the veil had been pulled aside. The pale visage that looked back at him was almost familiar.

"Holly!" He lengthened his stride until he was standing close to her.

"I heard you'd come to see Mr. Vogel off."

"That's right." He gestured. "That's his ship. What do you know about Julius Vogel?"

"Just because I don't go out much, Robert, doesn't mean I'm completely ignorant of everything that goes on. When one doesn't talk much there is ample opportunity to listen to others, and church is full of chatter after services."

"Yes, of course, but. . . ."

Her hand reached through the window, the glove cool on his skin. "Let's go for a ride, Robert."

If Mount Egmont had suddenly erupted he couldn't have been more shocked. "A ride? Where?"

"Not here. Let's go out to the country, out of the city. I need to get out, Robert. I've been locked up inside myself for too long."

"You *are* better." He just stared back at her. "Dr. Hamilcar told me, but I had no idea. . . ."

"A prolonged period of mourning, he kept calling it. The dear man!" Her eyes fell. "I know—I know nothing I do can bring back Christopher. I realize that now. Just as I realize," and she looked up at him, "that you couldn't have prevented his death. I know you tried to keep him out of the militia. I needed someone, anyone to blame, and—well, I blamed the both of us."

"Just a moment." He hurried to his own carriage and instructed the driver to return home, then walked more slowly back to Holly's, glanced up.

"Jack, take the south road out of the city."

"Very well, sir."

"You know where Brooks Farm is?"

"No sir, but I can find it."

"Good. Let's go, then."

They rode for several hours. By the time they reached their destination Holly was chatting animatedly. She still wasn't the old Holly, the sly and vivacious Holly of before the wars, but she had talked more to him in the past hours than she had in the previous year.

He directed Jack to pull up atop a hill. When the carriage rolled to a stop Coffin climbed out and offered Holly his hand. She emerged gingerly, fragile as an old woman.

They stood staring down at the city and the matchless harbor.

"Beautiful," she murmured, pressing close to him. "I'd forgotten how beautiful."

Rolling hills reached down to the ocean. Behind them a vast flock of sheep spilled across one hillside like foam which had broken away from its wave to crash upon the land. Their rhythmic voices echoed off the still sky. They advanced slowly, individual white carpets whose mass odor stained the air.

"Are all of those ours, Robert?"

"All of them and more than you can see. This is just Brooks Farm. There are others. Bath, Regis—we own a lot of land, Holly, that you've never seen."

"I know."

"You'll see it all now. I'll make sure of it. We'll take the time, travel across the whole country."

"Not—right away, Robert." Suddenly she sounded tired and he realized how much the unaccustomed excursion had exhausted her.

"No, we've plenty of time. You've had a bad time of it for a while, old girl. You don't want to be doing too much too soon."

She smiled weakly up at him. "I'll take care, Robert. It's going to be better now, you'll see. I've been making myself sick, withdrawing from the world. It's time I rejoined it." She reached up to gently caress his cheek. "I know it's been hard on you. I know I've been unfair, but I couldn't control what happened to me. Things will be different from now on. I promise." She looked back toward the sea.

They stood quietly awhile before he spoke again. "You know about the depression, Holly?" She nodded slightly. "Then you know how badly we're hurting, how badly the whole country's hurting right now."

"Mr. Vogel will change that. He seemed like a very clever man."

"He'll have to be the cleverest man to set foot in England since William the Conqueror, or we'll all be done for."

"Is that his ship?" She pointed out to sea where a large vessel was making its way out of the harbor.

"Maybe. Hard to tell from up here."

What was England like these days, he wondered? He saw pictures in magazines but they could only hint, suggest. Though curious he found he had no desire to go and see for himself. Come what may this was his home. This was where he would live out the rest of his life. He no longer thought of himself as an Englishman. He was a New Zealander—whatever that was.

Holly was making conversation. "All that mutton. What a shame we can't do something more with the meat."

"The sheep are here to produce wool, Holly. You know that. We can raise sheep better and cheaper than anyone else in the world. But you're right: we can't do anything with the meat. I don't think salt mutton will ever be very popular."

"What a shame."

They stood there for a long time, Holly watching the ship, Coffin staring far out to sea. They did not return home until well after sundown.

6

"He's back! Vogel's back!"

Coffin looked up from his desk as Elias Goldman burst into the office. Before Goldman shut the door behind him Coffin was able to hear the sounds of men busy at their own work. As the easy-to-mine placer gold vanished from Otago, clerks and accountants began drifting back to their old jobs. Coffin was only too glad to oblige the best of them. Most had to emigrate or take lesser-paying work. In the midst of depression, only a few could be rehired.

All morning he'd been agonizing over whether to sell Regis Farm. He didn't want to. Selling land was like selling blood. But the offer was a good one, surprisingly fair considering the low price of produce. It had been made through an intermediary on behalf of Rose Hull. If she'd thought to fool him by employing such a childish ruse she'd failed miserably.

Not that it mattered. He needed the money, needed it badly. The thought of selling hundreds of acres of prime land to Hull House was mortifying.

He was grateful to Elias for breaking his train of thought.

"Where is he?" Coffin rose and strode out from behind the desk. "What has he told you? How did he do?"

Goldman glanced back toward the hall. "I haven't seen him myself. A runner came with the news. I was told he'll come here first, since you were his first supporter."

"No, not I." Coffin put an arm around Goldman's shoulder, a gesture so shocking that the older man was taken aback. "You were his first supporter, Elias. He's coming to tell you."

"What matters, sir, is that he's back."

"Yes, but with what news?"

"It must be at least partly good, sir, or we both know he wouldn't have returned," Goldman said carefully.

"Well, come on then! We'll go and meet him." Coffin led

the way down the stairs. Heads turned and people stopped what they were doing to watch. Such uncharacteristic activity on the part of their lord and master was worth a stare.

Vogel was already there, standing in the hallway like a spectacled elf while the employees of Coffin House struggled unsuccessfully to ignore him. Enough knew who he was and they passed on the information to their colleagues. His gaze rose and his expression grew beatific as he espied the two men descending the stairway.

"Coffin! And Elias."

In an instant all three were shaking hands. Then the smiles were replaced by looks of concern. Goldman tried to sound encouraging.

"You're looking well, Julius. London must have agreed with you."

"Ah, well." Vogel sounded indifferent. "It's all right. The theater, the concerts, the parades, all very edifying, you know. But it's not New Zealand."

"Never mind your social life," Coffin said hastily. "What about our loan? Did you have any luck?"

Vogel studied his fingernails. "A little. They were very skeptical, very. It was as difficult as we thought it might be, Elias. The Bank of England is not the Bank of New Zealand."

"How did they receive you?" Goldman asked him.

"With barely veiled contempt. Despite that I managed to convince them to extend some small credits to the colony." When he looked up there was a sly gleam in his eye. "I convinced them that our situation here was desperate, that we stood on the very precipice of disaster."

Coffin frowned. "Seems an odd way to convince a banker to invest more money."

Vogel shook his head, smiling. "You never will understand modern economic theory, will you?"

That was Julius Vogel's manner. He was as tactful as a shark and just as efficient. Coffin quelled the instinctive surge of anger that welled up inside him. Besides, Vogel was probably right.

"Perhaps not. Possibly you could explain this particular aspect of it in terms simple enough so that even I can understand it."

"Certainly. You see," he said excitedly, "once I had them convinced that we not only were in the midst of a severe depression but were on the verge of complete collapse, it was a simple matter to persuade them that unless they agreed to extend additional credit, every one of their outstanding loans would default. They would thus lose not only the interest they were due but the principal as well. My intention was to frighten them and I am happy to say I succeeded beyond my wildest hopes.

"In that state of mind it was easy to convince them that if we just had some real help our business here would recover and they would get all of their money back. I assured them that our troubles here were more a matter of insufficient credit leading to a lack of confidence than to any inherent faults of the colony itself. Furthermore, if we could just hang on until the price of wool and corn rebounds, trade would expand exponentially."

"That's all well and good." Coffin was fighting his impatience. "But *did you get any credit*?"

"As I've said, a little." Vogel removed a satchel from beneath his left arm and began fumbling through it until he found the paper he was looking for. It was attached to forty others, all covered with fine print. He flipped through them rapidly until settling on one sheet near the middle. Then he refolded the rest and passed them to Coffin.

Robert Coffin was a good reader, but not good enough to plow rapidly through the mass of legalese Vogel had handed him. In disgust he handed it to Goldman, whose experienced eyes scanned the small print far more rapidly.

"Well, well, what does it say?" Coffin prompted him anxiously.

Goldman adjusted his glasses, read aloud. "Agree to extend to the Colony of New Zealand new credit in the amount of. . . ." He swallowed, went on. "Credit in the amount of—ten million pounds?"

Everyone within earshot on the ground floor looked up sharply from their work.

"Let me see that!" Coffin ripped the papers from Goldman's fingers, read the impossible last line for himself. When he looked up at Vogel, that worthy was leaning on his cane and smiling diffidently.

"It was the best I could do on short notice." Reaching out, he took the sheaf of papers from Coffin's limp fingers and slipped them back into his satchel. "Once we've spent that I intend to go back and ask for another ten million."

Somewhere someone dropped a glass. The sound of its shattering was enough to break the spell. Everyone rushed forward, all talking at once, to crowd around the prodigal son. Vogel tried to shake everyone's hand, accepting their excited accolades with as much modesty as was in him. There was little of that, but somehow no one seemed to mind.

It was astonishing how fast business recovered. In his wildest dreams Coffin couldn't have predicted it, nor could McQuade, Wallingford or any of the others. Even Rushton made a special visit to commend Vogel.

It was as though the economy had simply halted itself in mid-slide, turned about like a cart in the middle of a street, and resumed marching in the opposite direction. Suddenly people who had been desperate to sell their holdings at a tenth of their real worth announced intentions to expand. The new credit gave confidence not only to the old-timers but to potential investors in Australia and elsewhere. Additional credit was forthcoming without anyone having to request it. There seemed a huge number of people who had wanted to invest in the colony all along, but who had been waiting for a sign. The new money was all it took to set off a frenzy of expansion and buying.

Now the problem was not insufficient credit but too much of it. Business boomed before settling down to a period of steady growth. The large landholders and merchants like Coffin and his friends were delighted with these new developments and planned their futures accordingly. The boom didn't have the spice the discovery of gold had carried with it, but neither did it contain the seeds of sudden collapse or desperate risk.

Those who had hung on through near bankruptcy had their determination vindicated. For the first time in years people could make plans with a feeling of security. As if to emphasize the success of Vogel's policies the price of wool began its long hoped for rise. New settlement expanded the market for every kind of product and produce.

Once again Coffin could concentrate his energies on the takeover of Hull House. Regis Farm and the rest of his enterprises were saved. For its part, Hull House continued to expand under Rose Hull's administration, growing and thriving beyond anyone's expectations. It had to be admitted she'd done well in spite of every obstacle both commercial and social that had been placed in her path.

Coffin's reaction was unexpectedly ambivalent. On the one hand he'd not forgotten the promise he'd made to her to consume her company and merge it with his own burgeoning empire, already the largest in the country. What he hadn't thought to feel and what he was careful not to express to anyone else was his admiration for what she'd managed to accomplish under circumstances adverse enough to have broken most other human beings.

While he didn't speak of it, he was not the only one to take note of it. Goldman spoke of Hull House on more than one occasion.

"Perhaps we have been going about this business in the wrong fashion."

"What business, Elias?" They were walking down Auckland's main boulevard side by side, nodding occasionally to those they knew.

"The business of how we treat our women."

"What's wrong with how we treat our women?"

Goldman must have noted the disapproving tone in his employer's voice but pressed his point regardless. "Let us take Rose Hull by way of example. It must be admitted she has done as well as any man in the running of Hull House."

"I don't have to admit to any such thing. She's had the sense to hire good people, that's all. Good *men*."

"That in itself requires a certain knowledge and expertise." Goldman was unusually persistent. "The world is changing around us, sir. Largely for the better, I should say."

"I won't disagree with that, Elias. What's your point?" They turned a corner.

"There's been talk of trying new things, new ideas. This is after all a new land still. There's been talk of—well, of allowing women to have the vote."

Coffin stopped abruptly in the middle of the street. "Vote? You're joshing me, Elias."

Goldman stared back at him through his thick glasses. "No sir. Not a bit of it. There has been talk of exactly that, in certain circles."

"People who spend too much time in circles get dizzy." Coffin resumed his stride. "The day women vote'll be the day you grow hair again."

Goldman laughed. Beneath his top hat was a streak of bare skin smooth as polished marble framed by a fringe of rapidly graying hair. "I think there's more to this than talk, sir. You'd best prepare yourself. It may happen in spite of what any of us believe."

"You and your dreams, Elias. You'll do better to confine your imagination to your bookkeeping."

"Yes, sir. I try to, sir."

Conversation shifted to more prosaic subjects. Coffin had no trouble putting Goldman's absurd ideas out of his head. Lately Elias had exhibited a disturbing tendency to engage in all sorts of wild speculation. Women voting! Coffin shook his head in disbelief. Why, the next thing you knew Elias would be proposing the vote for the Maori.

He could afford to be tolerant of such nonsense. Business was excellent. The colony was going to survive and prosper. Holly continued her slow but steady improvement. She still suffered from occasional relapses which would find her sitting in that damnable chair staring out the parlor window, but they were becoming far less frequent. Much of the time she was all but her old self, when her lively determination would again come to the fore to delight all who happened to be near her.

Next week he was due to make his monthly inspection of the inland estates. That would mean a week to ten days at the country house. A week to ten days with Merita, who never seemed to age.

It was no wonder as he and Elias entered the city's finest restaurant that he was content.

7

"Andrew! Get out of there, you little *aputo*." At the sound of his mother's voice the boy looked up from whcre he was digging in the garden. "What are you doing in there, anyway?"

"Just chasin' lizards."

"Well you do it somewhere besides in my vegetables."

She spoke it softly, shaking her head. She loved him too much to be mad at him for long and besides, that wasn't the Maori way. "Go and get yourself cleaned up."

"All right, mother." He smiled back at her, ran and easily cleared the low fence that protected the garden from marauding chickens.

He was going to be tall, she mused. All legs now, but when he filled out he was going to be an impressive man. Bigger even than his father.

She was wiping her hands on her apron as she turned to go back inside when a noise made her pause. Someone was coming up the lakefront road. As the fame of the silica formations known as the Pink and White Terraces spread beyond Tarawera, the little town was becoming positively crowded.

It was a fine coach, though not a tourist one. She moved to close the front door to keep the dust of its passing outside the house. Then she noticed that it was slowing. A wealthy pakeha tourist sight-seeing alone, or perhaps just someone in quest of directions.

Sure enough, it halted across from the gate. A tall gentleman clad in top hat and fine suit emerged. Only when he'd opened the gate and raised his head was she able to recognize him. As she gaped in amazement he came toward her with a now familiar confident stride.

"Flynn? Flynn!" She took a step toward him before

375

catching herself. Isolated the great house might be, but it was still best to maintain a sense of decorum when outside. You never knew who might come riding or walking up the road at any moment. Maybe even Father Spencer. Better if no one, not even the driver of the coach, witnessed the mistress of the house and her handsome visitor embracing passionately. She looked around but there was no sign of Andrew. Probably he was out back washing off garden dirt as he'd been instructed to do.

Flynn stopped a foot in front of her, two steps down. "Hello, Merita."

"Come inside."

The door hadn't finished closing when he crushed her to him. She could smell the newness of his fancy clothes, the subtle yet distinct scents of silk and linen. Stepping back, she studied him in disbelief.

"Where on Earth did you find that outfit?"

"You like it?" He spun on his heels for her, grinning. When he was facing her again he gave the brim of his hat a flip, cocking it at a rakish angle. He stood posing for her, one leg crossed slightly in front of the other, both hands resting atop the amethyst-and-diamond tipped cane he carried.

"It's just fine, just fine, but it's not you. How did you ever afford such a get-up?"

He straightened, smiling down at her. "Merita, where do you think I go when I'm not with you?"

"I don't think about it. You've always told me you go and work. Rotorua, I always assumed, or Taupo."

He shook his head. "When first I came here that was where I worked. Then they discovered gold in Otago. Have you ever been to South Island?"

She clapped her hands together. At thirty-six she could still display the enthusiasm and delight of a little girl. "No, never, but I'd love to. The old chiefs speak of it many times."

"One day I'll take you there. I've been spending a lot of time on South Island, Merita. At first I was all alone, but that was all right. I don't mind being alone.

"After a while I fell in with some young fellas. They knew even less about gold mining than I did, but we watched those who knew and learned from them. And we worked. It's cold in Otago, Merita. Colder than you can imagine. It didn't stop us. The harder we worked the more we learned. We took chances the other miners wouldn't.

"One day we decided to go dig far up a creek no one else had tried. The older miners laughed at us. They said since there was no gold in the lower reaches of the creek there wouldn't be any higher up. And you know what we found?"

She shook her head, wide-eyed as she listened to the story.

"We found a sharp bend in the creek where the water slowed. In the middle of that bend was a big pool full of sand, and that sand had so much gold in it, Merita, you didn't even have to pan it. You could pick it out with your fingernails. Gold that had been washing down off this one mountain for a million years, all of it slowing, falling, and collecting in that pool. Enough gold to make even rich men tremble.

"We packed it carefully, mixed with pyrite to fool the curious. Then one of us would convoy it to New South Wales and bank it there while the others stayed behind. Three of us did all that, Merita, and to this day none of the other miners down there suspect we found anything at all. They just kept laughing at us, and we had to fight with ourselves not to smile when we passed them.

"Charlie Bigelow's taken his share and gone back to America to buy himself a farm in Virginia. Ho Teek's set himself up like a damn mandarin in Hong Kong. And me—I'm still here. Still here."

"You never said anything, Flynn. I never guessed—you stayed the same. The same clothes, everything."

"It wasn't easy not telling you, Merita. I think that was harder than working through some of the snows we had down there. But I wanted it to be a surprise."

"It certainly is."

A sound made her turn. Flynn looked past her. A back door slammed and footsteps could be heard ascending the back stairs. Small footsteps.

"How is the boy?"

"Growing like a fern," she said proudly. "He looks much like his father."

"Yes. Like his father." Flynn was staring off into the distance. Then he remembered his manners and looked down at her, said in a more normal tone of voice, "I think he looks like you."

"Like both of us, I imagine."

"What have you been telling him about us?"

"That you're just a 'pretend' uncle, a friend from Rotorua. Like Father Spencer or 'Aunt' Leola."

Flynn nodded. "How old is he now? Must be all of eight."

"Nine," she corrected him.

"He's going to have to be told why I come around so much. It won't be enough to say I'm a 'friend.' He's too smart for that."

"One of these days he will, but not right now."

"I'll leave that to you." He grabbed her shoulders. "Merita, you have to come someplace with me."

"Now? But I can't. Robert will be here in a week."

"A week is plenty of time. I only need you to come for a few days."

Her gaze narrowed. "Away from Tarawera? For what? What would I do with Andrew?"

"Send him to stay with the Spencers like you do when I stay in the house, or another of his friends' families. I have something very important to show you."

"A surprise? I love surprises. This has been a day for surprises. Dear Flynn, that's one of the things I love about you. I never know what you're going to do next." She reached back to begin untying her apron. "I'll do it! Andrew can stay with the Trapnells. He gets along so well with their two boys. It's practically a second home to him."

"Good. I have a little business to attend to in town and then I'll meet you back here. We can go in my coach."

"What kind of surprise is it to be? What shall I wear?" she asked excitedly.

"Wear something comfortable for riding."

"All right." She halted in mid-spin. "Wait a minute." She nodded past him. "You said we'd go in *your* coach. That's your coach out there?"

"All mine, yes. As well as the four horses drawing it and the coachman. I own it all, down to the smallest piece of tack. There was a *lot* of gold in that creek, Merita."

"I'm beginning to believe you."

He turned and headed for the door. "Get yourself and the boy ready. I'll be back for you in an hour."

"Where are we going? Rotorua, where?"

"You'll see."

The ride took longer than she expected, but the sight of the ocean raised her spirits as it always did. The ocean had brought her people to Aotearoa, in the Long Canoes, from the mysterious land called Raiatea. It was the Maoris' connection to their past, to their ancestors.

They'd followed the Kaituna River much of the way before crossing it to turn northward. When they were within the very shadow of Mount Maunganui Flynn moved close to her.

"Almost here." His hand was on her knee, sliding upward.

"Stop that!" She slapped at his roving fingers. "Not in the coach."

"Why not?" he asked mischievously, nodding in the direction of the driver. "He sees only the road, and the wheels are making too much noise for him to hear anything."

"Because if that's what you've brought me all this way to see it was a waste of time. I've seen it before."

"Are you saying it isn't worth a coach ride to see again?"

She closed her eyes partway and smiled over at him. "Do you really want me to answer that question?"

He removed his hand, grinning. "Never mind. I've brought you to show you something more substantial still." He reached for the speaking tube and directed their driver to stop.

The coach slowed until it was silent in the cab for the first time in hours. Flynn let himself out, walked around to open the door on Merita's side and help her to the ground.

She saw it right away, and was struck speechless.

It was one of the most beautiful places she'd ever seen. Off to the left rose the towering bulk of Mount Maunganui. To the right the unspoiled coast stretched southward toward the open sea.

Directly ahead lay a small, perfect beach nestled between rising masses of wave-weathered rock. Inland from the sand stood something that looked as if it had been lifted from the top of a wedding cake. It was all turrets and domes, gingerbread trim and bright white porches, a spun-sugar confection come to life.

"What a wonderful house!"

"You like it?"

"Like it? Who wouldn't like it? It's like something out of a pakeha fairy tale."

He put his arm around her shoulder. "Would you like to see the inside?"

"Won't the owner mind?"

"I don't think so. He's a good friend of mine."

At the base of the winding path that led to the house a pair of elderly Maoris stood waiting. Both bowed politely.

"This is Naputo and Anane," Flynn told her. "They're your servants."

Merita hesitated, looked from the old servitors to Flynn and found him grinning down at her. "What do you mean, my servants?" She turned back to the house. "Where is the owner?"

"Right here. This is your house, Merita. Really your house. I built it for you."

She stared at the beach home the equal of which was to be found nowhere else in the South Pacific. She took a couple of uncertain steps toward the front porch, then whirled, the anxiety she was feeling unmistakable in her expression and her voice.

"Flynn, I can't go in."

"Why not? It's yours. No one else need know." He rejoined her and grabbed her shoulders, lowering his voice. "Merita, this can be *our* house. Yours and mine—and yes, Andrew's, too."

When she looked up at him there was so much pain in her eyes he almost stepped away from her. "Flynn, it's—it's so beautiful. It's the most beautiful place I ever saw, the most wonderful present anyone ever offered me. But I *can't* live here. You know that. I have to stay at the house at Tarawera."

"Why?" he said caustically. "Let the great Robert Coffin find himself another housemaid."

"I can't do that."

"Then at least let me hire someone to take your place when Coffin and his family aren't at the lake, so you and I can spend our time together here, in our own house."

"Flynn, you have to understand, I can't."

He turned away angrily. "I won't believe that, Merita. You forget how well I know you. You can do anything you want, if you wish it enough. If you want to leave the house at Tarawera all you have to do is pick up your belongings and move." He spun to face her again. "Don't tell me you *can't*."

There were tears in her eyes now. "I know I can do that, Flynn. I can do it with my body, but not with my heart. Don't make me say the other thing."

"What other thing? Tell me, damn it! You owe me that much."

"I can't do it because I *won't* do it."

It was silent then save for the lapping of the waves on the perfect beach. The two elderly Maoris stood motionless off to one side, enigmatic as graven tikis.

"I see. That's clear enough even for me." He turned sharply and started up the path toward the waiting coach. She ran to catch him, putting both hands on his arm.

"Please, Flynn, please! Don't be mad. It's a wonderful house, a house in which to dream happy dreams. We could come here sometimes. I'm sure I could manage that. Yes, many times! Just you and I. I can't bring Andrew because he might speak of it to others. But don't ask me to move here with you. I can't abandon Tarawera and what I have there."

He halted abruptly to stare down at her, tight lipped and tense. "Does he love you more than I? Or is it that you love him more than me?"

She retreated a step, frightened by the uncharacteristic venom in his voice. "I—I love you both, but differently, in different ways. You know that, Flynn. I've never tried to hide it from you. When we came to love each other you said you could understand that, that it wouldn't trouble you."

"Well it troubles me now. Merita, I don't want to share you anymore. Not with him, not with anyone. Especially not with him."

Her fear and concern suddenly turned to curiosity. "Why not especially with Robert?" He looked away but she moved to where she could still see his face. "What is it about Robert that so angers you?"

"Nothing. Nothing at all. I'm upset. Forgive me. The thought of having to go on sharing you is driving me crazy."

"No." She was tugging insistently at his arm, trying to drag him down so she could peer into his eyes. "No, there's more to it than that. Something about Robert specifically. What is it, Flynn." Her voice was rising. "What have you been hiding from me all these years? Why are you trying to conceal this?"

"Very well. I'll tell you. I don't like rich people. I know that's ironic since I now find myself in the position of being one myself, but it's true. I've always been that way. I don't like people like Robert Coffin who use it to play God. Who puff themselves up full of false importance so they can push the rest of us around on their private little chessboards. Like he's done to you."

"He hasn't pushed me," she shot back. "No one pushes me around. My relationship with Robert Coffin is a willing one."

"Well then," he said with a sigh, trying to change the subject as well as defuse her curiosity and anger, "if I can't have you all to myself then I guess I'll have to continue sharing you."

"That is the way of things." She sounded mollified.

"One thing I must know. If you did have to choose between us some day, who would you choose?"

Now it was her turn to look away from him. She stood staring out to sea, the wind toying with her long black hair. "I honestly don't know. I only hope that day never comes. Since I am the one to make these choices I can say only that I love and will continue to love you both. It was my choice to love Robert Coffin when my father sent me into his service, and it was my choice to love you when you came to my door and stole a part of my soul." Her eyes shifted to the gleaming white house, the little palace above the beach.

"You know I mean what I say, Flynn. So you know I am being truthful when I tell you that I love this house. But I can only visit it. I cannot make it my home." When she turned back to him she was smiling apologetically.

"I am sorry. I've spoiled your grand surprise. We will come here often, dear Flynn. But don't ask me to live here."

"Very well. I accept that because I must." He put his arms around her. "Now—no more arguing, no more confrontations. It's too fine a day. I'll have as much of you as you'll let me as often as I can and will satisfy myself with that." He bent to kiss her gently.

She pressed her mouth to his, drew back slightly and said huskily, "When we are together, Flynn, you have all of me. Isn't that enough?"

"As I said, it will have to be. *Now* will you come inside?"

She skipped back from him, pursing her lips naughtily. "Only if you will too."

But his thoughts were elsewhere as he let her lead him down the path laughing and happy again. He would be satisfied with what she gave him, yes.

For now.

8

Holly Coffin looked up from the book she was reading and called to the maid. "Is'bel, where are you? There's someone at the front door."

"Sorry ma'm." A few moments later the sprightly lass entered the room.

"It was a delivery boy, ma'm." She set a tightly wrapped package on the nearest table. "He said it was for you."

"For me? You're sure he said it was for me?"

"Yes ma'm. I asked if he didn't mean Robert Coffin and he said no, his instructions were to deliver it to Mrs. Holly Coffin sure."

Holly put the book aside and rose to inspect the package. "How strange. It just has my name on it. See here?" She indicated the writing on the top of the box. "No address or return address or anything. No stamps, either. This didn't arrive via the post office."

"No ma'm. That's what I was thinkin', too. May I go now? I've cleaning to do."

"Yes, of course." She waved the girl out of the room.

Most peculiar. Who would be sending her something so inexplicable and mysterious? Her birthday was well in the past, the holidays far in the future. It might be her good friend Frances, she decided. Frances was a devil, always playing little jokes on her and the other ladies at church.

It was very slim. She picked it up, hefted it, and thought it must be a book of some kind. Better to see than to speculate. Taking a pair of scissors from the drawer table she cut the twine, only to find another package similarly bound within the heavy brown paper. Now she was smiling. One of Frances's tricks for sure. Buried inside all the twine and paper would be a dinner invitation or some such personal message.

When it became known Mrs. Coffin was going out again,

albeit infrequently and only as her strength permitted, the invitations started to pour in from people she'd all but forgotten. An identical barrage arrived from her husband's business associates, all seeking to curry favor. Amused by his new social standing, he turned them all over to her. There was a time when Robert would never have thought of attending anything as stuffy as a formal dinner, but over the years he'd changed. Having adopted the accoutrements of luxury and wealth he'd decided reluctantly it would be worthwhile to accept some of the social conventions that went along with his status in the community. That meant dining alongside people he might not like but wanted to do business with. Anything to get her out of the house, as he'd said.

No dinner invitation inside the final envelope; only a letter written in a hand she didn't recognize. That, and what appeared to be a bundle of photographs. She was delighted. Photographs were still something of a novelty, especially the new kind printed on paper. An expensive as well as mysterious package, then.

She recognized the first picture the instant she turned it over. It was the house at Tarawera, shown from a distance with a bit of lake and mountain in the background. It had been taken from a little hill that rose behind the house. Quite a charming scene.

The second was also of the house, only the camera was much closer this time. Lake and mountain had been excluded. The third picture was nearer still. It showed the back of the house, the garden, and the fence that surrounded the yard. The photographer was still high enough on the hill to shoot over the fence. He'd focused on the sitting bed that occupied the screened-in rear porch. That was where one slept in the summertime when it grew too hot on the second floor of the house.

The fourth photograph was a blowup of a portion of the previous one. The sitting bed was occupied. She stiffened slightly and the smile which had appeared on her face as she'd begun leafing through the pictures disappeared.

There were two figures lying on the bed: a man and a woman. Both were naked. What had started out as a joke was no longer amusing.

One photograph remained. She didn't want to look at it but she was unable to stop herself from raising the sheet and turning it over. The man and the woman were both sitting up in bed now. To be more precise, the man was sitting up and the woman was on his lap. She had her arms around him and he around her.

The image was fuzzy. It was difficult to discern expressions but not features. She was able to recognize the man instantly, even through the screening that shielded the porch. A voice inside kept insisting it had to be someone else, that it couldn't be him. But there weren't many men Robert's size.

It took a minute longer for her to identify the woman he was cradling in his arms. It was Merita, the housekeeper who looked after the lakeside villa. Her features were not distinct, but there was no mistaking that long black hair and the voluptuous figure.

Holly set the pictures down carefully, even though they were paper and would not break. The hand that held them was trembling. She felt for the nearby chair and sat down slowly. For a long time she stared across the room, not really thinking, too numbed to react.

After some time had passed (she didn't know how much time), she remembered the letter that had accompanied the photographs. Picking it up, she began to read. . . .

Coffin dug into his supper with gusto. It had been a profitable day. Word had come that the price of wool was up sharply. As if that weren't enough to stimulate a cheer, one of his ships, the *Albatross*, had arrived more than a week early from London thanks to unusually favorable winds. He and Elias had gone aboard to check the cargo and satisfy themselves that everything was as promised by their English shippers.

And Cook had outdone herself tonight. The duck in particular was succulent and tasty. Across the table Holly didn't seem to feel similarly. She was hardly eating at all, picking indifferently at the dark meat. Since they'd sat down to eat she'd said hardly a word. Chewing on a slice of duck breast he wiped at his lips with a linen napkin.

"What's wrong, woman? You're pale as a ghost and about as lively. Have you forgotten we're due at the Hamptons' later for tea and dessert?" To his surprise Coffin had found he was beginning to enjoy their nocturnal excursions. He was particularly looking forward to tonight's visit. The Hamptons had imported a chef from Paris who excelled at concocting the kind of sugary insubstantialities Coffin would never have touched years ago. Such delights were more to his taste now. He was beginning to acquire a waistline, but then he no longer spent the day riding the back country or climbing the rigging of a ship.

"I'm not going, Robert."

He had to strain to understand the words. When he did he frowned and put the napkin aside. "What do you mean you aren't going? What kind of nonsense is this? You enjoy the Hamptons' company more than I."

"I said I'm not going."

"What's wrong? Not feeling well tonight?"

Instead of answering she rose from the table, walked to the bookcase behind her seat, and extracted a sheaf of paper. Approaching him she dumped the pile unceremoniously next to his plate. He stared at it uncomprehendingly.

"What's this? Bad news from home?"

"No. Not from England."

Curious, Coffin took a sip of his wine before picking up the papers. Now he saw they were photographs, the exposed sides facing down. When he turned the second one over his expression darkened.

He stared at the last one for a long time. When he finally set it aside with the others he became aware she was still hovering close by, watching his face. Violently he shoved the pile toward the center of the table.

"Nonsense. All nonsense," he muttered.

"Nonsense?" A strange sound came from her throat, as if she were choking. "How can they be nonsense, Robert?"

He didn't look up at her. "Photographs can be altered. Treated and changed around. All you need is a clever photographer, a chemist, and an artist."

"Are you trying to tell me that's not you and that snippet of a housemaid in those pictures?"

"All I'm saying is that faces can be altered."

She took a step away from him, the loathing in her voice unmistakeable. "You must think I'm still half mad. I suppose that porch and that bed has been 'altered' as well. And the house of course. How could you, Robert? You and I slept in that same bed." Her voice was cracking now. "And with a *native*."

He said nothing. There was really nothing he could say. But she wasn't finished yet.

"A Maori woman. Like a common farmer. Animals, rutting in the yard."

"Who brought you these?" He gestured toward the damning images. She ignored him as she rambled on wildly.

"All these years. How long, Robert? How long? You told me you built that house for me, for us!"

"I did."

"The hell you did! You built it for you and that woman! Your secret little love-nest, wasn't it? All those 'inspection' trips you made to the lake district. Did you do a lot of inspecting, Robert?" She stalked down the length of the table, picked up the photographs and shook them at him. "It must've been very painful for you. All those times you came home so tired, so worn out, so exhausted by your exertions on behalf of the 'business'!" She threw the pictures across the table. They separated and drifted to the floor.

He looked up at last. "Holly, she's nothing but a housemaid. She means nothing to me."

"Lies compounding like interest! Don't lie to me, Robert. Not now. You won't save yourself with that. You've been lying to me for years, haven't you?" She picked up a letter, glanced briefly at it. "Eleven years, to be precise. All the happy summers we spent at that house, riding around the lake, bathing in the hot springs. All the time we ate there while that *woman*," and she spoke the word as though referring to an incurable tropical disease, "cooked for us and served us. How many secret smiles did I miss, Robert? How many grins and little touches did the two of you exchange when I wasn't looking. When I went early to bed did you have her on the kitchen table, Robert?"

"Holly, I. . . ."

"You want to know the worst of it? What really hurts? I liked her. I really liked her."

"She likes you as well, Holly."

"Likes me?" She gaped at him, her expression unbalanced now. "*Likes* me? How could she? How could she?" Her voice had risen to a steady scream. "To talk to me the way she did, do my laundry, be my friend—and then lie with you behind my back."

"She's Maori, Holly. Among the Maoris it's not uncommon to love more than one person."

"Heathen ways. They're all heathens, the lying bastards. They killed Christopher. Now I find one of them has been deceiving me with my husband for more than a decade." Her expression changed, her eyes narrowing and her voice tightening. "And the two of you even have a little bastard of your own. How charming."

Coffin had dealt as well as possible with each succeeding accusation. Only now was he unnerved. "How did you know that?"

"Andrew," she hissed sarcastically. "That cute little boy who has the run of the house and grounds and calls you 'Uncle' Robert. I knew from looking at him he was a half-breed, but I never suspected he was your half-breed. You even deceive your own child." She leaned forward, resting both hands on the polished table.

"Who else have you deceived, Robert? What about this poor, ignorant native girl? Did you tell her you would leave me some day so you could marry her?"

"No, that isn't necessary with her. She didn't need that."

"How open-minded she is."

"How did you find out about Andrew? He's not in any of the pictures."

"Oh. The pictures didn't come alone. There was a letter." Turning, she strode around the table and lifted the paper from her chair. "*This* letter. It's very long, Robert. Very detailed. Whoever wrote it didn't want anyone seeing those pictures to have the slightest doubt what they implied."

Coffin rose and moved toward her. She backed away from him, breathing hard. He tried to keep his voice level. "Give me that letter, Holly."

"Why not? Here!" She threw it at him. It floated to the floor like a severed palm frond. "Why should I want to keep it from you? There's nothing in it you don't already know."

He bent to recover the several sheets of paper which had been clipped together, and began reading. She was right about the detail. Whoever had written the missive had been clinical in the descriptions. It described everything he had worked to conceal from her for the past eleven years.

"Who sent it? Who!"

"I've no idea." She had backed herself against the bookcase. "Is'bel took them from a messenger boy who came to the house. There was no return address on the package." She laughed then, a sad, unhappy sound. "I am not surprised. Whoever sent these couldn't have been proud of their work."

"There must have been *something*. Some indication. A postmark, anything."

"Nothing." She was sneering at him now. "There was nothing. It didn't come through the post. I thought that unusual at the time. I thought it came from one of our neighbors. From one of our friends." Again the despairing laugh. "For all I know that might be the truth. After all, what do I know? Who else knows about you and your Maori tart? How many of our friends have been laughing at us, laughing at me behind my back over the years?"

He continued studying the damning letter. "No one knows about it," he muttered. "No one."

"Someone does. Someone who knew enough to have a photographer in just the right place, Robert, at just the right time. Someone who knew your secret life pretty well."

"Yes, that's true. But who?" Anyone who knew this much about Robert Coffin must also know that what they'd done had marked them for death, yet that hadn't dissuaded them. But how to trace letter and pictures back to their origin?

"I'll interview every photographer in New Zealand until I find out who's responsible for this!"

She was staring at him and shaking her head. "Thinking of yourself. You're always thinking of yourself, Robert. No picture-maker's responsible for what's happened. You're responsible. You. All you can think of right now is revenge, isn't it? Revenge against whoever knew the truth about you. The truth hurts. So easy, it's so easy when it's just your own little secret, nothing complicated, nothing painful. Maybe whoever wrote the letter also took the pictures. What about that?"

"Then I'll trace cameras."

"You can't trace cameras. You might as well try to trace stoves or bridles."

He crushed the letter in his fingers. "I'll find out. You'll see. Someday. Someday." He sat down heavily, still clutching the crumpled letter as he stared at the floor where the photographs lay scattered like so many playing cards. "Who would do such a thing? Why?"

She was trembling all over. It was amazing so small a body could contain so much fury. "It doesn't matter. What matters is that it's true." She ran at him then and he flinched from her anger. Her spittle landed on his face as she railed at him. "It's true, it's true! Deny it, Robert. Sit there before God and deny it!"

He inhaled deeply and rose, backing her away. "All right. It's true." He walked away from her. "I thought you were going to die, Holly. Everyone did. The servants, the doctors. But you did everything *but* die. You stared out the window overlooking the yard. Day after day you sat in that damned chair and stared! When you weren't staring you walked the halls like a statue. Can you imagine what that was like? Can you conceive of how oppressive my life became?

"I took it as long as I could. Dammit, woman, I'm not a corpse! Nor am I a relic. I still had feelings, emotions, needs. Merita was there when I needed her. You weren't."

It was silent then, until she said quietly, "And if I had been there, Robert, what then? Are you trying to tell me this never would have happened? That you wouldn't have made love to her behind my back? That you wouldn't have had a child by her when I couldn't give you another one?"

"That's right. That's right. I wouldn't have."

"I don't believe you. How can I believe you? I think you would have had this affair whether I was depressed, crippled, or healthy as a horse. Because you wanted this woman. And what the great Robert Coffin wants, he takes. How you must have enjoyed the planning! Keeping your sordid little secret, setting her up in her own house pretending it was ours—don't try to deny that, not now. I won't stand for it. I am the visitor at Tarawera, the guest. Oh no, it wouldn't have made any difference if I'd not become ill."

"It would. I swear to you it would have, Holly."

"Don't speak my name, you miserable adulterer! Look at you, standing there trying to deny your own lust, trying to appear the outraged one."

"Why would someone do a thing like this?" He gestured toward the fallen photographs. "Ask yourself that?"

"Why should I? What are you trying to do with such words? Put the blame on the poor unknown who revealed the truth to me? It doesn't matter. All that matters is the truth. That exists by itself, separate and apart from the letter and the pictures and the motives of whoever is responsible for them. None of them are as important as the truth, and the truth is that you love your little Maori whore, don't you? You love her!"

"Holly, I love you as well."

This time her laugh was frightening. She was walking the edge now, the thin line she'd traversed during her long, slow recovery.

"You don't love me, Robert. You value me, as you value all your possessions, all your successes. As you probably value that poor woman. Why did you really do it? Because I couldn't have another child after Christopher?"

"That had nothing to do with it. I've told you why it happened. Because I was lonely and you were here but not here."

"The great Robert Coffin. So you are as weak as any of the rest of us after all."

"I never denied that. I'm a human being. Do you condemn me for that?"

"I don't know." She spun away from him. "I don't know. All I know is that when I spoke the marriage vows to a hopeful young man in England oh so many years ago, I meant them. And you did not."

"Father Methune. We should talk to Father Methune. He can explain to you what I was going through, living with the shadow of the woman I'd married."

"I'm sorry if you suffered, Robert. Believe me I am. But bringing Father Methune to talk to me won't wipe out what you've done, won't extricate you from your own filthy machinations. Nothing you can say or do can alter the truth. That's the funny thing about truth, isn't it? It's quite immutable. You can try to cover it over, try to hide behind an avalanche of excuses and apologies, but it's too big for that.

"And now if you don't mind," she said suddenly, "I'm rather tired and I am going to bed. As you may have noticed, I've no appetite tonight." She turned toward the door.

He took three strides to block her retreat. "No. Neither of us is going anywhere until this is settled."

She stared calmly up at him. "Until what is settled? What is there to settle, Robert? Nothing has really changed. You still have everything you want. Your dutiful wife and your Maori whore."

"Don't call her that. Whatever you may think of me, that's not what she is."

"Oh?" Her voice was shaking. "Why not? Isn't a whore someone who sells herself for money?"

"She never did that."

"Really? She appears to have done fairly well from what I can see. A fine house, an independent income. Or are you going to tell me you pay her for cleaning and cooking?"

"Whether you believe me or not, that is the truth."

"More truth from Robert Coffin, the master of deception?"

"She did it for me."

"She did it for you. For you?" Holly laughed. "Am I now to be forced to acknowledge the nobility and self-sacrifice of your trollop?"

"She," he hesitated, "she loves me. She always has."

"Well of course she does! How could anyone not love the great Robert Coffin? Why else would she lie with you and bear your son if not out of love for the irresistible, the all-conquering Robert Coffin? How foolish of me to think otherwise." She turned to leave.

He grabbed her arm. "Don't end it like this, Holly. You don't understand."

"No. No, I guess I do not, Robert. I don't understand. I'm just a simple girl from London who thought she knew what life was all about, what love and marriage were supposed to be about. Obviously I was wrong. That's all different here, halfway around the world. It would be so much simpler if I were Maori, wouldn't it? Isn't that right, Robert?" Her stare and words were so cold he let go of her.

"You may come upstairs whenever it suits you." This time when she tried to laugh she failed miserably. "After all, with your country tart unavailable you will have to make do with whatever you can find in the city, won't you?" She put a hand on the handle of the dining room door intending to twist it 'round. Then she crumpled, silent as a rag doll, as if her legs had simply given out.

"Holly!" He ran over to kneel beside her. "Holly?" He put his ear to her chest, heard her heart still beating. "Is'bel, Edward! Edward, damn you, get in here!"

A moment later the door was pulled aside to reveal the butler and maid. The girl put her hands to her cheeks and made a small gasping sound.

"Don't stand there, go and fetch the doctor. Now!"

"Yes—yes sir." The butler turned and ran.

Coffin looked down at his wife. Her limp body suddenly felt weightless, insubstantial. "Holly," he whispered, "it can all be worked out. We can still make it work. My God, this isn't the way. This isn't the way." He looked up sharply. "Is'bel!"

"Yes sir." The maid continued staring down at her unconscious mistress.

"Go and get some water. Hot water. And towels."

"Yes sir." She whirled and disappeared.

Coffin lifted the small form off the floor, walked across the Persian carpet to set it gently on the nearest couch. He stayed by her side until the maid returned. Warm compresses were applied to his wife's forehead. She continued to breathe but her eyes remained shut.

Damn Edward! What was keeping him?

Suddenly conscious of the maid's presence in the room Coffin rose and quietly gathered the photographs from where they'd fallen. He put the letter on top of the first picture, sat down in his chair and began reading anew. His eyes burned into the paper as though by dint of sheer concentration he could somehow make a name, an address appear between the neat lines of script. As if in the rereading he might recognize the handwriting, or spot a watermark indicating where the paper had been purchased. But there was nothing. The careful, detached tone of the letter mocked his efforts to unravel its origin.

Meanwhile there was only silence. Silence in the room and in the hallway beyond.

9

"Mr. Coffin, sir, I have some bad news. Mr. Coffin?"

Lost in himself as he shuffled slowly past Goldman's office, Coffin looked up only when Goldman emerged to block his path.

When he saw the expression on his employer's face, Goldman found himself hesitating. The eyes were tired, lost. For the first time in all the years of their long acquaintance, Robert Coffin looked like an old man.

Now he tried to smile. You could see the effort it cost him. "I'm sorry, Elias. I guess I didn't hear you. My mind was elsewhere."

"Yes sir. I'm afraid John Morydon has left us."

"Left?" Coffin frowned, seemed to return from a place far away. "What do you mean, he's left?" After Elias Goldman, John Morydon was Coffin House's most valuable employee, a fine manager and master of half a dozen languages. Whenever Coffin had any serious trouble with his contacts in China, India or the Indies he dispatched Morydon to straighten out the problem, which he inevitably did.

"Why would he leave? I thought John was happy here."

"So did I, sir. Apparently he received a better offer elsewhere."

"So much better that he would leave without giving us the chance to match it?" Coffin's gaze narrowed. "Rose Hull."

"No sir, he didn't move over to Hull House, sir. Nor has he gone with Rushton or Wallingford or any of the others. At least, not insofar as I have been able to discover."

Coffin sagged. "Ah well. Then I don't imagine there's much we can do about it, is there?" He walked around Goldman.

His assistant came after him. This wasn't the Robert Coffin he'd known most of his life, the man who once would have

fought a whole crew of whalers or an entire government to
protect his interests.

"Don't you think we should make some kind of an effort,
Mr. Coffin?"

"How do you mean, Elias?"

"Well sir, to try and find out what happened. To hire John
back."

"If John's decided he can do better for himself elsewhere
then what's the point in our hounding him?" A gleam came
into Coffin's eye. "Though I would like to know who made
him the offer. Try to find out where he ends up."

This was better. "I will do the best I can, sir. If he's left the
country it won't be easy."

"I know it won't, Elias. But you've been doing the difficult
for a long time, haven't you?" They were outside Coffin's
offices now.

As Coffin moved to enter, Elias Goldman did something he
hadn't dared in more than thirty years. He physically prevented
the bigger man from proceeding. Coffin halted, though
whether out of consideration or shock Goldman didn't know.

"Mr. Coffin, sir—Robert. What's wrong?"

Coffin hesitated before speaking. "It's Holly again." He
talked slowly with visible reluctance. "She's had a—relapse."

"I see," Goldman replied carefully. "I am truly sorry, sir. I
didn't know."

"No one knows except for the household staff, myself, the
doctors and now you."

"I didn't mean to pry."

"I know that, Elias." Coffin put a reassuring hand on his
friend's shoulder.

"Is there anything I can do? I could send my wife around."

"No!" Coffin spoke so sharply Goldman retreated a step and
his employer hastened to reassure him. The thought was a kind
one, but the appearance at her bedside of Goldman's attractive
Maori wife was not the sort of therapy Holly required just now.

"Thank you Elias, but no."

"What of the prognosis?"

Coffin tried to sound hopeful, wondered if he was succeeding. "The doctors continue to consult. They say she has lapsed
into a coma, alive but yet not. She could awaken at any time,
or. . . ."

"Or?" Goldman prodded gently.

"Or she might never come out of it."

"I'm sorry."

"So am I." More than you'll ever know, Elias, he thought. "But I'm not the only one who's going to sorrow over this."

Goldman frowned. "I'm afraid I don't quite understand, sir."

They entered Coffin's enormous office and Goldman watched while the head of Coffin House sat down behind the desk. When his employer at last looked back to him it was as if the old Robert Coffin he knew so well had suddenly returned. The transition was abrupt and startling.

"I have some work for certain of our people, Elias." In contrast to Coffin's previous slow, tired speech his words now came fast and crisp. A relieved Goldman whipped out pad and pencil.

"Which people, sir?"

"The ones we occasionally employ for atypical purposes. I want them to find the names and whereabouts of every professional photographer in the country. I want to know the ages of these people, if they're independent artists or if they work for a service. I want to know if any of them worked in the Rotorua District at any time within the past two years. I want to know how many private cameras there are in the colony, who sells them and most importantly, who provides developing services and supplies. I want to know if any professional photographers have arrived from Australia or anywhere else anytime in the past year and any who've left recently.

"In brief, Elias, I want as thorough a breakdown of the photographic community in New Zealand for the past two years as it's possible to compile."

Goldman finally looked up from writing furiously. "Yes sir. May I inquire why you need this kind of information?"

"No Elias, you may not. Someday maybe I'll be able to explain it to you. If I find who I'm looking for." His voice fell. "I may not, but by God I'm going to try." Before he died he would know who had done this to him.

Then he would crush whoever was responsible like a fly.

10

Flynn Kinnegad rolled over to stare at Merita. She lay on her side next to him, sleeping soundly, as much a natural wonder as the hot springs of Ohine-mutu.

Everything was proceeding according to plan. His overseas investments continued to provide him with all the money he needed to do as he pleased. The gold he and his partners had wrenched from the hills of Otago had been channeled through offshore financial centers so as not to trigger any alarms in Wellington or Auckland. Yellow metal traveled from Melbourne to Hong Kong, New York and Rome, to be converted into pounds sterling and dollars.

His latest triumph had been to have a Glasgow company hire the resourceful and irreplaceable John Morydon away from Coffin House. The bewildered but delighted company had been more than glad to do so since the necessary money had been provided by an insistent and anonymous shareholder. The small company could never have afforded a man with Morydon's skills on their own. As for Morydon, he accepted the position and the outrageous bonus without bothering to inquire as to its origins, assuming quite naturally it had been provided by his new employer.

No one in Scotland or New Zealand suspected that all that money and maneuvering had been for one purpose only: to deprive Coffin House of a valuable employee.

It was a small blow, as had been the incriminating and revealing package that had been delivered to Coffin's home. First blood. After endless years of waiting at last he was beginning to move.

He drank in the sight of Merita. *I have your woman, Father,* he said to himself. *Soon I will take everything else.*

He knew he would have to be careful. A wounded bear was

more dangerous than a healthy one. Coffin House was such a vast enterprise it would be difficult to take over quietly.

If he moved boldly and openly he could achieve that end far sooner, but that wasn't the kind of revenge he'd spent his entire life planning. How much more satisfying to slice up his father's precious business a little piece at a time while Coffin went mad trying to unmask his tormentor, wondering who was demolishing him and why. Far more interesting to move slowly, like playing chess blindfolded. Only near the end would Kinnegad show Coffin who had broken him.

There was noise out in the hall, innocently loud and uncaring. That would be young Andrew off to play with his friends in the village. Some day he would learn that his mother's friend was in reality his own half-brother. A good boy, Andrew, and blameless. A magnanimous Flynn could leave the child out of the plans for his father's destruction. He smiled contentedly.

There was no way he could fail.

BOOK SIX

1886

1

"Damn all liberals!"

The shouts seeped from behind the heavy closed door to halt the two clerks in their tracks. The one nearest the door winked knowingly at his colleague.

"The Old Man's at it again."

"You better not let him hear you say that." His companion kept his voice to a whisper. "Better not let him hear you referring to him as the 'Old Man,' either. You know how vain he can be."

"Don't worry." Additional oaths and curses boomed from the big office sealed off by the door.

The smaller of the two men was staring nervously down the hall. "Come on, Mick. We'd better get away from here. If Goldman or Ellsworth catch us listening we'll be out on the street in two minutes, without severance pay."

"What are you worried about?" His foolhardy friend was straining to hear as the voices on the other side of the barrier fell. "It's lunchtime. Everyone else has cleared off. Besides, Goldman's in there with him. You can hear him muttering 'yes sir, yes sir' all the time. You know how the Old Man uses him for a sounding board."

"Yeah, I know, but this is still dangerous country." He took his friend by the arm and started trying to pull him away. "Come on!"

"Oh all right." The other clerk allowed himself to be led off. But he was still striving to listen as they started down the stairs.

Elias Goldman stood patiently in the middle of the floor while Robert Coffin strode angrily back and forth between his desk and the window that overlooked the city beyond. As he raved, Coffin gesticulating violently, using his fingers like knives.

401

"I just don't understand what's wrong with people today, Elias. What do they want, anyway?"

At seventy-three Coffin was a straight-backed, imposing figure, with the body and bearing of a much younger man. Not so Elias Goldman. Never impressive physically, now he was bent and wrinkled, so thin it seemed Coffin's bellowing must surely blow him across the carpet. But like a reed in the wind, Goldman knew how to cope with his employer's occasional tirades. He stood nodding understandingly while Coffin's violence slipped around him.

Coffin stopped to stare out at the bustling, busy street below. "Sure we're in debt, but business is good and improving. The country prospers. Even this fool Te Kooti and his passive resistance campaign have just about run out of steam."

"That's true, sir," said Goldman, venturing cautiously into the first gap in Coffin's sermon. "I hear tell he's going to surrender himself any day now."

"About time," Coffin said huffily. "At last we'll have an end to the Maori problem." He turned from the window, grinning ruefully. "Remember when the resistance first broke out, Elias? We thought we'd clean up the Maoris in a month. Instead it's taken almost twenty-five years. A quarter of a century!"

"Yes, sir, if you go back to the burning of Kororareka."

"Kororareka." Coffin stared off into the distance and his voice was suddenly thick with remembrance. "Now there was a *real* town! Not boring and stuffy like this." He swept a hand toward the window. "We've gotten too civilized, Elias. That was a place where people *lived*."

"I know, sir." Privately Goldman thought old Kororareka the most heinous blot on the country's history but he was far too sensible to offer his personal opinion to Coffin. "Remember, I lived there too."

"That's right. I'd forgotten. You know, you're a funny fellow, Elias."

"Am I, sir?" said Goldman noncommittally.

"Yes. You keep a lower profile than a kiwi, yet you're always around. Whether you're needed or not."

"I'm not naturally an obtrusive type, Mr. Coffin. I try to anticipate."

Coffin laughed. It was good to hear him laugh, Goldman mused. He didn't laugh often these days. Only when he'd stolen a march on a competitor or ground another into dust. Even Angus McQuade came around but rarely. Goldman often saw Coffin eating in silence at the Club or one of his favorite restaurants instead of participating in his friends' debates the way he used to do.

It wasn't that he saw them as enemies trying to steal information from him. It was simply that he wasn't good company anymore. Unless he was in one of his rare good moods, like today.

He sighed wistfully. "So many years gone. Poor old Kororareka. Now they call the place Russell. It just doesn't sound right." Coffin glanced sharply at Goldman. "I don't know what I would've done without you, Elias."

"Neither do I, sir." Goldman smiled through his thick gray mustache and Coffin grinned back. "If I may say so, it's good to see you feeling so well."

"I know I haven't been very cheerful lately, Elias."

Lately, Goldman thought? You haven't been very cheerful for years. But who was he to criticize Coffin's deportment? That was not now and never had been his job.

"How goes the cable laying?" Coffin asked him.

"Coming along on schedule, I believe, sir."

"Amazing, isn't it? Science and all that? It's hard for a simple seaman like myself to accept the fact that soon we'll be able to telegraph our Sydney and Melbourne branches directly. Think of the savings in time—and money."

"Speaking of time and money, sir, the *Corinthian* is overdue from San Francisco."

"Nothing to get excited about, Mr. Goldman. Even these days a transpacific voyage still involves many variables. It's only a few days late."

In an exceedingly good mood, Goldman told himself, even as he thought he knew the reason why. He would never voice his suspicions aloud, of course. Tolerant as Coffin was of their long relationship, he still had limits beyond which it was wise not to push.

"Staggs is rarely on time, but he always gets here."

"That's true, sir. He always does."

"And with his cargo and crew intact. I've watched other Captains, Elias. They drive their men so hard half of them jump ship as soon as they make port. All to shave a day or two off the crossing. Good sailors are more valuable than a few days."

"Quite so, sir." He swallowed pointedly. "Although as I'm sure you're aware, the *Marathon* docked yesterday."

"A Hull Company ship." Coffin chuckled. "A tough gal, that Rose Hull. Always was, even as a child. So she'll be the first to offer in stores the latest in bric-a-brac and fashions. No matter. Business is good enough that we'll still make a handsome profit on the *Corinthian*'s cargo. Maybe next time it'll be Skaggs who's first to port. There's enough profit to go around."

"I must disagree with you there, sir." Goldman had decided to test the depth of Coffin's good mood. "There isn't enough to go around."

"What? What's that?" Coffin eyed him in surprise. "Elias, we're not going to have a political disagreement, are we?"

"I'm afraid we are, sir. You spoke briefly earlier of the liberal sentiment in this country. It's not just a youthful aberration, sir. It's serious."

"You, a liberal?" Coffin let out a desultory laugh. "You of all people, Elias."

"I'm afraid it's true, Mr. Coffin."

"Well I'll be damned. I wouldn't have believed it possible if you hadn't told me yourself."

"That's because you don't go into the city, sir."

"What are you talking about, Elias? I'm in town every day."

"In the financial district, yes. In the better sections. You don't visit the fringe, the smaller towns. It's true Julius Vogel spent this country back to prosperity, but it was prosperity for a chosen few."

Coffin's smile was fading. "What are you driving at, Elias?"

Goldman took a deep breath and plunged ahead. "You've done well, sir. Coffin House Limited and Hull Company and Rushton and McQuade and many of the others have done equally well. But I'm afraid that the money generated by Mr. Vogel's policies has failed to trickle down to the common folk."

"Elias, I'm surprised at you. I always thought you were a great admirer of Julius."

"At first I was, sir. When his policy started working and the country began to rise out of depression my admiration knew no bounds. Even now I am ambivalent about his work. It is true there are more jobs and more work and on the whole we are better off. But the people at the lower end of the economic scale haven't the kinds of gains we have. The small farmers and tradesmen see the rich growing richer while they stand still. They don't find that equitable, sir."

"I see." Coffin looked thoughtful. "What would they have us do? Play Robin Hood? Rob from the achievers to give to the failures, like that crazy English chap—what's his name? Marx?"

"Not exactly, sir. All the common man sees is that the country itself is deeply in debt, and that they all share in that debt without having shared in any benefits."

"Some people are never satisfied, Elias." Coffin put his hands behind him as he turned back to the window. "Ten years ago the ones who are complaining now would have been overjoyed to have any kind of work at all. Now that most of them have work it's not enough for them."

"The work is good enough for them, Mr. Coffin, sir. It's the system that's failing them."

"That's because they can't see things over the long term, Elias. Such people don't have the overview available to you and me. Many of these constant complainers are young, so I suppose we should look on them tolerantly." He turned back from the window.

"I'll give you an example of how spoiled they are. Everyone takes refrigerated shipping for granted now. Some of your howling liberals forget that the first shipment of refrigerated lamb went to England barely four years ago. That made marginal ranching profitable. Do they give credit for that? No." Goldman said nothing.

"Think of it, Elias. Thousands of tons of perfectly good meat wasted down through the years because there was no way to preserve and ship it. Now we have not only a whole new industry but one that will come to dominate the economy. And we can still sell all the wool we can raise. We're using the entire animal now.

"Remember all the land I bought on South Island? Those 'useless' mountain ranges? We'll put an ocean of sheep on them, supply the whole world with mutton. We have the best land and the best people for doing that."

"The people I'm speaking of can't afford great estates, sir, like you and Miss Hull and Angus McQuade."

"There'll be plenty for all," Coffin insisted, refusing to let Goldman darken his vision. "But only for those willing to work. These utopian radical socialist schemes your liberal friends keep proposing bear no relationship to reality."

"Nevertheless, the sentiment is there, the feeling that something has to be done to ensure a more equitable distribution of income."

"Well, sentiment never harmed anyone, I guess."

What was this, Goldman thought? A concession from the immovable Robert Coffin? An expression of concern?

"Sir, may I inquire why you are in such a pleasant mood? I think I know, but I'd like to be certain."

"Implying that normally I'm not in a good mood, Elias?"

"No sir, not at all, but. . . ."

Coffin interrupted him with a laugh. "Rest easy. I'm off tomorrow to Tarawera. First light." He made a quick scan of his desk. "I've taken care to put everything in order."

"What about the *Corinthian*?"

"Cap'n Skaggs will be delighted if I'm not there to harry him with questions when he docks. You can handle the details. You know, it's been a long time since you've seen the lake house, Elias. You and Kamine and the children should visit there more often."

"I would, sir, but then who would run Coffin House? Patrick?"

"Ellsworth's a good man, but he's not Elias Goldman."

"Thank you, sir." Astonishing how Coffin could wound a man deeply one moment and lift him to the heights the next. "How are Merita and the boy?"

Coffin sat down in the leather chair and put his legs up on the desk. When he was completely relaxed like this, Goldman mused, he looked anything but the merchant tycoon. His employer's face was lined now, but he was still in remarkable physical condition. The heritage of so many hard years at sea. Had he wished to, Coffin could still outwrestle or outload any longshoreman.

"Merita, you know, Merita doesn't age."

"So I have heard, sir. So your pictures show. A most remarkable lady."

"Yes." Coffin's voice lowered thoughtfully. "Most remarkable."

Coffin did not publicize his relationship with Merita, but

neither did he need to keep it secret any longer, Goldman knew. Not since Holly Coffin had died. Coffin could speak of her death now, years later, without the bitterness that had first attended it. The woman had simply faded away. No one had been able to explain why.

She'd been ill for years following the death of her son Christopher, but then there'd been a period when she seemed to be recovering. Just when prospects for a complete recovery had been strongest she'd suffered a serious relapse, falling into a coma from which she'd never emerged.

Coffin had been a terror to be near in those days, and for a time everyone feared he might have suffered irreparable mental damage himself. Gradually, very gradually, he'd returned to a semblance of his old self. Goldman gave the credit for that to his Maori mistress. He had yet to marry her, but he had gone so far several years earlier as to give their son the Coffin name.

Goldman knew the young man well. Andrew was a tall, lanky whirlwind who reminded him of the young Robert Coffin, though much darker of appearance because of his half-Maori ancestry. Andrew had a good head for figures, but whenever Goldman or his father tried to persuade him to learn something of the business, the young man would vanish the instant their backs were turned. He wasn't ready to settle down, he kept telling them. Goldman thought twenty-five was old enough to commence a career, but it wasn't his place to press the matter.

Nor did Coffin. He was delighted simply to have Andrew around, expanding proudly in his son's presence. Nor did Andrew seem to mind the revelation that the man he'd known as a child as "Uncle" Robert was really his father. Perhaps that was the Maori in him, Goldman mused. It might also explain why there was no resentment toward Coffin for not marrying Merita.

It wasn't as though Coffin hadn't proposed. It was Merita who had turned him down, explaining that she was happy with things as they were. She did not wish to complicate his life, and she had no desire to be shunned by "proper" Auckland society. Coffin remonstrated with her but she was insistent. Better to let things stay as they'd always been. She loved the lake house at Tarawera and had little use for the city anyway. Eventually he acceded. As he'd so laughingly mentioned on more than one occasion, in addition to being the most beautiful woman in New Zealand, Merita was probably also the most stubborn. So she remained at Tarawera, visiting the city but rarely, and Coffin went to her every chance he had.

He'd sold the great house on the hill and moved into a spacious group of apartments in the city's best section. It was more convenient to Coffin House's headquarters and had a masculine air very different from the mansion. There was no question, Goldman knew, but that his old friend and employer was happier than he'd been in a long time.

"You'd think she'd get lonely, out there in that big place all by herself," Coffin was saying, "but she never does. As for Andrew, well, you know what he's like."

"Yes sir. Very much like yourself at that age, if I may say so, only not nearly so grim."

Coffin laughed, ran a hand through his still thick, silvery mane. "At least he got his mother's hair and won't have to play the old man before his time like I did."

"You never looked as old as you thought, sir."

"Perhaps. I expect I worried about it too much, but then I worried about everything too much, didn't I?"

Goldman said nothing.

"Anything that will concern you while I'm gone? Anything you can't handle, Elias?"

"I think not, sir," Goldman replied dryly. "Everything seems to be in order. If you could review these papers from the manager of Goldview Farm before you leave I would appreciate it." He handed Coffin a neatly clipped sheaf of letters. Coffin began scanning them rapidly, mumbling and nodding to himself. "Also there is the matter of the new general store in Wellington."

Coffin looked up thoughtfully. "Redline Company's putting that one in, aren't they?"

"Redline, yes sir. I remind you we still haven't been able to find out who's financing that lot. Neither has anyone else. There has been much talk of secret mergers and buyouts, but Redline's books are closely guarded. Meanwhile they continue to expand, primarily into our territory and regardless of their realistic commercial prospects. I wish we had that kind of liquidity. We no longer will have that portion of the Wellington market all to ourselves."

"It'll hurt," Coffin agreed, "but it won't be fatal. We've fought Redline's predatory pricing practices before. Sometimes

I think those people aren't as interested in making money as they are in a good fight. Anything else?"

"Not really, sir, unless you change your mind and decide to wait for the *Corinthian*."

"Don't worry about Skaggs. He'll be here tomorrow, or the next day. There's always the possibility of a disaster, but none of the other arriving transpacific ships have reported dangerous weather. Skaggs hardly knows how to put two words together but the man's got salt water for blood. He'll be here."

Coffin's expression softened. "Christopher could've been a Captain like that. Would have been if he'd been given the chance. Now. . . ." He sighed and looked up.

"I know, sir." Goldman politely lowered his gaze.

Coffin tried to recover his good spirits. "What's done is done, and we go on with our lives. Right, Elias?"

"Very right, sir. I may not see you in the morning so I'll wish you a pleasant journey now. Say hello to Merita for me."

"I will that. I'll be on my way before sunup. The older I get the more precious the days at Tarawera become to me. I don't want to waste any of them."

"I understand sir. You need not worry for the business."

"I know that, Elias." There was a long pause, then, "I never will get you to call me Robert on a regular basis, will I?"

"I'm afraid not, sir. It doesn't sound right and I'm never comfortable with it. Besides, that would cheapen the effect it has when I choose to employ it."

"You'd think I'd have figured that out by now."

Coffin chuckled as he took his top hat and coat from their places on the carved Kauri rack and headed for the door. "Well, you know me, Elias. Stubborn to a fault."

True enough, Goldman reflected as he watched his mentor depart.

2

Andrew Coffin tried to stay off the road as much as possible. Usually that wasn't a problem, since the places he preferred to ride were devoid of anything more elaborate than animal tracks. He delighted in picking his own way through the bush, whether it was behind Lake Rotomahana or along the rugged shores of the Tarawera River.

A few times he'd climbed the mountain itself. Those expeditions were a source of worry to his Maori friends. They told him that Tarawera was home to demons and devils and all kinds of indescribable monsters, not to mention fractious ancestors. Andrew just laughed and called them natives, which made them furious until they saw he was laughing with them and not at them. Then they too would laugh.

Today, however, he was compelled to ride a more frequented path. His mother needed certain supplies that were available only in Rotorua, so he'd agreed to make the ten-mile journey and pick them up for her. Though it slowed him, he kept to the woods as much as possible.

He'd risen early, even before his father was up, and had stopped at the McRae's hotel for breakfast. He tried not to play favorites. Next time he would eat at the other tourist hotel, the Terraces. You never knew who you might meet or strike up a friendship with. Because of his mixed parentage he was something of a curiosity to the many tourists who now visited the area. European women in particular were attracted to him. Being the polite, obliging fellow that he was, he was more than willing to satisfy the curiosity of the younger, prettier ones.

His numerous conquests were facilitated by the fact that the last of the Maori "troubles" had petered out some years earlier. There'd been no actual fighting for some time and he no longer suffered the occasional ignominy of having to identify himself to patrolling soldiers. Not that he'd ever had any

410

real problems. His last ñame took care of that. Everyone in the country knew the name Coffin.

Seeing a cloud of dust approaching he nudged his mount deeper into the trees, watched as a tourist coach came rumbling up the road. It was filled to capacity with sightseers on their way to view the Pink and White Terraces on the far side of Lake Tarawera. The Eighth Wonder of the World, people had taken to calling the spectacular silica formations. To Andrew, who'd grown up on the lakeshore and had often canoed over to the terraces with his Maori companions, they were no longer unique.

His opinion was not shared by the owners of the two modern hotels which had been built at Te Wairoa specifically to house European tourists. Nor was it shared by those local Maoris who'd given up farming to convey visitors to those two natural wonders. Some of the families who shared ownership of the land on which the terraces stood were clearing more than four thousand pounds a year in tourist fees.

He grinned at the irony of it. No pakehas had been interested in that steaming, inhospitable, unfarmable land. There must be early land speculators who were turning over in their graves for having passed on the opportunity to purchase it. It would have galled them to see how the Maoris were profiting from their oversights.

As the coach bounced past he tried to see if there were any attractive young women inside, but there was too much dust. When it began to settle he urged his mount back onto the road and continued on toward Rotorua. He hardly lacked for feminine companionship. To the European women the fact he was half Maori was exotic and exciting, while the fact he was half pakeha made him an object of intense interest on the part of the local Maori maidens. Those who thought his mixed ancestry subjected him to the worst of both worlds had it exactly backward, he knew.

It wasn't just the combination of races which made him attractive, though. It was the fact that the best of both seemed to have merged in him. He had his mother's sensitivity, black hair and fine features to go along with his father's height and strength and dark-blue eyes. It was a startling combination and as soon as he was old enough to recognize it he began using it to full advantage whenever possible.

School had been awkward. He was too impatient to sit and

study. Too wild, according to his tutor. Only his mother's insistence had made him endure the long hours he'd spent with texts. That, and his father's obvious love for the fine books which filled the shelves in the library.

"I didn't have much time to read when I was your age," the man he'd known for years as "Uncle" Robert used to tell him. "Don't you go making the same mistake."

Though he was close to Ohinemutu, the Maori part of Rotorua, it was difficult to make out through the mist. The village sat on the great thermal plain which bordered seven-mile-wide Lake Rotorua. Living here was very much like living on a piece of toast floating in a cookpot, he knew.

The analogy went farther than that. Down through the centuries the Maoris had adapted their Hades-like land to their own needs. As he passed one house he saw a woman placing a pot full of chicken into the steaming pool that filled her backyard. In a little while it would be ready to eat, thoroughly cooked through.

You had to watch your step in Ohinemutu. The same pools that readily cooked supper had also parboiled not a few Maoris and the occasional careless pakeha.

There were other pools, not quite as hot or stinking of sulphur, where people went to bathe. "Taking the waters," the Europeans called it. He'd first heard the term spoken by a visiting gentleman of German extraction.

Andrew didn't believe in the supposed therapeutic values of the waters, though bathing in them was relaxing. As a child he and his companions had gone swimming in similar if less extensive pools along Tarawera's shores. It was a simple matter for mindless young boys to find out which pools were cool enough to bathe in. They would find a frog and toss it into the water. If the frog swam it was safe. If it turned belly up it was time to seek elsewhere.

More houses became visible as he rode on. It was still early. If he made it back to Te Wairoa in time he could stop at the hotels to inspect the latest group of arrivals.

His mount balked unexpectedly. There was a startled scream ahead and he wrenched on the reins. Not even enough time to curse, he thought angrily.

When he finally got his horse under control again and saw who'd stepped out in front of him, all thoughts of upbraiding the unknown pedestrian were forgotten.

The girl stared back at him, breathing hard at the near miss, one hand pressed to her bosom. No, not a girl, he corrected himself. She looked to be about eighteen.

"I'm sorry," he said in perfect Maori. "I didn't see you."

"It's—it's all right. It was my fault. I was running and didn't look." She swallowed. "I should have been more careful while crossing the road."

A small bundle peeped out from beneath her left arm. She was tall and curvaceous and bold enough to have cut her hair short in the pakeha manner. Her face reminded him of the pictures of the Madonna in Father Spencer's books.

"Then we are both at fault," he replied with a smile. "Where are you going?"

"To bathe."

"Really. Don't let me stop you." He sat on his horse, waiting.

"Who are you? Where do you come from? I've never seen you before." Her tone was open, disingenuous.

"My name's Andrew. I'm from Tarawera." He purposely didn't mention his last name. If she was unfamiliar with the name of Coffin it would mean nothing to her and if she was it might intimidate her. Andrew had seen it have that effect on both pakehas and Maori. Something about this particular young woman, though, told him she would be difficult to intimidate.

"That's a long ride," she said.

"Long and dusty and hot." He continued to smile down at her as he paced alongside. It took a few minutes before she looked back up at him and grinned.

"Well then, if it is long and dusty and hot perhaps you need a bath."

"A little early in the day for me to get wet, but you may be right. I'd be better received in polite company if I first got some of this dirt off."

"In polite company, yes. We barbarian Maoris, of course, would not mind."

"Naturally not."

The trail led away from town. Within minutes he was quite lost, having been swallowed by the steam. This was an especially active part of the volcanic plateau that covered the central part of North Island and they were surrounded by mysterious hissing and bubbling noises. It was as if the ground itself were gossiping about them, the rocks and pools whispering mischievously to each other. In the thick mist one's imagination was easily stimulated. Hisses became words, mud pools bubbled with actual laughter.

Had he misread her? If so and she decided to abandon him it could mean real trouble. Already they'd picked their way around pools large enough to boil horse and rider together. Twice he'd lost sight of her when the steam had thickened to swallow her completely. He'd spurred his mount then, only to hear her giggling off to one side. The whole area was crisscrossed with faint trails. Just when he was sure she'd left him to his own resources she would reappear. She was teasing him and he restrained himself from chiding her. Such conduct was unbecoming to a warrior.

Then the mists on his right parted for just an instant and he had a glimpse of her standing naked by the side of a turquoise pool. Like a curtain the steam closed around her. There was laughter, then a small splash. He dismounted, tethered his horse to a broken stump, and tentatively approached.

When he reached the pool he bent and tried to see through the steam. It was a cool day and there was more mist than usual. Several times he called out, but there was no answer.

Then she burst from the pool almost at his feet, splashing him with hot water and giggling like a girl. He staggered back a couple of steps, arms wide, and stared down at himself.

"Now look at what you've done! I'm soaked!"

"Oh, you aren't soaked. You're just a little damp. But you'd better get out of those wet clothes. You wouldn't want to catch cold."

That made him smile despite his momentary distress. He was more upset at having been so easily surprised than he was at being damp. In this region of steam it was all but impossible to catch a chill. That didn't stop him from shedding his clothing and slipping into the pool. The moist heat invaded his body like a massage.

"All right, you." He spread his arms wide, feeling the water as he waded in deeper. There were spots on the bottom of the pool where the rocks were so hot you could barely touch them.

Something clutched at him and he whirled. "You better hope I don't catch you," he shouted in mock warning.

The touch came again and once more he grabbed only water. She was elusive as a lizard and fast as a mermaid.

But when he finally did catch her she didn't resist.

They were alone in the pool at the end of the world. Gradually he forgot about the tourist coach and its passengers, about visiting the hotel, about the errand he'd come to run for his mother. He forgot everything save the young woman in his arms.

Only later, as he dressed himself with her sitting and watching him, did he wonder what had brought him to this place. Some wondrous coincidence, a magical serendipity had caused her to step in front of his horse at just the right moment.

"Will I see you again?" she asked. She sat quite naked on the rocks beside the pool, as unself-conscious as a child.

"Tomorrow." He struggled with a damp boot. "I'll be back tomorrow. I have to do some shopping in Rotorua and return home tonight, but I swear I'll return tomorrow."

She rose then and walked over to him, her brown form seemingly a mobile part of the misty, mysterious landscape. Both hands went around his neck.

"Tomorrow? Just tomorrow?"

He stood there with one boot on and one off and wrapped his arms around her. "No, not just tomorrow. The day after that, and the day after that, and on until we run out of days, I think."

"I'll wait for you, then. In the third house at the end of the main road." Abruptly she skipped out of his grasp.

He watched while she dressed, a quick and simple task. She led him back to the main road. Only when they parted did he think to ask her name.

"Valerie," she told him. Then she became again one with the mist.

3

She was not, as he'd feared on returning home that night, an apparition. Not a dream but real. On his fifth visit to Ohinemutu she brought him to meet her family.

A stocky older Maori stared hard at him when he entered the house. His first words were anything but friendly.

"You are half pakeha." It was clearly an accusation, not an observation.

"Father!" Valerie said sharply.

The man glanced at her and seemed about to say something when Andrew took another step forward.

"It's all right, Valerie. I'm used to it." She looked mollified, but only a little. He turned to the man she'd called father.

"I am also half Maori, sir." He then recited several things in that language which caused the older man to relax slightly.

"Well then, young man, it seems I must greet you as a guest."

They moved to a table. A woman brought drink and cookies and cakes from the bakery at Rotorua.

"I understand you are fond of my daughter."

Andrew glanced over at where Valerie was making a pretense of busying herself with the refreshments, then turned back to his host. "We are fond of each other. I want to marry her."

The rangitira nodded, neither shocked nor surprised. "She has said as much."

"I want your permission."

The chief looked toward his daughter, who caught him staring and quickly turned away. He was well aware that a girl of age no longer needed parental approval to choose a husband-to-be, not in these days of permissive pakeha laws. It was a sign of respect for the old values that this young half-breed had come to request it.

"This is hard for me. I fought the pakehas for many years."
He looked up evenly at his visitor. "I have killed many
pakehas."

"The wars are done. There is no more fighting. Valerie and I
are interested in our future, not your past."

A faint suggestion of a smile twisted the rangitira's lips.
"You speak like a warrior. Also with the confidence of youth.
Once I had your confidence. The pakehas beat it out of me. But
I have learned to live with what I am. It is one thing to do battle
with the pakehas, another to welcome a white family into my
own."

"Not just any family. My father is very wealthy. His name is
honored in houses throughout the country."

"Not in this house it isn't." There was silence for a long
time. Valerie and the old woman who'd brought the food
whispered among themselves. Finally the rangitira sighed.

"Once I swore to fight the pakeha to the death. Then I
learned you cannot fight them to the death because for each one
you kill ten more wash ashore. And they breed like flies." He
nodded at the far wall. It was lined with Maori spears, fine
greenstone clubs, swords and pistols.

"I have survived twenty-five great battles. Ten times I had
pakeha bullets cut from my body. You must know by now that I
was of the Hau Hau." Andrew nodded.

"And yet here I sit, still alive despite all my wounds and
boasting. I have a fine house and the pakehas in the village
wave good morning to me and call me by name. 'Opotiki,'
they cry, 'how are you today!' Or 'fine day, Opotiki, isn't it?' "
He shook his head wonderingly. "When I meet the gods my
first question to them will be to explain the pakeha to me, for
surely a stranger breed of man never lived on this Earth. They
fight you for years and years, slaughter women and children,
and then when the fighting is over and the memories of spilt
blood grow a little dim they think of you as a romantic figure.
Or so a remarkable pakeha once told me. I will never
understand them."

"My father fought in the wars too. Yet my mother is a
Maori."

"Then your father is a man twice brave. Family." Opotiki
considered a moment longer, then sounded resigned. "Would it
matter if I did not give my permission?"

"Not to the law, but it would to me. It would matter very

much, sir. As much as I love your daughter I tell you I would not marry her without your permission."

That made Valerie whirl. "Andrew!"

"It's true, Valerie. Remember I'm as much Maori as pakeha." He looked back at Opotiki. "Under pakeha law I can marry your daughter without your permission, but by Maori tradition I will not."

The war chief sat a little straighter in his chair, wincing with effort. With a bullet still lodged near his spine it was a wonder he could sit at all.

"Truly you are a man of two worlds. I warn you both, this will not be an easy thing for you. What of your pakeha father? What will he say to this union?"

"How can he object, sir? He lives with a Maori woman himself. He can't deny me the right to the same."

"Can he not? The pakehas can be very unpredictable in such things. Though what does it matter if a man and a woman love each other? And it is plain this is true. I must give my consent."

"Oh, Father!" Valerie abandoned the drinks she'd poured, upsetting the bottle in the process, as she raced to embrace him. He stood it for a little while before pushing her away, whereupon she threw herself into Andrew's arms, kissing him repeatedly.

"Where will you live? What will you do? I would not want you to take my daughter far from me."

Andrew managed to partly disengage himself from Valerie. "Don't worry about that, sir. This is my home too. We'll build a place of our own. Maybe here, or at Tarawera. As to what I'll do, well, I hadn't given it much thought. My father owns many businesses. I guess I'll have to find one I can tolerate that will also let us continue to live in this region."

Opotiki was nodding approvingly. "You are thoughtful and respectful. You will make a good son-in-law, I think."

"I'll try, sir." He slipped clear of Valerie's grasp and walked over to shake the rising Opotiki's hand.

"We must have a celebration," the rangitira announced. "Tonight! Can you stay with us tonight or will your parents be concerned?"

"I'm a grown man, sir. I go off on my own all the time. Of course I'll stay." He took one of Valerie's hands and smiled down at her. "Tomorrow I'll introduce Val to my parents."

"Won't they be surprised when they learn what you've been doing all this time in Rotorua?" she asked him.

"It won't make any difference," he replied, laughing at her. "Nothing makes any difference so long as two people love one another. My mother told me that once. She said that if you love each other anything is possible." He bent low enough to meet her lips while Opotiki looked on approvingly.

Among many peoples having a good time is little more than necessary relaxation, but to the Maori it is an art. The dancing and feasting went on late into the night. Light from lanterns and fires seeped through the mist so that from a distance the ground appeared to be ablaze.

Opotiki had invited all the members of his whanau as well as friends and distant relations. There were even a few pakehas among the celebrants. None of them recognized Andrew Coffin. Even a close friend would have had trouble espying him through the mixture of firelight and steam, not to mention the smoke from the innumerable Maori pipes.

Though it was early morning the celebration was still going on when Andrew took Valerie by the hand and the two of them stole away through the rear entrance of a long house. By now he knew the path that led to their secret place as well as she did. He held an oil lamp in front of them as they tiptoed their way through the mists, threading a course between mud pools and fumaroles until they reached the special pool where they'd first met.

They slipped silently out of their clothes and into the shallows. In the chill of early morning the hot water was a stimulating shock to their systems. Surrounded by the palpitations of an uneasy Earth they swam and splashed until finally he grabbed her and pulled her close. Smiling, Valerie spread her legs as she floated next to him, wrapping them around his waist.

Later they lay side by side on the warm rocks, their bodies drying in the cool air with only a pair of towels to cover their naked forms. The fingers of his left hand clung reassuringly to hers. The swirling mist offered only brief, fitful views of the stars above. They did not mind. The steam was a vast damp blanket, shielding them from the world's prying eyes.

"Tell me, Andrew: will we be happy?"

He turned to smile gently at her. "As happy as two people have ever been."

"Will we have children?"

"As many as you want."

"I wonder whether they'll look like me or you, or your parents, or mine."

"They'll be all colors. Brown and white and every shade in between. Maybe we can have some blue and pink ones as well."

She laughed at that and he laughed back and their eyes met. Their laughter faded as they rolled toward each other.

It was Valerie who saw movement out of the corner of an eye. At first she thought it was merely a large rock revealed by a momentary parting of the mists, but it was too straight, too symmetrical for stone. The light from their lamp flashed off polished paua shell set in a staff taller than a tall man.

She gasped and sat up fast, clutching at the towel that did little to cover her. Andrew was on his feet in an instant, not bothering to conceal his nakedness.

"Who the hell are you—sir?" When he saw the stranger more clearly he repeated his angry query in Maori. "Why are you spying on us?"

"I was not spying on you." There was no anger in that calm, slightly irritated voice. Andrew relaxed a little.

The stranger looked to his left, let out a soft sigh and stepped forward. Now he sounded amused. "I have seen more nudity than you will ever see, young man, and been witness to more coupling than you can imagine. Neither hold any mysteries for me."

"What are you doing out here this time of night? Andrew was still wary. Their visitor might be old, but he was tall, and the staff he carried was a formidable weapon.

"Do you own this land? I was out for a walk. I often walk alone late at night the better to commune with the spirits of the Earth. I heard a noise that was not a hot pool and came to see what it was. Now that I have done this, I will leave." Tugging his blanket higher on his shoulders he turned on one heel.

"No, wait." Andrew looked at Valerie in surprise. The figure halted. "You're a tohunga, aren't you?"

He turned back to them. "I have some wisdom."

Andrew was bending over Valerie, whispering earnestly. "What is this, Val? Let him leave."

"No." There was excitement in her voice. "Don't you see, Andrew? This is a sign."

"It's no sign," he snapped, "unless you call it a sign of spying."

"Nonsense." Wrapping the towel around her as best she was able, she rose and took a step forward. "Wise sir, Andrew and I are about to be married. Can you tell us if we will be happy in our life together?"

Not all the light that gleamed in the eyes of the tall, shadowy figure was a reflection of what issued from their single lamp. Andrew blinked once and the suspect glint was gone.

"You ask me to see into the future. What makes you think, woman, I can do such a thing?" He looked sharply at Andrew, who stared back unwaveringly. The old man's gaze was intense, but not threatening. "This one knows none can see the future. He has enough pakeha in him to know that. Superstitions, young man! Is that not so?"

Andrew stepped forward to put a protective arm around Valerie's shoulders. "It is. But I am Maori enough to listen with respect to whatever a tohunga cares to say."

That cracked the old man's frozen expression ever so slightly. As the mist parted around him Andrew saw he was much older than he'd initially supposed.

"I think you will be content. Any fool can see you love each other. That is important. I think also you respect one another. That is more important still. Also you laugh together, which is the most important thing of all. But," he went on, his expression darkening unexpectedly, "you will *not* be happy if you stay here."

"Why not?" a suddenly concerned Valerie wondered.

"Do you know how the pakeha visitors sometimes describe this country? They say it is like their Hell. That is what it is going to become, and soon."

Andrew was frowning in confusion. "What are you talking about?"

"I mean that this entire region is going to be overturned. You should leave."

"But I can't leave," Valerie told him. "This is my home."

"And mine." Andrew had begun to slip into his clothing. "What do you mean, 'overturned'?"

"Just that. Overturned." He sounded sad now. "Perhaps you will be happy here anyway. I am an old man and very tired. I don't see anything clearly anymore."

"We'll be all right," Valerie told him. "Don't worry for us."

"I will not. Worry is bad for the belly." He turned to leave.

This time it was Andrew who called out to him, holding up their lamp. "Wait! We'll come with you. You can't find your way through there without a light. You'll fall into a boiling mud pool or something."

"I have six gods." The old tohunga smiled thinly. "I cannot be harmed." With that he seemed to slide into the mists.

"Hold on a minute." Andrew hurried forward. "We'll take you back with us. Why don't you. . . ," his voice trailed off. He held the lamp as high as he could. A lost breeze momentarily swept the immediate vicinity clear of steam, but there was no sign of the old man. It was as though he had vanished from the face of the Earth.

Valerie slowed as she drew abreast of him. "Andrew, what did he mean, 'overturned'?"

"I don't know." He continued to stare in puzzlement into the reforming mist. Where had the crazy old fool got to? Eventually he shrugged. There'd been no splash, so he hadn't fallen into one of the pools. Probably gone behind a rock somewhere. In any event it was no business of theirs.

"It all sounded like nonsense to me."

"Yes," she agreed doubtfully. "It probably was." She looked down at her feet. "Maybe he meant the ground here is going to collapse. That happens from time to time, you know."

"I've heard the stories." While an infrequent occurence, sometimes the thin crust of ground overlying the thermal regions gave way in places, sucking down the occasional unlucky traveler. "If that's the case we'd better get you away from here."

"Not to bed," she said, pouting. "Not already."

"No." He grinned down at her. "We'll go back and rejoin what's left of your father's celebration. We belong there anyhow."

"Do you think we were missed?" She was wiggling into her own clothes as she spoke.

"I don't know, but nothing could have kept me away from this place tonight."

"Nor me," she assured him boldly.

4

Andrew reined in his mount, staring. The inlet was only a minor arm of Lake Tarawera but that made the sight no less puzzling.

Valerie halted her horse and rode back to rejoin him. "What are you looking at?"

He nodded. "This little bay here. I used to play in this place when I was a child. There was always water in it."

"Maybe the level of the lake is down."

"Not this much." Dismounting, he walked his horse over to where the ground became soft, gazing at the mud drying in the sun, at the crumpled water plants and dying snails. "I wonder what happened."

Suddenly Valerie straightened in her saddle. "Andrew, look! The water is coming back!"

He rose from his crouch to stare. As they watched, a six-inch-high wavelet was racing shoreward from the middle of the lake, advancing silently like a moving carpet of quicksilver. It splashed up against the dry banks of the inlet, rolled back on itself once, and was still. A moment ago the inlet had been empty. Now it was full again. A freak tide, he thought?

"I've never seen anything like this before. I wonder what it means?"

"Maybe a hot spring caused it," she suggested. "That happens sometimes."

"That might make water come in, but what made it go out? Tarawera's six miles across. The action of one hot spring couldn't affect it like this."

She put a hand on his arm. "Leave it to the gods, Andrew. If we don't hurry we will miss seeing your parents."

"That's right." He turned back to his mount. Today of all days he wanted to make sure he found his mother and father at home.

He could see Valerie's eyes widen as they turned the last bend in the lakefront road and the mansion came into view. It looked larger than it was since it stood all alone on the low hill.

"Is that all one house?"

"It is. And my father owns other houses. I've been told he used to have an even bigger place in Auckland, but I never saw it."

"It is like a palace. Like the god-homes in the legends."

"It's just a house. This is where I grew up."

They tied up out front instead of going around to the stables in back. He wanted her to enter through the main door. Two Maori gardeners looked on curiously as they mounted the steps and crossed the sweeping porch that dominated the front of the house.

Before they reached the door Andrew swept Valerie up in his arms and carried her the rest of the way. She put her arms around his neck, giggling.

"Andrew, I don't understand."

"This is an old pakeha tradition. Carrying the bride across the threshold."

"But I'm not your bride," she reminded him coquettishly. "Not yet."

"Details."

She reached up to kiss him and he responded readily. It was left to him to pull away. "At this rate we'll never get past the door." He reached out, balancing her awkwardly, and pushed down on the latch.

He could have rung for the downstairs maid, but servants had always made him uncomfortable. Once inside he set Valerie down, watched as she *ooed* and *ahed* in astonishment over the imported furnishings and exotic artwork. It really must look like a palace to her, he reflected.

It didn't take long to locate his father. Robert Coffin was sitting in the big chair on the screened-in sun porch out back reading the *New Zealand Herald*, which he had brought to him every few days by coach. Andrew hesitated, took Valerie's hand in his. They stepped out together.

"Good morning, Father."

"Eh?" The powerfully built older man turned in his chair to look back toward them. "Oh, Andrew. Didn't hear you ride up." His gaze shifted to Valerie, who instinctively took a step backward. Andrew squeezed her hand tightly and she held her ground. "Who's your pretty little lady-friend?"

"This is Valerie. Valerie, this is my father, Robert Coffin."

At his urging she tried a half-curtsey. "How do you do, sir?"

"Very well, thank you, young missy." He then added a few flattering comments in perfect Maori.

Her expression softened. His Maori was accentless, as good as Andrew's. And why should it not be, she thought with a start? Wasn't Andrew's mother as Maori as herself? She glanced around the porch but there was no sight of that remarkable woman.

Coffin moved his chair the better to see them. "No wonder I can't get you to tend to business, Andrew. You spend all your time at sport and play."

Andrew shifted uncomfortably. "This isn't play, Father. Not this time. Valerie and I, well—we intend to marry."

Coffin's benign expression vanished. "Marry?" His tone turned cool and he now regarded Valerie with considerably less tolerance. "Quick decisions are valuable in business, son, but not in life."

"Father, I'm twenty-five. If anything I'm overdue to settle down."

"I won't argue that, but this sort of thing takes careful consideration."

"I have considered everything, Father." Andrew's voice had tightened. This wasn't going at all as he'd hoped.

Coffin studied the floor for a long moment. "Andrew, one of these days you're going to inherit everything. Not just this house, but the majority share of Coffin Ltd. Ships, estates, farms."

"Spare me the inventory, Father."

"Very well." Coffin looked up at his son again. "The point is that in your capacity as head of the company you're going to have to deal with certain people of a similar class. People who would not look kindly on. . . ."

"On what," Andrew said sharply, interrupting. "On a Maori wife? What about you, Father? What about Mother?"

"Merita is special. She's an exception to everything Maori *and* European."

"I'm aware of Mother's uniqueness. You speak of it often." He released Valerie's hand and put his arm around her shoulder to pull her close. "Valerie is that way to me. Who's to say she's not as special as Mother?"

"Now you listen to me, Son." Coffin was ready to rise from his chair. "I know this is hard for you to understand, so I'll make it as brief and simple as I can." Abruptly he broke off to stare past them. Andrew and Valerie turned to follow his gaze.

"Hello, Mother." Andrew threw his father a ferocious glare before turning back to the woman who stood in the doorway. "Mother, this is Valerie. We're engaged." He said it as defiantly as he could.

"Engaged?" Merita hesitated, then smiled at their uneasy young guest. "How interesting." Pitcher and glasses filled the tray she was carrying. She poured lemonade for herself and Coffin.

"I am very pleased to meet you, my dear."

"Pleased to meet you too, ma'm," said Valerie, showing off her English.

Merita was nodding approvingly. "I'm sure you'll both be happy together. What a delightful surprise."

"Father doesn't think so." Andrew couldn't keep the bitterness out of his voice. "He doesn't think it's a good idea."

"Robert? Why not?"

"Well, because, it's just—because," Coffin sputtered.

"Foo! Look at them. They make a beautiful couple." Andrew beamed and Valerie essayed a hesitant smile. "Now then: wouldn't you two like some lemonade?"

"I don't think I have ever had it," said Valerie.

Merita laughed. "It is one of the better pakeha inventions."

"I'm not through with this," Coffin growled.

"Of course you are, dear," said Merita, placing one hand on the back of his neck.

"Father, you've always told me I could have anything I wanted. Well, all I want now is your blessing. Valerie's father has already given his."

"Blessing," Coffin harrumphed. "I've just met this girl. We know nothing about her."

"I live in Ohinemutu," Valerie volunteered quickly. "My mother's name is Numeni and my father is a chief."

"An ariki?" Coffin asked sharply in Maori.

"No, not an ariki. Just a rangitira. But he has much mana. He was a great fighter in the wars and—oh!" She put a hand to her lips and looked worriedly at Andrew. "Maybe I should not have said that."

"It does not matter," Merita reassured her. "The wars are over with. From now on we all must live together in peace, for good or bad. What is your father's name, child?"

"He is called Opotiki, ma'm."

There was a crash as the tray struck the floor, one of the remaining glasses shattering, the pitcher not breaking but spilling pale yellow liquid across the smooth wooden planks.

"What is it, did I say something wrong?" Valerie hugged Andrew for protection. He gazed curiously at his mother.

"Yes, what's wrong?"

"Opotiki?" Coffin was out of his chair now, standing. "Opotiki the son of the great chief Te Ohine?"

"That was the name of my grandfather, yes." Valerie was staring nervously at Andrew's parents. "What is it? What is the matter?"

"Nothing. It's all right. It's all right." Merita was already recovering from the shock and her breathing was returning to normal. She managed a weak smile. "It doesn't matter. It is nothing to stand between you."

"Stand between them?" Coffin roared like a wounded bear. "What do you mean it needn't stand between them? I didn't want this marriage when Andrew first mentioned it. Now it's impossible." He turned to face his son, who stared back at his father unyieldingly. What had begun badly had become worse, and he had no idea what had gone wrong.

"Why? What difference does it make who Valerie's father is? He's already told me he was a Hau Hau."

"That's not it, that has nothing to do with it." Coffin sliced a hand toward the floor. "He killed without mercy but so did many of us. As your mother said, the wars are over with—and we won."

"Nobody won," Andrew insisted. "It was a standoff. You know that, Father. The Maoris fought the British Army to a standstill. I've read the papers and the histories. No 'native' people ever did anything like it before. That's why peace was made. Because the Maoris couldn't be beaten." He frowned suddenly.

"You spoke of Valerie's grandfather. Didn't I hear you talk of him when I was a boy?"

Coffin turned away slightly. "Te Ohine was a great man.

One of the greatest ariki of all. He was slain by a traitorous band of renegade pakehas. Opotiki was his son."

"This girl," said Merita, who was recovering rapidly from the initial revelation, "is not Opotiki."

"It doesn't matter." Coffin was insistent. "The marriage cannot happen."

"But *why*, Father?"

"First, because I don't think it a suitable match for you, and second because of her father's reputation." Valerie had shrunk back to try and hide behind Andrew. "To marry with the Maori is not itself a bad thing." Coffin flicked his eyes at Merita and his tone softened somewhat. "I've done so myself though we've had no ceremony and signed no papers. But that's different from having the future head of Coffin Ltd. marry the daughter of one of the worst of the war chiefs."

"My father has made his peace with the pakeha," said Valerie boldly. "He lives among them and they speak to one another as friends."

Coffin nodded understandingly. "Here in the central highlands that is common enough. It's different in Auckland or Wellington. People there aren't as forgiving." He shook his head. "It's impossible, just impossible. Besides, there's another reason you can't marry."

"There are no reasons I will accept," Andrew told him.

His father said it almost apologetically. "You and Valerie are cousins."

Neither of the lovers had a reply for that. Open-mouthed, Valerie looked up at Andrew, who was staring dumbfoundedly at his mother. She was nodding slowly.

"It is true, Andrew. Valerie's father. . . ," she seemed to choke on the words, "Valerie's father Opotiki is my brother. Did you not tell them who you were?"

"Only my first name," a dazed Andrew replied. "I never. . . ." He shook himself and his voice strengthened. "What is all this? This is crazy!"

"My father never spoke of having a living sister," Valerie was murmuring, staring at the woman who claimed to be her aunt. "He said all of them had been killed at the same time as my grandfather."

"It pleases your father to think of me as dead. I became dead to him when I took a pakeha for my lover." Merita sighed deeply. "So you see, not all the unreasoning hatreds are on the pakeha side. But it doesn't matter. If you two love each other. . . ."

"We do, Mother." Andrew pulled Valerie into his arms.

"Then the marriage should take place."

"Merita!"

She turned to Coffin. "It makes no difference, Robert. All that matters is that they will be happy together. Among the Maori marriage within the whanau is common."

"When Opotiki finds out who his daughter is really marrying he'll put a stop to this nonsense faster than I."

"He will do no such thing," Merita said firmly. "He might, if Andrew were all Maori. But we can have a civil ceremony in Father Spencer's church. There is no way Opotiki can stop that. Are you so sure, then, he will want to? Valerie says he has made peace with his old enemies. He might remember that you were a friend to his father more than he would remember you as an officer in the colonial militia. All will go well."

"Damnation, it will *not* go well! I won't stand for it. The idea of Andrew marrying his own cousin, the daughter of a war chief to boot, is impossible."

"A war chief whose father was your great friend, Robert. Remember that Te Ohine was my father, too."

Coffin was nodding slowly. "I remember. Just as I remember that he died because he was too trusting, too ready to merge Maori ways with those of the pakeha. Your brother fought on because he didn't trust us. Now you expect me not only to give my blessing to this unnatural union but to invite such a man into our house, to sit at our table and break bread with us."

"I do."

"He might come to meet me," Coffin said slowly, "but what makes you think he will come to meet you?"

Merita blinked, obviously hurt. But she recovered immediately. Nothing could dampen Merita's spirits for more than a moment.

"If he will come and sit across from me, then will you give your blessing?"

"Now wait," said Coffin quickly, "I didn't agree to. . . ."

"Will you do that?"

"I—you're a devil, woman." Merita grinned slyly at him. "You've always been a devil, and you've passed it to your son." He sat down heavily in the chair, eventually looked back up at Andrew.

"You were right when you said that I would never refuse you anything. If you want this marriage then I won't stand in your way. But neither will I give you any blessings. That I can't do. I want nothing to do with the whole business. I wash my hands of any consequences, do you hear?"

"That's good enough, Father—for now. You'd only get in the way of the arrangements anyway." He smiled reassuringly at Valerie. They'd won, though she didn't realize it yet.

"Leave the details to me." Merita approached the two lovers. "We can either use Father Spencer's church here or the big one at Rotorua. We'll have a grand time. There will be such dancing and feasting as hasn't been seen around this country in years!"

"Yes, oh yes!" Valerie was starting to relax. "And I can invite all my friends."

"And I mine, if I can find any of them in time," Andrew added.

"There are going to be some disappointed young ladies in this part of the world, Andrew."

"Mother! Not in front of Valerie."

"Why not?" She smiled mischievously at her niece. "Surely, Valerie, you knew when you set eyes on my son that he might have encountered one or two other young ladies before yourself."

"When I first saw Andrew he was about to run over me with his horse." The two women shared a gentle laugh.

"There will be problems, though." Merita cut her eyes back at the chair where her husband sat brooding and pretending not to listen. "For example, I do not know whether to have you call me mother-in-law or auntie. Since we are already related it will only be a matter of settling on terms."

"It can't work," Coffin muttered aloud. "Don't any of you see that?" He was shaking his head regretfully. "It just isn't done."

"But it is going to be done." Merita was full of confidence now, and she imparted some of it to the youngsters. "It will be done in the most splendid wedding anyone has ever seen." Her voice was full of joy. "As long as you love and respect one another you will always be happy. That is one thing that is true for both Maori and pakeha." She hugged her son, then stepped back.

"She is very beautiful, Andrew. And you, little niece who I did not know I had, it seems you have been family all along."

"I am going to have to tell my father what has happened."

"Do not worry. If he has made peace with those he fought against he can make peace with me. Send him my best wishes. Tell him I am sorry it has been so long since we have spoken. A foolish thing, us living so near and not knowing of it. The ways of the gods are wondrous indeed."

"What—what if he changes his mind? What if he withdraws his consent?"

"Having already agreed, he will not now change his mind. I remember Opotiki that well at least. Let nothing stop you." She made shooing motions with her hands. "Go now, go on and tell Opotiki he must suffer some happiness whether it pleases him or not. If he so wishes it we can have two weddings: one in a church and another at Ohinemutu in the Maori fashion."

"Two weddings. That would be fun," Valerie said.

"Yes. Now go on, get out. When you return we can begin the preparations."

"Thank you, Mother. I love you." Andrew bent to kiss her, as did Valerie. As they turned to depart, he glanced back toward his father, sitting silent and motionless in his chair. "Good-bye, Father."

Robert Coffin did not offer a reply.

Merita watched until the lovers had exited through the front door. Then she returned to the sun porch. Coffin sat as he had when they'd departed. The spilled lemonade had seeped into the wood.

She stopped behind her husband and put a hand on his shoulder. "It will be all right, Robert. The fact they are cousins makes no difference. Is it not remarkable that they should discover each other so?"

There was a long pause. Then Coffin sighed resignedly. "No, not really. Andrew always did have an eye for the ladies. The girl *is* remarkably pretty." Moving around in front of him Merita saw that his expression had softened. "In fact, she looks a bit like you. Hardly surprising, I suppose, given the circumstances."

"Then you will give them your blessing?" He looked away from her and said nothing. "Then do not, but promise me at least that you will not interfere with the wedding."

"Very well. I won't interfere with the wedding, Merita." He looked back up at her. "On that you have my word. But your brother could still make trouble."

She sounded surprised. "He cannot. We have already spoken of that. Under pakeha law he cannot stop the marriage."

"Not under the law, no. But there are other possibilities. Illegal but effective."

Her expression indicated she hadn't considered that. At last she said, "I do not think even Opotiki would go so far. But now you worry me, Robert." She looked back toward the hall. "Do you think Andrew will be all right?"

"Andrew can take care of himself, though I don't think he's acted very maturely in this. How long can he have known the girl? A few days, a week?"

"How long," asked Merita softly, "had you known me when you decided you wanted me for yourself?"

"As soon as I set eyes on you. But that was different. You're different."

"Not so very much, Robert." She stepped away. "So much to do. I must get started immediately."

"By all means, immediately," said Coffin sarcastically. "What's the hurry? Invitations will have to travel the length and breadth of the country."

"Those intended for your friends will, Robert. All my friends live in this district. If you wish your friends to attend it is you who must invite them. I have everything else to plan." She bent to plant a kiss on his lips, then hurried back into the house, calling back to him as she ran. "I will send someone to take care of the lemonade."

Coffin found himself staring through the screen. You do that, he thought coolly. Make all the plans you want. I have some to make myself.

5

"Where are you going, Robert?"

Coffin stopped at the gate and looked back toward the house.
Merita stood on the porch wiping out a large bowl. She was the
bane of the servants, always pre-empting their work, cleaning
and washing. It was unseemly for the mistress of the great
house by the lake to do such work but Merita insisted. Sitting
all day would drive her mad. So despite the disapproval of the
servants she participated in the daily chores, doing more work
than any two of them."

"Just over to the landing. There's a group going over to the
terraces this morning. I thought I might go with them."

Merita's expression changed to one of puzzlement. There
was nothing unusual in her husband's tone or demeanor, but
still she wondered.

"You have seen the terraces a dozen times, Robert. We both
have."

He shrugged. "I didn't say I was going for certain. I might
change my mind." He hesitated. "Would you like to come
along?"

"No. I have much to do here. You know Andrew and Valerie
are coming in from Ohinemutu tonight."

Indeed he did. It was another reason why he had to be on
that tour boat this morning. "I'll be back in plenty of time to
greet them." He gave her a cheery wave and reassuring smile
before departing through the gate. She watched until his horse
had crested the rise in the road that led toward Te Wairoa.

He rode slowly, wanting time to think. It would have to be
done with the utmost care. It had already been arranged for
Valerie to stay at the Terraces Hotel. While her presence in the
Coffin household would not have troubled her Maori relations,
it would have provoked unnecessary gossip among the local
pakehas. An unmarried young woman did not stay overnight at

433

the home of her fiance. Or so he had argued. Hadn't he agreed
to attend the wedding? This was such a small thing to ask.
They finally gave in, Merita too. The newlyweds-to-be would
only be a few miles apart, and then only for a couple of days.

He was the last to arrive at the boat landing. If he'd lingered
at the house ten minutes more he would have missed it
completely.

The tourists stood chatting excitedly, the men in their
traveling suits, the women in their long dresses, as they waited
for the boat to push off. There were half a dozen Maori rowers,
three of them women, and guide Sophia. She smiled as she saw
him approach. They'd seen each other in Te Wairoa many
times but had only become friends when Coffin learned that she
had been born in, of all places, Kororareka. That brought back
too many memories to ignore. Though she'd been little more
than a girl when Hone Heke had burned the old whaling town
to the ground, it was enough to form a bond between them.

Sophia was a handsome, mature Maori, widely respected as
the best guide on the lake. Her solid A-frame home was one of
the biggest and sturdiest Maori structures in the village. She
greeted him warmly.

"Mr. Coffin. I am surprised to see you this morning. Do you
come to see someone off?"

"On the contrary, I'd like to come along." He looked past
her. "Think there's room for me in the boat?"

"Always room for yourself, Mr. Coffin." She nodded in the
direction of the waiting Europeans. "With you there will be
eight, but I think everyone will fit."

"Thank you."

Coffin joined the party. Two of the men moved to make room
for him on one of the benches. He chatted briefly with several
of the other passengers without mentioning his name.

The Maoris all knew him. Everyone in the district did. But
they were more interested in talking among themselves.

Eventually Coffin's attention focused on a large man in his
mid-forties. His hair and beard were a ruddy red-brown. One
time the man made eye contact. It lasted until Coffin nodded
imperceptibly.

As the rowers prepared to shove off, Coffin moved to the
front of the boat. The other man sat near the back. They
ignored each other intentionally, the man watching one of the
female rowers, Coffin leisurely studying the lake and surround-

ing mountains. Around him the other tourists nattered on endlessly about the beauty of the landscape: the deep blue lake, the forest hills encompassing it and the vast gray lump of Mount Tarawera on the far side.

After the usual long crossing they drew within sight of the Pink Terraces. The rowers docked and Sophia led her charges along a crude path toward the remarkable thermal formation where warm water cascaded over bright pink limestone steps, tumbling fifty feet to the steaming shoreline below.

Coffin remained in the boat, waiting for the sightseers to return, listening to the idle conversation of the rowers. After the usual interval the tourists returned and resumed their seats, talking excitedly of the wonders they'd seen.

The White Terraces were even more spectacular, a seemingly endless succession of travertine pools that descended gradually to the lakeshore. Coffin had heard many visitors call it one of the wonders of the world.

Several of the pools were of a size and temperature ideal for bathing, and in fact had been marked for this purpose. Those designated for men and women were located on opposite sides of the terraces to allow privacy. However there would be no bathing today, since none of the visitors had contracted for the required longer stay.

Spilling over the pure white travertine dams, the water sparkled like molten glass. The tourists were appropriately impressed. They strolled off in different directions while Sophia bustled back and forth between them like a mother hen, warning of places where the ground was too fragile to support their weight.

Now that the group had dispersed, Coffin casually sidled over to where the large redhead was standing near the top of the terraces. Water steamed and boiled behind them, emerging from bubbling geysers to flow over the crests of the uppermost dams.

"Halifax?" The bearded man nodded, spoke without turning. Anyone watching could see that his attention was concentrated on the terraces.

"And you'd be Mr. Coffin, I take it." Coffin nodded in return and the man acknowledged it with a grunt. "Knew it couldn't have been any of the others." He grinned through his whiskers. "Thought for a minim it might've been the priest in disguise, but you've no need o' that, have you? You're an important fella."

"Sufficient for my needs. You saw the girl?"

The man who called himself Halifax nodded a second time, chuckling as he did so. "Identified 'er at the hotel. Pretty little thing—for a native. You folks seem to mix pretty free with the blackfolk here. Don't see much o' that over in Sydney."

"This isn't Sydney, and the Maori aren't the same as your Aborigines."

Halifax spat into the nearest pure pool. "Maoris, blackfolk—they're all abos to me."

Coffin's gaze narrowed and his voice took on an edge. "Listen close to me, Halifax. The girl is going to be indentured, and only for two years at that. While she's in your charge and up to the time you deliver her she's not to be mistreated. Understand?"

"Understand? Oh, sure, guv'nor." Halifax didn't try to hide his amusement. "Why, this'll be the politest kidnappin' anyone ever saw. I'll be sure an' tip me hat to the lady every chance I get. Seems a rotten shame, though."

"I'm warning you. No harm is to come to her. If any does I'll know about it. She's going to work for an honored, respectable Dutch family who'll treat her properly."

Halifax looked bored now. "Don't worry, guv'nor. I remember your instructions. The ship's already anchored at Tauranga. Me and the boys will hustle her out o' here before she's missed. We'll be out to sea before anyone, white or brown, has a chance to organize a search. And we'll keep her well hid, don't you worry. Nobody'll know which way she went. Providin' you does your part, o' course."

"I'll delay any search parties long enough for you to weigh anchor, don't worry about that. But keep in mind I'm holding you responsible for her safety. My contacts in Batavia will let me know in what condition she arrives."

"Now, now, guv. You've hired me to do a job. Rest assured I'll follow your instructions to the letter. Why would I even think o' doin' anything else?"

"Because the girl is beautiful," Coffin said evenly, "and you and I both know what kind of price she'd fetch in Hong Kong or Calcutta or the Arabias. I won't stand for any funny business, Halifax."

"You're upsettin' yourself needless-like, sir." Halifax went quiet while a pair of tourists strolled past. They talked animatedly between themselves, ignoring the two men standing on the edge of the travertine cliff. In a business of this nature one did not take chances. That was why Coffin had arranged to meet Halifax here, all the way across the lake from Te Wairoa and well away from any likely witnesses.

"You treat her gentle, now."

"Righty-right, guv'nor. Seems unnatural for an old sailor like yourself to spoil another's fun, though."

"Halifax, I'm paying you and your men enough to buy half the women in Sydney for a month, if that's what you want. You'll keep your hands off this one, or else."

"Now guv'nor." Halifax looked hurt. "It's not good for business to part with threats."

"I'm not threatening you. Do the job as we discussed in our letters and there'll be no trouble. Just don't cross me."

"Ah now, you just said you'd not be makin' any threats, sir." Halifax grinned. Coffin didn't like that, but at this stage there was little he could do. There was no time to plan anew with another group of men, and besides, Halifax had come highly recommended for this sort of underhanded business.

Everything had to be done tonight, while Andrew was at the house discussing wedding plans with his mother and Valerie was at the hotel away from her family at Ohinemutu. He had to admit Halifax had been discreet and inconspicuous. If the abduction was carried off as smoothly, all would be well.

"My apologies, but you should understand my concern. This matter is—delicate." He looked past his hireling. Several tourists were approaching. "We'd best break this up now. You know what to do and I wouldn't want anyone to remember that we talked for more than a minute or two."

"Wotcher, guv. Don't want 'em to think we're friends or nothin' like that."

Coffin studied Halifax as the redhead began to make his way toward the waiting boat far below. After a decent interval he followed. He still didn't trust the man completely, but how could you trust anyone completely in an enterprise of this sort, whose very nature required the employment of people generally recognized as untrustworthy?

It would work. Halifax would receive the other half of his pay only upon the successful delivery of the girl to the waiting family at Batavia. The abduction would take place late tonight, when everyone including Maori servants and the rest of the hotel staff were fast asleep. It likely wouldn't be discovered until several hours after breakfast. By that time the ship at Tauranga should be on its way.

Valerie would spend two years serving as a well-treated indentured servant to a respectable Dutch family, at the end of which period she would be "miraculously" rescued and returned home. If Andrew pined for her that long, then Coffin would admit the impossibility of preventing their marriage. He doubted such would be the case. It *had* to be no more than another infatuation. In six or seven months Andrew would find his attention wandering toward the other young ladies of marriageable age. Coffin hoped to be able to steer the lad toward women of his own station.

He didn't much like Halifax, but then, he hadn't expected to. That didn't matter. Coffin was sure the man would adhere to his instructions.

It was late afternoon when the boat started back across the lake. Once more the silently smiling Halifax sat at the opposite end of the craft from Coffin. Under Sophia's direction the rowers mechanically propelled themselves and their cargo toward the little dock at Te Wairoa.

They were out in the middle of the lake when one of the tourists let out a cry and pointed to his left. "Look there, everybody! Another boat."

Coffin whirled along with everyone else.

"Strange sort of boat," declared one of the other tourists.

Coffin said nothing, unable to believe what he saw drifting out of the mist that clung to this part of the lake. "That's no boat." He rubbed at his eyes, blinked at the apparition.

Getting old, he told himself. Got to be getting old.

But if it was an apparition, everyone else in the boat saw it too.

"Good God," Father Kelleher muttered. The Maoris were conversing excitedly among themselves. Coffin concentrated on the vision, expecting it to disappear at any minute. It did not.

It was a Maori war canoe, a huge double-hulled craft designed for ocean-going travel. Both the high stern post and sweeping curved bows were intricately carved. The line of Maori warriors in the nearest hull paddled steadily and strongly while those in the second hull stood at attention, holding greenstone clubs and long spears. All wore exquisite flaxen robes. Those who stood had their heads bowed. As befitted warriors, iridescent feathers had been worked into their hair.

Kelleher carried a sketch pad everywhere he went. Now he had the presence of mind to extract it from his pocket and begin drawing furiously.

Coffin kept waiting for the canoe to vanish. It remained as solid and real-looking as their own boat. Without straining one could see the water glistening on the paddles as the line of rowers dipped and stroked, dipped and stroked. He would have ordered their own rowers to turn toward the canoe except he knew they would ignore him.

There might be no need for directives since the canoe seemed to be angling toward them. Soon it was so close you could make out individual expressions on the rowers. Like the standing warriors, those wielding the paddles were elaborately tattooed.

When it was half a mile away, it vanished like a mirage.

"Where did it go?" Similar expressions of confusion came from all the tourists. Coffin glanced toward the rear of the boat, saw that Halifax was as baffled as anyone else.

Another man pointed. "Toward the shore, there, where the mist rises. It went into the mist."

Except it hadn't gone into the mist. It had simply disappeared. Coffin sat very close to Sophia. The old guide was staring out at the lake, hunting something which one minute had been plain as day, the next invisible as air.

"You saw it," he said to her in Maori.

At first she didn't seem to have heard him. Finally she blinked. "Yes, I saw it, Mr. Coffin."

"I didn't think there were any canoes of that size and design anywhere on the lake."

"There are not."

It jibed with what he knew. There was no reason for any of the local tribes to have an ocean-going war canoe. Why haul such an enormous vessel overland, and to what purpose? Even on Lake Taupo, which was a good deal larger even than Tarawera, there was no need for a craft of that size.

"Then what was it?"

"An *atua*. A spirit. A very particular kind of spirit. You saw the feathers in their hair?" He nodded. "Emblems of death.

Have you never heard, Mr. Coffin, of the *waka-wairua*? The death canoe?"

He shook his head. After all these years there were still Maori secrets he knew nothing of. He nodded toward the excited tourists.

"What are you going to tell them? The truth?"

"No." Sophia shook her head slowly. "They would not believe me anyway."

"It couldn't have been an atua. I've seen illusions before. That was *real*. Eighteen people don't experience the same hallucination."

"Then you tell me, Mr. Coffin. What was it?"

He looked back at the empty lake. "I don't know, Sophia. I don't know."

Everyone was still talking about the vision when the boat pulled in to shore. At the same time another boat was arriving from a short cruise to the eastern side of the lake. It contained the usual complement of rowers, a smaller group of tourists, and guide Kate.

Coaches stood waiting to convey the visitors back to their respective hotels, but everyone was too excited to board. Coffin stayed too, watching as Halifax mounted a tethered horse and rode briskly toward town. Everything was going as planned. Halifax would carry out his part of the scheme.

So why was Coffin worried? Because he'd been one of the many witnesses to an elaborate hallucination?

He was heading for his own mount when the conversation behind him intensified. Curious, he paused and looked back. The occupants of Sophia's boat were talking to those from guide Kate's. Torn between a desire to be on his way and an interest in what was being discussed, he rejoined the milling group. Besides, he wanted one more look at the priest's drawing.

Kelleher was showing his sketch of the death canoe to someone else. Coffin recognized Squire Martin. The man had made an extensive survey of the Rotorua District and considered himself something of an expert on the region.

"Coffin. Did you see it too?" Martin asked him.

Coffin frowned. "You mean, the people in your boat also saw it?" He found himself gazing unwillingly at the lake. "That's crazy. We never saw your craft. You were at least a mile away from us."

"Nevertheless, we saw it." Martin removed a piece of paper from his coat pocket and held it next to Kelleher's. It was a hastily-drawn sketch of a large canoe.

The same canoe. A mirror-image of the mirage.

Why was he wasting his time with this nonsense? He should be concentrating on tonight. On how shocked and surprised he was going to act when the news of Valerie's disappearance was made known.

Everyone was going to need his support, and they would have it. Robert Coffin would be in the forefront of any search party, comforting Andrew, reassuring Merita, giving directions and bellowing orders while calling down imprecations on whoever had committed the foul deed. Oh yes, he would be very convincing. Even Andrew would believe him without hesitation. Andrew, on behalf of whose future he had formulated the elaborate plan.

He tried to concentrate on details as he rode back to the house, but something else kept creeping into his thoughts: the image of the canoe. He could see it plainly in his mind, as clear and sharp of outline as it had been out on the lake.

It *had* to have been a mirage. But mirages were only reflections of real objects far away, and a canoe of that size and design hadn't been seen anywhere in years. More than twenty people, Maori and pakeha, had seen it.

Abruptly his mount shied and he had to fight to steady her. Then he heard the noise, saw the leaves moving, the bushes trembling.

Earthquake. A gentle one. Such tremors were common in this part of the world, with its bubbling hot springs, geysers and thermal pools.

A shaking this strong was rare, though. At least they had been, until a year or so ago. Since then the district had experienced roughly one good jolt a month. Today's lasted but a few seconds. Ordinarily he would have paid it no mind, but coming as it did on the heels of the canoe sighting it unsettled him badly.

It was only when he drew within sight of home that he realized he'd been whipping his horse to an unnecessary gallop.

6

There was another mild quake during supper. It was hardly strong enough to cause Merita to look up from her plate. The servants ignored it. Coffin tried to.

He hadn't told anyone in the household about the mass sighting of the waka-wairua. He was tense enough already.

He waited nervously for the ground to move again. As the evening passed and the ground remained stable, he was able to relax a little. He tried to lose himself in the book he was trying to read: one of the American James Cooper's frontier novels. Merita sat in the big chair opposite his, the two of them flanking the blaze in the fireplace as she worked quietly at her sewing. They did not have the advantage of the natural steam-heating that the citizens of Rotorua enjoyed.

It was late when Merita looked up from her fine needlepoint. "Robert, it is good that you find what you are reading so fascinating, but it would be nice to hear from you now and then. I have never seen you read with such single-minded intensity as you have these past few days."

"Really?" He lowered the tome and glanced at the clock, then changed the subject. "It's getting on. Andrew should be here by now."

"No he should not. You know that he and Valerie are having dinner at the hotel. He will stay as long as he desires. I am surprised to see you worried. The road is not long and Andrew knows it well." She leaned forward to peer out a window. "There is ample moonlight for him to ride by."

"I know, but I still worry." Though he could hardly tell her what he was really worrying about. "Maybe I should send one of the servants after him."

She smiled. "You know what Andrew would have to say about that, don't you?" She rose from her chair, holding her needlepoint. "I am going upstairs. I have some things to do and will be back down soon. Go to sleep in your chair if you wish. And don't worry. Andrew will be back before you know it. You should have more confidence in your son."

She walked over to kiss him. He returned her embrace, watched her fondly as she exited the room. Still graceful, still full of energy, still beautiful, he told himself. The past quarter-century had been kind to her, the brush of age only highlighting her extraordinary beauty—whereas he had gone from handsome to simply old.

Merita preferred to call him "rugged," though Coffin wasn't really vain enough to care.

He took another look at the clock. Though Merita had no way of knowing it, his concern for the time had nothing to do with his son's safety. There were no highwaymen in this part of the country. The few die-hard Hau Hau who still held out in the deepest forests had been reduced to the status of bandits. Even the Maori shunned them.

No, he was worried because the longer Andrew remained in Valerie's company, the longer Halifax and his men must delay their work and the less time they would have to ride to Tauranga before morning.

Andrew should not be a problem, though. Coffin planned to keep his son occupied and away from town. Discussion, sleep, celebration, drink—anything to keep him at the house until Halifax was safely away.

He thought he heard the large castiron knocker boom against the front door. Odd, he thought. Andrew wouldn't knock, and it was hardly the hour for a friendly visit. The buzz of what sounded like a violent argument filled the hall outside the parlor. Not Halifax, surely. Something else unexpected.

As he was rising from his chair the doors parted. The butler stood there, apologetic and upset, with a well-dressed gentleman waiting behind him.

"I am truly sorry, sir. I tried to tell him that it was too late for strangers to call, but. . . ."

The man stepped forward, his face partly in shadow. "I'm no bloody stranger."

Coffin grunted, peered hard at the intruder. Something about the other man's voice made him frown. The visitor was fifty-odd, tall, prosperous by the cut of his clothes and straight of bearing.

"It must be something important, sir," he said formally, "to bring you out so late."

"It's important, all right."

That rough tone! Coffin tried unsuccessfully to place it. A South Island burr, perhaps, but he wasn't sure. He remembered they were not alone and spoke to the butler.

"It's all right, Edward. I'll handle this."

"Very well, sir." The butler regarded the visitor with unmistakable dislike.

"Anyone who feels the need to barge into another man's house in the middle of the night must have something urgent on his mind." The visitor simply smiled at that and handed his hat and muffler to the butler, who took them with obvious reluctance and silently closed the doors behind him.

"Come in then, sir," Coffin said graciously. "What brings you here? You have the look of a tourist come to view the terraces, but not the manner of one."

"I am no tourist." The man was still grinning, though without evident humor. "You don't recognize me, do you? Well, I suppose that's not surprising. It would've been foolish to expect otherwise."

Coffin's vision was sharp as ever. What kind of deception was this? He'd never cared for riddles, far less so in the middle of the night, in his own house. This fellow had best have a reason for his nocturnal intrusion or Coffin intended to see to it that he left by the seat of his pants instead of on his feet.

"I'm afraid you're right. I don't know you."

"Just as well." He was surveying the parlor, examining it, appraising. "You've made a lot of changes."

"Changes? I think you'd better explain yourself, sir. You try my hospitality."

The fellow acts as if he owns the place, Coffin mused. Either he's supremely confident in what he's come to say or else he's all brass.

"It's been a while. Harder for me to visit than it used to be, since you began spending so much time here. Have to have my assignations elsewhere."

Now Coffin was fully on guard, though outwardly he exhibited no change in voice or posture. Clearly this man was no casual traveler. Not only his words but his manner proved that. But then what was he? Not that Coffin was worried. There

were two loaded pistols in the drawer of the reading table two
steps away and he was still a crack shot.

"What are you raving about, fellow?"

"Raving?" The smile vanished. "I know this house as well
as you, Robert Coffin."

"If you are an escaped maniac, sir, you are the best-dressed
one I've ever encountered. Who are you? You have the
advantage of me."

"I've had the advantage of you for years, Coffin, only you
didn't know it."

"How do you come to know my house and how it has
changed?"

"In time I'll tell you. But first a name. You should recognize
it easier than you do my person. It's Kinnegad."

Coffin's gaze narrowed. "What? What's that you say?"

"Kinnegad. Surely you've not forgotten the name as well?"

There was silence except for the crackle of the fire. Coffin
was staring straight at the visitor, slowly shaking his head.
"That's insane," he muttered.

"Insane? If sanity be at stake here tonight it will not be
mine—Father."

"I thought you were dead." Coffin's voice had dropped to a
tense whisper.

"Might as well have been, for all you cared."

The ground was not shaking, but Coffin was. He felt his way
back to the chair, sat down heavily as he regarded his
implacable visitor. "I—I never would have recognized you."
The pistols in the drawer, the intricate plans for the evening—
all forgotten now as he stared.

Flynn Kinnegad laughed then, the sound of sandpaper on
splintered wood. "How could you? You don't care about
anything or anyone except yourself." He spread his arms and
pivoted neatly. "As you can see, Father, we've both done well
despite your indifference."

Coffin said nothing.

"In fact," Kinnegad continued, "I'd say I'm doing better
just now than you. Coffin House has been having some
problems lately, hasn't it? A business deal gone sour here,
some unexpected and unreasonable competition somewhere
else?" When the elder Coffin still didn't reply, Kinnegad
shifted his attention to the portrait of Merita, which adorned

the mantle. "Those problems, Father? I must admit I'm responsible for most of them."

That finally provoked a response. "You? How could you be?"

"Because I'm Redline, Father. The relentless competitor who's more interested in market share than profits? That's me. And half a dozen other companies as well. I've worked long and hard to make things as difficult for you as possible. That's nothing compared to the trouble I'm going to cause you in a little while.

"Twenty-five years I've been preparing for this day, biding my time, restraining the urge to confront you directly. It's not easy to wait twenty-five years for a moment of truth, you know? You must admit I've done well at hiding myself, concealing my identity behind a dozen interlocking corporate boards. I doubt if half my own subordinates know who their real boss is. It takes time to place trustworthy people in strategic positions, not only within my own concerns but within yours as well. Oh yes, I've been responsible for any number of little difficulties you've experienced over the past years, though I couldn't give you any new gray hairs. Those you had always."

Coffin was thinking furiously. The unexpected collapse of a trading venture in Melbourne, the loss of his irreplaceable number-three man to Scotland, the bankruptcy of a lumber company and sawmill in Christchurch: all catastrophes for which there had been no obvious explanation. He mentioned them to his visitor and each time the younger man nodded complacently.

"Yes, those were me. Every one of them. Except for the sinking of the packet *Victoria*. I had nothing to do with that, though I praise Nature as my ally."

"Your ally in what?" Coffin inquired cautiously.

"Why, my life's work, which is to reduce you to nothing. To lay you low. To bring you down to the miserable level I lived at when you abandoned my mother, my sister, and myself."

"I abandoned no one!" For the first time since he'd learned the intruder's identity Coffin spoke sharply. He found himself thinking back, back through the years, to make certain he got it right. "We had—an argument. Your mother was a very stubborn, hard-headed woman."

"Oh yes, she was that."

"She was the one who made the final break. Not me. I never wanted that."

"Of course you didn't," Flynn sneered. "You wanted to keep screwing her on the side while you lived the proper married gentleman with your fancy lady from England. A mistress in the country and your wife in the city. That's what you've always wanted, isn't it?" He spat on the fine carpet. "You know, I'm glad you didn't give me your name."

Suddenly feeling his years, Coffin slumped back into the chair. He found himself unable to meet the stare of the man who called himself his son.

"How did Mary die? Your mother."

"That's right. Sometimes I forget you never heard. Syphilis."

"God." Coffin's eyes closed tight. "When she fled the burning of Kororareka I lost track of her."

"Yes, I'm sure you exhausted yourself in your efforts to find her and apologize."

Coffin's eyes snapped open. He gripped the arms of the chair with both hands. "Flynn, listen to me. It was your mother who made the break between us. It was her who sailed away without leaving word. She made it plain she wanted nothing more to do with me and I—I was pig-headed enough in those days to take her at her word. After Kororareka I tried to find her, but it wasn't a simple matter in those days to search this country. Kororareka's refugees scattered in many directions."

"There weren't that many people in this country then, either. If you'd really wanted to you could have found us."

"Don't you understand!" Coffin rose angrily. "She didn't *want* me to find her! Why should I have broken myself to find someone who'd made it plain she never wanted to see me again?"

"I don't believe that. I can't believe it. This is just some story you've invented to assuage your own guilt. Even if it's true, what about us? Sally and me? We didn't drive you away. Did you ever give a thought to us, Father? To what we might be going through? Mother was full of love, but she was never much of a provider, bless her poor, sad soul. Didn't you wonder about your children's situation?"

"What could I have done?" said Coffin earnestly. "Even if I'd managed to find you? Stolen you away from your mother? That would have made things ten times worse."

"Worse for whom, Father?" Flynn asked bitterly. "For us—or for you?"

Coffin looked toward the fire. "I won't take the blame for what happen all those years ago. It was Mary's decision, dammit! I won't suffer for it."

"Oh, but you will. Tomorrow I instruct my bankers to commence a complex series of sales and acquisitions. I've been planning them for the last ten years. When all is done Coffin Ltd. will be but a memory, a footnote in the economic history of this country. And you, *Father*, will be as broken and destitute as were we when mother died in our filthy little hovel. Others will suffer as well. That is unfortunate but unavoidable. In a financial panic it's impossible to single out one company for destruction."

Coffin was silent for a long time. When at last he turned back from the fire his voice had returned to normal. "You'd actually do it, wouldn't you? Damage the whole country just to get back at me."

Kinnegad stood stiffly. "I'd bring down the world if necessary. The Maoris have a word for it, Father. *Utu*. Revenge. You should understand that."

Coffin was shaking his head sadly. "All these wasted years. All this hatred festering inside you. What a pity."

"Not if you have something to live for, Father. Something meaningful."

"Your mother wouldn't approve. She wasn't one for that sort of thing."

"You think not? She hated you until the day she died. Oh, she didn't speak of it, but I know that itself was a sign of how deeply she hated."

"It doesn't matter. None of this matters. You've overestimated yourself. Coffin Ltd. is too sound financially, too stable to be hurt by anything you can possibly do."

"You think so? We'll see."

"Coffin Ltd. can shake but it cannot fall. I've built it too solidly."

"Perhaps. Why such an effort, anyway? So that your other bastard will have something to inherit?"

Coffin's voice fell dangerously. "Leave Andrew out of this. He knows nothing of my early life, nothing of you or your mother. He's a fine young man. I won't have something like *you* injuring him."

"Injuring?" Kinnegad threw back his head and laughed. "How could *I* injure him? You haven't even bothered to marry his mother. For that you might thank me for not interfering."

A glint of madness had appeared in the younger man's eyes and Coffin took a wary step toward the reading table.

"Thank you? What are you raving about now? Why should I want to thank *you*?"

"Because I made it possible for you to be with Merita. I wanted her all to myself, you know. On that we agree. Someday I'll have to show you *our* house."

"You're babbling."

"Am I? Come now, Father, we both know what a lively, energetic, exciting woman Merita is. Always has been. Surely you don't think you're the only man on North Island to have slept with her?"

Coffin stared at him, finally whispered, "You rotten bastard. What a monster I sired."

"Monster? It wasn't I who drove Mary Kinnegad to her death. It wasn't I who lived with one woman and claimed to love her alone." Some of the edge slipped from his voice then. "I didn't mean for her to die of the news."

For an instant Coffin stopped breathing, remembering a day long ago. A mysterious package containing photographs. And a letter. When he spoke again his voice was so soft it was barely audible above the crackle of the fireplace.

"Holly—that was you? You sent those pictures."

"Did it shock you, Father? I hoped it would. You never were one for sharing the truth. My intention was only that Holly Coffin should learn what her husband was really like. I did not intend for her to die."

"She'd been in poor health for some time," Coffin murmured. "The news broke her. I never did find out who'd sent the photographs or the letter. You, even then."

"Even then, yes, but if not me she would have learned it from someone else, eventually." Kinnegad refused to be put on the defensive. "Did you think you could conceal your infidelity forever? At least she learned the truth from a member of the family, as it were."

"Monster," was all Coffin could mutter.

"Whatever I am, I am my father's son."

"You caused the death of a good, innocent woman who never harmed you."

"I said that wasn't my intention!"

"Intentions matter not. Only results matter. You murdered Holly with those pictures as surely as if you'd used a knife."

Kinnegad's reply was thick with disdain. "Look at you, Coffin, standing there babbling your innocence. Even now you refuse to admit to your lies."

"You can go straight to Hell."

Kinnegad's laugh came out as a bark this time. "When the time comes I'll take my chances. Are you so confident of your own passport to Heaven, Father? Such a blameless life you've led!"

Suddenly too weak to stand, Coffin sat back in the chair. "I only tried to be fair," he was mumbling. "I only tried to be fair."

"*Fair*?" Flynn's voice rose to a shout. "You were never fair to anyone in your life, Father. Except to yourself."

7

Merita set the last of the papers aside. She didn't need them to help her picture the wedding. There would only be one, she'd decided. It would be unique, combining the best rituals of both the Anglican Church and Maori tradition. A good time. A healing time during which both Maori and pakeha could join in celebration and feasting. The Maoris had always celebrated the end of a war. Now that the fighting was all but over, the wedding of her son and Opotiki's daughter could stand as a symbol for a country reborn.

So much to do! Entertainment to be arranged, food to be catered: she hardly knew what to do next. Surely Father Spencer would be willing to perform the ceremony. Living among the Maori for many years had changed him from a somewhat stiff-backed missionary to a more cheerful and pragmatic gentleman. She could envision him standing alongside a Maori tohunga where another churchman would not.

They would have the actual ceremony at the Terraces and the reception afterwards at McRae's. That way neither of the local hotels would feel slighted. It would require the cooperation of both to successfully bring off so extensive a production anyway.

The discovery that she was related to Valerie only made her more protective toward her. It was true the girl was a good deal younger than Andrew, but that needn't stand in the way of a healthy relationship, as she knew well herself.

There was a pounding on her door. "Miss Merita?"

"Not now, Edward. I am busy."

"Please, ma'm." The door opened inward. "You must forgive me. Mr. Coffin has a visitor and—well, it sounds to me as if they might be fighting."

"Fighting?" She shut the drawer full of plans and spun on

her chair. "What do you mean, Edward? Mr. Coffin does not fight with his guests."

"Perhaps not fighting, then—but they are yelling and shouting something fierce and I am concerned. I thought you should know."

Merita chuckled. "Yelling and shouting? It's probably just business, then. I have listened to Mr. Coffin yell many times where business is concerned. It is part of what I believe he calls his technique. Pakeha business is often conducted by shouting."

The butler was insistent. "This does not sound like business to me, ma'm. It all sounds very personal."

"That is strange." With a sigh she rose from her seat. "I guess I should see what is going on. Besides, it is too late for someone to come calling on business. Perhaps that is what Mr. Coffin is yelling about."

Edward held the door for her but remained behind. As Merita descended the front stairway the noise from the parlor grew in volume. The butler was right. It didn't sound like business, though with Robert there were times when it was difficult to tell. She heard two voices clearly but they overlapped so much she couldn't identify either.

"Now then," she said briskly as she opened the parlor doors in front of her, "what is all this about?"

At the sound of her voice all discussion ceased. The occupants of the room turned to stare at her.

"Merita." Flynn Kinnegad essayed a crooked smile. "Didn't know you were still awake."

"It is not so very late." She replied without hesitation—and without thinking.

It was confirmation enough. Coffin's gaze flicked from Merita to his son, back again. "Then that's true also."

"What is true?" Merita's heart was pounding against her ribs.

"How does it feel, Father?" Kinnegad's voice dripped venom. "Cuckolded by your own son?"

Coffin had passed beyond anger. This time he merely shook his head sadly. "How you must hate me."

Merita mechanically shut the doors behind her, then turned to stare in disbelief at the younger man. "Flynn, you didn't."

"He didn't have to." Coffin regarded her out of sad eyes. "It is true, isn't it? You've slept with him?"

Merita had never been one to hesitate. Now she straightened as much as she was able. "Yes. It is not an uncommon thing among the Maori."

"But you're not just Maori. You're mistress of the Coffin lands."

"That is so. Yet I remain Merita, daughter of Te Ohine, granddaughter of. . . ."

"Never mind the genealogy." Coffin cut her off sharply. "I'll deal with you later." He looked back at Kinnegad. "How long has this been going on?"

Flynn shrugged as if it were something of no consequence, wandered behind an expensive couch and made a show of examining the upholstery. "Quite a while, Father. Longer than you'd think possible. Ironic, isn't it? You made your visits here to deceive your wife and while you were back in Auckland with her, I was here deceiving you with your mistress. One would think we were a line founded on deceit."

"I wish I'd known." Coffin stared into the fireplace.

"Known what? About Merita and me?"

"No. I wish I'd known what happened to you after Kororareka. All this might well have been avoided. All this pain and hurt."

Kinnegad was nodding. "You're right there. A lot could have been avoided. You're such an expert at avoiding things, aren't you, Father? Tell me: what would you have done if Mother had lived? Kept two mistresses? Your Maori woman here and Irish Mary in Napier, or maybe at New Plymouth? Wouldn't that have complicated your travels?"

Merita sounded confused now. "Robert, what is this? Who is he talking about?"

Coffin forced himself to reply. "Merita, I haven't had two sons, Christopher and Andrew. I've had three."

She gazed at him blankly, finally turned to Kinnegad.

"My mother," Flynn explained with icy calmness, "was an Irish whore. The soul of kindness, but a woman of no common sense. Your 'benefactor' here slept with her, used her for a few years, then cast her aside. This happened rather a long time ago."

"I did not cast her aside!" Coffin bellowed.

"Yes, yes, so you say." Kinnegad sounded bored. "It was all her fault and you bear no responsibility. You're as innocent as the driven snow."

"I didn't say that." Coffin subsided slightly. "I don't think anyone in this is wholly innocent. But I did not plan the demise of our relationship, as you think. I never intended for us to part, much less in the manner we did."

"How can you expect anyone, myself least of all, to believe anything you say? You've been as devious in your personal relationships as in your business." Kinnegad glanced to his right. "He's a clever chap, isn't he, sweet Merita? You should know that if anyone should. I expect you're finding all this quite fascinating, as you know both generations intimately. Now if only I'd been able to get you pregnant. . . ."

Robert Coffin roared like a wounded lion as he charged. Though slowed by age he was still an immensely powerful man. He struck the startled Kinnegad straight on. The two of them went backward over the couch, Coffin's callused hands tight around his son's throat.

"Stop it!" Merita screamed. "Stop it, the both of you!"

There was a loud crash as both men tumbled over a cherry-wood table, shattering crystal and pieces of fine imported porcelain before they landed heavily on the floor. Kinnegad emerged on top, an expression of twisted bliss on his handsome face, the reflection of the culmination of decades of planning and brooding.

The older Coffin gave as good as he got, bloodying the younger man's nose. They battled with single-minded intensity and in frightening silence, the only sounds that of heavy breathing and of bodies bumping into furniture, of clenched fists striking flesh.

Tears were pouring down Merita's cheeks. "No more, please, no more!" The two men ignored her pleas, lost in their own private furies.

She ran to the library table and wrenched open the drawer. Grabbing up one of the pistols she clutched it tight in both hands and pointed it at them.

"That's enough! Stop it! Stop or I swear I'll shoot the both of you!"

When they still didn't respond she aimed the barrel at the ceiling and pulled the trigger. She didn't close her eyes as she did so. Robert had taught her how to handle firearms. Besides, she was Maori. A weapon was the last thing she'd be afraid of.

What her pleading and crying had failed to do the single gunshot accomplished. The pistol's echoing report caused both men to pause. Kinnegad sat atop his father, blood streaming from his nose, one fist raised to strike. He gazed blankly at the wild-eyed woman with the revolver.

"Get off him," she said, her voice dangerously low.

"Dear Merita." He smiled, sniffed blood, wiped it away with the sleeve of his formerly immaculate jacket. "You wouldn't shoot old Flynn, now would you?"

"I'll kill the both of you if you give me half an excuse. Now *get off him*."

"All right. Sure." Kinnegad raised both hands, favored the man under him with a last look of pure hatred, and climbed slowly to his feet, backing away. Coffin sat up shaking his head, his silver-gray hair thoroughly disheveled. Sweaty strands were stuck to his forehead. He pushed them aside, grinned up at her.

"Thanks, Merita. I wouldn't have thought of that."

"Don't thank me. Don't you thank me!" She was still crying. "Why didn't you ever tell me about this woman? I would have understood. But you hid it from me, Robert. Why? Are there others? The women I could forgive you for, but not the secrets and the lying."

His smile vanished. "No. There are no others." He climbed to his feet and took a step toward her.

"Stop!" She steadied the revolver.

Coffin obeyed, his expression pained. "Merita. What's got into you?" He looked angrily to his right as Kinnegad began laughing uncontrollably.

"This is wonderful! Better even than I had planned, better than I could have imagined."

"And you!" Merita swung the muzzle of the gun to point at Kinnegad. "All the years I made you welcome. All to salve your anger and your hurt. You never hinted, never told me it wasn't me you really wanted. All that time you were just using me. Both of you, using me." The tears continued to flow, but not enough to impair her aim.

"You both used me, and I let you, I let you. And the worst of it is I still love you both." She added a pitiful addendum in Maori.

Kinnegad sat down on a chair and used a hankerchief to dab at his nose. "Of course we used you. Didn't we, Father?" He smiled humorlessly at the older man. "That's the way it is with us Coffins. We're always fair and honorable and just—except when it suits us to behave otherwise. Then we make up our own private set of rules and values."

"No." Coffin glared down at him. "That's not how it is. I could never have done what you've done to Merita, much less what you've done to yourself."

"How profound!" Kinnegad turned in the chair. "I suppose the time has come, sweet Merita. Now you're going to have to make a choice between lovers. Come now, which is it to be? Which of us will you choose? Or will you shoot both of us?"

"I—I don't know what I am going to do."

"Merita. . . ." Coffin took a step toward her. Immediately the gun shifted toward him. He saw her finger tremble against the trigger.

"Don't, Robert. Don't try to push me. Not now. Not now."

"Very well." She was right on the edge, he saw. Beyond the anger in her eyes and the anguish in her voice were the beginnings of hysteria. Carefully he retreated and spoke in what he hoped was a soothing tone. "But what are you going to do?"

"Yes, what are you going to do?" Kinnegad was enjoying himself thoroughly. "Stay with me. Cast aside this sham of a life he gives you. I'll marry you in an instant, give you my name. A proud name, Kinnegad. We're the same age, Merita. How can you think of staying with this lying old man who's deceived you all your life?"

"Listen to me, you little bastard, when this is over I'm. . . ."

"You're going to what, Father?" Kinnegad challenged him. "Don't think to insult me so easily. I know what I am, thanks to you." He looked back at Merita. "Choose. Which of us will it be?"

"I can't choose. I love you both. I always have."

"Then I must say," Kinnegad sighed, "you have rotten taste in men. Perhaps you'll choose neither of us." He looked back at his father. "What will you do then, Coffin? Live in this great empty house by yourself? No, I imagine you'd be quick to find yourself another. You have a talent for it, I suppose. She's going to choose me, you know."

"We—we have a family," Coffin muttered.

"Ah yes, your charming half-breed Andrew. I've met him, though he had no idea who I was. Seems like a fine chap, not a bit like a Coffin. Not like you and me. I understand he's to be married in a few days. What a pity the wedding isn't going to take place."

Coffin had thought he was beyond shock. He was wrong.

"Open your mouth about this and you're a dead man, Flynn. Dead, you understand? No one will know who did it and they'll never find your body."

Kinnegad shrugged. "Seems I'm about to be shot anyway." He'd risen from the chair and worked his way around to the other side of the couch. Now he kept one eye on his father while he spoke to Merita.

"You couldn't know, of course. It's planned that way. Even as we speak, the thugs your wonderful, sweet Robert has hired are preparing to kidnap your son's fiancee and spirit her away to Batavia. Only for a while, of course. Until they've forgotten each other."

"Damn you," Coffin said through clenched teeth. "Damn you to Hell!"

"You can't damn what's already been damned, Father." Kinnegad was grinning.

Merita gazed blankly at Coffin. "What men? What kidnapping? Robert. . . ?"

"He's making it all up," Coffin replied quickly. "It's all part of his attempt to turn you against me, to poison what we have together. Can't you see he's only been using you all along so he can get at me?"

"No!" Kinnegad spoke so sharply even Coffin looked back at him. His voice softened when he spoke to Merita. "No. I admit that was my intention at first, but that changed. She changed it. I didn't plan to fall in love with her, but I did. I still love you, Merita. I thought I'd planned for everything, but I was wrong. I fell in love with you in spite of myself. You spoiled that part of my plan, Merita, and I'm happy that you did.

"As for what I've said, ask him." He nodded contemptuously toward Coffin. "Go on, ask him if it's true or not. You can see it in his face."

Coffin was ready to deny again, until he saw that Merita already believed.

"How did you find out? No one knew except myself and one or two others."

"Money buys most anything, Father, as you taught me.

Your man Halifax wouldn't tell me the time, but his accomplices are less principled."

"Robert." The muzzle of the revolver dropped as the strength drained from Merita. The warrior blood that had sustained her thus far deserted her.

"Go on, Father. What's wrong? What's holding you back? Lie to her some more."

Coffin was breathing painfully. "I'm doing it for our son. For Andrew. Don't you see, Merita, he can't marry that girl. One day he'll be head of Coffin Ltd. He'll need a woman at his side who can deal with society, who'll know the right things to say and how to say them. Not some half-wild child from Ohinemutu."

"Like me, Robert?" she said quietly. "A wild Maori girl like me?"

He turned away from her. "I've told you before and I tell you again now, Merita: you're different. I looked for some of that in this girl, believe me I looked, but she's not like you. No one is. She's not right for Andrew. You'll see." He tried to force a smile as he turned back to her. "In a few months he'll have forgotten all about her. As soon as he finds someone more suitable I'll bring the girl back, return her to her family. There'll be no harm done. She'll be well compensated for her enforced vacation."

"Enforced vacation?" Kinnegad laughed anew. "You've always had a remarkable way with words, Father."

"I can't believe. I can't. . . ." Slowly Merita raised the revolver, though her hand was shaking now.

"Rightly or wrongly, Merita, you must believe me when I tell you I'm doing this for Andrew." Coffin stared unwaveringly at her.

She might have done it, might have shot him at that moment. But Flynn Kinnegad, reveling in the situation, was too eager, too anxious. "Go on, kill him! Do it now!"

The muzzle shook. Coffin gazed calmly back at her, having prepared himself for whatever might come.

Instead of pulling the trigger she looked across at the younger of the two men. "That's what you want, isn't it? That would be your grand achievement. To have me murder Robert for you. You see, I can understand how your mind is working, dear Flynn."

"What are you hesitating for? Shoot him, shoot him!"

Kinnegad's face was convulsed, his voice a banshee shriek. *"Kill him, dammit!"*

Her voice was calm. "That is why you told me this story."

"It's not a story!" he howled.

"I know. It is truth. All truth." She was no longer crying. Voice, eyes, expression—all were cold as ice. "At least he finally spoke the truth." Her eyes, those exquisite dark eyes, darted from one man to the other, appraising. Taking the final measure of each. "I loved you both. I love you both still. The gods take pity on you." She aimed the gun very carefully.

Coffin's eyes widened. He opened his mouth to shout. "Merita—no!"

He jumped, but he was halfway across the room. Too far. At the last, too far.

She placed the muzzle of the gun in her mouth and pulled the trigger.

8

"Dear God." Coffin knelt next to the body. Strong. She'd always been so strong.

Behind him, Flynn Kinnegad looked on in horror. All the anger, all the self-confident power he'd brought with him had drained away like water from a broken bucket.

"No." He was mumbling to himself. "I didn't mean for this. I didn't plan it this way. This is wrong, wrong, wrong." His face was alight with terror and the final flickering vestiges of an always uncertain sanity.

Coffin gazed back at him. "You've had your revenge now, haven't you?" Gently he lifted the body. As he raised her, the gun fell from Merita's hand. "Isn't this what you wanted?"

"No, no. Keep away!" Kinnegad's bulging eyes never left the bloody, limp form Coffin held. Something held taut for decades had finally snapped inside the younger man. He no longer resembled the confident individual who had come striding into the parlor less than an hour earlier.

As Coffin watched him, a noise inside his head caused him to wonder if perhaps he wasn't losing control of himself as well. Then he realized the whole room was shaking. A soft rumble came from beneath the floor. He expected it to cease at any moment. Instead it rose in volume, until he was reminded of a troop of cavalry passing close by at the gallop.

The house jumped. Jarred from its hooks above the mantle, the ornately framed portrait of Merita crashed to the floor. Glass and candlesticks toppled from their places. An oil lamp on the far wall leaped into the air, to smash on the floor and spill its flammable contents over wallpaper and carpet. Flames erupted from the stains.

Ignoring the blaze, both men continued to stare at one another.

"It's over, Flynn. You got what you came for. Now get

out." Tenderly Coffin laid the body of his beloved Merita on the couch, the same couch around which he and his son had sparred not long ago. He knelt beside her. Her hair was thick with the blood, which continued trickling from the back of her skull. Coffin didn't see the ugly wound. He saw only the still-radiant face, no longer contorted in confusion, no longer suffering.

"I didn't mean it." Kinnegad was babbling as he stumbled backwards. "I didn't mean it." A sound made him look sharply upward.

Coffin looked also. It sounded like rain, except one should not have heard rain on the roof, not down on the ground floor. Certainly it was the loudest rain he'd ever heard, much more violent than the largest hail.

The "rain" shattered a north-facing window, then the one alongside it. Black, sulphurous pumice began to filter into the house.

The parlor doors were parted by a tall, powerful figure that took two steps into the room before halting.

"Father! You've got to get out of here!"

Coffin rose quickly, realizing that Merita's wound was not visible to Andrew from where he stood. His son's attention had been diverted by the sight of the wild-eyed Flynn Kinnegad, who now stood pressed into a corner with his knuckles jammed against his teeth.

"It's all right, Andrew." Coffin was surprised how calm he sounded. "I'll handle this."

With an effort, Andrew forced his gaze back to his father. "It doesn't matter what's going on here. Everyone must get out. The servants have already fled."

"Why? We've had earthquakes before, though none have lasted as long as this." Coffin deliberately ignored the dark scoria now pouring through the shattered windows.

"It's not a quake, Father. It's Tarawera. The mountain is blowing up."

Coffin stared hard at his son. "What are you talking about?"

"Come and see for yourself."

Coffin followed his son out the front door. The porch roof offered protection from the stone deluge.

"It can't be." Even as Coffin murmured the words, the evidence of his eyes contradicted them. "Tarawera's just an ordinary mountain. Dead rock."

A mountain yes, but silent no longer. Three distinct craters had appeared near the summit of the vast gray bulk. An immense cloud black as ink was boiling out of the mountain's guts. Gigantic lightning bolts ripped the sky, crackling and spitting thunderously. The air itself seemed on fire, though it was actually the reflection of the magma lake oozing up from below.

Harmless, docile Tarawera thundered in full, violent eruption.

The lightning, the glow from the belching magma, and the tremendous volume of white-hot rock the mountain was blasting skyward provided enough light for them to see the lake and the surrounding landscape clearly. Then ash and pumice began to fall thicker than ever and their view grew intermittent and obscured.

Coffin and his son gazed in awe and wonder at the sight. As they stood listening to the debris rattle against the roof, Coffin fought to recall something from long ago. Andrew interrupted his reverie.

"This was foretold, Father."

"Eh? What?" Coffin blinked at his son.

"I mean that I was told that this was going to happen."

"You're talking foolishness, foolishness. There's no time for that." The Robert Coffin of old now reached out of the past to clutch his son with both hands. His fingers dug into the younger man's arms. "Listen to me and do as I tell you. Find your horse before it breaks its tether and bolts. Get back to the hotel. You've got to get Valerie out of there."

"Surely she'll be safe enough there, Father. The Terraces is new construction. It'll hold."

"If this gets worse nothing will be left standing. I've read about such things. Your mother," he swallowed painfully, found his voice again, "your mother liked to read pakeha books. She had one called *The Last Days of Pompeii*, I think it was. About a city buried by a volcano long ago. I read part of it."

"This can't get that bad, Father. Tarawera's not a real volcano." He made himself smile. "It'll stop soon."

"We don't know that, just as we don't know what Tarawera really is. You know what the Maori always said about it. Get back to the hotel, *now*. Find Valerie. The two of you ride like blazes for Rotorua. Go on, quickly!"

Andrew looked back into the house. "What about you and Mother?"

"We'll take care of ourselves. Don't worry about us, dammit. I've one or two things, irreplaceable papers, to get together. Then we'll take the carriage and come into town. Go on, boy. Think of how frightened Valerie must be."

"All right." Andrew started down the steps, holding an arm over his head to protect himself from some of the falling ash. A rock that must have weighed five pounds slammed into the ground near him. Another crashed through the roof of the porch.

"Go!" Coffin whirled, vanished back inside and slammed the door behind him.

With hot pumice falling all around him, Andrew Coffin hesitated. Everything was happening, had happened, too fast. Then he thought of his father's words, of Valerie. Turning, he ran and cleared the front fence in a single leap, fairly flew into the saddle of his favorite mount. Ordinarily nothing upset the three-year-old, but now it was wrenching at its tether, rolling its eyes and frothing at the mouth. Coffin cut the rope and fought to get the animal under control. When the stallion finally heard its rider's voice it calmed a little. Then Coffin was able to turn it up the road. It took off without having to be urged.

Though he concentrated on the road ahead and trying to see through the clinging ash he couldn't avoid the spectacular sight off to his right. The entire lake was heaving and bubbling like a gigantic cauldron. The black cloud vomiting out of Tarawera rose higher and higher, until the entire night sky was alive with lightning and brilliant flashes of pure white light.

Robert Coffin stood at the broken window until he was certain his son would not be returning. Only then did he let the curtain drop and turn. A great calm filled him as he walked back toward the couch and its precious burden.

They might be all right here. The huge house was one of the sturdiest structures in the area. He found he didn't really care.

Flames continued to lick at the far wall. Ash and pumice began to form miniature black talus slopes against the north wall. Overhead were the echoes of nature's bombardment as large rocks began to split the roof shingles and crash into the attic.

He stood over the couch gazing down at Merita. The

bleeding had finally ceased. The cushions, the carpet, all were soaked with her life.

A glance showed Flynn Kinnegad sitting in his corner. His knuckles were bloody now where they pressed against his teeth as he continued to stare unblinkingly at the couch.

"It's all right now, Flynn." There was an ineffable sadness in Coffin's voice. "You've done all you can do. You came here to hurt me, and that you've done. I should be sorry for you, but I'm not. For your mother I can feel sorrow. Poor Irish Mary. Oh, I do remember her, despite what you think. I remember her better than I ought."

He flinched and stumbled backward as a boulder weighing several hundred pounds ripped through the second story to bury itself in the floor. Dust and pulverized plaster filled the air. He felt the heat of the blazing wall on his back now.

Flying rock struck him above the left ear, stunning him and dropping him to his knees. He stayed like that, swaying numbly.

"I'm sorry, Merita." He could hardly hear himself above the crash and roar of still larger volcanic bombs. "I was so good at planning everything, except my own life. First Mary, then Holly. Now you too. I never meant to harm anyone."

He leaned close, placing his head against her breast, one hand on her forehead and the other on her belly. She was still warm.

As for Robert Coffin, he still lived, but only on the outside. Within, he was already dead.

9

Twice Andrew had to pull on the reins with all his strength and scream at his mount. Otherwise the animal would have bolted into the woods. Ash and cinders were falling faster than ever, blinding him as he struggled to see the road ahead. The ground heaved unceasingly.

He kept wiping the volcanic debris out of his eyes and nostrils, hoping his horse wouldn't choke on it before they reached the hotel. As he considered abandoning the terrified animal and continuing on foot he saw the hotel directly ahead, lit by the eerie light of the eruption. He slowed and used the reins to secure the horse, hoping they'd hold against its spasmodic bucking.

Lightning stenciled the sky. Behind him volcanic rock fountained more than a thousand feet high.

An excited crowd milled about in front of the hotel, mesmerized by the spectacular display. A couple of the women were crying but there was no panic as yet. Everyone was more interested in watching the eruption than in running. After all, Tarawera was miles away, across the lake. No lava could reach them here. Surely the ash and pumice would stop falling soon.

The Terraces Hotel was a stoutly built two-story building with upper and lower porch. So far it looked none the worse for wear. The larger volcanic bombs had yet to fall here. Shoving past the crowd Andrew forced his way into the hotel. As he did so it occurred to him that it was likely none of the guests had ever witnessed a volcanic eruption before. They might not know enough to be frightened.

"Isn't it a grand sight, Mr. Coffin!" someone yelled to him. He would have taken the time to reply except that his father had warned him to hurry. In a crisis it was usually best to take Robert Coffin's advice. He took the stairs two at a time, heading for Valerie's suite.

"Valerie! Valerie!" Her rooms were located at the far end of the hall. As he drew near he slowed, breathing hard. The door was slightly ajar and sounds issued from within. He frowned. It sounded as though someone was fighting.

He peered through the half-open doorway, his mind trying to make sense of what his eyes showed him. Valerie, in her night dress, lying on her side on the bed with a gag in her mouth. A man kneeling next to her, binding her wrists. Two others at the foot of the bed opening a large burlap sack.

One of them happened to glance toward the door. "Get lost, friend. This ain't none o' your business." In front of him Valerie twisted futilely as she tried to escape her bonds.

Another man leaned into view. When he saw Andrew his eyes widened. "Be damned! I think that's the bleedin' fiancé!" He reached for the knife at his belt.

Coffin burst into the room. The man who'd first noticed him dropped his end of the burlap bag and fumbled for his own blade. Coffin hit him so hard he could hear the muffled *crack* as the man's jaw broke. He went down as though he'd been struck by a runaway train, the knife falling from his fingers.

His companion jumped on Andrew's back while Halifax, growling, left Valerie's bonds unsecured and came to help. Coffin pivoted. The man on his back hung on with both arms, but his legs swung in a wide arc to smash Halifax across the face. The big redhead stumbled back, crashed into the dressing table and slid to the floor like a man bumping down a series of steps.

Coffin swung madly in the other direction. His attacker's flailing legs shattered a full-length mirror. Under ordinary circumstances half the guests in the hotel as well as most of the management would have arrived by now seeking the source of the commotion. Most were outside, however, and Tarawera was making too much noise for anyone to hear anything.

Valerie watched the struggle as she fought to dislodge her gag and the cords binding her wrists and ankles.

With utter disregard for his own safety, Coffin threw himself at the far wall. The man clinging desperately to his back was crushed between him and the unyielding wood. Andrew felt the man slide away as his grip loosened. He crumpled up like a broken doll.

Halifax was back on his feet and moving toward him. His right hand held a big, ugly skinning knife. He was grinning through his beard at Andrew, who was bent over the bed working on Valerie's bonds. Now he slowly backed away, his eyes fastened on the thick blade.

"You shouldn't have interfered, fellow. No harm would've come to you, or her. Now you've made a mess. I'm afraid in cleaning it up I'll have to make a bigger one."

Coffin's gaze never left the weaving knife as he continued backing up. "Get out. Get out now and we'll call it done. You haven't hurt anyone yet."

"Yet. Now that's the key word, ain't it?" He lunged suddenly, stabbing with the blade. Coffin jumped clear, feeling the bed against the back of his legs. He stepped up onto the mattress, still retreating. Halifax followed, readying the blade for another swipe.

Suddenly he was fighting for balance. Valerie had kicked out strongly, catching the preoccupied kidnapper at the ankles. As he flailed wildly Coffin tackled him and the two men went down together.

Halifax's knife went sliding as they hit the floor hard with Coffin on top. Andrew tried to position one fist to deliver a solid blow, but it was like wrestling a bear. Halifax clung to him tightly. They rolled over several times, slamming into the door and knocking it shut. Meanwhile Valerie had struggled into a sitting position and was trying her best to scream through the tight gag.

Halifax tried to break clear and make a dive for the knife where it lay gleaming against the carpet. Andrew hung on desperately, clawing at the other man's waist and legs. Seeing what was taking place, Valerie swung her legs off the bed and hopped toward the door. Though bound at the ankles she managed a short, sharp kick with one foot. The deadly blade went skittering clear across the floor.

The kidnapper bellowed a curse and kicked back at Andrew, catching the younger man in the nose. As Andrew's hands went to his face Halifax scrambled toward the knife. Andrew recovered, leaped to land on Halifax's back as the other man's right hand closed on the handle of the knife. They fought like that, Halifax fighting to turn to bring the blade to bear, Andrew struggling to keep him on his stomach.

Valerie had backed herself against the washstand. She felt with her fingers until they closed around the handle of the ceramic water pitcher. It was full of lukewarm water. Now she hopped toward the two men, positioned herself as best she was able, and released her grip. The pitcher landed heavily on Halifax's skull. He uttered a surprisingly high-pitched yelp and then was still. Warm water spilled across the floor.

Gasping for breath, Andrew rose from the unconscious kidnapper's back. He took the skinning knife from the man's limp fingers and began cutting Valerie's bonds. When he had her wrists free she removed the gag as he went to work on her ankles.

"What is going on? Who are these men? Why were they doing this to me?"

"I wish I had some answers for you, love." Andrew straightened. "Are you all right?"

"Just scared. They didn't try to hurt me." Across the room the man with the broken jaw was starting to moan. "I was getting ready for bed when Tarawera started to blow up. Someone knocked on the door saying everyone had to leave the hotel. When I opened it these men rushed in on me. They wouldn't even talk to me." She started to shake as she pointed to the burlap sack. "I think they were going to put me in that. But why?" She shook her head, dazed and disbelieving. "I don't recognize any of them."

"Neither do I, but we haven't time to wonder about it now. We've got to get away from here."

"No." She held onto his hand, holding him back. "This is the best place to stay, Andrew. The hotel is the strongest building in Te Wairoa."

He hesitated. "Father insisted we ride for Rotorua. I'm not sure he's right, but when he's that positive it's usually a good idea to take his advice. Come on."

Still she held back, clutching the neckline of her night dress against her throat. "I can't go like this."

"Get a coat then."

She nodded, pulled her one winter garment from the closet and followed him out of the room. How beautiful she was, he couldn't help thinking, even in the dim light of the hotel with the heavy coat enclosing her completely.

Descending the stairs they nearly fell as another quake rattled the building. They plunged out into the crowd on the front porch, ignoring the comments of those around them.

Andrew's horse was gone. Bolted or stolen, it didn't matter now. He looked around wildly, wiping ash from his eyes.

"This way!"

The hotel stables were around back. He led Valerie that way, half pulling, half carrying her. The stables sheltered riding horses and the long-bed carriages used to convey tourists to the lake and boat landing. Lifting Valerie easily, he set her on the driver's bench.

"What are you doing?" She held her coat tight at the front.

"We're taking this one." He ran to the first stalls and brought two frightened horses out, began hitching them up. They bucked and pawed the ground but allowed him to secure bits and tack.

"Andrew, we can't do this. It is. . . ."

The rest of her words were obliterated by a colossal explosion from the mountain across the lake. Coffin didn't look in that direction. He worked at the hitches with single-minded intensity.

Then he was swinging himself up onto the seat next to her. He yelled and chucked the reins. The horses hesitated uneasily, then bolted. With a violent lurch forward the carriage burst clear of the stables. Andrew had thoughtfully put blinders on both animals.

"Andrew," Valerie shouted, "this is stealing!"

"I'm not stealing, I'm borrowing. We'll bring it back."

No one saw the carriage as it careened out the stables and swung wildly onto the road leading to Rotorua. With the blinders in place the horses concentrated on their running. It helped that they were racing away from the lightning and noise.

Heavier rock and volcanic debris began to rain down atop the carriage. The rain lip which normally protected the driver kept the bulk of it off the two desperate refugees. The horses enjoyed no such protection but if anything the intensified ashfall spurred them to gallop faster.

They were nearing the crest of the highest hill when Valerie happened to look back. She let out a cry in Maori. Holding the reins, Andrew turned also. As he did so a light so bright it hurt his eyes filled the entire lake basin.

With a roar neither of them would forget for the rest of their lives the entire right side of Mount Tarawera split open as though blasted by a titanic axe. A crack twelve miles long appeared in the earth, running from the mountain along the far side of the lake. The ground wrenched beneath the carriage and the terrified horses somehow increased their pace. All along the vast fissure magma began to fountain into the sky.

"The world is coming to an end!" Valerie moaned.

"Just this part of it!" Andrew turned back to the road and shouted at the panicky horses, trying to give them the reassurance he could not enjoy himself.

Tarawera and the town of Te Wairoa were miles behind them when something began to splatter on the top of the carriage. It was a wet, smacking sound, very different from the dry patter made by falling pumice. Valerie extended an arm, brought it back to gaze in amazement at what lay in her hand. She showed it to Andrew.

"Mud. *Ungwa.*" Despite his mastery of the language, that was a word he didn't know. She tried to explain.

"It comes out of geysers sometimes. But there are no geysers on Tarawera."

"Nobody knew Tarawera was a volcano, either." Grimly he urged the tiring horses on.

They'd fled another half-mile when they first heard the sound. At first it was a soft whistling. It grew rapidly in volume and intensity. Coffin fought to slow the horses.

"What the Devil is that?"

"Wind," Valerie murmured, "but it is all wrong. I have never heard the wind sound like that."

He rose and tried to penetrate the gloom that surrounded them, could see little but falling mud and ash. "I think we'd better try and find some shelter."

"But your father said we should go to Rotorua."

"I don't think father anticipated anything like this. Besides, the horses are about done."

Squinting hard, he thought he could see a squarish shape in the center of the cornfield that bordered the road. Finding a spot where the fence was down, he urged the horses through.

It was a storage barn, solidly fashioned of pine. The horses were relieved to be in out of the mud and ashfall. Outside, the eerie wind continued to rise.

He tried to determine which end of the barn was sturdiest, tied the horses up nearby. Then he and Valerie walked to the open, far end and stared outside.

As they stood gazing into the night it finally struck him what was so peculiar about the wind. He'd been through many storms, but never one like this.

"It's rushing toward the volcano," he whispered to her. "Toward the lake, and Tarawera." He put both arms around her and drew her close.

As he did so the full force of the gale struck like a hammerblow. Valerie screamed as the hurricane hit. The wall blew inward, timbers splintering and planks flying apart, knocking them to the ground. Dazed, they crawled until they bumped up against something solid.

Exhausted and aching, they fell asleep while the unnatural storm raged around them.

10

Andrew Coffin opened his eyes. As they slowly grew accustomed to the feeble light he made out posts and planks lying everywhere.

He sat up, saw they had crawled into a corn crib. The sturdy walls still stood, though the ferocious storm had collapsed most of the barn.

Valerie lay curled up in her coat next to him. He reached down to shake her. "Val. Valerie, wake up."

She let out a tired groan, rolled over and rubbed at her eyes. Her exquisite face was dirty with ash. "Andrew—what is it?"

"Can't you hear? It's stopped." Indeed, the horrible wind had subsided, though mud and ash continued to land on what remained of the roof. "Are you okay?"

Slowly she sat up. "I think so. That was a great wind. The Devils were sucking the air back into the Earth."

"Something sure as Hell was."

He rose on shaky legs. Every muscle and bone in his body felt bruised. He staggered through the darkness toward where he'd tied the horses. They were still there, trembling and damp with nerve sweat. Patiently he talked to them, stroked and petted until they calmed down enough to be secured to the carriage.

It felt as if he'd been asleep for days, though it was still dark as night outside. Rejoining Valerie, he removed his pocket watch and struck a match in front of it.

"Ten o'clock." He flipped the protective cover closed, looked out through the ruined wall. "In the morning. It's the ash, the ash and the mud. There must be a huge cloud above us." She nodded in agreement.

He gave her a hand up. "We can't stay here forever. We should try and make it to Rotorua—if Rotorua's still there."

472

"No." She threw her arms around him. "Andrew, I'm frightened. What if another wind comes?"

"I don't think it will, but if it does we'll find shelter elsewhere. There isn't much left here anyway. If we stay and this stuff keeps falling like this we'll be buried alive. Come on now."

He helped her into the carriage. The horses refused to move and for the first time in his life he had to make use of a riding crop. Though it cut him inside he kept whipping them until they started forward. Blood showed on their hindquarters.

What they could see of the cornfield in the darkness was gone. Where there had been neat rows and furrows and bound bundles of cornstalk there was now only mud and lumpy ash. Pumice continued to fall, striking the roof of the carriage as soon as they exited the barn.

Memory more than sight led them back to the road. The numbed, dispirited horses would not move faster than a fast walk despite Andrew's best efforts to encourage them. But at least they moved.

It was still dark when they reached Rotorua. The town was quiet, the first panic having spent itself much earlier. Now people moved with purpose, employing a startling assortment of coverings to protect themselves from the gritty rain.

Andrew and Valerie made for her father's house. Neither Opotiki nor her mother were there, but a number of other relatives and friends were. Anxious discussion followed tears and hugs of greeting.

No one else from Te Ariki, Te Wairoa, or the villages that lined the shores of Lake Tarawera, Lake Rotomahana, or the Blue and Green Lakes had arrived in town. They were the first, and so far the only refugees from the Tarawera District.

"Don't expect anyone else soon," Andrew told his audience. "We got out fast, before the mud and ash really started coming down. At that point I don't see how anyone could have made it up the road, but if the buildings held against the wind there should be plenty of survivors."

"It was Tarawera," Valerie explained. "It blew up. All the ground around it blew up. The whole Earth was on fire."

"We could tell that something very bad was happening," said old Makewe, one of Valerie's uncles. "Geysers here that have been many years dead are now active again, and all of the hot pools and mud pots are bubbling violently.

"Many wanted to flee from here to the sea, and some have. They worried the ground would open and swallow them up. But most of us were too afraid to go outside for fear of being suffocated by the ash and mud."

Andrew glanced outside. What the old man was saying was clearly true. Volcanic debris was falling as heavily here as it had been at Tarawera when they'd fled. Rotorua was ten miles from the lake, sixteen from the mountain itself. The volume of solid material being ejected from the volcano must be nothing short of incredible.

What must it be like at the hotel now, he wondered?

"We'll stay here as long as the roof holds," he told Valerie. "If the buildings start to go we'll load the carriage and make a run for the coast."

"If the horses will go that far," she reminded him. "They are worn out, and so am I."

Everyone agreed to remain unless the town became completely untenable. Andrew helped Valerie to one of the beds, knelt next to her. It was afternoon outside, but you still needed a lamp to see by. She'd washed her face. In the golden glow of the lamp she seemed to radiate her own inner light.

"It's going to be all right."

She smiled and reached up to caress his face with both hands. "The important thing is that we are together."

"Always." He bent to kiss her. She began to laugh softly and he pulled away. "What's wrong?"

"Your face." He had yet to wash and volcanic dust coated him from head to toe. "You look like a wild man. Like one of the old warriors." One finger traced patterns in the dust. "There. Now you are properly tattooed."

"Until I bathe again." He grinned. "Now try and get some rest." She nodded, they kissed again, and then he rose to leave.

He returned to the front part of the house where a group of Opotiki's relatives had gathered. They were dressing in pakeha clothes. Andrew approached Makewe, who was wrestling with boots.

"What's going on?"

"We are going to climb the big hill and try to see Tarawera. Do you want to come?"

"My mother and father are still back there. I'll come."

Makewe nodded solemnly. When the Maoris had dressed,

Andrew followed them out, adding the light of his lamp to those of the others.

"Look there," one of the men in the lead said, pointing to his right where hot water could be both seen and heard as it fountained twenty feet high. "That geyser has been quiet for ten years."

"That is nothing," said one of the others. "There is a hot spring in the middle of the big meeting house. It burst right through the floor where I was standing. I and those with me barely got out alive."

They struggled up the hill through the falling ash. At first nothing was visible in the direction of Tarawera. Then the wind must have shifted because the dark ash cloud parted enough to enable them to make out the distant glow sixteen miles away. Lightning crawled across the sky as they stared in awe.

As they watched, a tremendous blast echoed across the land, as if the biggest cannon in the world had gone off not far away. From the twelve-mile rift that snaked its way down the mountain a shaft of light climbed skyward. Then the dust cloud closed tight around them again.

Something struck Andrew a sharp but light blow on the head. As he knelt to recover the cooling missile more of the pea-sized pebbles fell around the climbers. They could hear the volcano blasting away in the distance.

"We are all going to die here," one of the men muttered as he crossed his arms over his head to protect himself.

"Shut up," Makewe snapped. "The gods will decide that. Meanwhile we stay." He turned and started back down the hill towards town.

All through the afternoon and another terrible night the inhabitants of Rotorua and Ohinemutu cowered in their homes and places of business. Morning of the following day brought welcome if weak sunlight, and not a few cheers of relief.

The whole village wore a blanket of ash and dust. The eruption had ceased and the dense black cloud which had lain over the district had dissipated. Life took on a semblance of normality. Those without immediate responsibilities began to form rescue parties. Riders left to carry word of the disaster to Tauranga on the coast since the telegraph lines were down all over the region.

Andrew had joined one of the first rescue parties and was readying the horses when Valerie joined him.

"I am going with you," she told him.

He shook his head. "No. It's too dangerous. We don't know what Tarawera's going to do, or what it might still be doing. I have to go. I have to find out what's happened to my parents."

"And what of my Aunt Merita? I am going also. If I have to I will walk."

"All right. I know that tone. Get aboard." She climbed up onto the driver's bench.

Men were working frantically, hitching horses to wagons, loading everything that might be needed by the survivors at Te Ariki and the other villages. The hotel carriage which had carried Andrew and Valerie to safety was already loaded down with food and barrels of clean drinking water.

They were in the vanguard as the first vehicles pulled out onto the muddy road. Wagons and coaches strung out behind them while individual riders pushed on ahead.

They expected to pass scenes of devastation, but the enormity of the destruction far exceeded the worst anyone could imagine.

Within six miles of the lake everything had been destroyed. Herds of dust and mud-covered cattle wandered aimlessly through muddy fields searching for something to eat. Carcasses had already begun to litter the landscape. Of the native wildlife there was nothing to be seen: not a lizard, not a bird, not even insects.

Closer to Tarawera even the forests had been blasted from their hillsides. Every bush, every tree had been flattened by mud or ripped from the earth by the hurricane-force wind. They rode past clumps of earth clinging to upturned tree roots ten feet and more across.

"The world has died here," Valerie whispered. "There is nothing left."

"There has to be." Coffin grimly urged the horses to greater speed. "People aren't animals. They wouldn't be caught out in the open."

"It does not matter, Andrew. Even the forest is dead. The land has been stripped bare."

She was wrong. There were survivors. Not as many as had been hoped for, nor as few as had been feared.

A number had taken shelter in guide Sophia's house, whose sharply angled walls shed mud and ash much better than the European buildings. She had kept her charges together during the ashfall when many had wished to flee. Thanks to her obstinacy they had survived, for if they had run outside the mud and dust would surely have overwhelmed them.

In some places the mud was so deep only the tops of fences remained visible. Rats and mice could be seen skittering around the ruins. Birds hopped blindly, their eyelids glued shut by drying mud.

The Terraces Hotel still stood, battered and crushed as if by a tsunami. McRae's had been completely obliterated. They were focal points for the rescue work which was already under way. Survivors were being given food and drink, clean clothes, and blankets.

As soon as the carriage had been unloaded, Andrew headed west along the altered lakeshore. "We've got to get up to the house." Valerie said nothing, watching him silently.

Road signs barely peeped above the mud. Remnants of the great dust cloud continued to sift down around them.

As they topped the last rise Andrew had to force down the lump rising in his throat. The vast, magical house in which he'd spent most of his life was completely gone. Nothing remained but a pile of broken, muddy lumber and a mass of rock where the main fireplace had stood. The neat picket fence which his mother had tended as zealously as any Crusader's fortress wall lay buried beneath six feet of mud and ash.

"I am sorry, Andrew." He felt Valerie's hand on his arm as he stared at the ruins.

"It's all right, Val. It's just, I expected *something* to be left."

As he stepped down from the carriage his feet sank several inches into the still cooling mud. The deep ruts left by the vehicle formed a pair of parallel lines leading back toward town, a trail other rescuers could follow. Not that there was anyone left here to rescue.

That didn't stop him from removing a shovel from the back of the carriage and fighting through the muck toward the site of the house.

Valerie watched him dig until both the sunlight and his strength gave out. Then she tenderly wiped his face clean and drove the carriage back to Te Wairoa. In the fading light of evening they noticed that Tarawera itself had been changed by the eruption. A giant had taken his own shovel and scooped out a great gap in the side of the mountain.

By morning rescue efforts were in high gear. They were

finishing a simple but satisfying breakfast when Andrew spotted Alfred Warbrick. He and Andrew had been casual friends for several years, not only because they were about the same age but because Warbrick too was half Maori and half European.

"Took a boat across the lake," Warbrick told them.

"That took courage," Valerie said admiringly.

Warbrick shrugged. "Had no choice. I had relatives at Moura."

"Any luck?" Andrew asked hopefully.

Warbrick wasn't smiling beneath his huge, curly mustache. "The whole town's gone. Must be five feet of mud over everything. You remember the *karaka* forest?" Andrew nodded. "It's floating in the lake, every last tree."

"What about Te Ariki?"

Warbrick laughed bitterly. "The mud there must be hundreds of feet thick. You wouldn't believe it unless you saw it."

"Oh, I'd believe it, all right."

"We tried to make it over to Rotomahana. It isn't there anymore."

Rotomahana was a good-sized lake, not as large as Tarawera but a mile across in places. The image of it Andrew had carried with him most of his life didn't square with Warbrick's comment.

"What do you mean, it 'isn't there'?"

"It's gone. Blown dry," said Warbrick tiredly. "The bottom's just mud and steaming craters. All the water's gone. We couldn't get any farther. No telling what it's like on the other side. If you'll excuse me." He tipped his hat toward Valerie. "I've got work to do."

Andrew nodded, turned back to her. "I knew some people at Te Ariki. It wasn't a big village. Maybe fifty people. All dead now."

"Come, Andrew. Our help is needed."

While they worked word came trickling in from other rescue parties. The Pink and White Terraces, the loudly proclaimed eighth wonder of the world, had vanished. Whether buried or blown to bits no one knew for sure. Of the one hundred and fifty houses at Te Wairoa, only two remained standing.

"What are we going to do now, Andrew?" Valerie asked him as they ate lunch.

"We'll stay here and help until we aren't needed anymore,"

he decided. "Then we'll go to Tauranga and take ship to Auckland. Elias Goldman must be told what's happened here. He's going to need my help, and we'll surely need his." He took a bite of an apple, chewed reflectively. "It's funny."

"What is?"

"I never thought I'd have to work at the business. Now it seems I've no choice. With Father gone I'm the only one who can make certain decisions, sign certain papers. He would've been pleased."

"I know he would," she said comfortingly.

Other rescue workers and survivors ate around them. The despair of the previous day had given way to animated discussion, to purpose and activity. Life of a sort had returned to the shores of Lake Tarawera.

"I want to go back to the house tomorrow," Andrew murmured. "Maybe with some help. I want them to have," he surprised himself by choking on the words, "a proper burial."

"Of course." She hesitated a moment, then added, "You will not mind if I engage a tohunga to say the right Maori words?"

He smiled. "That would only be right."

As no one had yet claimed the hotel carriage he felt comfortable using it to transport a group of men to the site. They set to work with picks and shovels, the work going much faster now that he had help.

They found Merita first. At the digger's cry Andrew came running, but when he was close enough to see the condition of the body he pivoted and walked away to resume digging elsewhere. Others gently removed the broken form and slipped it into the large sack that had been brought for that purpose. Andrew preferred to remember his mother as she had been: regal, full of life, laughing and supremely beautiful. Not crushed and battered by falling debris and the collapsing house.

He was beginning to despair of ever finding his father when the diggers let out their third shout of the afternoon. This time Valerie joined them.

Andrew bent to help remove the heavy timber and shattered chunks of plaster which had once formed part of the ground floor ceiling. It was only then that the burly digger close to the body cried out.

"Good God! It's still warm."

"Here, let me!" Andrew fell on his knees to put an ear against the massive chest. He looked up in astonishment. "His heart's still beating! Let's get him out of here."

The men worked frenziedly, shards of wood and plaster flying in all directions. When they had the body freed they lifted it carefully and carried it to the waiting carriage. It was all Andrew could do to maintain a steady pace and not spur the horses to a wild gallop as he drove back to the refugee camp.

One of the doctors, who'd ridden out from Rotorua to help, examined his new patient and hastily ordered the comatose elder Coffin transferred immediately to the hospital. Andrew would have accompanied the makeshift ambulance except that much remained to be done at Te Wairoa. Every available hand was needed to assist the living. The doctor assured him there was nothing he could do and warned him it was quite possible that even should his father survive his injuries, he might never regain consciousness. Andrew struggled with himself, finally went to Valerie for advice.

"Stay awhile longer here," she urged him. "I have relatives missing also. We can go back in a few days, when things here are under control. Perhaps at that time the doctors at the hospital will have better news."

He considered. "You're right. There are others here who need our help." He turned to follow the hospital wagon as it crawled out of town up the muddy road leading to Rotorua. "I can't do anything for him now. He'll make it without me, I think. The old man's too tough to die."

11

They were digging in another part of the village on the fourth day after the eruption when a series of piercing screams drew the attention of everyone working in the vicinity. Andrew put up his shovel and Valerie moved to his side.

As they stared, four Maori workmen came running madly from the buried outskirts of the town. Andrew intercepted the last of them. The man was breathing erratically and his eyes were wild.

"What's going on over there?" Andrew nodded in the direction the men had been working. "Get ahold of yourself, man!"

"He—he's still alive," the terrified man gasped. "The old devil is still alive. Let me go, let me go!" He was looking over his shoulder as if all the hounds of Hell were close on his heels.

Andrew held on. "What are you mumbling about? Who's still alive?"

"Let me go!" The man tore his shirt as he stumbled off after his friends.

Andrew watched him run, then picked up his own shovel. "Stay here," he ordered Valerie.

She shook her head. "You have tried that before. It will not work with me now either." She hefted her own, smaller spade.

Several other men had been drawn by the shouting. As they marched toward the site Doctor Chambers joined them. All Europeans, Andrew noted. By this time there wasn't a Maori to be seen—not counting Valerie and himself, of course.

They found another man leaning over the recently excavated pit. He was talking in a concerned voice, directing his words into the hole. "Come now, sir. You must climb out of there. We only want to help you."

"Go away and leave me alone." The sepulchral response

did not seem to come from a human throat. "The world has died here. I do not want to have to see it."

"You must come out." The workman looked pained. "You can't stay down there."

"I will not come out."

The man stood, shaking his head as Chambers, Andrew, Valerie and two other men gathered around him.

"Has he been down there all this time?" Andrew inquired incredulously.

"I expect so." The digger nodded in the direction taken by the now departed Maori workers. "A couple of the fellows were digging this hole when they heard a voice and realized there was somebody alive down there. When they figured out who it was they just took off."

A disbelieving Chambers was staring at the excavation. "This place has been buried for four days. No food, no water—no air. Nobody could live through that."

The digger was not put off. "It seems somebody has, sir."

Chambers knelt and cupped his hands to his mouth as he shouted into the pit. "Look here, friend. If you'll come out of there we'll get some hot food into you, give you a drink and fix you up so that you'll be all right. We can't do anything for you if you stay where you are."

"I will be all right." The voice was insistent.

"Let me try." Chambers stepped aside so Andrew could take his place. "You must come out, sir!" he said in Maori. "It's not right to live in a hole like a rat. You're a man, not a rat."

This time there was only silence from below. Rising, Andrew saw that Chambers and the others were looking at him expectantly. Instead of speaking, he hefted his shovel and began to dig. They fell to with him, the dirt flying silently, Valerie helping where she was able.

They soon uncovered the front wall and door of a buried whare. The house had lain sealed under ten feet of mud. As the open entryway was cleared Andrew could see far enough inside to make out a hunched-over, motionless figure. Long bony arms were crossed in front of folded legs. At first he thought he was looking at a dead man. Then the head lifted to peer at him.

"I know you," an aged but strong voice declared calmly.

"And I know you." Andrew leaned in. "I'm sure of it. Yes! Valerie and I were bathing in a hot pool when you surprised us.

You told us," his voice momentarily failed him as he remembered, "you told us that this whole country was going to be overturned. That was the word you used. Overturned."

The man who'd been buried alive did not smile. "What the gods willed."

"Please, come out. You can't stay here." Andrew glanced back, then leaned in as far as he could and whispered. "The pakehas won't let you stay. They'll come down and drag you out."

The oldster looked away from him. He sighed deeply, then unfolded himself. On hands and knees he crawled from his house, putting an end to his four-day entombment. He needed help to climb out of the hole, but once on the surface he stood without assistance, blinking at the sky he had not seen for a hundred and four hours.

He was an impressive sight as he turned a slow circle, surveying his land. Andrew was the tallest of his rescuers, and the old man overtopped him by four inches. Silently he examined the devastated terrain, the ruined hillsides, the annihilated town.

"As I foretold," he murmured.

Valerie had recognized him immediately. Now she moved close. "There has been talk in the village. Some blame you for the disaster."

Tuhoto looked down at her, shaking his head sadly. "I tried to warn them. I tried to warn them all. But they would not listen. Naturally some would blame me. In their own way the Maori are as ignorant as the pakeha."

Chambers had produced the thermos he carried with him. He offered the old man a cup of warm milk. "Here you are, friend. This'll make you feel better."

Tuhoto shook his head imperiously. "I eat nothing but potatoes and water."

"But you must have some real food! You've had nothing to eat for four days down there." Chambers was about to add that the old man had also had nothing to breathe, but could not make himself say the words. He was trying to cope with a living impossibility.

"I have six gods. I am one hundred and four years old. I will not die."

Chambers poured the milk back into his thermos. "Very well. But you must go to the hospital at Rotorua for a check-up. All the survivors are going. As a doctor I must insist upon that much."

"I will not go," said Tuhoto obstinately. "I do not need pakeha medicines. They would be bad for me."

Chambers sighed. "Look here, old fellow. You must go. If not for your own good then for mine. Don't you see? If word got about that I'd let someone in your condition go wandering off as he pleased without at least having him examined, it would be professionally embarrassing for me."

Tuhoto was not impressed. "I have six gods." He looked down at Andrew. "What of your father and mother?"

"My mother's dead. I think she was killed when the house collapsed on her. My father is, well, he's still alive, but barely."

There was a flicker of interest in the old tohunga's eyes. "I have known your father for a long time. I would see him."

"They took him to Rotorua in the hospital wagon."

Tuhoto considered, then turned back to Chambers. "I will do as you ask. I will go to the white man's hospital. But not for the white man's medicine. I will go to see my friend."

"Fine," said a relieved Chambers, "so long as you go. You can come along with me if you wish. I'll be heading back that way myself shortly."

Tuhoto nodded, then turned back to Andrew and Valerie. "How is it with you?"

"We'll be all right, sir." Andrew put his arm around Val's shoulders, hugging her close.

"That is good." Exhibiting no ill effects from his four-day interment, he turned and strode off in the direction of the refugee camp.

"Wouldn't have believed it if I didn't see it with me own eyes," muttered one of the other men.

"The human body is capable of extraordinary accomplishments when under extreme stress," said Chambers.

Andrew and Valerie did not comment. They knew that the old man had survived because he was a tohunga, maybe the greatest of all the tohungas. Certainly he was the most remarkable person either of them had ever encountered. Modern medicine had accomplished much, Andrew knew, but the wise pakehas did not know everything. Not yet.

Valerie was looking up at him. "What did he mean, that he

was a friend of your father? I never saw him around here before that night at the pool."

"Nor did I, not even when I was a boy." He shrugged. "My father had friends scattered all over the country. He traveled many places without mother and myself. It doesn't surprise me that he had an old tohunga for a friend, along with captains of industry and princes of commerce."

She frowned. "What are those chiefs?"

Grinning, he kissed her softly. "Father always referred to them as cheap royalty. Come, let's get back to the camp. There's still plenty to be done here."

They did not think about the remarkable old man again that day. Later, that night, wrapped in each other's arms, they did not think of him at all. That would not have displeased Tuhoto. It only meant things were once more as they should be.

12

The hospital was a strange place, but the strangeness did not trouble him. Tuhoto let them move him silently from place to place, from room to room. Many pakehas poked and prodded him, asked him questions. He answered as best he could, politely but with indifference. This was not what he had come to this place for.

Now that word of the disaster had been passed, the whole country had been mobilized to help the survivors of Tarawera. Supplies and help were pouring in from Auckland, Wellington, Christchurch and the smaller communities. Even those busy unloading or marking supplies or helping the physicians and nurses paused to gaze at the giant old Maori who towered over everyone at the hospital, much as the ancient moa had once loomed over the Maoris.

"We'll just get you checked in for a couple of days. As a precaution." the cheerful young pakeha who'd taken charge of the old tohunga spoke briskly, patronizingly. Tuhoto did not have to use much of his mind to listen to his words.

"Wait over there, please, while I fill out some papers. Then we'll find you a room." the young white man adjusted his glasses. "One more check-over, it says here, and then you can have a nice rest."

Tuhoto nodded compliantly and moved to the other side of the busy room. It was filled with people who had suffered from the disaster. They mostly ignored him, involved as they were with their own afflictions.

He looked to his left, then to his right. The earnest young pakeha was busy with his papers. Tuhoto knew that white men needed four things to live: food, water, air, and papers to fill out. Silently he started up the nearest corridor.

It was quiet. No one challenged his right to be there. He turned a corner and continued down another deserted hallway.

Once he paused, as if listening, before heading off in another direction.

All the doors he passed were identical except for the numbers on them. He stopped outside one, not bothering to read the numerals. It opened at his touch. Entering the shaded room, he closed the door quietly behind him.

On the single hospital bed an old man lay beneath clean sheets. He was not as old as Tuhoto nor as tall. The tohunga approached the bed until he was gazing down at the barely breathing figure. The eyes were closed tight.

"Hello, my friend Robert Coffin. This has been a bad time. But your son lives, and his woman. I thought you would want to know that, so I came to tell you."

The figure in the bed did not reply, did not move, did not respond in any way to the words, but Tuhoto knew Coffin heard him anyway, with his body if not with his ears. That was all that mattered. Sighing deeply, the tohunga raised both hands over the bed and began to sing softly in the voice of a man much younger than one hundred and four. He sang a *karakia*, a prayer. A very important and powerful one.

When he was finished he lowered his arms, listening to the last words of the incantation as they dissolved in the sterile air. Moments passed. Then Robert Coffin's eyes fluttered open. The body did not react, did not move. But the gray-haired head turned slightly. *Makawe Rino*, Tuhoto thought.

Coffin's voice was feeble, confused. "Tuhoto?"

The tall, angular figure looming over the bed nodded once. "Yes, Captain Coffin. It is good to see you again."

The eyes shut momentarily, signs of strain etched deep on the heavily lined face. Then they opened again. "I'd greet you, but I don't think I can move. I'm very tired."

"It does not matter, my friend. You have already greeted me."

Coffin's words came faintly, barely perceptible. "It was terrible, terrible. Andrew?"

Perhaps he had not heard, Tuhoto thought. "He is well. And the woman he would marry."

"That's good. That's very good. Tuhoto, I'm sorry, but I don't think I can talk anymore. I need to rest."

"The world needs to rest. This part of the land has been hurt. Even the gods are tired."

"I haven't done the right things recently, Tuhoto. There are things I wish I could take back."

"You would not be a man if you did not wish that, Captain Coffin. All of us wish things we could take back."

Coffin managed a feeble smile. "I tried to make up for a little, there at the last. But there's never enough time, is there?"

"No, Captain Coffin, there is never enough time."

The eyes closed again. This time even Tuhoto's singsong prompting could not reopen them. The old Maori leaned over and placed four fingers on Coffin's forehead. He whispered softly.

"Once, long, long ago, you gave me a ride from one place to another, Captain Coffin. You did not insult me. You treated me with respect and did not ask for payment. Now I will help you along your path from this world to Po, the land of peace and darkness. The torment within you will be stilled as the torment in the Earth has been stilled. I will miss you, my old friend. Perhaps when the time comes I will join you in Po and we will take ship there together for some interesting place, and talk as we once did of the people and gods, of the land and the sea, as we sail the ocean of darkness."

He removed his fingers. The painful, barely noticeable rise and fall of Robert Coffin's chest had ceased. Tuhoto turned and left the room without looking back, closing the door behind him as silently as when he'd entered.

The man who intercepted him in the corridor sounded exasperated. "There you are! Where did you get off to, old man?" He muttered under his breath. "Maoris! Just like children." He smiled a smile he did not mean. "Come along, then."

"I do not need to come along. I am done here."

"Oh no you're not." The young pakeha was insistent. "You can't leave looking like that. What would people think of our hospital?" Tilting his head to one side he eyed the long, stringy locks that tumbled from the old man's head. "You need a bath and a haircut."

"You cannot do that. If you bathe me and cut my hair I will die."

The youth couldn't resist smirking. "As I recall when they brought you in here you said you had six gods and couldn't die."

"If you do those pakeha things to me I will die."

"Nonsense! And I thought you were an educated native. Now come along." He reached out and locked his fingers around one thin wrist. The old man was much taller, but thin as a rail. The strength he had left was not of the physical kind. He could not stop the young man from pulling him up the hall.

Tuhoto looked back over his shoulder toward the room where he had bade farewell to an old friend. He thought of the country of his birth, where he had spent many pleasant times resting between his travels. It had all been destroyed. Though the birds and animals, the forest and the lakes would come back, he knew this would not happen in his lifetime. Not even with six gods to aid him.

So he did not object when the nurses washed him cleaner than he had ever been, or when they trimmed his hair in a style that was well thought of by modern Maoris.

"There, much better," said the young orderly whose care he'd been given into.

Tuhoto looked at himself in a mirror, thoughtfully considered the clean face that stared back at him. "I would like a glass of water, please."

"Certainly. Then we'll see about getting in touch with your family or friends to take you back home, if you won't stay and rest here."

"I have no family. I have outlived all wives and all my children and now I have outlived all my friends as well. Those who know me scorn me as a sorcerer and devil."

"More nonsense," said the orderly briskly. It seemed to be his favorite word today. "You just lie down on that fine bed over there and we'll find you some new clothes. It'll take some searching, but among all the goods that have been donated I'm sure we can find something close to your size. Then we'll get you a nice, hot, fresh-cooked meal. And you needn't worry. The government will take care of you if we can't contact anyone who knows you."

"I am not a child." Tuhoto obediently walked over and sat down on the indicated bed. "The pakeha government is not my father."

"I'll be back in a couple of minutes to check on you," said the orderly, ignoring the old man's words.

He was on his way to the main desk when he was stopped by a priest.

"Excuse me, young man."

"What is it, Vicar?" The orderly tried to restrain his impatience. With all the interruptions he'd never get anything done today.

"I saw your name tag." The Vicar indicated the name pinned to the young man's shirt. "You are the one attending a Robert Coffin, are you not?"

"Among others. We're full to overflowing here, Vicar."

"I know. I was doing work of my own elsewhere in the hospital when I was informed he had passed away. I'm here to perform the final rites."

The orderly looked resigned. "All right, Vicar. Come along. I'll take you to him. Didn't know he'd expired, myself. I'm trying to do a dozen things at once."

"We all are, my son."

"Don't know that I've seen you in here before, Vicar." The orderly was trying to make conversation as the two men walked down the empty corridor.

"I am only yesterday off a ship from Auckland. I've come to offer my services to those in need. My name is Methune." He spoke absently, his attention on the hallway ahead.

"Heaven knows we need all the help we can get, Vicar." The orderly stopped outside an open door. "If you can wait just a moment, I need to check on a patient." He poked his head inside while Methune waited impatiently.

"Hey! I'm helping someone else out here. If one of you can get that old Maori up to the front desk, someone there'll take him down to the commissary for a feed."

One of the nurses approached the door, rubbing his forehead with the back of an arm. "Doesn't matter anymore, Will. The old boy's dead."

The orderly gaped at the nurse, speechless. Then he looked toward the bed where he'd left his charge. The bed was empty.

"Took him already," the nurse explained. He was shaking his head. "Funny old bugger. One minute he was lying there fine. When I turned around he was gone. Just like that. Damnedest thing I ever saw." Noticing Methune out in the hall he added, "Sorry, Father."

"How—did he say anything, do anything?" The stunned orderly couldn't take his eyes from the empty bed.

"Naw. He didn't cry out or anything. Don't think he even moved. He just kind of went away, like. Had his eyes wide open, staring at the ceiling. Like he was concentrating on something. I don't know." He looked past the dumbfounded orderly. "Do you believe in a soul, Father?"

"Naturally, my son," Methune replied. "How else is one to believe?"

"Yeah, that's what I thought. I've seen a lot of men die, Father. Here, in the wars. But I never saw one go like that. Like his spirit just evaporated."

"A man who is truly at peace with himself can die so quietly you don't realize what has happened."

"That's what it was like. Guess even a Maori's got a soul, right?"

"We are all children of God." Methune turned his attention to the motionless orderly. "Mr. Coffin's room?"

"What? Oh, yeah. Yeah. This way, Vicar." Pulling himself back together, the orderly resumed his march down the hall.

When they reached the right room, the young man paused with his hand on the latch. He seemed lost in himself. "Vicar, what you said back there, about all of us being children of the same God?"

"Yes?"

"I don't suppose—I don't guess there could be more than one, could there?"

Methune eyed him disapprovingly, but the orderly didn't back down. "Young man, I have worked among the Maori all my life. They have adopted many of our ways, have married among us, entered wholeheartedly into our churches. They have fought against us and alongside us. I am not one to say what is possible and what is not in this world. I don't believe any man knows the answers to the great mysteries. But as a Christian I can give you only one reply to that question."

"That's what I thought you'd say, Vicar. A man in your position, I know he couldn't say much of anything else."

But the orderly was not satisfied. As he opened the door admitting them to the silent room he knew he would not be able to believe exactly as his friends and neighbors did any longer. He would go to his own grave burdened by an unresolved question. Knowing that the one man who might answer it for him had already preceded him on that long journey.

EPILOGUE

1893

Rain had never bothered Rose Hull. It had been a welcome part of her life ever since she could remember. Rain kept people indoors, and those were the times when she and her friends had turned the city into their private playground. The feeling carried over into adulthood. Where others withdrew from the rain, she delighted in it.

It would have been better, though, for it not to rain on this particular day. Even as she considered this, the skies began to clear a little. A deluge could not have kept her at home this morning, but bad weather might affect the turnout for the election. There were candidates to be supported and beyond that, a much more important reason for certain citizens to get out and vote. Also, the rain would make trouble for the photographers. They would be more disappointed than anyone else. They had the job of recording a historic moment.

A voice reached her via the carriage's speaking tube. "We're almost there, Miss Hull."

"Thank you, Ed."

She leaned back in the plush seat and stared out the window. Hard to believe this was the same Auckland where she'd grown up. Now it was a city of fine buildings and paved streets. So much changed from her childhood. So many things changed.

She'd never really been a child, she reflected. Not in the accepted sense of the word. Her playmates had been mostly boys, like Edward, and Joby. Street urchins, ragamuffins, ship's orphans, the offspring of whores and Maori transients. It was to be regretted.

As they parked outside the courthouse she saw two groups of people assembled on the steps. To the left was a small line of citizens waiting for the polls to open so they could cast their ballots. To their right, higher on the steps and trying to keep dry, were the reporters and photographers. Not just from New

Zealand but from all around the world. It was an impressive gathering.

She smiled to herself. Four years the liberals had held power. They owed a large part of their success to her behind-the-scenes maneuvering and substantial financial support. Since they'd taken control life was beginning to change for the better for the common people.

Today she intended to do something she usually avoided, which was to purposely seek the limelight. To emphasize the importance of this day, this moment, she would accept a role in a historic drama.

She'd prepared herself for the reporters to rush the carriage, but the rain was as much her ally today as it had been when she was young. It kept them huddled beneath the overhang of the courthouse roof. Joby had climbed down from his footman's position to intercept the one man who braved the elements to greet her. She recognized Simpson, the party representative. The expression he wore had nothing to do with the rain.

"Something wrong, Simpson?" She spoke without leaving the protection of the carriage.

The party man was obviously distressed at having to serve as the bearer of bad news. "I fear so, Miss Hull. We seem to have a bit of a problem." He glanced back toward the courthouse entrance. The polls would be opening any moment now.

"What sort of problem?" She used the voice she had been forced to develop over the years, the voice that reassured whoever was listening that anything, absolutely anything, could be fixed.

"Well, Miss Hull, it's just that—there are some Maoris here."

"Not with greenstone clubs in their hands, I presume?" She smiled to indicate she meant it as a joke. Though the Maori wars had been done with for over a decade you still had to reassure the uncertain at times. And while Simpson was an effective orator and legislator, he wasn't quite what one would call bold and brave. Not like the early settlers who'd fought a continuous war with a tough and relentless enemy while building a country. She decided he would not have lasted long back in the fifties.

Different eras call for different skills, however. The man was a marvelous organizer.

"There aren't many of them," he was telling her, "and they

don't appear to be armed, but they are being difficult. Causing something of a commotion. So far we've kept it quiet, but we can't keep the reporters and photographers away forever."

"I see. What is it they want?"

"There are several women in the group. They're saying that since today New Zealand will become the first country in the world to allow women to vote, they feel it would only be just if a true New Zealander cast the initial ballot. By that they mean one of their own kind. They have selected one of their number and insist they'll block the polls unless she is allowed to vote first. I've argued with them, but they won't see reason."

"Depends whose reason you're looking at, doesn't it, Simpson?"

"Miss Hull?"

"Never mind. Be silent and let me think."

There was no guarantee that whoever voted first here in central Auckland would actually be casting the earliest ballot. That could take place in Wellington or Napier or any of several dozen other cities and towns if the polls there happened to open a minute or two earlier. But attention was focused here, because while Auckland was no longer the country's capital (that honor having passed to Wellington) it was still its largest city, the center of commerce, and the place where the world's attention would be focused. Since it was the city best known to Europeans and Americans, this was where reporters from around the world had come to document this unique moment in the history of women's rights.

"I'll speak to them," she said abruptly.

"I don't know—well, if you think it best, Miss Hull."

"I do." Joby opened the door and helped her out as Simpson stepped aside.

"There's something else." He hesitated a moment. "Andrew Coffin is with them."

"Andrew Coffin? Here?" Another unexpected development. She wondered at its import. She'd had no trouble with Coffin Ltd. since its founder and namesake had perished years ago at Tarawera. Neither had she been able to absorb the great company into her own. Wily old Elias Goldman kept his eagle eye on the daily operations while teaching the son the intricacies of the business.

One of these days Goldman would retire, or collapse atop his beloved ledgers. Then she could move in—if she still

wanted to. Empire building was losing its spice. She had
nothing left to prove, not to herself or any of her competitors.
More and more she preferred to leave operations to her
managers, retiring to her house to enjoy the company of close
friends, or participating in the expanding social and political
life of the country.

Robert Coffin had once vowed to take over Hull House.
Now that it was her turn she found she no longer cared to try.

"Do you have any idea why he's here?"

"Apparently he is related to these natives. He is half Maori
himself, you know. His mother."

"I've heard the story," she replied crisply as she started up
the steps. A tall shadow, Joby the footman walked silently
alongside, holding an umbrella over her. "Let's see if we can't
work this out."

Simpson appeared relieved she had arrived to take charge.
Let's see these natives try to bluster their way past Rose Hull!
he mused expectantly. He stayed close to her as she ascended,
not out of any particular concern for her safety but because that
was the place of power. It was useful for any politician to be
seen in her company.

He's hoping for a confrontation, she thought. It's written all
over his face. They want someone to put these Maoris in their
place. Her expression twisted. How easily some of her
colleagues forgot that the Maoris were also citizens.

They reached the top and entered the shelter of the
overhang. The Maoris had packed themselves against the main
doors, refusing to be moved or to let anyone ahead of them.
Most wore European clothing. Automatically she looked for
tattoos, but there were few visible. Except for one man about
her own age and a tiny, elderly woman clad in ceremonial
dress, the group consisted of young people.

Andrew Coffin she recognized immediately, not only because he was taller than his companions but because he so
resembled his father. Darker skin, of course, and gentler of
countenance. She saw none of the bitterness and frustration in
him that had scarred Robert Coffin. He was holding hands with
his handsome Maori wife. What was her name? Oh yes,
Valerie.

She walked straight toward him, her hand extended in
greeting. The Maoris eyed her approach warily.

"Good morning to you, Mr. Coffin."

He smiled courteously as they shook hands. "Miss Hull."
He nodded to his left. "My wife."

"Valerie, of course! How do you do, my dear?" The woman
smiled reflexively. A real beauty, Rose thought. Almost noble,
yet childlike. She shifted her attention to the old couple
standing nearby. "What seems to be the problem here?"

The man stepped forward. He used a cane and his eyes were
blinded with cataracts, but his voice was strong. "I am
Opotiki. Son of Te Ohine." He gestured briefly. "Valerie
Coffin is my daughter."

"I see. This is primarily a family affair, then?"

"If you consider that all Maori are family," Andrew Coffin
told her with a smile.

"And who is this?" Rose's gaze dropped to the matriarch
who still stood close by the doors.

"My name is Ane," the woman said softly. While embarrassed at having so much attention focused on her, neither did
she seem inclined to step aside.

"My mother," Opotiki explained proudly. "Wife to the
great Te Ohine. Today she will be eighty-five years old."

"My congratulations." Not for the first time Rose regretted
her ignorance of the Maori tongue. She knew a few words, but
not how to say happy birthday.

Opotiki drew himself up importantly. "Today is the first day
women will be allowed to vote anywhere in the pakeha
world."

Rose nodded. "That's right. That is why we're all here."

"The Maori have always acknowledged the role and
importance of women. We think it would be the right thing for
a Maori woman to be the first to cast a vote today." He glanced
behind him. "A woman of wisdom and importance like my
honored mother."

"I see." Rose looked past him, at the lady who had survived
so much for so long. "And what do you think about this, Miss
Ane?"

The old woman's English was awkward but intelligible. "I
think would be a good thing."

Simpson's line had broken and reporters and photographers
had crowded close, ready to record the historic moment. The
politico positioned himself next to her. Now he whispered
intently.

"You can't let that old native vote first, Miss Hull! It will make a mockery of all the work and legislation."

"Why will it make a mockery of that, Mr. Simpson?"

"Because," he hesitated as he hunted for the right words, "it's not expected. It will look like a concession to the Maori. Don't you see that?"

"It's only a gesture."

"You know how important gestures are in politics, Miss Hull."

She sighed. "Yes, you're right." Simpson knew his business. She looked back at Ane.

"You know, I never knew my own grandmother. I imagine she must have been rather like yourself. I hope so, anyway." Ane's smile banished the damp chill of morning. "I didn't even know my mother. She died when I was born."

"A bad thing. I am sorry for that."

"Thank you. I have an idea, if it's acceptable to you. These people here," and she indicated the reporters even as flashbars began to pop around them, "have come to record an important moment. I think we can make it even more important, if you will help me."

"What is it you wish?"

Rose Hull leaned forward to whisper into the old woman's ear. As she talked, the smile on Ane's ancient face widened. Finally Rose straightened.

The Maori matriarch gazed up at her and nodded. "A good idea. Very good thing. Let us do it."

"Let's. This way is better than any other. This will be the best way. If you will allow me?" Rose Hull extended her right arm. The old woman slipped her much smaller arm through that of the tall pakeha.

"It's time," Andrew Coffin declared.

The courthouse doors opened inward. The clerk who'd unlocked them stared in surprise at the two women waiting side-by-side in the entryway. Then he shrugged and stepped aside.

With flashbars exploding and reporters scribbling furiously, the two women entered the courthouse arm in arm, making history with their entrance.

Cheers began to rise behind them, from a few of the watching pakehas, from the Maoris who'd escorted the senior mother all the way from the country to the heart of the great stone pa. Now they could rightly claim this as their city too.

Ane and Rose Hull did not hear the cheers and shouts. They were too busy conversing with each other. Not about the forthcoming election or whom each intended to vote for, nor about the weather or their families or themselves.

They were talking about the old days.

Te Tapea
(The End)

Among those who helped in the writing of this book, the author particularly wishes to acknowledge the assistance of the Consulate of New Zealand at Los Angeles, California, and the account of the eruption of Mt. Tarawera in 1886 as related in the book *Tarawera*, by Eugene and Valerie Grayland. Those seeking a more detailed account of the actual eruption and its aftermath are invited to consult this fine report.

Although real and fictional personages mix freely in this tale, the sighting of the death canoe by two separate parties of travelers and the entombment and subsequent rescue and death of the one-hundred-and-four-year-old Maori tohunga known as Tuhoto are a matter of historical record.

Fantasy from Ace fanciful and fantastic!